Wasteland

ABOUT THE AUTHOR

Jo Sinclair is the pen name of Ruth Seid. She adopted this pseudonym in 1938, when *Esquire* magazine would accept stories written by men only. Using the name Jo Sinclair, she sold two stories to *Esquire*.

Sinclair, who was born in Brooklyn in 1913, began writing poetry when she was 14 and then went on to write fiction. *Wasteland* took her three years to complete. It was first published in 1946, when it won the $10,000 Harper Prize of that year. Sinclair, who never went to college, has been during her lifetime a publicist, a factory worker, and a ghost writer. She received her "degrees" in the public libraries of Cleveland, Ohio, where she moved with her family when she was three years old. Today, she is writing her seventh novel in a comfortable old house in Jenkintown, Pennsylvania; when she can, she spends her afternoons gardening.

Other novels by Sinclair:
Sing at My Wake
The Changelings (winner of the National Jewish Book Award)
Anna Teller

ABOUT THE SERIES

GEMS OF AMERICAN JEWISH LITERATURE is a new series devoted to books by Jewish writers that have made a significant contribution to Jewish culture. These works were highly praised and warmly received at the time of publication. The Jewish Publication Society is proud to republish them now with introductions by contemporary writers so that a new audience may have an opportunity to discover and enjoy these timeless books.

Other titles in the series:

Allegra Maud Goldman by Edith Konecky
Leah by Seymour Epstein
Coat Upon a Stick by Norman Fruchter

Wasteland

JO SINCLAIR

INTRODUCTION BY VIVIAN GORNICK

THE JEWISH PUBLICATION SOCIETY

Philadelphia • New York • Jerusalem   5747 • 1987

Library of Congress Cataloging in Publication Data

Sinclair, Jo, 1913–
  Wasteland.
  (JPS gems of American Jewish literature)
  I. Title. II. Series.
PS3537.E3514W3 1987   813'.54   87–2631
ISBN 0–8276–0280–4

Designed by Bill Donnelly

Introduction

Jews in America have accumulated a complicated social history in a short fifty years. Nowhere is this history more apparent than in the literature they have made. The novels American Jews have written over the past half century tell us what it has felt like, at every stage of the way, to be inside Jewish lives in this country, not so much through their content as through the quality of their prose. From *Call It Sleep* to *Zuckerman Unbound* —the compass swings from the fluency of the outsider to the fluency of the acculturated, and as it moves it takes in the groping, puzzled expressiveness of those who occupy all the spaces in between.

In 1935, *Call It Sleep* stood alone in Jewish-American literature. Driven by a pressing need to convey the taste of his own life, Henry Roth had produced an extraordinary novel. To read *Call It Sleep* is to enter a trance: The reader moves inside the writer's skin and stands behind his eyes, feels as he feels, sees as he sees, and is changed by what is felt and what is seen. The book transcends time and subject. Yet part of its greatness turns on the degree to which it seems to embody its time as well. Although the novel is set in the early decades of the century, Roth published it in 1935 and the reader cannot help feeling that something important is being said about Jews in America in the mid-1930s: so much political noise in Depression America, and so many Jews identified with the noise, yet such a profound silence welling up in the pages of *Call It Sleep*.

From the stillness of *Call It Sleep* to the tumult of *Portnoy's Complaint*. Faster than the speed of light, some might say, but the world turned upside down and inside out during those thirty years. For those of us in America who had gone into the Second World War as the children of intimidated inner-city Jews, 1945 signified an astonishing change in the atmosphere. The end of the war brought frozen food and nuclear fission, laundromats and anti-Communists, Levittown and a breakup of the college quota system. We were about to enter the new world as our parents had never imagined entering it. That was the big difference between us and them. We could imagine ourselves out there.

Jewish-American novels of the forties are filled with the fear and longing that came of imagining ourselves out there—downtown, in the city, more American than Jewish. These novels are among the most interesting written by American Jews. They are neither depressed nor manic, neither silent nor tumultuous. The word that best describes them is thoughtful; they have about them an air of thoughtfulness. It is as though the writers are straining to understand the transitional place in which they find themselves, and to figure out how they feel about being half in, half out. They seem to linger in the doorway of a room they are not certain they wish to enter. Only as the writing progresses do they (and we) realize that the sense of choice is illusory. To stand in the open doorway is to be compelled to enter the room. The larger world is inside the room. To turn back from it is to turn back into the smallness within ourselves. The writers know this. Knowledge brings pain and anxiety, exhilaration and an undreamt-of courage.

Published in 1946 and winner of the prestigious Harper Prize, Jo Sinclair's *Wasteland* was startling for its psychological precocity and for a boldness of social feeling that linked Jews, blacks, and homosexuals as cultural outsiders in a time when very few were able to make that parallel. Sinclair had grasped whole the language and drama of psychoanalysis, and she brought to her story of American working-class Jews great understanding of the anxiety that lies behind social exclusion. She knew such anxiety originated in a sense of shame and worthlessness that social experience might mirror but did not actually cause. She also knew that anxiety chased its own tail. With a writer's instinct for the timeliness of a metaphor, she made the ghetto in which her inner-city Jews live a reflection of the ghetto within themselves: that vast dark continent of the unknowing self she called a wasteland.

The time is the early forties, the place a large midwestern city, the characters a family called Braunowitz. The family is ignorant and depressed, lumpen and vacant-eyed, inarticulate, frightened of emotion. Mother, father, brothers, sisters, all wander about the house, each exiled from the others, each compelled to deaden himself or herself to the misery of this primitive isolation. Inside the deadness a live wounded self is daily being twisted out of shape. This, Sinclair observes, is early damage. A common heritage. Into this we are all born, out of this we must all struggle. The only way out is through self-understanding. To climb out of the swamp of early inner deadness one must become conscious. One must know how one came to be.

The genius of *Wasteland* lies in the strength of feeling the novel's structure imparts to this most hard-won of human wisdoms. Sinclair makes the Jewishness and the homosexuality of her characters symbolic of the disenfranchised inner state and psychoanalysis a paradigm of the struggle for self-possession. In 1943 it was exactly right to make ordinary social phobias and early analysis serve metaphorically. Sinclair's characters would not be accused of either paranoia or pathology.

Jake Braunowitz, thirty-five years old and the youngest son in the family, enters psychoanalytic treatment at the urging of his still younger sister, Debby (already an analysand), because he feels bad about himself. Inside, he says, it's like a wasteland. Jake had thought all he had to do was get away from the house, and from being Jewish, and he'd start feeling better. But it hadn't worked. He'd quit school, changed his name to John Brown, gone downtown, gotten a job on a big daily newspaper, become apprenticed to the photographer, and in time had discovered he had the talent himself. He becomes a press photographer, moves out of the house, drinks heavily, sleeps with gentile women. But nothing changes. Jake still feels bad about himself. Very bad. He drifts back home, back to his old room, back to the painful gloom and silence of his father's house . . . back, back, back. No one sees the pain except his sister Debby. It is she who begins the rescue operation.

The fact that Jake has changed his name, and that no one at work (including the woman he sleeps with) knows he is Jewish, is startling to a contemporary reader. Yet the prose is quite calm about the matter. No, it's not a good thing he's doing, and yes, we've got to get to the bottom of why he's driven to do it, but after all, it's not really so shocking, is it? It happens every day of the week. The reality is, it's hard to get a job out there if you've got a Jewish name.

True. All true. It makes perfect sense that Jake should change his name to John. The social invisibility inflicted on Jews in the forties matches perfectly the invisibility Jake feels within himself. He doesn't exist inside, or outside. He doesn't know who on earth he is, and no one "out there" will tell him. But this powerful sense of invisibility, of not actually existing, that didn't begin downtown, that began at home. In fact, it began in the very moment that the Braunowitzes, as Jews, were declaring tribal loyalties central to their identity.

The first major revelation in Jake's analysis is his memory of the Seder the year he was fifteen. He remembers being suffused by the ceremonial occasion. He loved the smell of the clean house, the wonderful food, the table beautifully set, the entire family gathered. He felt surrounded by love and beauty, safety and prosperity. As the youngest son he has read the four questions. They have always moved him deeply, and now for the first time he is aware of how fully the Jewish holiday provides him with meaning and centeredness. Here at the Passover table he knows who he is. The boy falls into a trance of emotion. Then:

> His eyes lifted from the page, the dish was set down on the table, and his father's voice began again.
> That was the moment it happened to him. . . .
> It struck him, with an appalling clarity, that they had not been listening.

Suddenly, Jake "sees" it all. The blinders of innocence are lifted from his eyes. The boy of fifteen is initiated into a sickening piece of knowledge. They do not love each other. They are not really a family; neither are they believing Jews. It is an empty ritual they are going through, as empty as their relations, one to another. He is alone here, more alone than he will again be anywhere else in the world, or in his life.

Jake looks around the table with new eyes:

> And now it was strange, now it was of terror and of trap, of the knowledge that his father was a dirty stranger and his mother a frightened, sad, incapable woman, that his older brother was a stranger with bored, cold eyes, that his sister was overly rouged and her flesh restless for he knew what—yes, he knew what in his own body, and that was more of the terror and lostness. And the other sister was a soft, dreaming baby with solemn eyes, a baby who might cry out in her own fear some day because she did not have mother or father strong enough or clean enough or loving enough. . . . All of it, the sudden, not-to-be-understood knowledge, the abrupt premonition, the shaking of earth's foundations, all of this suddenly was tied up with the fact that they were Jews, with this Jewish evening (how beautiful it had been up until a split, jagged moment ago! how full of secrecy and meaning!). . . .

This is the central moment in *Wasteland*. Around this moment the entire novel collects. It is toward the resolution of conflict as it is here described that all action and all meditation is structured. Within the context of this event Jake will "remember," on Saturday afternoons in the analyst's office, his groping adolescence and lonely manhood, his fragmented work life (he fears his own talent, takes "good" pictures in secret), and his fragmented eroticism (he cannot sleep with the woman he loves or love the woman he sleeps with). And, of course, one by one he will "remember" the entire family: his father ("a dirty, stingy, silent man who didn't flush the toilet after he'd used it"); his morbidly helpless mother; his sister Roz, who lives off men; his sister Sarah re-creating the same family horrors with her own children; his brother Sig, a flashy dresser who loses his job and deflates into silent listlessness; and

Deborah, the youngest sister, a lesbian whose lonely courage leads Jake out of his own wilderness.

The novel ends—it will come as no surprise—with Jake, having battled through to sufficient understanding, once again at the Seder (even photographing it this time), reading the four questions with an eased heart, in tender acceptance of the people at the table, fortified by the secret knowledge that he has, this very day, enlisted. Tonight he can be a Jew. Tomorrow he becomes a soldier in the armies of the western world.

Wasteland is a problematic novel in many ways. Its characters are somewhat shadowy, its structure at times too mechanical, its prose often as depressed as the story it is telling. But these failings do not weigh in the balance. What weighs in the balance is a strong intelligence at work that makes believable the pain felt by those who bear a double load of existential misery. This intelligence perceives clearly that, ultimately, freedom lies with conquering the demons (or squeezing the slave out of oneself drop by drop, as Chekhov said). It also knows that inner freedom inevitably releases one into the larger world.

Analysis takes Jake as far *in* as he can go so that he may emerge from the chrysalis of his own arrest. He is required to experience the pain and fear of all the others in the house so that he may free himself of their dark influence. He must "learn" that they languish even as he does, that within each of them is also a wasteland. (Sinclair mimics the analytic process wonderfully but crudely; in three or four Saturday afternoons Jake "sees" what it takes others five or seven years to see). Diving down into family life he gains the strength and courage to surface into his own life.

In exactly the same way, Jake must accept his Jewishness so that he will be free to leave it for the larger world. In his life the denial of Jewishness is the sign of a man at war with himself. On the other hand, Jewishness accepted is a negotiated peace between intimates whose feelings are mixed. Jewishness, as the Braunowitzes have known it, is the anxiety-ridden, childlike state of life in the ghetto. Now, for the first time in America, the barriers between the ghetto and the larger culture have been lowered, and Jake is compelled to pass through. It is the instinct of the healthy organism to fill available space. Jewishness, as such, is therefore now behind him, not before him.

To leave the family and the ghetto is neither to deny nor to shrink from them; it is only to detach properly from them. However, detachment is clearly a prelude to assimilation. Jake must abandon his childhood grievance if he is to mature, and in a very real sense he must abandon Jewishness as he has known it if he is to integrate his own experience. Jake's children will be only half Jake, and their children a quarter Jake. The handwriting is on the wall. The writer reads it quietly and with interest.

Wasteland is a remarkable social document, a state-of-the-art observation of the American-Jewish situation in the early forties, made calmly, clearly, and in an undefended manner. Never again would there be such calm in American-Jewish novels. As the process of assimilation went inexorably forward (and American Jews simultaneously learned the full truth of the Holocaust), a kind of frenzy seized the writers. It was as though they were terrified of what they were doing . . . or rather, of what they were no longer free *not* to do . . . and they became slightly hysterical. Saul Bellow and Philip Roth made the words Jewish and manic synonymous. "What are we doing? What are we doing?" their novels scream at us, from *Augie March* on. Jo Sinclair reminds us of the quiet before the storm, of that moment of speculation and insight that precedes the turbulence of engagement. Her novel, unquestionably, is part of the record of an absorbing and complicated piece of life.

Vivian Gornick

Wasteland

For *Helen Buchman*
Who Hates
Any Kind of Waste

And that one talent, which is death to hide,
Lodg'd with me useless, though my soul more bent
To serve therewith my Maker, and present
My true account, lest he, returning, chide . . .

Milton

One

Even in the secrecy of his own mind, Jake called him "the doctor." He hated the word psychiatrist. He hated it even if Debby
did say it was a beautiful word.

"I looked it up in the dictionary," he had told her harshly.
"Treatment of diseases of the mind! What in hell's that got to do
with me? Jesus, if anybody at the office knew I was going to a
guy like that!"

"But don't feel that way," Debby had said. Her eyes had got
that same look they had when she was listening to the radio
music at night, that program of recordings that came through
every night about half past eleven.

"It has the word soul in it," she had told him, with that look
in her eyes. "Psyche means soul. That's beautiful, isn't it?"

But then Debby was funny about words. "Hate is an ugly
word," she had said to him once. "You can't really bear to say a
word like that about Pa, can you? Even if it's true. Can you?" He
hadn't answered.

This was his third Saturday. He sat in the small, simply furnished office and watched the doctor open his notebook and
unscrew the top of his fountain pen.

He watched everything carefully, grudgingly liked most of

1

the things he saw. The two doors, for instance. Debby had told him about the two doors. You came in by the regular door but you left by the other door, not by the one you'd used to come in here. That was so's you wouldn't see the next guy, and he wouldn't have to see you. He liked that. He'd hate like hell to see that next guy, all right.

This was his third visit, but today things seemed different. The room looked warm, the quiet gray walls further away from the big desk, the ceiling higher. It was as if there were a feeling of space in the office. Jake did not feel so closed in, so anxious. Maybe he would talk today.

The first two visits had come to exactly nothing. He had jittered through the hour of talk that first Saturday without really saying a thing. Then, last Saturday, it had been examinations. Of course there was nothing wrong with him. He'd told the doctor that in the first place; still, it was a good thing to know for sure that there was nothing wrong. He'd told the doctor about his back hurting all the time, sometimes as if it were hammered bent and couldn't straighten up, but all the doctor'd done was nod and write in the notebook.

After the exams the doctor had said, "It's always better to know for certain, isn't it? That nothing is really organically wrong. I agree with you, John."

He liked that. The way the doctor called him John, instead of Mr. Brown. He was a lot like a father was supposed to be. He reminded him a lot of Pete. Except, Pete was a lot older. The doctor's voice and eyes. Those were the two things he kept remembering during the week, between visits.

Both Saturdays he had come away from this office with his hands sweating. "I didn't tell him anything important," he had said to Debby in the living room late at night, when he'd come in and she was still sitting there. "Maybe it won't work for me the way it did for you. I couldn't talk. I didn't really say a damn thing, even though I did some talking."

"Listen, Jack," Debby had told him quickly, "you'll talk. Just don't worry about it. You'll be going to him every Saturday for a long time. Every Saturday, three o'clock, you'll be there. It'll just start by itself. The talking, I mean. Just don't worry about it."

"He didn't tell me to lie down on that couch in there, either," Jake had said stubbornly. "He told me to sit down in the chair in front of that big desk he sits at."

He was sitting in the chair now, waiting for the doctor to say something. There was a long window high in the wall back of the desk, and the bright afternoon light came streaming down through it, directly onto Jake's head, warming it. The doctor sat in a kind of dimness, exactly as though a strong electric light were behind him, so that his head was outlined but his features seemed gentled and far away, and his eyes that gray-blue color. There was an anonymity about him that reassured Jake. He didn't seem quite a real man sitting there, though his handshake had been hard and warm. He wasn't like a man Jake might meet in the street and stop and talk to, or a guy who might drop into the office and stand around outside the darkroom, yelling some casual thing from behind the curtains.

Jake thought of some other words Debby had called beautiful. The words made the doctor seem even more anonymous, more wonderfully unlike other people, when he thought of them in connection with him.

"How can you hate the idea?" Debby had said to him. "Do you know what you could call a psychiatrist, if you wanted to? A catalytic agent. You've had chemistry, you know what I mean. Well look, Jack, he's like a vessel through which all these parts of you pass. The parts that are all confused, that—well, that can't get together and are making you feel so rotten. They have to get together and work together, or else you'll just feel more and more rotten. Well, a psychiatrist is the agent that's going to make the changes in you. And he's going to stay unchanged himself, just like a catalytic agent stays unchanged. Once you don't need him any more you just don't go to him any more; he's nothing that will have to stay with you the rest of your life. Don't you see, Jack? What's there to feel ashamed of in chemistry?"

Sitting in the chair, he remembered how he had used to spend his Saturday afternoons before Debby had persuaded him to go to the doctor. In the Brass Rail mostly. (Though when Laura had been around they had gone to her apartment; in the summer they had stopped there and picked up the dogs and had driven far out on the lake road, then stopped to swim. The drinking hadn't started until late afternoon then, or early evening, and the crowd would drop in, and Katherine would be sitting at the piano playing, singing the old, slow, heartbroken songs, everybody starting to sing, too, after a while.)

Jake glared about him at the walls. They seemed good, too, anonymous, gray, deep and far back. He was nervous but he felt fine. Full of words; all he needed was the signal to start. Nothing in the room was too sharp today. He remembered how sharp and tense he had felt all that morning, all the way through his three assignments. Then, when he was through in the darkroom, about one-thirty, he had gone down to the Brass Rail. He had got one sandwich and coleslaw down, no potatoes, and then he had had three, one after another, quickly. Then he'd had a fourth before leaving.

The sharpness had left him in the car, as he drove toward his appointment, and when he had got to the doctor's outer office it was completely gone. The secretary had taken him right in. He felt nervous now only with wanting to talk. He wanted that very much. He wanted to tell Debby tonight that it was O.K., that he had talked, that he was starting to feel better.

The doctor's voice came into his thoughts, softly as usual, unabruptly, as though it had been talking for some time. "How do you feel today, John?"

"Lousy." Jake's muscles tensed. He was so anxious to talk that the word had come out in a harsh lump.

"Do you want to tell me about it? What's bothering you, John? Can you talk today?"

"I can talk, all right!" Jake hitched his chair closer to the desk, became aware, almost painfully, of the watching eyes.

"I'm not drunk," he said immediately. Heat sluiced down over his face and into his neck and collarbone. "I had a few drinks, sure. It's always easier to talk when I've had a few."

The doctor nodded. He didn't look surprised, or disapproving, or anything but waiting and listening. His eyes were the same, gentle, that blue-and-gray mixture which was the quietest color Jake had ever seen. Debby's were blue, but not quiet. Strong, like her hands, like the things she talked about. Laura's were brown. Kathy's were brown, too, but so different from Laura's that they seemed a different shade.

"What are you thinking about?" the doctor said. "Tell me. What's in your mind right now?"

Jake glared. Very suddenly he felt resentful, thought, Aw nuts, why in hell did I ever come?

He said it deliberately, feeling the half drunkenness tighten into anger as he talked, "Why, I was thinking of the way I always have to get tanked up before I can talk to anybody. What do you think of that?"

"All right, now you're what you call tanked up," the doctor said quietly. "Now you're all set to talk. What do you want to talk about?"

Jake stared at him. His heart sank a little as he thought, Jesus, I won't even have to get drunk to talk to him.

It was too unfamiliar a thought. He began to stammer. He did not know how to start so he clung to Debby in his mind. "How—how do I know what to say? I came here because you helped my sister."

"I helped her help herself," the doctor told him gravely.

"Oh sure, I know! She told me that. She said she got two things from you. They're what I want, too! One, she found out what she really wants. Two, she found out how to get her hands on what she wants."

He began to feel panicky, on the treacherous edge of slipping into the leaning on Deborah again, feeling the comfort of her hard shoulder and arm.

"You feel confused, don't you?" the doctor said.

Jake nodded.

"But take it slowly, easily." The doctor's voice was that way, too, slow, easy, and Jake pulled the breath slowly into his chest. "What bothers you very much? At this moment? Tell me about that one thing. Never mind all the others right now. We'll talk about all of them eventually. What bothers you most right now?"

Jake shoved the words out almost frantically. He did it in shame, the way he had come here, half afraid, the way he had been half afraid coming here.

"It's my nephews. My sister Sarah's kids. That's why I really came to you. I don't give a damn about myself! But those two kids—my God! When I think of it, how they're going to go through the same hell I did—and wish they were dead. Young kids like that! I can't stand it when I think they're going to be knocked out, too. The same as all of us. Every Goddam one of us. Except Debby! She's O.K. She's the only one of us who got away."

He watched the doctor write, and the quiet movement seemed natural, a part of the quiet room, and the doctor's eyes seemed scarcely to leave his, so that the writing had much of that automatic and anonymous quality which made him feel safely away from the ordinary world.

He himself felt himself at the beginning of a wonderful exhilaration. It was the tremendous and almost shattering relief of telling something he was ashamed of; and he knew that he would tell it all, just as Debby had, all the secret things no one knew, just he, the things which sucked at the core of him, which had corrupted him from the very beginning of his being.

"Listen," he said suddenly, "don't you want me on the couch? Instead of sitting here?"

"I beg your pardon?" the doctor said.

"Debby said she lay down on the couch," Jake said hesitantly. He wanted to lie there. It seemed to him that it would be wonderful to lie on the couch, relaxed, being held his full length, not to have to think of anything but the words spilling out of him.

"Look here, John." He started. The doctor's voice was still gentle, but very firm. When he looked up hurriedly, the eyes seemed all blue with warmth. "Your sister lay on the couch, you sit in the chair. There are good reasons for both. If I think, as your doctor, that you should sit, don't you think that's a good enough reason?"

Jake's voice flared nervously against that sympathetic look. "I wouldn't even be here if it weren't for my sister! You think I'd have come to a head doctor if she hadn't said it was a good idea? She did it, and that was good enough for me. If anybody as wonderful as Debby came here, I figured I didn't have anything to lose!"

"That's fine," the doctor said casually. Jake saw the gray anonymity in the eyes again, the glint of firmness in abeyance. He felt abashed. His hands were wet, and he pushed them out of sight, into his pockets. Oddly enough, he felt relaxed completely now, even sitting in the chair.

"What's this about your nephews?" the doctor asked. "Are they being harmed by someone? Are you worried about them?"

Jake did not know how to say it. He stared miserably at the doctor's notebook.

"How old are they?" the doctor said.

"Bernie's thirteen. Allen's eight. Bernie's the one right now. But the other one'll be there, too. Before you know it." He looked up, into the watching eyes, saw shore for an instant and the words rushed out. "Jesus Christ, Doctor, they're going to be wasted! That's what gets me. It isn't enough that all the rest of us were wasted—now those little snots have to go exactly the same way! That's what I can't take. Why in hell do their lives have to be wasted, too?"

"Wasted," the doctor repeated. Jake was not aware of being questioned with the word, but he felt savagely that he would cram it across the desk.

"Wasted, wasted," he cried. "Like garbage. Just throwing things down the drain. You know what the word means, don't you?"

"Yes, I think I do. You say, just like all of us. Who is all of us, John?"

"My brother. My father and mother. Me. My sisters." But then Jake looked up, the savagery halted. "Not Debby."

"Everybody in your family with the exception of your sister Deborah," the doctor said. Again, it was not a question but a gentle underscoring of what had been said. "And you yourself? You believe that your life has been wasted. What makes you think that?"

"What makes me think that! My God, I don't even know what it's all about. I get up every morning and I'm—I feel like it's still night. I feel black, pitch black. For Christ sake, what's bothering me? I don't even know! Black all the time. Heavy. Like the whole world's on my back. All right, I call it being wasted!"

"What's it like at home?" the doctor asked.

"Home?" Jake said, and he was beginning to stammer in earnest. "Why the devil bring that up? All I want is to help those two kids. I don't give a damn about myself. Honest, I mean it! They don't live in our house. Why talk about that damn trap of mine?"

7

He could not stare the doctor down, and he began to shout. "I wouldn't want to talk about it. I never talk about it to anybody. It's nobody's worry but mine. O.K., O.K., and Debby's, too! But nobody else gives a damn. I wouldn't want anybody to know about the house." He stopped.

"There is no shame here," the doctor said to him. "Here, in this room, nothing is shameful. Even if you've believed it is all your life. When you talk about it, John, when you get it out into the open, you'll discover it's not shame."

Jake nodded bleakly. A kind of numbness had come into his mind with the shouting, and now it was a numb relief at having said the first words about the house. (As soon as you talk about it, Jack, Debby had said. As soon as you say it out loud and think about it. It changes. It gets a kind of perspective.)

"So it's not only your nephews' potential waste," the doctor's patient voice began to point out to him. "It is also your own wasted life behind theirs. That's what bothers you so much, isn't it?"

Jake nodded again. His throat ached. If that's what it was, he hadn't known it. He hadn't given a damn, but when the words had come out they were true. And it wasn't true that he hadn't given a damn.

"Wasted lives everywhere you look," the soft voice said, like a pointing finger. "Wherever you turn, in your own family, your own house. And now the babies are starting to be wasted, too. Is that it, John? Is that what you mean?"

"I didn't care so much about me," Jake said hoarsely. "The way I can't do anything. The way I worry all the time. I figured, all right, I'm through, I'm no good. The whole bunch of us, we're through. Then, all of a sudden, I saw the kids starting it all over again. I'd forgotten they were alive. I never paid any attention to them. All of a sudden, I see Bernie. Going exactly the way all of us went. Like—like garbage!"

"Except Deborah, you say."

Jake's voice was lower. "She's different. She's the only one. I wouldn't even have seen Bernie if she hadn't told me about him. The way he would be wasted, too, if I didn't do something. She's the one who made me see that."

"And what do you see when you look at Bernie?"

Jake swallowed. "What?" he said. "What do you mean, what do I see?"

"Do you see only Bernie?"

"Well, I see what's going to happen to him. Is that what you mean?"

The doctor's voice seemed hard and gentle at the same time. It made him grope and probe, it made him anxious to answer right. "And what else do you see?"

"What else? Maybe Allen. Yeah, I see Allen, too, the way he'll be like Bernie soon. Another couple of years, and he'll be tough and swearing all the time, too." He looked into the eyes to see if he had answered correctly.

"Anything else?"

Jake tried hard. He brought out a picture of Bernie as he had seen him last. "I don't know what you mean, Doctor," he finally said.

"Could it possibly be that Bernie is a mirror for you?"

"I don't get it," Jake said doggedly.

"Could it possibly be," the doctor said, "that in looking at Bernie you see your own wasteland as a cause, a reason, for that child's approaching wasteland?"

Jake listened closely to the strangeness, the remoteness, yet the appalling familiarity, of that. He had never put it into words. The blackness and heaviness had blotted out words.

"I never called it wasteland," he said carefully.

"Could you call it that?" the doctor asked, his voice as careful as Jake's.

"Wasteland. That's like a desert, isn't it? Nothing grows there. It's all dry. It's all—dead. Is that what you mean?"

"Is that what you mean?" the doctor stressed gently.

Jake looked at him. His throat was dry and scratchy. He felt frightened because he had never said it in words. He had never brought it out into the open, out of the dark and heavy obscurity of his thoughts.

"Land that's barren," the doctor said, almost absently. "Where nothing will grow. When a flower, or even a blade of grass, is put there, something seems to choke it. It dies. Isn't that what you'd call wasteland, John?"

Jake nodded, thinking of the other thing. His heart was

9

pounding. Was that why he'd been so worried? Because a kid like Bernie could be caused by—all of them? Including him? My God, like you catch a sickness; you go into a house where it is, and then you catch it!

"Tell me," the doctor said almost carelessly, "is there any love in the wasteland? Has John Brown ever been in love?"

Jake flushed heavily. "What's that, a joke?" he said.

The doctor watched him now, Jake could see. "There is no reason for me to joke," he said gravely. "Is it possible for love to exist in a wasteland, John?"

Jake shook his head miserably. "I have to get used to you, maybe," he said, his voice very low. "I just don't talk about such things. I mean—Jesus Christ, I'm not used to talking about things like that!"

"Would you rather not talk about it just yet?" the doctor said. "You can talk about anything here. You're in your doctor's office. But there's no hurry. You can talk when you like."

"She isn't even in the city," Jake said harshly. "The one I'm in love with. Laura. Her name's Laura. She's in Washington. Why talk about her? She'd never marry me, anyway. Hell, that's another thing about me. I haven't even ever had a Jewish girl friend."

He looked up quickly, anxious to see the doctor's reaction.

"Don't you like Jewish girls?" the doctor said, as casually as he had asked any of the other questions.

"Oh, sure. They're—well, they'd be the real thing. You wouldn't kid around, or—well, I mean, that would be the real thing. I just never had any." He wondered if he could tell the doctor that he had never understood that part of it.

"Maybe I'm just not good enough," he added suddenly. "I don't want to—to get into any trouble with a Jewish girl, that's all!"

"I see," the doctor said. "But Laura's gone to Washington. Do you ever see her?"

"No. We write once in a while." Sullenly, he added, "I see this girl, Katherine. She's in the same office with me. A reporter. We go out a lot."

"In love?"

Jake laughed. "My God, no! We're not in love. Katherine would laugh like hell if you said that to her. She's a good friend of Laura's, she knows how I feel about Laura. Hell, the whole office knew about that! But we like each other a lot. She's swell fun. Likes to drink. Plays the piano like a champ." He stopped laughing. "She isn't Jewish, either."

"Oh, do you mean you couldn't be in love with a woman who wasn't Jewish?"

Jake tensed in the chair. "I don't know about that! Laura isn't a Jew. I mean—well, maybe I don't think I'd ever marry anyone who wasn't Jewish."

"But you would have sexual relations with such women."

"Well, but look," Jake said uncomfortably, "I never thought about it, that's all. I just never thought I'd marry anybody who wasn't."

"You must be very proud of being a Jew," the doctor said to him.

For a moment, Jake felt stunned, as if the words had crashed into his chest like a bar of iron. Then he cried sharply, "That's wrong! That's all wrong. I hate being a Jew. Nobody in the office even knows I'm a Jew. My God, I used to wake up sweating because I dreamed they found out I was—." He broke off, suddenly aware that he had said it. After all the years he finally had said it out loud.

"Come now, is it so difficult to tell the truth?" the soft voice said.

"It's tough," Jake admitted. He felt depressed, shaken to some secret part of himself, where the words had lain in silence for so long.

"Listen to me, John," the soft voice went on. "In this room you can tell the truth about everything. This room is you now. The rest of the world is removed. The rest of the world will not have to know what is said here. You know that, don't you?"

"Sure, sure," Jake said. He wanted to cry now. Talking aloud. He had never talked aloud, only to himself. What made him want to cry? This feeling of relief, or the fear? He was terribly afraid. He was afraid of what he'd say now, and afraid of what it would mean to him when he said it.

He was not even surprised when the doctor said, "Are you afraid?"

He nodded. The doctor would know everything about him. Then it would be all right. Then he wouldn't have to worry. (It isn't that he tells you what to do, Debby had said to him. It's not magic, Jack. It's just that you get all those confused, terrible thoughts out into the air, then you figure out what to do with your life. You can't figure out things you have hidden away, secrets. He helps you, Jack. He's a doctor, he knows how to name things, he helps you find out what's the matter. It's not magic, it's that he's a doctor and he knows what to call all kinds of sickness. He knows all the medicine, too.)

"What's the matter with me, Doctor?" Jake said dully. "What do you call my sickness?"

"Let's not talk about that now, John. Let's talk about two favorite words of mine. Truth and fear. Do you ever say those words to yourself?"

When Jake remained silent, the doctor said, "Let me tell you what I know about those two words. People are afraid when they don't know the truth. In this room you can talk, you can get the truth out of yourself. Pleasant or unpleasant, it must be the truth. And then you can face it. Do you understand? Once you know the truth, there's very little to be afraid of. Tell me now, do you understand?"

The voice was gentle, firm, a sound of decision he had wanted all his life. When Jake looked up his eyes were wet.

"That's why I get scared. Worried." There was no shame for him in crying. There was only the wonderful relief of sharing the fear and of sitting here and asking for help, openly, with no shame.

"Because I don't know. I can't figure things out, and who is there to ask? There wasn't ever anybody to ask! That's when I feel so rotten. When I try and tell myself what it's all about—and *I don't know*. I can't find out." (It's not magic, Debby had said. You talk, you tell him all the secret stuff that's in you, that knife stuff. I know, Jack, I know how those knives feel. And then both of you figure it out. People go to him for help because he's trained, he's a doctor. Some people can't figure it out for themselves. I couldn't. I asked for help. I'm not ashamed to ask for help when I need it.)

He wept for a while, not harshly but in a relaxed, silent way, his handkerchief at his face. The warm, still room seemed to hold him very peacefully, and it was all right for him to cry. The words were out of their corners now. He could no longer feel the furtive creep of them, they were beginning to come out into the open room.

After he blew his nose and was wiping at his eyes, he said half seriously, "It's like when I'm drunk. That's when I cry sometimes, when I'm drunk."

He shoved the handkerchief into his pocket. The doctor was regarding him in the anonymous way he found so good. "Have a cigarette," he said.

When Jake took the first drag, the doctor said, "Don't you want to talk now?"

Jake thought he heard a kind of compassion, and he cried gratefully, "I do, I do! I never talked to anybody, except a little to Laura. And then I found Debby—talked to her. But that didn't happen till a couple of months ago. It's tough, Doctor!"

"It's very tough. I agree, John. Too tough?"

"No. No, I'll do it. I've got to." He used the cigarette for fierceness, puffing out the smoke furiously, all the time conscious of the mounting relief, the lightening of that heavy, black thing pressing on him.

He looked up, across the bars of blue smoke in the sunlight. "Debby said I could do it."

The doctor nodded. "What does she think of the situation? The nephews' situation. You seem to respect her opinion very much."

"She thinks I could help them," Jake said slowly.

"In what way?"

"I told her I didn't know how I could," Jake said. He looked frightened, an expression he tightened from his mouth and eyes as he rubbed out the cigarette.

"She said I was probably the only one who could help them. Bernie, especially. His parents aren't any good with him. Hell, they aren't any good with anyone! He—well, Debby said he likes me. He thinks I'm a—a big shot. You know the way kids get about certain people. He knows I take pictures at prize fights and ball games. He thinks that's big-shot stuff."

"But you don't think you can help?"

"My God!" Jake said. He wanted so much to tell the doctor what he meant that his throat felt raw. "How the hell could I do anything for him? I'm as wrecked right now as he's going to be

13

some day! I mean, I'm through. I don't know what to do next for myself. How can I tell a *kid* what to do? I'm trapped. And he's going to be trapped in a year, maybe two, three years. Just like the whole bunch of us. How in hell does Debby expect me to tell him what to do?"

"Well now, take it easy," the doctor said. The pen was moving, and Jake watched it gratefully, thinking, That's my guts he's writing down.

"Talk as much as you like, John, but don't get so excited. There's time for everything you want to say. There's time to open every trap you see."

Jake glared. "Time! I'm thirty-five. How much time do you think I've got left?" But another thought clicked in his mind. "But hell, there's nothing to do with the time I've got left! Sure, it's like that wasteland you talked about. I want to enlist, but what'll I do about my mother?"

Now he was confused again, all that weight of words backing up in his chest and throat, and choking him. "That's only one example! There's so damn much to tell you! Debby said I should enlist if I really want to. Everything will work out all right, she said. But I keep telling her—how'll they get along without me? And now these kids, Jesus! Every time I think of Bernie I just feel sick. Absolutely sick."

"Why do you want to enlist?" the doctor asked.

"Why? I don't know. There's a war on. It's something exciting, new. You get away from all the old things. You leave the house, your job." (But I'll tell you, Jack, Debby had said with a kind of sadness. You wouldn't really get away from all these things. It doesn't work that way. You'd be taking them right along with you unless you cleared them up first. Before you enlisted and went away. It's like you would be carrying them around inside of you, no matter where you went. You can't leave things like that behind. I know. They stay with you. It's like they're in your blood.)

"What about winning the war?" the doctor said crisply. "Does that enter into your plans?"

"Oh, sure. I don't care. The war—hell, what do I know about the war? There's a war on, and you get into it." Jake reddened. "Sure, that's one of the reasons. Anybody enlists so he can help win the war!"

The doctor pushed the square box across the desk toward him. "Tell me," he said as Jake lit a cigarette, "do you ever think of the Jews of the world when you think of enlisting? The suffering, the way they're murdered and tortured?"

"No. I don't know. No, I never think of them." Jake winced back into the chair, watched the doctor miserably. "Why should I think about the Jews of the world? I'm an American. Why should I have to call myself a Jew all the time?" He blew out smoke, tapped the cigarette harshly against the ashtray on the desk.

"Maybe Bernie wouldn't be in such a tough spot if he weren't a Jew," he said in a low voice. "You haven't thought of that, have you?"

The doctor smiled, nodded. "Tell me about Bernie," he said.

"I don't know too much," Jake said quickly. "I don't see a hell of a lot of my family. It's a funny family, sort of." He was talking faster and faster. He had never said so much about the family before, to anyone. The old, apologetic strain went through him but he talked faster, with a kind of desperation, against it. "We're not close, see? We don't like each other much, and we don't have much to do with each other. I've never been to Roz's apartment, or to Sarah's house either."

"Yes, but tell me the little that you do know about Bernie," the doctor said.

"All right, I'll tell you. Sure." Jake smashed out the cigarette, thinking back to about a month ago, Friday. He had come home early from an East Side assignment, close to the house. Instead of going back downtown, he thought he'd print his stuff the next morning; he was on the seven o'clock shift, and he'd have plenty of time to make the night edition if he worked on them when he got to the office.

"Bernie came over to the house to pick up the fish and bread for his mother. You see, my mother always bakes bread on Friday. And she makes this *gefüllte* fish—I don't know if you've ever had any. It's Jewish fish, sort of stuffed. We have it every Friday night for supper. It's wonderful. Then we have chicken and soup, and this bread she bakes. *Cholah*, it's called. You know, Friday night is when our Sabbath begins, and we always have this special food. I don't know if you know anything about it."

"I know," the doctor said softly.

"Well, my mother always bakes for Sarah, too. And she makes twice as much fish, too, so Sarah's family can have some, too. It's hard to make. I don't think a lot of people could make that kind of bread or fish. I guess my mother learned how in Europe. You know, in Russia, where she was born and raised."

"And you're always home for that Sabbath meal?" the doctor asked.

"Oh, sure," Jake said. "That's about the only meal I eat at home. Yeah, that's one night I eat at home. All of us do. Roz and Sig and Deborah, too."

"And Bernie came to the house?" the doctor reminded him.

"Well, that Friday was the first time I'd had a really good look at him in a long time. He's so big. He's even got the beginnings of a mustache, and his face is starting to break out. He's a little cross-eyed. Debby says it's because he had measles when he was around seven. She says he was supposed to wear glasses, and he did for a while—the school gave him a pair—but then he quit wearing them. You know how kids are, he just quit. His parents never did anything about it. That's the way they are, the kids do anything they want to."

"Did you talk to Bernie?" the doctor asked.

"I tried to. He wouldn't even look at me, kept looking at the floor, and giggling a lot. I guess he's shy. I had to go out to the kitchen to see him. I heard my mother tell him I was in the living room, and to go on in and see me. But he didn't. Out in the kitchen, I asked him how he was doing. All he said was, O.K. He looked up at me for a second, then he looked at the floor again. I gave him a dime. He wouldn't take it at first. Kept on giggling, and said, 'Naw, I don't want it.' I told him, 'Go on, take it. Buy yourself something.' My mother kept telling him to take it, too. Finally he took it, kind of mumbled thanks, grabbed the basket of fish and bread and ran out of the house. Funny kid."

"Why is he funny?" the doctor said.

"Why?" Jake stared back at him, a little confused. "Why didn't he want to take the dime? After all, I'm his uncle. And the way he wouldn't look at me. Why shouldn't he look at me?"

"Maybe he wants more from an uncle than a dime. Maybe he wants to know you, but is too shy. He sees you rarely, you said that yourself."

"Oh, nuts!" Jake cried. "That's what Debby said, that maybe he wants something else than a dime. Why should he want other things? We don't even know each other. I'm a stranger to him. He is to me, too. A person doesn't want things from strangers." He hesitated. "My mother told me a couple of things about him—he sure is a stranger to me! My mother feels bad about him, but it's like she says, what can you do for a crazy kid like that?"

"Crazy in what respect?"

"They call him a moron, my mother says." Jake began to feel warm all through him, talking about Bernie. "See, he gets deficiency slips in school all the time. Last year he failed. He makes his mother cry a lot. My mother says he loses his temper, starts to holler and shout. Of course, everybody in Sarah's house shouts all the time. I remember when they were living upstairs of us—before we lost the house and had to move— Sarah and Max would be screaming at the kids all the time, and the kids would be hollering back. All kinds of swearing, in English and Yiddish both. Well, I guess it just got worse through the years. My mother says it's pretty terrible. Bernie swears at his mother, and Max beats him, and Bernie calls his sister a bum. You know, stuff like that."

"Is his sister a bum?" the doctor asked coolly.

"Leah?" Jake said. Then, heavily, "I don't know. Maybe she is. She's around twenty-one now, I guess. You know, she seems a lot like my sister Roz, runs around with a lot of guys with lousy reputations. Well, she and Bernie go at it hot and heavy, my mother said. Then Sarah starts screaming and crying. Then, when Max is home he finally tells them all to shut up. Ends up by whipping Bernie."

He lit another cigarette. "I got a lot more about Bernie from Debby. She feels sorry for him; none of the others do. She's tried to talk to him, but it doesn't do much good, I guess. Every once in a while she goes over to Sarah's and tries to talk to her, and to Max and Leah. She ends up by losing her temper, she says."

"What else did you get from Deborah?" the doctor said.

"Well, he doesn't like school. He loses his temper, then he won't eat for two or three days in a row. Not at home, anyway. Guess he fills up on candy and such stuff. But he can be a good kid, too, Debby says. Goes to the store for his mother. Plays games with Allen sometimes. The thing is, I don't think he's got much of a chance. I tried to tell that to Debby. She says it's pretty raw there. Maybe they don't mean it—I mean Sarah and Max, and Leah. I mean, they're not bad people. But they call him a cross-eyed little snot when they get sore. Or they call him moron, or half-wit."

"And what does Bernie do when they call him cross-eyed little snot?" the doctor asked.

"Hollers back, I guess."

"Gets back at them, doesn't he?" the doctor said. "Gets back at them the same way they attack him, by using their vulnerable spots. Calls his sister a bum. He's an adolescent, maybe he knows what the word bum means. Tell me, does he call his mother names, too?"

Jake felt tired suddenly. "Sarah's a big woman," he said. "Debby says when Bernie gets sore he calls his mother fat. Stands there and jeers, hollers that the only thing she's capable of doing is eating all the time."

The doctor asked him softly uttered questions. "Does she do anything but eat, as far as that child is concerned? Do you think that perhaps he senses that her size is her vulnerable point, just as his crossed eyes are his? Do you see a reason for his trying to strike out at her, just as she strikes at him?"

That tired feeling jabbed at Jake again. He knew he could not combat the doctor, but he tried again to accuse his nephew. "Debby says he makes fun of Allen, too, sometimes. Sneers at him. Allen talks with kind of a lisp, see, and Bernie mimics him."

The doctor examined his pen, his careful, cool voice going right on. "And perhaps Bernie thinks he can hurt his mother by sneering at Allen, the youngest child. Hurting Allen would give him a certain kind of satisfaction. Does the family like Allen? Is he clever, a good student?"

"I guess. Yeah, he is. In fact they're always comparing Allen's brain with Bernie's dumbness."

The doctor nodded. "When Bernie grows older he'll undoubtedly learn to keep his feelings to himself. Then, after a while, all that pain inside may turn against him. Did that happen to you, John?"

Jake was not surprised. Everything the doctor talked about made sense. "I'm sorry for the kid," he said, but his voice sounded empty and tired to his own ears. "I don't know, I thought I didn't give a damn about my family any more. But all of a sudden I'm thinking about Bernie. Pretty soon it'll be Allen, too. Calling her a bum. A man uses a word like that. It's all wrong about Bernie. It shouldn't be like that."

"Like what?"

Jake's feeling of tiredness mounted. When he lit a cigarette he saw his hands shaking, and he thought, It's because I'm saying it finally. And I'll say it all, too.

"Why should that kid go through the same kind of hell I did?" he mumbled. "My sister's house is just as rotten as ours always was—in a different way. At least we never hollered and cursed at each other. My father just never paid any attention. I mean, it's not fair, Doctor! All of us were wrecked, but I thought it was over with. Now it's beginning all over again. With kids again. Why shouldn't Bernie have the chance I never had?"

The office was silent and warm, with the scent of cigarette smoke drifting lightly on the air. Jake looked up into the gray-blue gentleness.

"To try to give Bernie a chance," the doctor said, "we'll have to know about the chance you never had. Do you feel like talking about it now?"

Jake said hesitantly, "I'd like to talk, sure. I really would. Where would I start? I feel as if I've got thirty-five years of words in me. Where do I start, for Christ sake?"

"You said 'a house as rotten as ours always was,'" the doctor said softly. "Tell me about that rotten house, John. Let's start from there."

And then, when he finally started to talk, it was easy. He had a crash and burn of words in him he wanted desperately to release. Sitting back in the chair, his eyes on the doctor's sometimes, but more often on the walls, where his remembering blossomed in pictures, he began to tell the doctor about the house. . . .

. . . He could not escape the house. Sometimes it seemed to him that someone or something had tied him to that house. A trap. Or to his mother. Maybe it was his mother who kept him tied to the house that way. Would that make it a trap? After all, he loved his mother. Did he love his mother? His mother was Ma, a short old woman with nearsighted eyes. Faded blue, gentle-looking, they never saw him. She never hollered. There was a weakness in the bones and lines of her face, a helplessness which sapped any strength from his own bones when he looked at her. Yes, she was the rope to tie him. Not the old man. The old man was Pa, a dirty, white-haired man whose eyes had been cold and expressionless for as long as Jake remembered. Stingy, whether he had it or not. He had some dough now, and a few years ago he'd been on relief, but there was no difference. Oh yes, there was! When the old man had a few extra bucks in the bank, he acted like a big shot. The old man with his lousy, old half-ton truck, that he loved more than anyone in the house. The old, filthy bastard. He was no tie. He was a hate. A hate all tied up with money and a rotten, sneering way of smiling, and the garble of half English, half Yiddish he spoke. He was a hate all tied up with shame, but he couldn't tie Jake to the house. It was Ma who was the tie. Or could hate be a tie, too?

Only once or twice had he called the word trap, and then only to himself. Hell, it wasn't a word to say aloud. It was a word that made him feel ashamed. How could somebody you love trap you?

If only he did not feel so guilty about her. As if it were his fault that it was so bad for her! Jesus, how did she get stuck with a guy like the old man? Pinching her for money all the time, never a nice word, shoving dirt all over the house, in every corner. How could she sleep in the same room with the old man, even if they slept in twin beds? But why should he feel guilty about things like that? Why should he feel as if he had to pay Ma back for all the rotten years she must have had? Those vague years he had never inquired into too closely.

"We were always poor, always," Ma had said often; he remembered hearing her, he a child and listening too hard, her voice like a groan. "Money is the world," she had said time after time. In Yiddish it sounded worse: *gelt iss duh welt*. "When did we ever have enough money?" And he, the child, clenching his fists; he remembered, oh, he remembered, all right! Just as he remembered how she would cry sometimes because the old man wouldn't give her enough, cry and beg, and then the old man would get that smile on his face, like a whip. That's why it was hate for the old man. All the vague years, the vague, bitter stories he had caught in tag ends of sentences, in little aching pockets of silence. The rotten, tormented years she had spent with that bastard.

Pay her back. But how could he pay her back? He scarcely knew what the debt was, or the extent of the guilt. He knew only that it seemed like his guilt, and that he must make it up to her, make up for the years and the tears, and the bitter things, however vague they were. How?—maybe by giving her enough money. But he could not talk to her. Could he love her? That bewildered, shy, peering woman who spoke to him in Yiddish, who wanted him to come home to the tasteless meals, the cluttered table. She was a woman who could be browbeat by grocers, who exchanged an article three or four times after she bought it, and even then the indecision dogged her about the house every time she thought of the dress, or the apron, or whatever it had been she had bought. She was a woman he could not understand.

Could he not love her, however?—his mother, who was tired and old now, who caught cold easily, who sat silently in the kitchen evenings, reading the Yiddish paper in that helpless, sibilant half-aloud whisper. What debt was he trying to pay, for God's sake, trying desperately and yet unable to pay, unable to know how, unable to know anything but this depressed, black, trapped way of living?

And now, for years, he had been searching for a kind of identity—for himself, away from these people who were unreal and strange to him. Away from the house, he had no identity; he was not alive, he was without framework of name, without flesh of heritage, without blood of pride or love. And yet, within the house he was without identity, too. Within that house, walking in the dim, dirty rooms, he was a shadow to the shadows of his parents, his sister and brother. And the shadows of his two other sisters, and of Sarah's family, all these lengthened on the walls of the house, too.

But now, suddenly, one of those shadows had taken on the

starkness of flesh and blood. The shadow's eyes had focused, were staring into his. And now, for the first time, he felt how eyes were asking him for help. Bernie. A stranger child had become nephew, had become the accusing voice of his own blood. His own identity a secret, he was forced now to identify the child of his stranger sister. It was not to be understood. He felt all confused. He felt powerless.

He could not escape that house. From its hated shadows of waste, he walked out into the world each morning, trying to escape them, to lose himself in the world, but the house walked with him, like a dark and heavy thing tied to his back. He could not escape.

Once he had tried having his own furnished apartment. For three months. On Church Street, near the office. He had kept on giving Ma the same amount of money each week. Every Friday he would come home for supper, into the Sabbath candle-light, into the aromas of still-warm bread, fish and chicken. Solemnly, he would carry into the house the pack of dirty laundry, as solemnly accept the paper-wrapped package of clean shirts and pillow-cases, sheets and towels and handkerchiefs. After supper, back he would go. To what? Not identity; to a loneliness that was, in its way, more tortured than the loneliness of the house.

Sometimes Katherine would come up to the furnished apartment, sometimes Wally and Bill, once Ted Pope had come. There was drinking, singing, dancing to the Magnavox portable Laura had sent him two years ago Christmas from Washington. But when they had gone, the apartment was too quiet. Out of the corners of the room had drifted that loneliness, that darkness and feeling of guilt.

So he had moved home again, mumbling to Ma that he couldn't afford two places. And Ma? Whatever he did was right. No word—of approval, disapproval. Yet he knew she was glad when he came home again. Was he glad? He did not know. Christ, he would never know! Coming home was like sinking into a dark, dirty, familiar bed. At least the pain was familiar. Away from the house, he was frightened. He could not believe in himself, either at home or away, but when he lived at home at least he could touch the things that bothered him so much— the guilt, the mysterious debt, the shame.

During vacations he had driven to Mexico, once to Canada, many times to Cleveland and Pittsburgh. Always alone, and in a melancholy way he had enjoyed the trips, feeling always how in the back seat of the car the loneliness sat, waiting for him to look around. The top down, and the sun warm on his bare head, the wind so clean, so sharp; but in the car was the loneliness and the namelessness.

And in the end, it was always that feeling of namelessness which brought him home three or four days before it was time to go back to work. Not that a name ever awaited him in this city, in this house where he lived, or even at the office; but at least here, in the house, or in the office darkroom, there were the familiar torments, the known things he could fume at, or get drunk about, or lie in the dark bedroom and jitter about (listening to Sig breathing heavily in the other bed). Away from the house, there were too many unknown things; he was afraid to visualize them. In the darkness of his house, he had no need to visualize them. In that house, there was no hope for him, nor room or strength for a tomorrow. He was so afraid of that word, tomorrow.

He had told himself, in the house, that he wanted to be like other people, not ashamed, not lonely, not weak, not a child of dirt. Yes, there was dirt of the mind, too. And of the soul—to use Debby's word. And yet, in that house, he had always known that he didn't have a chance. He was trapped, wasted, like a dead man. Yes, wasteland was a good word. That was exactly what he was—in the head, in the guts, in the soul. A wasteland.

He had tried so damn hard to cut the rope between the house and him. Nothing had done any good. Changing his name had not done it. Drinking had not, nor the things he did evenings. Three or four nights a week he stayed downtown. It was a date with Katherine, or with some girl or other he had met somewhere and then telephoned for a date. It was a solo movie, after eating at the Rail, or poker with Wally and Bill and a bunch they called up to Wally's place. Or it was drinking, alone, or with the fellows, or with a girl. At the Brass Rail, or the Lucky Seven Club, or the Mexican Room. Nothing had done any good. He always came home. To the smell of the house, the aloneness, the bedroom with the two hard, narrow beds. The sound of the old man snoring, or groaning in his sleep. Sometimes he sat in the living room and finished the bottle, and he would listen, with a kind of dark pleasure, to the familiar sound of the old man's clock (he kept it in his bedroom) bonging the half hour, and the hour. As far back as he could remember, the clock had always been in the house, in whatever street the house had been.

If Debby was in the living room, reading or listening to that classical music she was so crazy about, or if she was asleep on the couch, the sheets glistening in the dark room, he walked right through the living room, hung his coat on one of the dining room chairs and went right to the bathroom, or to the bedroom. If Sig was not in the other bed, he would read. If Sig was there, he might read in the kitchen. He read *Time, Life, Liberty, Collier's*, and the *Post* every week. He had a circulating library card and would draw books regularly, adventure sagas, foreign correspondent stuff, all books on newspaper life, an occasional novel.

When Debby wasn't home, at eleven or midnight, or one, when he let himself into the house by the front door, he always sat in the living room for a while before he went to bed. It was the only room he liked even a little. Debby's books were in that room, and the radio, and she had hung a swell picture, full of bright yellow, over the mantel. It was her room. Besides sleeping there, she read there, and wrote there, too. Nobody else cared to sit in the living room. Sig was scarcely ever home, and Ma and the old man always sat in the kitchen. Always. The kitchen was theirs. The living room was hers. As soon as she came home he walked out of it and left it for her. He himself had no favorite room, but he liked the living room. It was brightest, sometimes even warm and alive-looking; it reminded him of Debby a lot, especially when that classical music was coming from the radio.

Sometimes, once a week or so, he came home on a weekday evening to eat dinner. That was besides Friday night. Ma called it supper. Highly seasoned Jewish food, which he liked; bits of this, fragments of that. On Mondays, there was always fried fish and potato pancakes, some nights there was herring or sardines or smoked salmon, things like noodle pudding, salami. The table was never set. He would reach for a fork or a spoon out of the table drawers, cut a slice from the loaf of pum-

24

pernickel or rye bread in the middle of the uncovered table. There was always plenty of lettuce or green pepper or tomato in the house; Debby had seen to that.

Nothing was regular with him, habit or custom, or breakfast at home, or even Christmas (wonderful thing celebrated by all the others at the office). Oh sure, he celebrated with the gang. He gave gifts and sent cards, got drunk. He always received gifts, sure, but he knew all the time it wasn't *his* holiday. See, there again he was different from everybody else!

Well, he could amend that; there were two regular things for him. There was Friday nights, and there was voting. He always came home for supper Friday night, and he always voted.

Voting was something that belonged to you. You wrote your name in the registration book, and you stood in line and marked the names of the guys you wanted in. You and all the rest of America. You were just like all the others, all the voters. Your name was just as good as the next guy's. In a voting booth, nobody knew who was your mother, or your old man! That was something he would do all his life, vote.

And Friday night supper? Well, that was the one time in the whole week when all of them came home to eat. Even Roz, his sister who lived alone in her own apartment on the other side of town. She was divorced, worked as a waitress in a night club, but that was the night she came home to see Ma. Drove home in her car that she'd bought for herself, walked into the house dressed to kill, made up to kill, and sat down with Debby to eat the Sabbath meal, by God!

That was the one night when there was a full meal, in courses, and maybe they didn't all eat at the same time, but the meal was a big one and always the same. Ma's *cholah*, still a little warm. You started with *gefüllte* fish, then chicken, then soup and noodles. They had always eaten soup last in their house; it was a Russian custom, he guessed. Sometimes there were dumplings instead of noodles. Then you ended with fruit compote, or stewed prunes.

It was food he loved. All week he ate downtown, in restaurants. American food. Roast beef, steak, apple pie, salad. But on Friday night there was the Jewish food, regularly, always the same. And the house seemed cleaner, the kitchen and bathroom floors washed. And in the dining room, on the bureau, the candles were lit. The candles, like a feeling of hush even now, like yellow wavering hush, and he could remember back, way back, on their flicker, the way they had always been lit on Fridays, at dusk. Ma, with the shawl over her head, standing in front of them, swaying. Through the years, there had always been Friday, with its candles and Sabbath food. A custom, a landmark in the undirected week, a stable thing in a world that was insecure and perilous.

Through the years, yes. What kind of a house was it, what kind of people, that through the years had raised a fence around him? A fence, a wasteland, a trap—take your pick, all of the words meant the same thing.

Yes, ask me again what the house is like. It was always like that. All right, what makes a house? The people in it, sure. Oh yes, the people change a little. Not inside; but through the years they change a little on the outside—to fit the Depression, say, or the going on relief, or when they lose a job. But inside, the guts of them, that never changes. The soul, as Debby would say. What makes up a soul? The feeling of hate, for Pa. The feeling of guilt, about Ma. The shame, about the others. The sneering at Sig. The questioning of somebody like Debby. His family, his torture, his anxiety—all these made up the house.

They get old, sure. Ma and Pa. But you don't even remember when that happens. When you look at them now, you never remember when Ma looked otherwise but helpless, her eyes nearsighted, her hands gnarled and much older than her face. You know Pa hasn't changed from anything but money grabbing, silence, that smile like something rotting out of his eyes and mouth. The white hair, the gray, grizzled-looking mustache, the dirty baggy clothes. When had Pa been anything but a feeling of shame thick as oatmeal in your mouth and throat?

The smell of potato pancakes in the house when you woke in the morning. That silent, dirty man liked them for breakfast, made them himself. You brushed past him standing at the stove, silently turning the pancakes in the early morning dimness of the kitchen (he never put on a light when he could help it), when you walked out of the house mornings.

Sig had changed, maybe. A balding guy of silences and, when he did talk, of big-shot speeches. Smoking that perpetual cigar of his, but you knew now that he was a lot like a scared kid inside despite the big-shot cigar; something you hadn't known when he was the manager of a department at a big plant. Remember how he gave Ma money every Saturday night? Remember how he'd rent a tux every New Year's Eve? How Ma would have everything ready for him Saturday nights when he came home to change before he went out on dates? How he was the big shot, the classy guy?

Losing a job had done it to him. His silences had thickened over the years, and he was still well dressed, he still went out on dates all the time, but he hadn't been the big shot around the house since the good job had gone. Who handed over the money every Saturday now? Little Jacky. But look, a funny thing! He hadn't taken Sig's place in the house—the big-shot place. Sig didn't have it now, but neither did he. He hadn't had it even when he was slipping Sig money, before he'd got this job he had now, a salesman. If anybody was the big shot, the one to whom Ma looked, for whom she prepared meals, it was, of all people—Debby!

His sister Deborah. Well, she went with the house, too. But in an entirely different way. If he could explain how he felt about her! She was different, entirely different from any of them. Look at Roz. Make-up, high heels, divorced, a night club waitress. Look at Sig, a guy who could cry like a woman. Look at Sarah and her awful family. And he, Jack, ashamed, eyes down wherever he went. And then look at Deborah. As if she didn't belong to any of them. As if she had been put into that house by accident. Yes, she looked a lot like all of them, except she was more blond, her eyes much more blue. Yes, she re-sembled him, especially. They had the same shape face, kind of the same sort of jaw. But what resemblance was there between her brain and theirs? Her—all right, her soul! None, absolutely none. Everything she did was different, and the way she did it. She was the youngest in the family; you know, the baby.

His sister Deborah. She was a book person, a music per-son. He had always thought of her as a scholar; well, she wasn't really, but she was always monkeying with books and maga-zines. She was always sitting there in the living room, with a pencil in her hand.

He didn't know a lot about her, no. She had always made him feel funny. She was so damn odd. Smart. My God, you know that girl was the valedictorian of her class in high school. No, not college, nobody in the family had gone to college. Sig went to night college for a little while. He quit after a while.

Oh hell, a person like Debby didn't really have to go to college. Yes, he'd always felt funny about her. He thought that was a feeling of shame, too. The way she looked like a boy, her hair cut short that way. He used to look at her and keep out of her way. He used to think, My God, if the fellows at the office saw her they'd laugh like hell. They'd look at me and say, "Jesus, Brown, what kind of a thing is that? You mean that's your sister?"

Now, he wondered if it was shame. See, she was something special. She wrote stories. She was—well, it was hard to explain about Debby. When you looked at her you got a feeling of how strong she was. How—clean. See, she was the one clean thing in the house. Everything about her was different. The kind of things she read, the kind of music she liked, the way she talked.

She talked Yiddish to Ma and Pa, sure, and she liked those Hebrew things the old man sang on holidays. But she looked just like a gentile boy. Sure, even in a dress. Around the house she always wore slacks. She'd always worn pants around the house. He could remember when she was a kid; she wore a funny, little pair of shabby knickers, and her hair was cut Buster Brown in those days. She'd looked like a little, tough Dutch boy. Milk-white hair, just like now, only now it was cut like a boy's.

Well, he didn't know, maybe he was still ashamed of her. Would he take her up to the newspaper, introduce her as his sister, to the editor, to Pete, to Wally and Katherine? My God, no! See, she wasn't like other people. She was too different. And there was another example! The whole bunch of them; they were different, not like other people. That's what makes a fellow ashamed. When a fellow is scared to death anybody he knows will ever catch sight of his parents, his sisters. O. K., Sig was nothing to be ashamed about, in his clothes or his speech. But look at his insides! That was something, wasn't it? To be ashamed of your older brother because he's all beat up inside.

My God, compare the old man with Pete, for example. Pete was the head photographer at the office, the man who'd hired him about seventeen years ago. He'd always wished Pete was his father. From the very beginning. Pete was somebody you'd be proud to have for a father.

Well, why say anything more about the house! Sometimes it was like he carried it around with him wherever he went. Down to the office, even. Sometimes it was like it got between the job and him, and then he couldn't do his work.

The job? He loved the job. For him there was nothing in the world as wonderful as a camera. Nothing. He could use one, too. But there was a damn funny thing about the camera. Sometimes, when he took pictures, he was afraid. All he could think of was the house, Ma, the old man, the smell of the house in the morning. Then—God, it was funny!—then he wasn't sure of the camera either. It was like he carried the house right into the job at those times. And the way he felt in the house— well, that was the way he felt about his pictures sometimes, too.

And when he was with people the same thing happened. He'd get to feeling—well, he didn't know! As if the old man were sitting in the same room, and all the people were watching Pa eat, or listening to him talk, seeing the kind of clothes he wore, seeing the way he acted toward Ma. Then he, Jack, wouldn't even be able to talk to people. Until he got a couple of drinks into him! He could forget about the house most of the time, if he had enough to drink.

The trouble was, whenever he heard somebody say "dirty Jew" he thought immediately of his family. Sure, and of himself. Was he ashamed of being a Jew? It looked like it, didn't it! And yet, every time he read about what was happening to Jews all over the world, he wanted to smash faces, he wanted to get up and shoot all those bastards who were doing it.

No, nobody at the paper knew he was a Jew. He'd just never mentioned it. His name wasn't Jewish; he didn't look like a Jew either. Why mention it? Why make a point of it? All right, maybe he was ashamed of being a Jew! But that wasn't the big thing he was ashamed of. There was plenty to be ashamed about without having to be ashamed of being a Jew.

When his father went on relief, for example. My God, how could a fellow ever forget a thing like that? Sarah and Max went on relief too, at the same time. They were living upstairs then; Pa and Max owned the house together, partners. That was the year they lost the house. Well, I was paying as much as I could! Sig wasn't working, and Debby couldn't get a job either. Maybe it was her screwy haircut and the way she walked that kept her from getting a job, I don't know. The old man, well, the old man was doing little jobs of hauling with his truck, the same as now, only he wasn't making more than a few dollars a week. So he goes on relief.

My God, I felt terrible. For a hell of a long time after it happened, I never came home if I could help it, just to sleep, and Friday for supper. I used to have nightmares about the office finding it out, that my family was on relief. Well, they never did find out.

Debby got us out of that, too. What she did was take one of those WPA jobs, and that took us off relief. I never asked her too much about it, but Ma used to tell me a lot of things when she saw me every once in a while. Debby had a job on the WPA Writers Project, and she'd keep a little of her check for expenses, give the rest of it to Ma. She never gave it to the old man, naturally. Debby doesn't have any use for him either. The funny thing is, she doesn't hate him. That's funny, all right. I don't get that at all.

Well, that went on for about three, four years. You remember the cracks people used to make about WPA in those days? Shovel pushers, grafters, all the rest of the things they'd call WPA workers. I mean, I heard those cracks all the time right at the office. I figured if anybody ever tried to tell me my sister was on WPA, I could always laugh it off, I could say I never saw my sister anyway. Well, luckily, nobody ever found it out. I mean, I was *ashamed* of the whole damn mess.

Debby. Yeah, she's the peculiar one in that house. See, one day she was a kid, a little, tough tomboy in knickers. Then, all of a sudden, one day I notice she's grown up, out of school, a kind of tall girl with blond, short hair. I mean, I got a feeling of white and clean when I looked at at her. The white hair, the blue eyes. Sometimes it's like you can smell how clean she is. Well, there it was. One day, all of a sudden, she's on WPA, supporting the family right along with me, right along with the ten bucks a week I gave Ma.

One day Ma tells me she's sold a story.

"Who bought it?" I asked. A story, my God!

"Oh," Ma said, "they didn't even pay her for it. A magazine by the name of *New Masses*."

It took me a few weeks, then I finally met up with Debby in the living room. It was about eleven o'clock at night. I came in and hung my coat over the dining room chair. She was sitting in the big chair in the living room, in the lamplight. Ma and the old man were asleep, the rest of the house was dark.

I went back into the living room, walked around for a second. The radio was playing, the kind of music she always had on; I've never heard her listening to any other kind. I felt funny. She was reading, all curled up in the chair, the light on that blond hair so it looked absolutely gold. Slacks and a white shirt, sleeves rolled. Well, she looked like a fifteen-year-old boy sitting there.

"I hear you sold a story," I said finally.

She looked up. Her eyes are so blue sometimes, you get a feeling of water, or sky. Know what I mean? Well, that night I got a feeling of ice.

"I didn't get any money for it," she said, and kind of smiled, and that's where the ice feeling came in. It was like she didn't have any use for me, and her eyes were like blue ice even though she was smiling.

"Could I read it?" I said.

She pointed to the table. "Help yourself," she said. "It's on page nine."

I took the magazine and sat down on the couch, turned to page nine. By Deborah Brown, it said on the page, and I got a feeling like a pain in my chest. Just the look of the name did it, I don't know why. I read the story. It was as peculiar as she was. I didn't know what to think, what to say to her. It was about colored people. Why the hell she should write about colored people! And I kept thinking, See, she's different even in a thing like this! See, your lousy family, even when they get into a magazine they're different than other writers!

When I looked up, she said, "Do you like it?"

"I think it's swell," I said. I felt my face get hot, and I couldn't look her in the eye.

"It's my first published story," she said, and that low radio music was all around her voice, all over the room.

"I read it to Ma," she said. Her voice sounded like it was

laughing at a private joke. "After I read it she said, 'Why do you have to write about colored people? Maybe that's why they didn't pay you anything for it.'"

"Oh well, Ma!" I said, but my face was plenty hot by that time.

"I didn't tell her," Debby said, and her voice was very quiet, "that Negroes are very important to people like us. She wouldn't have understood."

I couldn't look at her. What was I, ashamed, afraid? I didn't know. All I knew was that Debby was part of everything that made me feel different from the rest of the world.

About a year later she sold another story. This time Ma was plenty excited when she told me. "They sent her a check for a hundred and fifty dollars! Imagine, for one story! The name of the magazine? *Sketch*, I think it's called. Do you know of such a magazine?"

I watched the newsstands this time. I wasn't surprised. Debby. She could do anything and I wouldn't be surprised any more. That blond, strong sister who was like a boy.

The magazine came out with the story three months later. Her name was on the cover. D. B. Brown, not Deborah Brown. I bought a copy and took it up to the office, to the morgue, where I hang out a lot to read between assignments.

It was a story about the war in Spain. She took a bunch of kids and wrote about what happened to them during and after a bombing. And she compared them to American kids.

I don't know how I felt. Kind of proud. I guess. This D. B. Brown was my sister. She lived in that house, along with the old man, in those dingy, smelly rooms. She had come out of that house different, clean and like—well, like an electric light. A person who could write stories, whose name was printed in magazines. How did I feel?

Sure, proud. And yet this story, too, was different, not like most of the stories I'd read in magazines and books. Why should this sister of mine write about Spanish kids? About colored people? Why didn't she write about love and about people who were happy? Was she happy?

That was the first time I had asked myself if somebody in our house was happy or unhappy. All I had ever thought about was my own unhappiness. Was Debby happy? I asked myself. Is she maybe trapped, too? Does she have that awful feeling of wanting to pay back Ma? Of hating Pa? Does she feel different from the whole world? As if she's all alone, in a shameful and different way? Does she wonder about things she's writing, wonder if it's any good—the way I wonder about my pictures?

It was around that time that I began to watch my sister Deborah as much as I could. Watched her, what she did, how she did it. It was around that time that I began to feel as if there was a secret in the house, in the family. I thought maybe if I could figure Deborah out, then maybe I could figure out that secret.

But I couldn't. How could I figure her out? She was like that music she tuned in on the radio, strong and far away from me, sounds I couldn't understand inside of me. She was a secret, half like a man and half like a woman. Yeah, I began to see in her face and her eyes a lot of what women have there. A softness, a kind of a tender business. The way she talked to Ma sometimes, as if she were the older and stronger, and Ma could lean on her if she wanted to. The way she had nothing to do with the old man, but would bring home candy for Ma sometimes, or a shopping basket, or an umbrella—you know, little presents.

Sometimes, when I turned the key and let myself into the house, at eleven or so, she wouldn't be sitting there under the lamplight. The radio would be playing very softly, her kind of music, and when I'd walk into the other part of the house I'd see a light in the bathroom, the door open. There she was, with a rag and scouring powder, scrubbing the washbowl. Or she'd be on her knees, scrubbing the toilet. I'd see such things often, and to me it was a secret that she did them.

Yeah, and her friends were a secret I couldn't figure out. I would see them in the house on Saturday nights sometimes, and when I'd let myself in, Debby would say, "John, I want you to meet a friend of mine."

I'd say, "How do you do," and walk quick into the dining room, take off my coat, beat it into my bedroom.

Her friends. They were as peculiar as she was. They made me feel funny, sitting there in the living room, smoking and talking, or drinking the coffee Debby had made in the kitchen and carried in.

There was that colored girl. There was this girl, Fran. Jewish. She ran her father's pawnshop. Ma told me she wrote things. Not stories, but *lieder*, Ma said. I finally figured it out, poetry. She was Debby's best friend, Ma said. A thin girl who looked dark and Jewish and sort of afraid. I never saw her smile. I think she was afraid because sometimes I felt inside the way her eyes looked.

There was a girl they called Toby. Short red hair, a plump girl. She looked kind of like a happy, smiling boy. There was a good-looking woman they called Barbara. Debby had met her in WPA days; she'd been Debby's boss. She was the one who brought a portable victrola with her sometimes, and books of records.

Then that same kind of music that Debby got from the radio would go all through the house, for hours. I could hear it in my bedroom.

I didn't dislike that music. It was really a hell of a lot like Debby. Some of it sounded strong, some sweet and tender, so that it made me feel funny. Music that was a secret to me, like she was, and behind her the house. You can't figure out a secret by watching it! I couldn't understand those people she had over to the house on Saturdays. All I knew was, they were different, too, and she was their friend. It all made me feel twice as hard how different she was. What if I were to meet her downtown some day, right smack on Main Street, and what if I were walking with Wally or Bill when I met her? Or anybody from the paper. "This is my sister Deborah. She's a secret to me, fellows. If you know what the secret of her is, why by God you'll have the secret of that house of mine! And maybe of me, fellows."

Debby. Yeah, and wasn't it a secret how he could feel so mixed up about her? Ashamed, sure, but what about the feeling he always had about her strength and cleanliness, her story writing, her intelligence? You know what? Part of that secret was that she was like Friday night in his mind. When he came home every Friday night to eat supper, he was always glad Debby would be there. She was a part of that night, a part of the small section of his life that was regular, that was there, that was for sure. Like the *cholah* Ma baked every Friday afternoon, like the peppery fish, the golden-colored, thin noodles in the chicken soup.

Friday night. Look, he could remember a Friday night not so long ago, about a week before his first visit here. . . .

. . . when he'd come home early. He had been on an East Side assignment, taking pictures of the golf tournament for next day's sports page. Wally was planning the usual big art layout, and he had taken about a dozen shots. Then, instead of driving all the way downtown, he went home. He figured he'd print the pictures first thing in the morning, in time for the night edition.

When he let himself in by the front door, immediately he smelled the *cholah* and the fish. The odors made him feel pretty good, and he thought he'd have a drink. He draped his jacket over the dining room chair and squinted at the glass bowl in the center of the table, where Ma put the mail. There was nothing. Instead of permitting himself to think of Laura, he carried his camera and case very quickly into his bedroom. The first dusk of early evening was beginning to shadow the rooms.

From the kitchen, his mother called in her usual Yiddish, "So early, Jake? You can eat if you want."

"I'm not hungry yet, Ma," he called back. "I'll eat later."

He took the bottle of whisky down from the shelf in his closet. It was half full, and he told himself to remember to pick up another bottle tomorrow.

In the kitchen his mother was standing near the stove, the semi-gloom thick about her, and he could scarcely make out her features.

"Nobody home yet?" he said uncomfortably, and took a glass from the cupboard.

"It's too early," she said. "Pa isn't even home from *shule* yet."

He mumbled something, went to the bedroom again and poured whisky into the glass. It took him a minute or two before he had the nerve to go back for water. His mother and he had never discussed drinking. He always felt odd, as if he were cringing a little inside, when she saw him with a drink in his hand. He had been drinking in the house only for the last few years; all the other years it had been away from the house, at the Brass Rail, or at Laura's, or at Wally's, or in the dozen bars he went to off and on. Never in the house. When had he started to drink here? Why here? He couldn't remember.

In the kitchen, he added water from the tap, got some ice cubes from the refrigerator in the hall. (Roz had bought it for Ma, a tall handsome white box which Ma kept scrupulously clean. Why?—because it was so expensive, because it had been a gift from Roz? It was the cleanest thing in the house.) All the while, he was conscious of how she stood in the shadows near the stove, her eyes looking off somewhere, he didn't know where.

"I'll read the paper," he mumbled. "Eat later."

He escaped into the living room, sat in Debby's chair, snapped on the lamp. The shadows sprang back, into the dining room, back toward the three windows. He spread the paper over his knees and looked at the front page. It was a stocks edition he had picked up at the country club after he had got his pictures. He stared aimlessly at the war headlines for a moment, conscious of his tiredness now and of the deadly dull feeling at the back of his head.

The first swallow made him feel better, and as he was rolling the whisky in his mouth he glanced about the room. It seemed clean, warm to the eye. It was that oil painting of Debby's that made the warmth, he decided. The wonderful bright yellow of it in the lamplight. He had asked her about it finally.

"It's a Van Gogh," she'd told him. "It's only a copy, of course, but isn't it marvelous? Barb gave it to me for one of my birthdays. Do you like it? She had it framed for me, too."

The name had meant nothing to him, but he had nodded. "It's swell," he'd said.

Secret, secret. Debby and Van Gogh, and the powerful brooding music which had been in the room the night he had asked her. Secret, secret on the wall. Secret, coming from the radio into this room, like the restless, powerful rush of waters.

"What's playing?" he'd asked casually.

"Beethoven. The Eroica symphony."

"Nice," he'd said, almost curtly, and he'd gone into his own room, away from the secret of her and of this music of hers, away from the secret of these strange yellows on the wall.

He took a second deep swallow, then stood the glass on

the floor near the leg of the chair. At that moment, his mother walked into the dining room, and he put the paper up quickly, pretending to read. He could see her around the edge of the print at the left.

She was ready to light the Sabbath candles. He watched intently as she placed the joined candlesticks in the center of the bureau on a small scarf, which would keep the dripping wax from the wood. She drew the shawl that lay around her shoulders up over her head, so that most of her hair was covered. Watching, he saw one tiny flame after another appear as she touched a match to each candle, and then the shadows appeared on the ceiling above her as she bent her head and covered her face with her hands.

He heard the whisper of prayer drift through her fingers as she swayed, and he remembered all the times he had watched her light candles, all the years of it, and how as a child he had come to stand close to her and look up at her hands in the candlelight, at her bowed head, at the secret and mysterious tips of gold light at the ends of the thick, white, penny candles. Then, as now, the beautiful shadows had sprung up to the ceiling and flickered there, and Ma had whispered the solemn-sounding prayers for the lighting of the Sabbath candles.

He had not seen her do it for a long time, nor heard her voice in this whispered ritual, but nothing had changed from the sound and sight he remembered out of childhood. Had her hands always had this gnarled and woodsy appearance in the candlelight? Had her shoulders always had this bowed and thickened look to them? When had she grown old, so that now he could not remember her looking any other way? The wispy brown hair, the peering eyes so faded blue, the hundreds of wrinkles. And her hands. When he saw those candlelit hands, which seemed aching and old and twisted, his guilty feeling became almost overpowering; a feeling of indebtedness, of anxiety to quickly, quickly do something for her.

It was over, the candles prayed into light. She went back to the kitchen, and he grabbed at his drink as the queer, familiar loneliness crashed inside of him like a loud noise. Then he wanted another drink, right away, but he was too lonely to move. He felt as if he were sprawling helplessly in the chair, pinned through the center of him to its mohair solidity. Child and man of him remembered at once, cried out in the shrill-deep voice of both. Ma, Ma, don't go away. Speak to me. Love me.

Then the kitchen door slammed. He heard his father's stolid voice, in Yiddish, "Good Sabbath." He lifted the paper and began, with an intense effort, to read the war news.

The others came in by way of the kitchen, too. That was because the kitchen was the only alive room in the house for the rest of them, he told himself behind the newspaper. Debby was the only one who could put life into this room. Nobody else sat here, talked here, felt gay or warm here.

He remembered how she and Roz had always slept in the living room of the various houses in which they had lived. Debby on the couch, just the way she still did, and Roz on a folding bed. Years after Roz had married that thin, smooth-talking little racketeer and moved out, the old man had sold the folding bed with one of his truckloads of junk.

The kitchen door slammed again. He heard Sig's sinus sneeze almost immediately, then saw him walk into the narrow hallway and disappear into their bedroom.

They had always had houses with two bedrooms, ever since he could remember. Always one room short. Always the boys had been given the second room; girls could sleep in makeshift beds when there was not enough money for a six-room house. Girls were unimportant; boys rated a bedroom. (Who had dictated that, the old man?)

Sig went back into the kitchen. "You'll eat now?" Jake heard his mother say.

"All right, I'll eat now."

Dishes rattled. Jake heard the clink of fork and spoon against a plate.

"So I'll eat now, too," the old man said.

And then there was silence, the sound of silverware on dishes. The paper dropped to his knees, and Jake stared blankly at the candles in the next room. They had burned down almost halfway. They were an aching loneliness in the shadows.

The back door again; this time it was Roz.

"Hi," she cried. "I picked up Leah, Ma. I saw her on the corner."

"Oh, you came for the fish and *cholah*, Leah." Suddenly his mother's voice had become warm and gay. Jake smiled.

His mother loved the bright and glittering quality of Roz, her clothes, her make-up, her gay voice. Friday after Friday, he had heard his mother's voice change as Roz came into the house. He had seen the faded eyes brighten, the woman herself become younger, bustling, full of those little giggling sounds he heard so rarely.

"I'll walk back, Grandma," Leah said. "Roz said she'd drive me, but I'll walk. I need the exercise."

The dining room light snapped on as Roz walked into the room. "Oh, hello," she said coolly, and shrugged out of her light coat, tossed her hat on the table.

She went immediately to the bureau mirror, peered into it as she applied fresh lipstick. "Leah," she said, "I brought you that purse you liked. I've got a new one. Get it out of the car when you go."

Without watching, he knew the look of her; the stiff, elaborate curls of her touched-up blond hair, the expert job of make-up, the expensive, stylish clothes she took pride in wearing. He knew the cool, clever stare of the eyes, the reddened mouth, lips a shade too heavy. And, without looking around his paper, he knew that Leah was a replica ten years younger, without the high-priced clothes, without the deliberate stare and the experienced grace of body.

"Oh gee, Roz," Leah cried, "thanks a million! I sure can use that purse."

The light snapped off. He felt thick-wrapped in the loneliness. Behind the fence of newspaper, he listened to Leah leave, to Sig wander into the bedroom, to the steady chatter of Roz and his mother in Yiddish.

A thought twitched his lips. What would Roz's patrons at the club think if they heard this cool, flashy woman speak Yiddish? Every Friday she brought her mother money, a slightly used purse or compact, some gift or other. What would they think of that at the club? Tired, he let his head drop back against the chair top. He wondered what had happened to the cheap, slender boy she had married and then divorced. He wondered if he would always be ashamed of her.

He heard the key in the front door and sat up abruptly. Usually she used the back door on Fridays.

She came in with scarcely a sound, as usual; she was the

quiet one in the house, loathing slammed doors and raised voices.

She was hatless, in a brown suit, with her worn-looking briefcase under her left arm. Her hair was blown and very golden in the lamplight.

"Hello," she said in her low voice, and turned to shut the inner door. He was so glad to see her that he felt a kind of choked lump in his throat.

"Have you eaten?" she asked, walked up close to him. He knew she had seen the glass, though her eyes looked straight into his, blue and tired. She looked like a tall, slim, scholarly boy, and he noticed her hands on the briefcase as she leaned toward him. They went with her. They were square-looking, lean, with square fingers, and thumbs that seemed to curl back at the tips.

"Not very hungry," he mumbled. "Guess I'll finish my paper before I eat."

"Don't you want to eat with me?" she said, smiling in her grave way.

He shook his head. He felt very shy with her now, still not knowing the exact shadings of what he was feeling for her, but knowing that the house had become alive and sharp with her in it.

In the kitchen, Roz laughed and then they heard their mother giggle. Deborah smiled down at him. "Nice to hear Ma laugh, isn't it?" she said.

He nodded, watched her drop the briefcase on the table, saw her eyes go to the candlelight as she passed the bureau. Then she was in the kitchen. He heard her voice, his mother's, Roz's, mingle.

His eyes came back to the briefcase. My sister Deborah. She's a writer. She kind of does it for a living, too. Publicity. Works for an organization called the League of Rights. That's her briefcase.

He drew a long, relaxed breath. Now that she was here, he felt hungry. After Roz went, taking Ma over to Sarah's for the evening, he would grab something to eat. Sig would be gone by then, too, and the old man would be either in bed or crouched over his paper at one end of the table. Maybe Debby would serve him. She usually did, if she heard him clattering dishes in the kitchen. She'd come in and say, "Oh, go on, sit down. I'll get it. Go on, cut the bread. I'll get you some tomatoes. You don't want to eat just plain chicken that way, do you?"

She'd come in, and then maybe they'd talk. What would they say, those people in the kitchen now, if they knew he wanted to enlist? Roz, Ma, the old man. What would they say if they knew Debby thought it was a good idea! Yeah, maybe she would sit at the other end of the table, as she had so many times, and talk. Light a cigarette and look at him in that serious way she had. Talk.

He no longer felt the loneliness. Leaning back, he listened to the voices in the kitchen. Now that she was there the voices were meaningful, flowed into single words, into definite snatches he could recognize.

He lit a cigarette, began to read the paper. The words, which had been a blur of print before, made sense now.

C · H · A · P · T · E · R

Two

. . . And though Subject complains of excessive backache much
of the time, examination reveals nothing. S' shoulders droop
badly; this seems worse when he is badly depressed. *Watch.*
Physical and laboratory examinations reveal no evidence of or-
ganic disease; fifteen pounds underweight. Sleeps badly, ap-
petite not too good, especially in the morning. Slight retarda-
tion of speech at times. S is extremely inarticulate until he
forgets shyness and sense of shame under stress of emotion,
then he talks with total unrestraint. Prevalent state seems one
of anxiety rather than depression. Dresses neatly but is careless
about color combinations and things like press of clothing, care
of nails.

S seems to disregard, for the most part, the fact that his
sister Deborah was a patient here and that doctor knows *her*
picture of S: weak, silent, morose much of the time, generous
to mother (often protestingly so, but giving way in the end).
However, S speaks freely of Deborah and her influence in
bringing him here. S' attachment for sister seems deep and
genuine and yet he is intensely jealous of her. He is five years
older than Deborah; strong similarity in features.

During first two visits, S found it impossible to speak
freely. Drank enough before the third visit to break barriers.

Spoke defiantly of alcoholism. S covers guilt feeling caused by alcoholism by explaining it as a release mechanism: "I can't really talk unless I'm drunk. When I'm drunk I forget, it's the only time I can be happy."

S feels deep shame arising from "Jewishness." Apparently, however, religion in itself means nothing to him. He is very confused, often making two or three conflicting statements within ten minutes. This was especially true of the "Jewish" question. The "Friday night" which he stresses so much seems a matter of identification, one of his very few possessions of security, stability. The matter of Jewishness, too, confused as it is, seems to be tied with identification. *Watch.*

S feels shame at being in a "head doctor's" office, but wants rather desperately to be here, to be helped.

Family situation not too clear as yet. Hatred for father. Curious, rather clouded, love for mother, which is almost inextricably part of interesting feeling of guilt. Interesting, because his sister Deborah felt same thing strongly, same feeling of "paying off a debt." Interesting, too, the way the feeling strengthened her, weakens him. Both assumed their father's guilt: the guilt of his failure as a husband to the little, mild, bewildered woman, the guilt of his failure as a father to all of them. S often has unconscious feelings of impotence and guilt in the face of mother's unaware need for fulfillment. S realizes, without recognizing it, mother's sexual and social barrenness. The feeling of hatred is tied up with father's selfishness, silences, personal dirtiness.

S describes feeling of being "trapped" by his house. Is it his mother? he asks. Is it his feeling of guilt? The dark and gloomy house itself? His feeling of namelessness? He did not seem to think it could be the hatred for his father. He does not attach too much importance to his father. *Watch.*

S does not understand his feelings about his sister Deborah. She seems to be the strongest person on his horizon at the moment. He leans on her, quotes her, yet he confesses being ashamed of her—what he calls—differences. He feels himself disgustingly different from most people, and that Deborah's oddness substantiates his own. Feels that the entire family is different. That he, as a member of that family, that house, is something to be scorned. He talks of Deborah's oddness, her short hair, her boyishness. He has not used the word homosexual, or Lesbian. Is he ashamed to use such words, or doesn't he know the words? Does he know what Deborah is; or is it pure feeling on his part?

The fact that S thinks he will not marry anyone but a Jewess seems like further search of identification: with a people, with the stability and security of that people. Unless it is a tag end of the confusion. *Watch.*

Strongest motif seems his frantic desire for identification within himself. His feeling for Deborah may be due to this desire. Closeness to her apparent strength and cleanliness and "smartness" may seem to him a way of touching her sharply defined identification, perhaps utilizing some of it for himself. In his mind, for all her differences, she has identified herself. Surely, he thinks, anyone as direct, as single-streamed, as she, must have named herself! Despite the house, the father, despite those other people in the family. Perhaps, he thinks, if he gets close enough to this strong sister of his, perhaps if he starts to understand her, he will himself achieve an identity! . . .

It was Saturday again. Jake sat in the chair, leaning eagerly toward the big desk. It was almost as if he had not left this office last Saturday, as if he had stepped from then across the shadowy, dreamlike quality of the past week into today, somewhat as one steps from a well-lighted, familiar room into a maze of dim, unreal corridors and wanders through their vague, half-familiar turns, then comes again into the warm, bright room where the conversation is alive and meaningful, where the faces are of those one knows.

He tried to tell this to the doctor. "See," he said, struggling to use the right words, "it's as if my life out there isn't real. The people are like ghosts. I meet them and talk to them, and they talk to me, and it's like everything is a dream. But here, in this room, everything is real. I mean, all the people I talk about and the things I used to do—well, they're the real things. The things I do every day right now, the people I bump into—honest, they're like ghosts. It's scary!"

The doctor nodded. "It's nothing to be frightened about," he said, so quietly and firmly that Jake felt immediate relief. "You see, in your mind you are going back, you are seeing new versions of all the people you thought you knew so well. You are beginning to understand them, and therefore re-creating them to fit their new meaning. It's your past and all those people in your past that bother you so. Your present way of living, and the people in the present, are relatively unimportant. Relatively unreal."

"But my family is in the present," Jake protested. "I see them every day. But they're just not real."

"That's right, they're not. They'll become real only after you understand them. After you understand what happened between you and them, and exactly when it happened, and why." The gray-blue eyes questioned him. "Your house is a trap, you say. The people in your house, you feel strange toward them. You don't understand them. You feel hatred, you want to sneer at them, and then again you feel lost. A man without a name, without an identity."

Jake nodded miserably.

"But all these things happened yesterday," the doctor said. "Your today is unhappy, that is true, but is today the source of the unhappiness?"

"No," Jake cried eagerly. "I know, I have to find out what made me feel like I do now. I have to figure out why certain things happened. Sure, I know that."

"That's the realness you're looking for," the doctor went on. "Everything else will be unreal until you go back far enough to discover the real meaning of what has happened. The truth, John. When you know the truth of what happened, the truth of those people who torture you, then your present will swing into focus."

Jake looked at him.

"It's not too easy to understand," the doctor admitted. "It frightens many people, this feeling of unreality during the time they are probing back and back into memory."

"I don't think I'm frightened," Jake said slowly, trying to think it out. "I think it's like you say. And Debby said it, too. As soon as I have a good reason for something happening, I can take it. It's just that—well, I felt so funny all week! Like I was split up. A little part of me was going to the job and to movies and home to sleep, but a big part of me was all wrapped up in what I told you last week. It's like I was still here, in this office, talking, trying to figure out my mother and father. Debby. My brother Sig. You know what I mean? All week I kept seeing them the way they used to be, not the way they are now."

The doctor pushed the box of cigarettes toward Jake, watched him light one and blow out the smoke excitedly. "That will go on," he said. "Then, one of these days, you'll really see them the way they were. You'll understand them. And then you'll understand the way things are now."

Jake tapped his cigarette violently against the edge of the ashtray. "One of these days! God, I hope so. I really hope so." He hitched his chair closer to the desk. "I keep thinking about last Saturday, Doctor. You remember what I told you, about that Friday night stuff?"

The doctor smiled. "Yes, I remember."

Jake shook his head, eager and impatient at once. "Sure you remember! Don't I say sappy things, though? Well, but I wanted to ask you. That Friday night I described last week, it happened only about a month ago. All this week, I've been thinking—do you think I should have gone into the kitchen and eaten supper with Roz and Deborah? Or with Sig and my father?"

"Why didn't you want to eat with them?" the doctor asked, instead of answering.

A kind of stiffening movement went through Jake. Slowly he mashed out his cigarette. His eyes stayed down, on the silvery, heavy ashtray.

"Do you know why?" the doctor said.

Jake looked up. Suddenly his back ached, that intolerable feeling of weight too heavy to stand up under; he pushed back into the harshness of the chair, trying to sit straight with the support of the chair's hardness.

"Jesus, my back feels like I've been carrying a ton of stuff," he mumbled, but he kept his eyes on the doctor's, on the gentleness, on the decisive and warm gradations of glance there.

"Is it too hard to talk?" the doctor asked.

Jake's eyes went to the pen, the notebook, came up again heavily. "I don't know where to start," he said vaguely. The familiar, depressed feeling was settling fast, and he could feel himself sinking under the dark, numbing sensation.

"Don't leave that particular Friday night," the doctor said

quickly. "You didn't want to eat with anybody in the family. Why? Is there a reason for that, John?"

"Sure there's a reason," Jake cried. "I swore to myself once that I'd never eat with the whole family again. It didn't mean a Goddam thing for all of us to sit down together, and I knew it, and I said then, Goddam it, I never would again! Never."

"Why did you swear that? When was it? This is where you can start, John. This is where you can start talking."

"Yeah," Jake said grimly, "that's where I ought to start, all right. That's when all my trouble started."

"What kind of trouble?"

"When I saw them all. Every single one of them. My family! It was at Passover, at the Seder, and I was just sitting there and asking the questions, and all of a sudden I looked up and saw them. My God, it was just like I'd never seen them before—the way they really were."

He stopped abruptly. Suddenly the face and eyes opposite him were no longer anonymous. He was aware of a person, a man, sitting behind a desk. A sunken feeling materialized at the pit of his stomach.

White-faced, he demanded, "Say, are you a Jew?"

"No," the doctor answered gravely. "Why do you want to know that, John? Will you tell me?"

Jake sat back, perspiring. He felt a closeness now, and was not frightened by it. The doctor had become a man, but not like any man he had ever known. Part of the anonymous and cool quality was still there, and yet, in addition, there was the living and breathing warmth of another human being in the room. Maybe a friend?

He tried to tell the truth. "If you were a Jew maybe I couldn't tell you. It's all about Jewish stuff. I hate it! But I don't hate it all the time, just certain things about it. Maybe I couldn't talk about all of that to a Jew."

"I'm not a Jew," the grave voice told him.

Jake nodded. "But do you know anything about Jewish holidays? I mean, we've got this one holiday called Passover. It comes in the spring every year, and it's nice. I mean, we use new dishes for those special days, and we eat matzoth instead of bread. A matzoth is like a big square cracker. Then, after the holiday, my mother packs the dishes away until next Passover and we go back to using the year-round dishes. I mean, it's something that comes every year, regularly. Every single year, like summer comes, or winter."

His voice petered out. "If you don't know anything about it," he said hesitantly, "it'd be pretty tough to tell you."

The doctor nodded. "But I know a lot about it," he said. "I've read so much about it, John, that I think I would understand anything you said in connection with it."

"You would?" Jake said dubiously.

"I know it's a happy holiday," the doctor told him immediately. "It goes with the spring, doesn't it? With a feeling of warm weather coming, and hope, everything clean and new."

Jake stared at him. "Yeah."

"I know it's a holiday celebrating the deliverance of the Jews from the bondage of Egypt, and that the holiday starts each year with two holy suppers, or Seders, as they're called. Matzoth is unleavened bread, the kind the Jews ate during their flight from Egypt."

Jake hunched deeper into the chair, restless with the relief of the doctor knowing and with the deep need to get on with it now.

"Jesus," he said, "you know more about it than I do. I mean, what the holiday really means. I never cared about that part of it, what it meant and all that. All I cared about was that it was such a nice holiday. The house was so clean, and all the dishes new, and we all sat at the Seder table, and there was wine and—hell, everything was so nice! See, we were all together, like—like a family. My father prayed, and we ate the holiday stuff, and then I asked the questions. I mean, it was—well, everybody was together, and all the Jews all over the world were doing the same thing. It felt—. It's really hard to say it out in words. It felt strong and—and old. As if the Passover and the Seder had always been there, and it always would, forever and ever. Look. I can't tell you what it felt like, but it was a good feeling."

"Let's see if I can help," the doctor said. "Tell me if I'm right about this, John. The entire family sat at the Seder supper every year. To celebrate a holiday that was thousands of years old, a holiday that would be celebrated forever, as long as Jews were alive to celebrate it. It's a holiday of fruitfulness, deliverance. It ushers in the spring, the fruitful joyous season of the world."

Jake nodded. "That's good."

"In your mind, then, the Seder supper is tied to words like family, like Jewish history and culture, security, strength. I want to know if you understand this, John, if I'm saying what you mean."

Jake lit a cigarette. "Well," he said, his forehead creased, "why would you use words like security or strength?"

"The strength of the Jews, who lived through the torture of Egypt?" the doctor asked.

"Yeah, maybe. And all the pogroms, sure. And all the hell people are always giving them," Jake said. "Yeah, I guess that's right."

"Security?" the doctor said. "Didn't you feel strong and secure at that holiday table? Your father at the head of the table, conducting the old, holy ritual. Your mother there, your brother and sisters there. Your family. And behind your family, tens of thousands of Jewish families, going through the dignity and beauty of each of these prayers, each of these holiday steps. How did you feel?"

"Good. I felt—happy. There wasn't anything to be worried about." Jake rubbed his cheek. His voice was apologetic. "Those two words you just used. You know, that's really the way it felt, dignified and beautiful. Really! I'm not kidding."

"That could make a man feel secure," the doctor reminded him softly. "Inside himself. Dignity and beauty, his family, the heritage of his people."

The room folded round Jake like layers of cotton. He felt tired, but his head had stopped whirling so violently. The room was softly full of confusion and aimlessness, but many of the thousands of words twisting and turning in the air seemed familiar now; they made sense. He felt that maybe he could reach up and hold others of them still for long enough to be able to recognize them, those words describing him and his family and their way of doing things.

"I get so damned mixed up," he confessed in a low voice.

"I know," the warm voice reassured him. "So many people do, John. But it's not impossibly mixed up, you know. Are you very mixed up about being a Jew?"

"I feel very bad about it," Jake muttered. "The way I hate

it, and still, at the same time, it's like—like candles burning all the time. I'm all mixed up about it, sure. I just never know what to do."

"This time you're going to know," the doctor assured him. "Let's go back now, John. Try hard. What made you swear never again to eat with your family? You say all your trouble started at one of the Seders. When was that? Do you remember how old you were?"

"I remember, all right! I was fifteen." Jake swallowed. "You see, Passover always comes out close to my birthday. And I always used to pretend that Passover was sort of half to celebrate my birthday, too."

The doctor leaned forward. "And the two Seder suppers were somewhat like birthday parties?"

Jake nodded. His jaw felt stiff, as though he had been clenching it for a long time. "We never celebrate birthdays in my house. Nobody ever mentions them."

"Nobody at all?"

Jake's mouth twisted, made a little rueful joke of it. "That'll bring us to my sister Debby again," he said. "She always had a word to say about my birthday. You know, that's something I forgot about until just this second. She never sent me a card or anything, but she always said something. Like, 'Well, this is the big day, isn't it?' Or, 'Say, many happy returns,' and then she'd walk right out of the room."

"Did she always do that?"

Jake's forehead wrinkled. "Well, not when she was a kid. Let's see, when did she start? After she grew up, I guess."

The doctor's voice impelled him back. "Twenty years ago. You looked around that birthday-Seder table, and 'saw' your family. What had you seen in them before that night?"

"What do you mean?"

"You say you really saw them that night. What had you seen in other years when you looked at them? You say there was a sharp difference."

"My God," Jake cried savagely, "difference! That night I felt as if the whole world—Well, I felt all lost. Like I was out in the night, and everything was black and freezing cold. I was scared to death, like I didn't know anybody there. My family, see? Like they weren't anything to me, and I didn't belong to them either. Hell, didn't you ever feel like the whole world was shaking and it was going to just fall down in little pieces?"

"But the Seder before that one," the doctor said insistently, "how had it been for you then? The year before, when you were fourteen? Do you remember?"

"Sure I remember! I'll never forget. I was happy then. Why should a guy forget when he's happy?"

"And then, one year later," the doctor said softly, "everything was changed. The whole world. Was that it?"

Jake's eyes closed; he went back and back, trying to erase everything smooth and blank from his mind and then printing on its blackboard with round, childish letters: Seder, fifteen, Pa told me to ask the questions.

His eyes opened to the gray-blue warmth opposite. "It didn't happen to me until the old man said it was time to ask the questions. I read them, in English, the way I always do. The old man does everything in Hebrew during the Seder, but I don't know any Hebrew. Then, when I looked up, after I was through asking, then's when it hit me. Like a rock had come down on my head."

"What do you mean when you talk about 'the questions'?" the doctor asked.

"It's part of the ceremony. The old man prays, and we all drink wine, and he goes on telling the story of what happened in Egypt. See, I know all that because when he's praying in Hebrew I'm following the story in English, out of the *Haggadah*." Jake shook his head impatiently. "There's so much to tell you! The *Haggadah* is a little book that's printed in English in one column of the page, and then the other column's in Hebrew—a book that's got all the prayers of the Passover in it. And pictures. You know, pictures of David and Moses, and how the Jews walked out of Egypt. I used to look at the pictures while the old man was praying. I remember how funny and wonderful they used to seem."

"All right," the doctor said gently, "now I know what the *Haggadah* is. Tell me about the questions.

"Well, he starts going through all the steps of the Passover story, see. I mean, we all drink a little wine when it's time, and we eat stuff like horseradish and parsley and a mixture of apples and nuts, stuff that shows things out of those days; you know, the hardships and the bondage. Well, at one point of this story, my father always stops and I read these questions out of the *Haggadah*. In English. See, the youngest son at the table is supposed to ask these questions. All about why is this night different. Then, when I'm through asking, my father starts again, in Hebrew, and he tells why this night is different."

"I see," the doctor said. "And these questions are always asked by the youngest son present."

Jake's face whitened. He stared at the doctor, his mouth tight. "Yeah," he said.

"What is it?" the doctor asked immediately.

"Nothing." But in a moment, Jake muttered, "I better tell you. Those questions— Well, once I asked the old man what if no sons are present, who asks then? He said, the youngest child present asks them then. But if a son is there, it's always the youngest son."

He was crouched in the chair now, making a terrific effort to tell it all, every confused and mysterious detail of it. He felt that if he did not impress the doctor with all of it, all the small things that nobody knew, why then being here would not help.

"See," he said, breathing rapidly, "you've got to know how this is. All of it. For instance, if I wasn't at the Seder, and everybody else was—Sig and Roz and Debby—then Sig would ask the questions. He'd be the youngest son present. But if Sig and I both weren't there, then Debby would ask them. There wouldn't be any sons there, so the youngest child would ask them. But usually, when everybody is there, I'd ask them because I'm the one. I'm the youngest son. It's the sons who really matter to Jews." He finished lamely, his eyes tormented. "That's—really, that's very important stuff, and I had to tell it to you. I just had to."

"Yes, of course you did," the doctor said soothingly. He was writing rapidly in the notebook, and yet at the same time his eyes were there to look into, cool and understanding, as if that garbled maze of words had gone into them and fallen into immediate order.

"John," the doctor went on, "I'd like very much to hear

about those two Seders. First, about the happy one. Then, I want to hear about the Seder which took place the year you were fifteen."

"Jesus," Jake said, rubbing his forehead, "both of them? I don't even think I can remember everything that happened. It was so long ago. Twenty years, my God! Why do you want to hear about that?"

"Do you understand what happened at those two Seders, what happened in the year between them?"

"No," Jake cried angrily. "You know I don't!"

In the hot silence following, he looked at the doctor. After a while, he said in a low voice, "I'm sorry. I didn't tell you, but it—it hurts to go back, to tell all that stuff. I get so tired."

"I know it hurts. I know how tiring it is." The voice comforted Jake. He thought then, sitting there and listening, that sometimes that voice was like a wall to lean against while he took a deep breath.

"We must try to re-create those scenes," the doctor said, and Jake knew it was true, he had known all along, but it had seemed such an impossible thing to do. "We must get them out, talk about them. Reason them out. There is a reason for everything. We must find the reason, the truth of what had happened."

"I know, I know," Jake said. He smiled, rather painfully. "Wouldn't you think a guy'd forget after twenty years? Why, I even remember the look on Debby's face!"

And then, after he had begun, it was easy. The remembered sound of voices, the etched glance of eyes, the dip of a finger into the wineglass in ritual gesture, the tiny sharpness of sound as a matzoth was cracked; back he went, and the office filled with words, and out from the words pictures gleamed, and from the pictures figures stepped into the room and looked at him, and he looked back, seeing them out of childhood but imbued now with the new meaning of what he saw as he looked back . . .

. . . and yes, it was true, for him the excitement always began at the table. Looking back, he always began remembering at the moment when all of them were sitting around the dining room table. It was the only time of the year when they ate in the dining room instead of the kitchen. Looking back at the Passover scene, at the first Seder of that year's holiday, he did not remember too well that Pa came home from *shule* around eight, or that Ma and Roz ran around in the kitchen from stove to sink to table, and that Debby carefully and lovingly arranged the wineglasses upon the table, upon the special, white holiday tablecloth. He did not remember, except dimly, that his brother Sig came home from work and got washed, and that he himself had had a bath and that Ma was wearing a nice dress under the apron, and that Debby was not wearing knickers but one of those little square-looking dresses that Ma sewed for her and which usually she wore only to school.

For him, memory in all its sharp and delighted detail began at the table, when all were at last sitting down, and Pa, at the head of that table, sitting on a pillow (remember the matzoth hidden, for its secret, ritual reason, at the edge of that pillow!), had filled each glass with the red wine. The big, shabby book was open before Pa, the electric light gleaming on the Hebrew print. And, before Jake's place, the *Haggadah* Pa had given him was open at the first page (then he would turn the pages backward, because in Jewish books you started to read at the end, then you went toward the beginning of the book). Pa wore his little, round, black prayer cap, and Sig and he wore their hats. Men had to cover their heads when they were praying, see; but those were not really the things to remember.

For him, after twenty years, memory lay in the warm, marvelous odors which pervaded the house on that night, and in the brightness of everything, the knowledge that the dishes were special—unused since last Passover—the walls and floors washed, the candles lit in the joined, heavy candlesticks (Ma had brought them from Europe) standing on the bureau. Sitting there, you smelled the chicken stewing in the pot, the soup (with the matzoth balls floating in it), the *gefüllte* fish cooling on the sink. You smelled the rich, sweet wine in the glasses and saw the gleam of the glass through the deep, red color of the wine (Pa had made that wine himself, special for the Seder). You sat next to Pa, and you saw Debby and Roz play the matzoth game. That was one thing to remember, the matzoth game. One person shut her eyes, see, and the other person broke a piece of matzoth (in twenty years you could not forget that tiny, sharp, cracking sound as the matzoth broke!), then she held the two pieces tightly together, trying to disguise the crack, and said: "O.K., open your eyes." Then the other person would stare at the piece of matzoth and try to guess where the crack was. Boy, what fun when you had guessed right—or even wrong! Sig would be sitting there, eating little pieces of his matzoth, and Ma would be running to the stove to see if the chicken was O.K., the soup hot enough. Debby always sat opposite him, next to Pa on the other side of the table, and she sure was cute; her hair was cut Buster Brown then, and she looked like a little Dutch kid, her round face and her blue eyes so serious.

Pa would be getting ready. "Have you got the eggs and salt water?" he'd say to Ma. "Where's the horseradish? Where's the *charoseth?*" All the little dishes of things that one dipped into during the Seder service. Everything was ready, Ma said breathlessly. Here is the new box of matzoths. Have you got enough glasses for the wine? Sig, you must be starved, it's so late!

Everything was beautiful, just beautiful. Jake felt excited and solemn at once, one ear cocked for when Pa would start to pray. He was wearing his new suit, gray, with knickers that came down past the knees and slipped neatly into knee-length socks. It was a wonderful suit! He began to read the column in English on the first page of the *Haggadah*, remembering the familiar words from last Passover, when he had read them to himself before everything started: *Almost everyone is familiar with the Biblical story of Passover—the festival of the emancipation of the Jewish people from Egypt, the festival of unleavened bread (matzoth), the festival of spring.*

In a dim, scarcely understood way, he felt part of something universal, something strong and ageless. The emancipation of the Jewish people from Egypt. How long ago, before Ma and Pa were born, and before their parents were born; and yet here they all were, sitting around a table the same way as those Jewish people, and all over the world Jewish people were ready to sip the wine and to take a bite of matzoth. All over the world, families were together, waiting for a father to start praying. All over the world, the youngest son present (just like him!) was getting ready to ask the questions.

Then, finally, Pa started. He followed his father's Hebrew in the English column, which was to the left of the Hebrew column in the *Haggadah*, followed his father's chanting voice that always seemed to cry when it prayed.

Oh, it was so beautiful, it was so strong and so much the-whole-world-is-doing-this. He pretended he could understand the Hebrew as he read the English. *Blessed art thou, O Eternal, our God, King of the Universe, Creator of the fruit of the vine.*

He didn't understand it, no, but it was so beautiful. And Pa went on praying. No, his voice wasn't like crying, it was like singing, but singing like a man would sing, way down low and kind of sad, but strong. Listening, you felt like you were dreaming about all those things that had happened such a long time ago, all the terrible things, but how the people had got away anyway, and how they were safe and they were going to start all over again in a new land.

Pa took a sip of wine, and everybody else followed him and took a sip, even Debby, whose face got all screwed up when she tasted it. That was something you remembered after twenty years, that first wonderful sip of wine at the Seder table.

All the details. Pa leaving the table to wash his hands. Then he comes back. He dips pieces of parsley into salt water, one piece for everybody, and passes the pieces around. A little prayer, then he eats his parsley. And, on the echo of that mournful, chanting prayer, everyone eats his piece. Even Debby, the baby, her eyes all shining and solemn as they watch how everybody is doing it—and she, too.

Then Pa breaks the special matzoth and hides some of it under the edge of the pillow, and he picks up the dish with the bone and egg on it and everybody touches it while Pa says the words in Hebrew (you read it in the English column): *This is the bread of affliction which our ancestors ate in the land of Egypt; let all those who are hungry, enter and eat thereof. . . .*

But you don't read all of that section; you wait tremulously for Pa to go through the prayer. Your moment is coming, the biggest moment of the Seder, the moment for which you have waited so shiveringly. The moment when the youngest son present asks the questions. This is your own momentous role in the service. You feel it vaguely, scarcely understanding it, but not vague is that feeling in your chest when the moment comes. Not vague, but fierce, strong, a solemnity and holiness you know must be terribly important. This is the part you yourself, as the youngest son at the services, must play. And you know that for thousands of years Jewish boys, the youngest present on those ancient, ageless, never-dying evenings, have been playing this same part. No, you do not quite understand, but you are happy in this moment because you feel what a meaningful moment it is, you feel that you are a definite, named (in the Bible, named) part of this holy thing. Behind you, in the shadow of history, in the thousands of years of Jews, stand other boys like you; ahead of you, in the future, in the tomorrow of the world, stand still other boys not even born yet, not alive yet, but you know they will all sit at tables like this some day, they will all ask the meaningful, historical questions.

Ma fills the wineglasses to brimming now. Pa is still holding up the dish with the bone and egg on it. You sit there, clutching the *Haggadah*. Your throat is so tight it almost hurts, your chest feels deep and arched, as if you are getting ready to start running a race, or start shooting a ball into the basket at gym, or as if you are ready to take a test, the pencil poised over the exam paper, only waiting for Teacher to say: "Go!"

How can you explain it, feeling it so dimly, not even understanding it? How can you explain that you felt like a cog in a monumental, ageless, beautiful wheel which had been turning slowly, with terrific meaning, for centuries, and would continue to turn forever, for as long as there were Jews alive? You were in that wheel, and your family, and the Jewish families on earth. How can you explain how you felt?

"Well, ask the questions," Pa said in Yiddish.

There was a little silence, and then Jake, his heart pounding, spoke in an odd, hoarse voice.

"Wherefore is this night distinguished from all other nights?" he read in English from the *Haggadah*. His heart knocked at each beautiful word, at each wonderful phrase. "Any other night we may eat either leavened or unleavened bread, but on this night only unleavened bread; all other nights we may eat any species of herbs, but this night only bitter herbs; all other nights we do not dip even once, but on this night twice; all other nights we eat and drink either sitting or reclined, but on this night we all of us recline."

And it was over for him, his individual, momentous part in the evening. Trembling, he saw the dish replaced on the table.

He heard his father's chant start again and rise in mourning Hebrew, and, looking across the table, he saw the solemnity and dream of the moment mirrored in Debby's shining, half-dazed eyes.

His eyes went back to the *Haggadah*. He read the English while his father's voice in Hebrew sang mournfully into the room. *Because we were slaves unto Pharaoh in Egypt, and the Eternal, our God, brought us thence with a mighty hand and an outstretched arm.*

His active part in the services was over, and now he sipped wine when his father did, trying to mimic all his gestures. He played the matzoth game with Roz once, and with Debby once, while the chanting went on. He felt all happy now, his nervousness at waiting for the questions gone. He, too, like Sig, ate small pieces of matzoth from time to time, the taste adding to his delicious feeling of hunger.

Languidly, he heard his father's voice falling like sonorous, mournful, rich rain on all their heads. In that soft, dreamy way, he followed the services, sipping when his father did, in the *Haggadah* coming upon the part about the ten plagues, the part about the bitter herbs, and reading to himself as his father showed the herb to everybody and then said it in Hebrew: *It is eaten because the Egyptians embittered the lives of our ancestors in Egypt. . . .*

It was wonderful and joyous to be sitting there, listening to his father pray, reading a little of the book or looking up to see his brother's face, his mother nodding, an abstracted, musing look in her eyes, and Debby's chubby hands folded on the table edge, as if it were a desk and she listening to Teacher.

Pa passed around the bitter herbs with a piece of matzoth for each one, and Jake ate his, the familiar tears springing to his eyes at the sharp taste, familiar and well-loved tears he remembered from last year's Seder. And his tearful eyes read in the *Haggadah,* as his father prayed: *With unleavened bread and bitter herbs shall they eat it.*

Then it was all over for a little bit, because it was time to eat supper. Ma and Roz started to run around, getting the food from the stove and some from the icebox in the hall, and even Debby helped, and Sig said, "Ah, food." And Pa kept saying little pieces of prayer.

What could he remember of that last happy Seder? That all of them seemed to laugh a great deal, and the house was full of words and that laughter and the scents of holiday food.

First they ate hard-boiled egg sliced into salt water. Then came the *gefüllte* fish, cooled but with an undercurrent of warmth in it, and Ma had remembered to put lots of slices of carrot on his plate. Then they had chicken, and he helped himself to the mixture of horseradish and beet. The taste of that made his eyes smart, but he smeared the wonderful red stuff on his chicken anyway and ate it, like Sig and Pa were eating it. And then, last, there was the steaming yellow chicken soup with the two matzoth balls floating in each bowl, the soft, delicious, yellow matzoth balls of Passover.

"How are the matzoth balls?" his mother cried gaily. "Soft, or hard?"

"Soft, soft," Jake cried back. "They're so soft, they're so wonderful!"

And when she smiled with pride, he felt happy, intensely happy.

After the stewed prunes, Pa gave each of them that last small piece of matzoth to chew, the last mouthful of the evening, and Ma and Roz started to clear the table. Pa filled all the wineglasses again, the third time, and started to pray again.

"Well," Sig said. "I've got a date. See you later." He went into his bedroom, and Ma and Roz started to wash dishes.

Sig was somebody you didn't understand, but he was pretty wonderful, all right. He had a job and he brought money home, and he always went out on dates in the evening. He drove a car. Sometimes he gave Jake money to spend. He was going out on a date now, but Jake and Debby would sit at the table under the rain of Pa's praying voice, and finish out the Seder because it was so wonderful. If Sig had had enough and had eaten supper, he could go away if he wanted to; that was his business.

Chant and chant the prayers of this night, and I will remember them forever. I will watch my stern-faced father drink the third cup of wine, and, imitating him and the Jews of all the world, I shall sip from the third cup, too.

Now my mother and Roz are sitting again, talking in low

voices of neighbors and relatives, but Debby and I are following the chant.

My father says, "Open the door," and I go to the kitchen door and open it wide.

Chant and chant the prayers of this night. Now the door is open, the Messiah will come into our house and drink from the full cup of wine which has been waiting for him all evening. Feel the mystery, obscurely feel the footsteps of long ago and far away in this room, and Pa praying them in, Pa praying them here.

At the signal, shut the door softly. The Messiah has been here, we have eaten and prayed, the last cup of wine has been drunk, and I have asked the questions; I too, have played my tiny, meaningful part in the Passover. The wine has lulled me. I feel lullaby soft, and I sit next to my father as he prays the last of the evening song.

Sleepily, I watch Ma take Debby's hand and whisper: "Come on to sleep now; it's late, it's after the Seder."

Chant and chant the prayers, listen and feel them inside you like song, and in the Passover dream you are sitting next to your father, you and he the only ones left at the table now as he finishes the services. Chant and chant, Pa, and I will hear and understand inside of me how it was, how the Jews were delivered from bondage and how we are here now, and Debby is going to sleep, and Sig has gone out to people, and Roz has gone outside to talk to other people in the street, and how only I am sitting with you here. I, having asked the questions, having read the *Haggadah*, having had my say as the youngest son, will sit here with my father as he comes to the end of the Seder. Tomorrow will be the second Seder, never so wonderful as the first but very nice in its way. And we will pray again, and we will all of us be here again, a family, all of us close and warm and together.

As his father and he sat alone at the table, the sorrowful deep chant became softer and softer. Jake's eyes closed and he heard his father's prayers, gentle and lullaby safe, go on and on even as he slept. . . .

"It happened at the next Passover," Jake said. "The one I just told you about was the last good Seder I remember. I was four-teen that year."

He felt deathly tired, as if he had been confronted by people long dead, and had walked with them and talked with them in rooms and streets long crumbled and covered with the dust of the years.

"Exactly what happened?" The doctor sat at the desk look-ing at him, his eyes compassionate. "You say *it* happened. What do you mean when you say it?"

Jake wanted to cry. He was afraid to take himself into that following year, afraid to trace its unknown mazes up until that one known hour at the Seder table.

"Exactly, exactly," he muttered, his voice hoarse. "How can I tell you what it was, exactly? There I was, sitting at the table, asking the questions, and all of a sudden it was as if entirely different people were sitting at the table with me. No, that's not right!"

He rubbed his forehead, scowling in an attempt to remem-ber. He was starting to feel excited again, the tiredness begin-ning to go somehow as the faces began again to come clear out of the shadows of the years. He smelled the pungent, sweet wine for an instant.

"No," he said excitedly, "they weren't different. No, that wasn't it! It was as if I'd been looking at them through a—well, a screen, all the years up until then. And then, after I'd read the questions, when I looked up from the *Haggadah*—that was the second when the screen disappeared! That was the second when I *saw* them. The way they really were. Yes, that's the way it happened, Doctor. Right at that second after I'd finished read-ing the questions."

He stared at the doctor in a panic. "Why did it happen at that second?" he cried. "I don't understand it! Why did it have to hit me then, at that second that had always been so wonder-ful for me? It isn't fair!"

"That was undoubtedly the only time it could have broken on you," the doctor said quickly, like a hand stretched out to him across the desk. "Any intense kind of consciousness or un-dertaking would have hit you at that time, John. That moment of asking your father the solemn questions of the Passover was the most meaningful moment of the evening for you. I can even say, I think, that it was the most meaningful moment of the year. As you explained it, that was the moment when you, an individual, the youngest son at the gathering, spoke up and took your solemn place in the Passover story of the Jews. To you, it was the most important time of the year. As far as religion was concerned, and culture, and your position in the family."

"But I wasn't religious! I didn't go to Hebrew school, or to *shule*. I never paid any attention to why we celebrated the Passover every year. I mean, I didn't know a hell of a lot about Jewish history, or praying, or anything like that."

"But you loved that holiday. When it came, each year, you were happy. The whole family was assembled. You loved sitting there, following the prayers in your book. And when it came time for you to ask the questions you felt glad that it was your place in the services. Would you willingly have given over the asking of those questions to anyone else?"

"Jesus Christ, no!" Jake cried. "They belonged to me. I was the youngest son there!"

The doctor continued his steady, cool pointing out of things Jake knew, and yet did not know.

"You may not be religious in the sense that your father is, but that Passover ritual and promise, that holding out of spring and hope, are religion to you, John. Just as surely as if you pray in Hebrew. They're your sense of God, your clasped hands in prayer. Other men get it from music. Or from poetry."

Jake stared at him. He felt as though he were swinging in a dream, shuttling back and forth from this dream to the one of the past.

"What do you mean, I *am* religious?" he asked painfully. "I was talking about more than twenty years ago, and why those things happened to me. Why do you say I am, instead of I was?"

"It strikes me you are a religious man," the doctor told him quietly. "Just as you were a religious boy. That's not the important point right now. We're trying to isolate that moment twenty years ago, when you looked up and saw your family. Has it occurred to you that you had been seeing your family all along, say for the past year, but that you were not conscious of seeing them? Not until all your senses were keyed up for that minute of asking the questions. That was the minute when you were emotionally ripe to see what you had known all the past year but had not told yourself in so many words."

Jake shook his head violently. "No! I don't get that. It's too tough for me to see that."

The quiet, calm voice continued. "People grow into their hour of maturity in a variety of ways. Sometimes they don't know the approximate hour. Let's say the consciousness of your hour came to you when you were fifteen, when you were at the holiday table, when you took your individual part in that evening's pageant of religious history. Will you please try to tell me what happened that evening?"

"All right," Jake said. He felt raw down the full length of him. Some of what the doctor had said made sense, but at the same time how could all those things be true? That he was religious! He, who hated Jews and everything Jewish.

"That's when I started to hate it that I was a Jew," he blurted out.

"Yes, I know," the doctor said. "But let's find out what it was you really started to hate that evening."

Lighting a cigarette, Jake tried to digest the exciting import of that. What it was you really started to hate. There was a lot to think about in words like that. Because, look at him, sure he hated the idea that anybody would think he was Jewish— like the old man, like Sarah and Max, like his family, sure. But look at how he always wondered, kept wondering, if he'd ever meet a Jewish girl, the kind he could marry.

"John," the doctor said at that moment, "talk all those things you're thinking so hard. Put them into words, so that we can examine them."

"I'm thinking how I felt that year," Jake said hesitantly. "I felt lots older. Sort of serious, you know what I mean? And I kept waiting for Passover. I don't know, that winter was so cold, and it seemed to go on for so long. I kept thinking it would be Passover soon, and my birthday, and then the warm weather would come. The grass, and then pretty soon it would be baseball weather, no school. I don't know, it seemed as if winter would never end. . . ."

. . . and then it had ended. Then it was Passover time, the night of the first Seder. He felt the familiar surge of excitement as he took his bath that evening and got into his suit. It was not a new suit this year, and as he buttoned the gray jacket and looked into the bathroom mirror he had a sudden, rather startling vision of his mother's face. It was tearful, the eyes pleading and the mouth trembling.

She wanted me to have a new suit, he thought, troubled. But the moment slipped away from him as he heard, beyond the bathroom door, his mother cry excitedly: "Roz, turn off the fire under the eggs! Put them in cold water. Pa'll be home soon. Debby, you found all the wineglasses?"

And then it was suddenly time. Pa was home, they were all sitting around the table and the house was crammed with the scents of holiday, the bright electric lights were reflected in the wineglasses, shone back from the dream in Debby's eyes across the table. His *Haggadah* lay open on the table in front of him, and he pushed his hat up a half inch on his forehead.

Blessed art thou, O Eternal, our God, King of the Universe, Creator of the fruit of the vine. His father's voice filled the room, and he blinked under the anticipated power and sonority of the Hebrew half chant, half song.

It was more than excitement this year, for some reason. He felt terribly solemn, almost tearful, as he followed his father's voice in the *Haggadah* English. When he lifted his glass, following his father's gesture, and sipped the wine it seemed to him that the taste was different this year; a powerful, mixed aroma of strength and solemnity seemed to come from the wine as he drank slowly, half afraid to swallow this strangely potent liquid.

He watched the familiar ritual steps, the washing of the hands, dreamily accepted the parsley dipped in salt water and ate it after his father had eaten, watched the elevation of the dish containing the bone and the egg.

He read the English, intensely curious this year about the import of each word and why it was uttered at that approximate moment. He read with a kind of avidness, not realizing with what fierceness he was searching phraseology. It was almost time for him now.

The tearful feeling mounted in him as he read the English which shaped itself on the page under the sound of the Hebrew over his head. *This year we are servants here, but next year we hope to be freemen in the land of Israel.*

"Fill the glasses," his father murmured, and his mother lifted the wine bottle and tipped it over each glass, and the red, rich color mounted to the edge of each glass.

It was time for him. It was time for his voice to go into the room, to join the prayers his father had uttered first, to prepare the way for the prayers with which his father would continue to tell the story.

"Ask the questions," his father murmured tonelessly.

Oh beautiful, Jake thought fleetingly, filled with a painful yearning. Oh mysterious, of God and of life, that is handed down through the thousands of years, oh beautiful that is so strong and meaningful that it will happen again and again, each year, forever, for as long as families sit down to tell and retell this story. And my voice has to come now, the way it's written that the youngest son has to talk at this second. Me, Jake. I have a place in this story.

"Wherefore is this night distinguished from all other nights?" he read, his voice trembling with the wonder and secrecy of life. "Any other night we may eat either leavened or unleavened bread, but on this night only unleavened bread; all other nights we may eat any species of herbs, but this night only bitter herbs; all other nights we do not dip even once, but on this night twice; all other nights we eat and drink either sitting or reclined, but on this night we all of us recline."

His eyes lifted from the page, the dish was set down on the table, and his father's voice began again.

That was the moment it happened to him. When his eyes lifted from the words and he himself was so full and deep with the tearfulness and the awe; at that moment, he looked around the table to see the eyes of his family because this had been his wonderful moment in the story and he wanted to see his feeling reflected in those eyes.

It struck him, with an appalling clarity, that they had not been listening. As he looked from face to face, clinging hard at that moment to the sound of his father's voice up there, above his head, it seemed to him that familiar and known masks had slipped from these faces and that now the bones and lines he had never seen before protruded in a terrible kind of sharpness.

Sig was tapping on the table with the fingers of his left

hand and whistling soundlessly; he kept looking at his watch, his lips shaped in that silent whistle.

He suddenly saw Roz as she sat restlessly cracking bits of matzoth. Her face was rouged and powdered, and he was aware, his heart sinking, of the petulant curve of her lips under the bright lipstick. What boy's name was she saying to herself!

His mother? His eyes flew to her face and studied it, but he knew nothing, the eyes seemed intent on the table, the face closed to him and to the entire Passover story.

His father's voice pulled his eyes up to the face. Stern, the head nodding, the upper body swaying slightly, the eyes focused on the big, worn-looking book from which he was reading; and now Jake sensed, with a kind of half-nauseated terror, that the prayers were being uttered mechanically, a singsong reading of one word after another, one automatic phrase after another.

Then Jake's eyes jumped to Debby. She was the same! Of all there, she was the only one with meaning left to her—the baby! The round, plump face under the Buster Brown hair (so neatly combed, so milk-white in the electric light) was turned toward their father. Her eyes were solemn, big with the dream of the chanted words. He saw her little, plump hands folded on the table, and he turned away impatiently, raging inwardly. That baby! she still believes everything, she thinks everything is still wonderful. Look at her, she believes every sound, every damn lie!

That was when he had first said the word. Lie. It's all a lie. Everything he's praying, every dish Ma cooked, every one of us sitting here—we're sitting in a lie.

That was when the terrible doubt hit him across the heart with a sledge hammer. It all stemmed from the focal point of that father, sitting so hypocritically at the head of a table. A father, the teller of the story about the Jews, the head of a family! Yes, but all the time Jake knew (my God, how long had he really known!) that he was stingy, without love for anyone, a smiler at tears, cold as ice and snow.

All the details of the past year (yes, and years!) sprang to life, sprang upon the Passover table and danced there like little horrid, grimacing idols. The eyes of his memory recognized them, approved their taunting steps. Seeing them now, he remembered that he must have seen them thousands of times without recognizing them. They were all the times his mother had asked for more money and his father had smiled that cold, jeering smile. Dancing there on the table were his mother's tears, her twisted lips as she cried and the half-whispered little cries of hopelessness. There, between the wineglasses, were the gloomy, dust-silent rooms of the house and the coldness of never a loving word, never a kiss. There, near the bitter herbs and the shabby book of prayers, danced his puzzlement at a brother's silence, at the never-closeness of a sister.

He never once put out his hand to me, Jake thought as he watched the stranger's face of his father. The Hebrew suddenly was an alien language, and in the room it sounded mechanical, flaccid rote. He never gave me a nickel, or asked me how I felt!

And she? he thought dismally as he watched his mother's face, seeing the tired droop of mouth, the grayness of skin. Did she ever kiss me? I don't remember. But she's warm, she I know, she's my mother! Just as I know he must have done it to her, he must have made her so that she doesn't put her arms around any of us, she doesn't make us all eat together every night, like Irving's mother does. It's as if something's wrong between them, between a mother and father, and something's wrong with all of us because of that, and with our house, too. Everything is a lie, because it's a lie that they're a mother and father.

He felt desperately alone. A frightened, shivering sensation accosted him as he felt how all the warm, prayerful ritual was false, and how his own part in this ritual was not true either. His identity as the youngest son asking questions of the head of the house— Why, it was not true! There was no head of the house, no identity for himself, no meaning to those questions he had thought were so beautiful. All the proud story of Jews and faith and strength, Moses smiting the Egyptians, David anointed by the prophet Samuel, all the pictures in the *Haggadah* through the years, were they all as false as this Seder table? Was it all pretense, just as his father pretended to be the head of a family, the leader of prayers, even though he had no right to be sitting there?

No right to be his father, no right to say holy words, no right to drink holy wine, no right to be asked those questions by the youngest son. A dirty, stingy, silent man who didn't flush the toilet after he'd used it, who squeezed his wife until she cried for enough money to buy a suit for a kid of theirs.

Sure, Jake said to himself grimly, why should she keep the house clean when he makes it dirty as soon as he steps into it? Why should she give a damn about everybody eating together, like a family, when he sits there and never says a word, just stuffs his face?

The wine seemed to smell sickeningly sweet, the color unreal for a moment in the glasses, and the mixed odors of the wine and the herbs and the food made him dizzy for an instant, his stomach rocking.

His father, a Jew. Was that the way it was to be a Jew? To be like his father in everyday life, then to sit at the Seder table like a patriarch of old—dignified, praying? It was a lie. His father, a Jew, lived a lie when he pretended to sit like this and tell a beautiful story. It was all a lie. If his father was a Jew, then he didn't want to be a Jew! And yet. Yes, yet how beautiful this Passover story had seemed. How could he bear not to believe it? And yet, there sat his father, a false man, a lie for a father, a Jew. How could he believe in both things?

His mother, who could cry, who could look so helpless, who could not be a strong mother full of love; how could he believe her? Sig and Roz, they did not live like a brother and a sister toward him, they lived like a lie, too. And Debby? She still believed all the lies. When he looked at her he could see how all the prayers were still shining in her eyes. She was the child he had been and was no longer. She was cut off from him because she still believed. She belonged to that father who was not a father; he no longer did. She belonged to the mother who was not really a mother; she had not seen those tears, the helpless eyes, the mother mouth twisted with crying.

He was alone. Like he didn't have a country, or a home, or a family—or even a name. He didn't want that man's name anyway! He'd make his own name. He'd get out, he didn't want any of them anyway. None of them, not even Debby with the dreamy eyes and the clean, white hair. He'd get a job, live his own life away from the lie of their lives.

But there was no comfort in these threats. As Jake sat there, the chant of his father's praying seemed to mount in a blurred, thick crescendo. He felt stifled by the heaviness of the sound and of the wine and food odors.

Listening intently, he heard Sig's amused, bored murmur in Yiddish to their mother: "Every year it seems to take him longer until we can finally eat." He heard their mother's half-apologetic whisper in answer, and tried to bury himself in the *Haggadah*, tried to match the English to the Hebrew words his father was chanting.

At that moment, a terrifying thing happened to him. It's because we're Jews, he thought, and then he was absolutely terrified because it seemed to him that he was trapped with that word, Jew. After all, he was a Jew, and it was something inside, in the blood and in the way one was born of Jews (King David and his harp, Moses smiting the Egyptians!), in the bone and in the flesh, something one could not cut out of himself, or run away from.

He did not dare lift his eyes from the blur of words on the page. How terrifying, but how strange, too, for never before had he called himself that—Jew—as if it were an extraordinary thing. Never before had he been conscious of being one or not being one. It had been simply Jake Brown, just as Passover had been, or eating chicken every Friday and every holiday, or staying home from school on holidays, like all the Jewish kids did. It had been part of life, something not to call by name or even to think by name.

And now it was strange, now it was of terror and of trap, of the knowledge that his father was a dirty stranger and his mother a frightened, sad, incapable woman, that his older brother was a stranger with bored, cold eyes, that his sister was overly rouged and her flesh restless for he knew what—yes, he knew what in his own body, and that was more of the terror and lostness. And the other sister was a soft, dreaming baby with solemn eyes, a baby who might cry out in her own fear some day because she did not have mother or father strong enough or clean enough or loving enough.

All of it, the sudden, not-to-be-understood knowledge, the abrupt premonition, the shaking of earth's foundations, all of this suddenly was tied up with the fact that they were Jews, with this Jewish evening (how beautiful it had been up until a split, jagged moment ago! how full of secrecy and meaning!).

Here they sat, these people and their lie of being Jews, of being solemn and prayerful, of being part of a story about deliverance from bondage. Here they sat, lying with every sip of wine. The old man pretending to be the head of a family on this one night, and all year round he made dirt, he made tears, he gave no love or pennies, or father words or husband looks.

Were all Jews like that? Liars. Come sit at the holy table and pray, sip wine, eat the bitter herbs, pretend to be beautiful, for this one night. Then, all the rest of the year, make your wife cry (my mother, my mother!). Sit, like a silent stranger, at the kitchen table drinking your tea and reading your Goddam Jewish paper, and belching. Not a word for your children. Not a smile for your wife. Not a reason in all the shattered world for all of us to live in this house, pretending to be a family. *Wherefore is this night distinguished from other nights?* It isn't, it isn't! That's a lie, too!

Then, finally, like the next step in a pageant, the terror left Jake. It seeped slowly out of him, and into its place stalked the next ghost, the lostness, the feeling that he was cut off from all of them (there they sat, not knowing, not feeling any of his emotions), from their blood, their kind, their name.

It was a caving in of walls, a lostness in which his identity was drowning (youngest son, wherefore is this night distinguished, but you aren't his son, or his name, so how can you ask the questions, how can you say father to him, so who are you anyway?). Motherless and fatherless, brotherless and sisterless. Nameless. Whatever name he had was a lie. And if his father was a Jew, then by God all Jews were like his father and he would not be a Jew! He would not, he would not, though David played on his harp and though there was a miracle at the Red Sea and though the ten plagues were brought down upon the enemy.

As his father chanted with a dry, automatic sound above his head, Jake searched the page of the *Haggadah* for some accusing phrase, some pointed and talismanic word. But now even the English words were alien, meaningless. *And we cried unto the Eternal, the God of our fathers, and the Eternal heard our voice, saw our affliction, our sorrow, and our oppression.*

It was all a lie. These words and his father and the Passover. Jews were a lie.

As he lifted his eyes from the book, he heard Roz cracking bits of matzoth and, without looking, he knew the sullen, hard shape of her mouth, the restless ache in her eyes.

Ma was at the stove, looking into the pots, and Pa's voice went on and on until he could feel how the mumbo-jumbo was parching his own throat. He would not look across the table, into Debby's rapt eyes. He would not look at Sig, because he knew now that the brother look had never been there.

Jake reached for his wineglass and took a sip. His throat was as dry as if he had been praying for hours.

A stern promise shaped itself in his mind as he felt this bitter and nameless moment of leaving all of them. I'll never again sit down with my family at one table. We lied enough. I'll never eat with all of them again and lie that we're a family. I'll never ask him the questions again, that dirty Jew.

And he swallowed the wine solemnly, as if it could seal the promise. . . .

"I remember how ashamed I was," Jake finished slowly. "Ashamed that he was my father, that I was a Jew. Because he was one. And all of us, the whole family, we were Jews. I blamed everything on that, I guess—on the fact that we were Jews. All the dirt and the stinginess and the way we didn't love each other. I guess I thought all Jews were like that, didn't I? I didn't want to be one, I know that. I blamed everything on that."

"You had to blame it on something," the doctor said. "You couldn't bear to face the fact that it was one man, your father, who must have been the source of all that misery."

He caught Jake's eyes, added slowly, "You couldn't face the idea that your mother had chosen this man for her husband, for your father. Did you think it would have been a betrayal on your part to face that choice of hers? To blame her? You had to blame it on the race, didn't you? You were unable to blame her. Did you think then that the Passover ritual, that beautiful thing in your life, had been betrayed, too?"

Jake thought hard about that. "Maybe I did," he said grudgingly. Then, he could not help it, he demanded: "Why should I have blamed her? It wasn't her fault that he was a dirty Jew!"

"But how could she deliberately have picked this dirty Jew for her husband?" the doctor said gently. "Did you ever ask yourself that? Did you picture them in the same bedroom? Did you want to accuse her of marrying a man like that, to ask her how and why she had dared?"

Jake shivered. "No," he said flatly. "I never thought of such things. I tell you I didn't!"

"What did you think of?"

"I remember when I'd bring my report card home," Jake said, tired. "Fathers signed report cards. Well, he'd finally sign mine. He never looked at it, or said anything about the marks I'd got. You should see him write! He sits all hunched over, and it takes him a long time, and then his name is all twisted on the card. You can hardly read it."

He sighed. "I remember how ashamed I was when I took the card back to school. I used to wait for my teachers to laugh at the way he'd written his name, all twisted up, the way it didn't look like English at all. I used to feel so ashamed."

"Did you ever think of your mother at those times?"

"She can't write at all, in any language," Jake said slowly. "She learned how to write her name in Yiddish, and that's all."

"And did you hate that?"

Jake talked more slowly, thinking it out as he talked. "No. She always seemed—. You see, I was always sorry for her. Nothing seemed to be her fault. She always seemed weak; I had to protect her. I knew if she couldn't write, it wasn't her fault."

"I see. What else did you feel about her?"

"I used to wonder," Jake admitted, "if she was ashamed of him, too. I used to wonder how she felt, especially at night, when she was—." He stopped, glared at the doctor.

"Yes?"

"All right! When she was in the same room with him! I used to feel glad, so terribly glad that they had twin beds, that they didn't have to sleep in the same bed. That she didn't have to be too close to him all the time at night."

He took a cigarette from the box the doctor pushed toward him, lit it, noticed with scarcely any feeling that his hands were shaking. Sitting back in the chair, he felt exhausted but intensely relieved, as if he had completed a job of hard labor.

"That's when you began to feel guilty about your mother?" the doctor questioned him softly.

Jake nodded. "I think so, I'm not sure."

"When you realized, however vaguely and without words, that her relationship with your father must be degrading?"

"Yeah!" His jaws seemed set. "Degrading! When I thought about them—together—I could smell how his underwear must smell. That long, thick underwear he'd wear for weeks at a time. I could smell the way it must have smelled in bed!"

"But think it out," the doctor's cool, quiet voice went on. "You can't make up to her for such a repulsive relationship. You can't make up for that dirty old man, for all the ignorant, foul personal habits to which he has subjected her." The voice became firmer. "You can't, John. That would be incest. You don't want that."

Jake looked dazed. "Listen," he said haltingly, "I was scared. Ashamed. When I looked at her I felt how she was asking me for something. I knew that, whatever it was, it was his fault. Just as it was his fault that I couldn't ask the questions any more. But I couldn't get it, I couldn't get the point. I knew he'd spoiled Passover for me. I knew he was dirty and rotten, that he was Jewish, that he had no business praying, no business making a Seder for his family."

"So you blamed it on the Jews," the doctor said.

Jake's mouth dropped slackly as he looked back.

"In Germany, a lot of people blame their fear and hunger on the Jews."

"Yeah, I know," Jake cried, his forehead gashed with sudden lines. "And they're not Jews themselves, like I am. That was peculiar, wasn't it? I mean that Passover business, how I loved it so much, and all of a sudden it seemed like a dirty lie."

"It seemed like a betrayal," the doctor said. "Beauty and meaning betrayed by the man who was leading prayers. The entire essence of Jewishness seemed to crumble for you."

"Yeah, I guess so," Jake mumbled. "Though I didn't know anything about such words, essence of Jewishness."

"Except inside of you," the doctor pointed out. "You knew all the words there. Shame for your father, who was dirty, a Jew, a man who did not give his wife a good life. If this man was a Jew, then one should be ashamed of being a Jew."

"Yeah!"

"But is it the Jewishness of your father you dislike? Or is it the personality, the mind and actions, of the man?"

74

Jake stared at him.

"Is it the Jews who are dirty and rotten, stingy, illiterate as far as their adopted land is concerned? Or are all those traits embodied in this one man, whom your mother chose to marry—who happens to be a Jew?"

The silence in the office washed over Jake warmly, softly, like slow-running, gentle water. He felt the thick, rigid bar of shame quiver for the first time, the bar he had thought so immovably fixed across his heart.

Three

It was Saturday again. Today he was eager to be here. Already he shared with the walls of this office the intimacy of secrets released, the wonderful freedom of shame and pain eased, even the inch of secret, the first few stumbling steps of ease.

The big desk was somewhat like a bridge between the doctor and him; at one end the doctor sat, and here at this end he sat, waiting for the moment when he could take a few further awkward steps upon that bridge into understanding, into reasoning.

"Have you seen your nephews recently?" the doctor asked casually.

Jake started. He had been thinking of Passover, wondering if he would feel differently about it this year. He had been thinking of the taste of matzoth, one whole piece with butter spread thick on it and plenty of salt and pepper sprinkled on.

"No," he said hurriedly. "I don't want to see them, to tell you the truth. It would make me feel lousy. Debby sees them. She tells me about them."

"When is the last time you saw them?"

Jake flushed, lit a cigarette. "I don't know exactly. Maybe two weeks ago, I don't know. It was a Friday. I was home because it was my day off. On the way from school, they stopped for the fish and bread my mother had made for Sarah."

"Why are you embarrassed about it?" the doctor asked.

"Embarrassed?" Jake took a quick drag of the cigarette. "I wasn't embarrassed. I was just thinking how I slipped them a dime apiece that day."

"But it doesn't do any good to give them money, does it? You still feel guilty about them, don't you? Do you feel 'lousy' when you see them, or is it really that you feel ashamed? At not doing anything for them. 'Lousy,' or guilty?"

Jake's heart started to pound. He fumbled with the ashtray. Then he decided to look up.

"All right, ashamed," he admitted finally in a low voice. Then he cried, "But honestly, they're like stranger kids to me. Both of them. I told you about when I saw Bernie. Well, I had the same feeling about both of them this time. They made me feel funny. Uncomfortable!"

His voice petered out, and he stared for a moment into the steady eyes watching him. "Not uncomfortable," he said carefully then. "That's not the word, is it? I guess it's a feeling of being ashamed. All right. But hell, I don't know what to do about Bernie! I wasn't like that when I was a kid, wild like that."

"What were you like?"

What was he like? Go back now. Go far and deep and twenty-five years back. Beyond the muddle and darkness, beyond the unhappy Seder, far and deep back beyond some of the happy Seders.

"I don't know," he muttered. "I never think about when I was a kid. It's like a blank."

"What was your father like when you were young? Did you like him?"

Jake studied that. "I'll tell you," he said thoughtfully, very slowly, "I can hardly remember. When I think of the old man I see him the way he is now. Old. Dirty. Those baggy pants he wears. The way he's always drinking tea, reading a newspaper or a Jewish library book."

He took a deep breath. "There's a picture of him hanging in the hall near the bedrooms. He put it up there himself. I don't even recognize him in that picture. He's got brown hair in it. The mustache is brown, too. It's a different man entirely. The picture's young."

He hesitated. "I don't look at it often. But every once in a while, see, I bump right into it on the way to my room. Well, it's nothing like he is now."

"A handsome man?"

"Yeah. I guess maybe he was handsome when she—when he was young."

He flushed, and the doctor said quickly, "Think back. Think hard for a moment. You as a child."

Jake hunched back in the chair, closed his eyes. When he began talking, the words came in ragged spurts. "I hustled papers. Downtown, after school and on Sundays. Gave the money to her. I didn't like school. I was dumb at it, not like Sig or Debby. Quiet. I was always blushing when a teacher talked to me. It was hard to talk, hard to read. I wanted to work, make my own money. It got worse all the time. When I had to ask her for money—for a book, or pencils and paper—I felt bad. Got worse and worse. I knew she'd have to beg for it. And even after she begged she wouldn't get it, most of the time. I thought, What the hell, what's the use? I wore a lot of Sig's old clothes."

His eyes opened. "I finally quit school," he said dully. "In my second-last year. I felt better then. I knew things would be better as soon as I got a job."

"And were they?"

"Well, the money business was better."

Jake scowled. For a livid moment he hated this doctor. What the hell was he pushing him for? Into those days? Into those lousy days he'd practically forgotten?

The quiet voice asked him a completely different thing now. "Tell me, John, how have you been sleeping?"

Sullenly Jake replied, "Not so hot. I have a tough time falling asleep. Then I keep waking up, and it's hard to get back to sleep. I woke up three times last night."

"Why? Were you anxious about something in particular?"

"Anxious?" Jake said. "I was worried, I guess. I kept thinking about some art I took on one of my assignments yesterday. I kept wondering if my boss had thrown it out. The city editor, you know."

"Well, had he thrown it out?"

"No." Jake tried to light a cigarette but the matches would not ignite; two broke off as he struck them. "Damn it," he said softly, almost tearfully, then he got a light.

"What were you saying?" the doctor asked quietly.

Jake tensed. "My pictures," he muttered. "They were in today's paper, all right. In all editions. I even got a by-line. I don't know what the hell gets into me. I worry all the time. That job of mine."

There was a tightness in the room for him. He dragged on the cigarette, felt himself straining against the man behind the big desk. He looked up against the cool, stone wall of eyes, felt his mind, too, pushing savagely against that wall.

"Listen," he started out very quickly, "I know it sounds crazy, but I'm really nuts about my job. Don't get me wrong! But I'm always worried about it. I mean, well, how the pictures are going to turn out. What people are going to say. What to say to them, for Christ sake!"

"Do you want to talk about your job today?" the doctor asked.

"There's too much to talk about," Jake said, groaning to himself at the impossibility of saying it all in words. "I don't know where to start. Jesus, I've been on the *Register* eighteen years! How do you start talking about eighteen years' worth of stuff?"

He watched the doctor's thumb press down on the notebook, the pen move without writing.

"Why did you quit school?" the doctor asked.

"Jesus Christ!" Jake burst out, "what was the use of finishing? I was a dope. I needed money. Every time I looked at my mother I wanted money more and more. Every time I looked at my father. . . ."

. . . he hated him more. He spent a lot of time dreaming of wonderful, triumphant things to possess, to flaunt in that man's face. A million dollars; and he could see the look in the old man's eyes when he was confronted with the money, the way his jeering smile would fade and dry out, blow off the bone of cheek and the fuzz of mustache, like yellow powder.

One early evening he was sitting at the kitchen table, trying to write an English composition. It was a desperate business for him. He disliked school, was poor in all subjects but gym and science. Grammar and writing, even the sheer physical movements of them, made him sweat.

He had come to the paper with a blank mind, and for minutes he had sat at the table staring around him. At his father, opposite him, and then at his mother, who was sitting in her favorite chair, next to the sink, reading part of the paper. He could hear Sig whistling in the bathroom. He could hear Roz tap-tapping sharply with her high heels as she walked from the dining room to their parents' bedroom, where some of her clothes hung in their closet. Next he stared at Debby, who was reading a book in the chair opposite Ma. She was reading with her usual absorption, something he had always envied her; the way her head leaned toward a book, her face intent and solemn with the words she was reading.

Jake began to write, laboriously, forming the letters big and sprawly and round, the way he had always written. For a change, his thoughts came swiftly and freely; he had decided to write about them.

> My father is sitting in the kitchen, drinking tea out of his special glass and reading the Jewish paper [Jake wrote]. In Russia you drink tea out of a thin glass, and you don't put sugar in the tea. Instead, you bite off a piece of a lump of sugar and hold the piece in your mouth, then you take a sip of tea and it tastes sweet because of the sugar you're holding in your mouth. It looks like lots of trouble but my father always drinks tea that way, just like he used to in Russia. I wouldn't drink tea that way, I'd drink it the American way.
>
> My mother is in the kitchen too. She's reading part of the same Jewish paper. I can't read Jewish. I don't want to either, but they can't read English so it's all right. My father can read it a little bit.
>
> My sister is here too, reading a book. She came in about a half hour ago from the street. She was playing with the kids. On our street the kids are mostly Jewish, but there are lots of Italians too, and a couple of colored kids. My brother Sig wants us to move soon because he says the street is not as good as it used to be. I don't know why he

figures that because I have fun on this street. So does my sister Deborah. She is leader of a gang. There's even two colored kids in her gang, but she's the leader. She's the only girl in the gang, but she's the leader anyway.

Just then he became conscious of his brother standing next to him. Sig was leaning over his shoulder and reading his composition. He was laughing!

"What the hell's the matter with you?" he demanded, his left hand lunging protectively over the paper.

"God, look at that handwriting," Sig said.

Everybody in the kitchen looked up; Jake could feel them look up, even though he could see nothing but Sig's smile. All of a sudden it reminded him of the old man's smile, and he swallowed a bubble of nausea.

"Leave me alone," he muttered.

"It's worse than a kid's writing," Sig said, and Jake had a sudden picture of Sig signing his name, Sigmund Brown, all flourishes, the letters beautiful and arched and flowing one into the other. He had been a big shot at school, too. All the teachers always looked hard at Jake, then they'd say: "Aren't you Sigmund Brown's brother?"

Sigmund Brown's brother. The class president, the smart guy, the guy whose handwriting was so beautiful all the teachers still raved about it, Jesus Christ! He'd even won prizes for his handwriting.

The fire began to burn quietly, very steadily, inside his chest. But Debby's writing is just like mine, he thought, and the odd comfort of being in any way like that blond, strong little sister quickly came to him. Several times within the past year he had traced certain similarities; the knowledge had given him that queer sense of comfort.

"Leave me alone," he muttered again. The hand that was smashed down on the beginning of the composition felt wet and clammy.

It was not only the hatred for the old man, and the way Sig was belittling him in front of Ma. It was the shame, too. The shame of being dumb, a lousy writer, a lousy student; the shame of being accused before his mother, before Debby and Roz. To hell with Sig himself, the accuser; he didn't even care about him!

Then the old man opened up, in Yiddish. The paper came down, he cleared his throat. He always cleared his throat before he started making one of his rare speeches, the bastard.

"School," the old man said. "School is for scholars, not for big, hulking boys who have long been ready to work. Some people haven't the mind for such subtleties as books. In Russia we knew which boys to send to school, which to send to work."

Not one word from his mother. Jake felt such hatred for this man that he knew how his hands would feel after they fisted themselves against his face. There was a hot tingling in all his fingers as he sat there.

Very quietly he said, "I'm quitting school after this term."

That was a surprise; he had not known he was going to say it. He had never said it to himself. A liquid, warm gush of gladness came up in back of his eyes.

"What!" Sig cried. "What did you say?"

"You heard me," Jake muttered, his voice furry with the glad feeling. When he looked up, he saw Debby's face. It was pale, and her eyes looked horrified. But his mother hadn't said one word.

"My God," Sig groaned, "he isn't happy just acting like a dummy. He has to quit school. Like the lowest kind of person."

His voice rose. "Ma, I told you we had to move out of this street. Look at him. He's acting just like the dagoes. Like the niggers. Our neighbors! I don't care about him, let him wreck his life, but how does he think I feel? My own brother, quitting school!"

Roz came tap-tapping into the kitchen. Her face was freshly made up, her coat wrapped tight around her hips. Who's she seeing tonight? Jake thought mechanically. Who's she kissing tonight, petting tonight, hugging tonight?

"Aw, let him quit," Roz cried. "It's his life, isn't it?" The kitchen door slammed after her; he could hear the tap-tap down the four hall steps, then faintly down the driveway, then the sound was gone.

There was not much more to it that evening. He sat at the table, confronting those words he had said out loud. All around the edge of those words peered the faces. Debby's, all white and frightened and as if she had seen something terrible. Sig's, disgusted and ashamed. Pa's, starting to look fat and satisfied, even though it was a skinny, gray face. Ma's—but she hadn't said a word, not the picture of one word in her eyes, on her lips to curve them or narrow them.

He looked up, into Sig's brown, indignant eyes.

"I'm warning you," Sig said. "Take the word of your older brother, you'll be sorry some day. But it'll be too late then. I'm warning you."

The old man cleared his throat. He put down the glass, swallowed the sip of tea. "He's smart." The familiar, hateful Yiddish swirled in murky lines around the kitchen. "He finally knows money is the world. It's time he found it out."

It made a harsh, many-timed echo. *Gelt iss duh welt.* "Money is the world."

That's a dirty, lousy lie, he said to himself very steadily and quietly, like the fire in his chest. Debby knows it, that's why she looks like she's seen a ghost. But I'll get plenty of *gelt*, all right. I'll burn it up in front of that bastard, but he won't see a dime of it. I hope he begs for it so I can laugh in his face.

Sig was talking, his voice shrilling in the kitchen, but Jake was not listening. He could not see his mother; Sig's body was between them. What was she really thinking? Behind that closed, shy face and the peering eyes, was she feeling bad, good?

But Ma, I'll give it all to you. All the money. All the *gelt*. You won't ever cry again. You won't ever look scared, or as if you were going to hit your fists against your head (I've seen you do that, when you didn't know anybody was looking!).

You don't care if my handwriting isn't nice. If Sig ever says anything about your not even being able to write, I'll kill him!

But he did not know, he could not possibly guess, what she was thinking. . . .

He'd had no trouble getting the job.

The logical thing to do, as he had been hustling the *Register* all along, was to see Joe, in the circulation department, the same guy who'd been slipping him the packages of papers all this time.

"What about on the truck?" he said. "Or checking on part-time workers, or on hustlers?"

"We're all full," Joe said. "But why don't you go up to the

editorial department, kid? It's right next door, up on the fourth floor. I hear they need copy boys."

It had been so easy. Everything had been easy, the job, the sliding into a name, the wonderful way the office had seemed like home from the very first moment.

He had seen a tall, lanky man with red hair, who had looked him over carelessly.

"You look like you can run," he said. "It's ten bucks a week to start—if you last you'll get a raise one of these days."

The clatter of typewriters came up at him from all corners of the huge room, and every second a telephone bell rang in some other direction. It was wonderful.

"What you do," the redheaded man said, stepping on his cigarette end, "you'll work in shifts, like the staff. See, what you do is run copy for all of us. Also you chase around for stuff, lunches and cigs and all that. See, we holler 'Copy!' or 'Boy!' and you come running. What do you say?"

"Swell," Jake quavered.

"Yeah, well you better fill out a paper." He tossed Jake a form. "Sit down right there. Better use that pen, kid."

So easy. He still remembered vividly the knocking of his heart as he wrote; the terrible, terrible moving of earth under the chair in which he was sitting, hunched over the paper.

John Brown, he printed. He felt the red heat climbing up into his face. For an everlasting minute, he sat there and studied that name he had printed for his own.

It was beautiful. It was as American-looking, as anonymous, as any name he could think of.

If Sig could change our name from Braunowitz to Brown, he argued savagely for a split second, then I can change Jake to John.

John Brown. It was like Indians, or Plymouth Rock, it was like American history. It hasn't got potato pancakes in it, he thought, the joy like an ache in his chest. It doesn't smell like the house, or like him. When you say the name, you can't hear the way he belches and the way he can't talk good English, and the way he never closes the bathroom door when he's in there.

Flushed to his hair, he passed the paper to the redheaded man. It was difficult to breathe while he waited.

Nothing happened. The man looked at it briefly, then tossed it into a wire basket on his desk.

"O.K., Johnnie. There's a head boy, name of Joe Harbor." He looked around the pulsating room, frowned. "Well, I don't see him, but he'll find you. What he'll do, he'll give you your schedule. Some weeks you'll be working mornings; some, days, and some, nights. He'll straighten you out."

Jake stumbled to his feet. They felt asleep, prickling in the soles.

"Want to start now?" the man said.

"Sure!"

"O.K. Run down and bring me a coke and a ham-on-rye. We use the Greek joint right next door. Tell Sam to put it on my account. White. Ernie White."

Jake ran.

He paused briefly at the open elevator door. The operator stared at him as he stopped abruptly.

"Hey, where're the steps?" Jake demanded, starting to grin.

The little man pointed toward the right.

"Thanks! Say, I got a job here! How do you like that? Say, who's that redheaded man in there?"

"Ernie?" The man stared again, then said with icy politeness, "Oh, he ain't nobody much. He's just the city editor, that's all."

"Thanks!" Jake cried, and sprang toward the door at the right.

He clattered down the steps. Triumph paced him, outran him, then jumped two steps at a time along with him. John Brown.

He was seventeen. He had a job. He had a name. . . .

The camera happened to him about a year after he had started working. The camera happened to him while he was on night shift; it was then, in the dead stretches which occurred so often at night in the city room, that he began to poke around in the darkroom.

In the darkroom, and in the small room just outside it, he became friendly with the Old Man at last. In fact, the Old Man finally sort of adopted him.

The Old Man's name was Pete Bartok. He was only about fifty-five, but everybody called him either Pete or the Old Man. He'd been head of the photographic department for one hell of a long time. Why they called him the Old Man is because some big shot in New York had written a letter to the editor of the *Register* and in the letter he had called Pete the "Grand Old Man of photography." They'd posted the letter on the bulletin board in the city room and from that moment on, part of the name had hung on.

The Old Man was a hunky, the head copy boy added to Jake while telling him about the bulletin board. That is, he'd come to America when he was about sixteen or seventeen, a hell of a long time ago, but he still talked with a slight accent, so that made him still a hunky.

Jake was afraid of him for a long time. Pete had a ragged mustache that was all gray, and his hair was partially gray, and whenever Jake saw him or heard him there was a fierce, blustering layer of air all around him. He'd come yelling into the city room and walk fast through the barnlike room, into the section where the photographers hung out. Later he'd come hollering out of the darkroom and glare all around him. Jake couldn't figure out why everybody was so crazy about him.

He'd stay away from the darkroom until the Old Man left, or if the Old Man was on a different shift it would be easy, he would hang around every free minute he could chisel, and pester Bill Thomas with questions on developing, filmpak, chemicals, the shutter on a camera and what happened if a person knelt and shot upward. The idea of photography began to fascinate him, for some reason. He was all muddled about it in his mind, but he could not wait to get his hands on a camera. The possibility of halting action in mid-air, a gesture, a look of eyes or curve of mouth, and getting that action or inflection on paper, seemed to him an absolutely marvelous thing.

The night the Old Man adopted him Jake was sitting on the floor of the little room which lay between the darkroom and the studio, the room in which the photographers sat around and smoked and told stories. He was going through a huge album of the Old Man's pictures, whistling to himself at how wonderful they were. Some of them looked like they were painted, and in one of them—a fire shot—the Old Man had got a woman's tears, and how her eyes were sad and afraid at the same time.

It was silent and warm in the room, and Jake was happy. He thought maybe if he worked like a dog, some day he'd do pictures like that. Where it was possible to get a look of tears in a shot, and how a woman's mouth twisted.

Quiet and warm; and when he looked up, the Old Man was leaning against the wall near the door and watching him.

All of a sudden, Jake was not afraid of him. The Old Man looked like—well, like a father is supposed to look.

"What's your name, kid?" the Old Man said, leaning like that. His voice sounded kind of like singing because of that hunky accent.

"John," Jake said tremulously, looking up from the open album. "John Brown."

"John Brown's body, eh?" Jake noticed how short and slight the Old Man really was, and how blue his eyes were.

"Lies a-moldering in the grave, eh!" The Old Man suddenly knelt, right next to Jake, and squinted his fierce eyes down at the picture of the woman. Only it wasn't fierce; that wasn't the word at all, Jake noticed.

"Like that one?" the Old Man said, studying the picture.

"It sure is a marvelous shot," Jake said, his face hot. He wondered if the Old Man would notice how he said the word shot, instead of picture.

The Old Man turned, looked squarely into Jake's eyes, at his rough-cut mouth and the dirty-blond hair hanging into his face. He was so close that Jake's eyes filled with tears, but he did not look away. There were tiny, fine lines sprayed at the corners of the eyes.

"What's the matter?" the Old Man asked. "You want to be a photographer?"

Jake nodded. There was a big lump in his throat, and he wanted the Old Man to put an arm around him. He looked like that, too, like he wanted to put an arm around him.

The Old Man nodded absently, as if Jake's nod had started him off.

"Bill Thomas says you keep hanging around," he said, his voice sounding absent, too. "So let's do it to him, I said to Bill.

What we'll do, any time you can snitch from the big room out there, why you come in here and Bill or me—we'll break you in. We'll show you. Like I said to Bill, Let's do it to him, let's make him a lousy photographer, the poor sap."

Jake started to say something but his voice came out all rough and hoarse, and the Old Man nodded again. He had started to turn the pages of the album, squatting over the book like a little gray, absent-minded monkey.

"It's not hard. Only you've got to have a feel for it. That's the only important thing you've got to have. Look at this one, Johnnie."

Jake leaned close, the skin of his face hot and quivering to that carelessly uttered Johnnie. The Old Man's short, dirty finger was pointing to a face.

"I took this at the hospital fire," he said. "Look at this guy's face. You gotta look for faces when you want to get the feel of a shot. Look at him. They'd just pulled him out. His wife was still in there. He was just standing and shivering, but why'd I pick this one face? Look at him. You got a face there that's full of fire and wife and how scared he is and how he wants to pray. How he wants to rush back into that fire and get her. Haven't you?"

Jake nodded. "Yes, sir, you sure have."

The hand turned a few pages. "Feel, Johnnie, feel! You gotta feel your way into things, into mugs, and then the camera'll just do like you say it should. Look at this. What do you see?"

Jake peered down. His heart was knocking, but he felt so close to the Old Man he wasn't scared to answer.

"It's a boxer and three guys," he said. "One guy is crying and the other two look like they want to cry. But the boxer looks like—well, he looks like he isn't feeling like anything."

"Good, good!" the Old Man cried. "Here's a man who just lost the world's heavyweight crown. What do you shoot? His deadpan, sure, he's just had his block knocked off. But you get his manager bawling, too, don't you? And his trainers looking like they're at his funeral. Look there, kid." The finger jumped from end to end of the picture. "Look at the detail on that shot. You gotta feel your detail, don't ever forget that. Look at those faces near the ring, will you? Those eyes just saw a crown drop, bang-o! Those mouths just got through yelling. Feel the whole shot, kid, and for Chris' sake don't ever forget your detail."

The pages turned. Jake relaxed, forgot his fear, his lie of a name, his shameful heritage. The Old Man sang him a song he'd never forget, he was offering him a gift he'd never stop grabbing for, and he knew it right now.

"After a while," the Old Man said in his absent way, "it'd be a good idea, maybe, to specialize. You know, maybe in sports. Or action shots. Or maybe even that theater and movie stuff. Get yourself a reputation. But you'll have to figure out what you've got the feel for first, kid."

Then he said, "Come on in the darkroom, I'll show you a couple of things."

Jake jumped up, ran to the door and peered into the city room. The long reaches of it were like a desert, the lights shining down on empty desks and silent telephones. He could see Ernie White in the AP room, his head bent over the sheet of white paper ticking slowly from the machine through his fingers.

"I'll leave the door open," he cried, and started to giggle. "He won't want a coke yet for a while, and I'll hear him call me. Hey, Mr. Bartok, when can I look at a camera?"

The Old Man looked at him absently. "You break any of my equipment, kid, and I'll break your head," he said, starting to go through the curtains separating the room from the darkroom. "Well, come on. Let's see if you got the feel for a camera, kid. Come on. And I'll tell you something," he added in that faraway manner, "people around here call me Pete. Let's see you get the feel for that . . ."

Jake had never called him father, even in the secrecy of his thoughts, nor had he ever gone to the Old Man for advice outside of work problems. Named or unnamed, however, Pete gave him a particular kind of strength. Being with him, working with him and under him, leaning over a bath with him as the print came out of it and both of them peering to see how good the shot really was, these were things of father to him, the strength and feeling a guy got from his father.

The way the Old Man had gone into the front office and talked to the editor, the way he had got Jake switched to the darkroom within six months, the way his hand tousled Jake's hair as he growled, "Hey kid, that was a terrible shot; what the hell did I tell you about watching your Goddam background?"—these were the things he never labeled father-son, but they were anyway, and they would be in his mind forever.

And the eighteen years of working on the *Register*; what did one remember of them? The way they flowed one into the next, and the next. The way the first fears faded (and yet somehow never quite completely faded), the fear of not fitting in, of being a Jew among hundreds of gentiles, the fear that the Anglo-Saxon name would not be enough to carry him, that some hidden, secret thing of Jewishness would creep out and mark his face, or his speech, or the way he worked.

The way he worked! In all the eighteen years, that was the fear that was most swollen, that would not go away. How, in what abrupt, sudden, secret way, would his Jewishness mark his work? He realized that there were certain scars which must be permanent. However deep you buried them, however far you left them, they were bound to stand out again some day, and there, starkly and permanently, would be your shame again! In all the eighteen years, he could not succeed in forgetting such a thing, but had to keep waiting for it. Imagine how it is to wait for something like that every minute of the day and night!

John Brown. It was a good name, a fine name, and yet always he waited for somebody to call him a liar. In eighteen years, no one on the paper knew he was a Jew. He had just never discussed it with anyone; it just had never come up. And yet, in all the eighteen years, he kept waiting for somebody to confront him with the words, "Well, well, hiya, Jake!"

He did not know who it would be, but he kept waiting anyway. He never saw any of his relatives, his numerous uncles or cousins, and even if Pa or Ma called him Jake he knew they would never come anywhere near the paper. Neither would Sarah's family.

Sig and Roz called him Jack, and Debby called him John. When he was drunk, he remembered, she called him Jack. But even they would not come up to the office; he knew they wouldn't. How did he know? He just did! See, none of them knew any of his business, any of his friends. He'd never told them anything at home. They didn't want to know anyway! So what was he afraid of, who was he waiting for? He didn't know. All he knew was, he was waiting. For eighteen years.

Yes, maybe it was true ("Yes, Doctor, I'm sure you're right!") that he would remain rootless, nameless, even with this fine John Brown of a name, until he named himself inside. Yes, maybe it was true that real identity happens inside of a guy first, and then the outside name does not matter much. But how does a guy get such an inside identity, for God's sake!

Because, look at him, how he had tried during those eighteen years. He hadn't finished high school and he'd been ashamed of things like bad grammar, so he'd read a lot. My God, he'd read books and magazines by the thousand! He even had a card at a rental library, and the woman there telephoned him every time she found a book she thought he'd like. What he liked to read was biographies and really good mystery stories and books by foreign correspondents, and naturally he had a standing order for books about newspapers, any kind of book as long as it was about a reporter or a publisher or a photographer. Magazines? Why, every week he bought *Time, Life, Liberty,* the *Post, Collier's* and the *New Yorker.* Also he read the Sunday *PM.*

At least maybe those books and magazines would give him an idea of what it was all about, even if he hadn't finished high school.

And over the eighteen years, look at how many important people knew him. And liked him! Mayors, governors, actors, lots of big businessmen, anybody in town who was a big shot. A lot of nationally known boxers and baseball players.

He had a good-looking car, a new one every year; what he did was trade in the old one every year. It was always a convertible coupe because he was so nuts about sun and wind.

Get a name inside! How do you do that? Because, look at him. Over the eighteen years (that's a hell of a long time! that makes me thirty-five!) he still was not sure of his camera. By God, until those pictures were in the paper and until the minute he examined them—on page one or on the sports page—he was never sure they'd be in. And what about a one-man show? Take a kid like Ted Pope, or take my pal Bill Thomas—he's an old-timer, but so am I—they put on one-man shows all the time. At the museum, or at the university. But I don't. Ask me why!

Identity. I tell you, a guy gets all mixed up. Let me tell you about this guy on the paper. For a while I watched him. I studied the way he acts, the way he talks, the way he walks. And I ended up by hating him. He's got a name, he's got an identity! I'll tell you, nobody in the office even likes him.

His name is Dave Adler. That's right, he's a Jew! He's got everything I haven't got. That's why I watched him so hard.

He's the music and drama critic on the paper. I asked people all about him. He comes from a fancy family, and he's married to a rich Jewish girl. I mean, he's the kind of guy that goes to concerts in full dress and he knows all the fancy Jews in town— you know, the doctors and lawyers and welfare chairmen.

Well, Jesus Christ, he never knows anybody's alive! I'll bet he doesn't even know my name. He's got his desk pushed off behind a rail, and he comes in when he wants to, and every other month or such he goes to New York, and then his column's full of actors and big shots. I read it every day so I know.

Well, there's a Jew that's one hundred per cent different from my kind of Jew. Would he even look at me? He's got it all, name and dough and fancy wife and a house in the Heights. And nobody in the office likes him! He doesn't make friends with any of us. O.K., he's a Jew and he's got an identity, but maybe I'd rather be me. Without a name!

I tell you, everything's all mixed up. You don't know where to look, where to go. All you know is, for eighteen years you've been trying to do a good job. To be happy. To talk to people and get them to like you. For eighteen years you go home to sleep and sometimes to eat, but your real life begins at the office. And yet that isn't home either.

You make pals like Bill and Wally Lowell, he's my boss when I'm on the sports desk. You make love to a girl like Katherine Adams and it's swell because you're pals with her, too, but it doesn't mean anything but that, just pals. You expect to see Laura wherever you go, like she's left her perfume all over the office—everywhere, in the darkroom, in the morgue, in the elevator, so that even if you know she isn't there you keep expecting to bump into her all the time anyway. And finally the Old Man retires, and then you miss him all the time in a way, like you feel a little toothache that never really stops hurting for a minute. You have a drink with Katherine. "What's new? What do you hear from Laura?" She knows how you feel about Laura, but that night you go to bed with her and it's O.K., both of you know how you feel about Laura.

For eighteen years. Things happen. You meet people, you fall in love, you say good-by to a guy that's more than your own father, you take pictures and take 'em, and you're still jittery, you're still waiting for the roof to fall in. You're still waiting every day for somebody to say, "Hey, I hear you're a Yid. Hey, I hear you're really Jakey the Yid."

For eighteen years. . . .

"Tell me, do you remember when you started drinking?"

"Hell, how should I know? Everybody drinks, Doctor. Jeez, you wouldn't call a guy a drunkard just because he wants to be a good guy. Like everybody in the office. Why hell, in the newspaper game—"

"I'm not calling you a drunkard, remember that, John. Do you recall just when it was you started to drink to excess?"

"I don't remember, Doctor! I just can't remember. Eighteen years, Jesus, it's a long time."

"Try to remember. Try right now."

God, God, how could he remember a thing like that? Had it begun with Laura? With Adler's look (his recognition of that snobbery, his mounting hatred)? With some sort of half-cocked realization: the feeling that his pictures would not turn out right, not ever? With the constant reading, the constant growing of confusion, muddle, emptiness?

Yes, and sometimes the drinking was tied up with the look in Debby's eyes. That kind of clean blue, that kind of unwavering. With the mutter of that special kind of radio music she listened to at night. The house silent, and that sister of his sitting there with a book, the lamplight yellow on her short hair. And when he let himself in, sure with a couple of drinks in him! those eyes of hers looked up. It was like touching cold, clean, blue water.

How the hell did he know when he'd started drinking? It felt like he'd always done it. It felt like he'd always tried to figure Debby out and to forget Laura. Always. Always been ashamed, kind of, to look in his mother's eyes. Always felt like a fist in his stomach when he came near that dirty bastard of an old man of his. Always is a hell of a long time! Maybe he'd always been a drunkard, huh?

"Look here, John, I want you to stop glaring that way, acting as though I'm your deadly enemy. I'm not, you know."

"Maybe I need a drink!"

"Relax now. Have a cigarette. . . . That's right. That's more like it. Lean back. Close your eyes for a moment. That's better, isn't it?"

"Yeah, yeah, that's better. . . . Sorry, Doctor. That stuff gets me. That digging into myself. With a shovel! But I feel better now. Honest, I do."

"Feel like doing some more talking?"

"Yeah, I think so. Yeah, sure. What should I talk about?"

"What bothers you most at this moment?"

"What—bothers me—most."

"What do you want talked out of you?"

What did he want talked out of him? Oh Christ, for God's sake, what did he want out of him! The stone, the slow poison, the pendulum weight of the earth, never still for a second, and on the upstroke screaming Laura, and on the down beat shouting filth and confusion and dark, dark, dark.

"I don't know where to start," Jake said painfully. "What to say. There's so much to say, and yet there's nothing to say."

"Start anywhere. Talk about what you remember."

"I met her ten years ago. She was the most beautiful woman I'd ever seen in my life. She's fifteen years older than I am. Can you feature that? But that isn't even important. It never was important."

Jake stopped abruptly, stared across the desk. "It's queer as hell to talk about it," he mumbled, his face gray. "I wasn't in love with her at first. She was kind of like a sister to me, or a— well, lots like a mother. She phoned the photographer's room once and asked for one of us to come to her office and take a shot of somebody. A society fashion plate or something. Well, I went. I did a couple of other jobs for her, and by that time we were talking a lot. At least I was. She was easy to talk to, and I felt pretty good that she'd spend all that time listening to me. You see, she was the fashion editor for our paper, and everybody knew she was about the smartest person on the paper. I mean, hell, the New York papers and magazines would use a lot of her stuff, see?

"And I felt sorry for her. I wanted to do things for her because of all the tough breaks she'd had. Everybody thought she was marvelous and was sorry for her because of Dick, her husband. . ."

. . . who finally died. Laura had divorced him, then married him again when he'd gone down on his knees and sworn he'd never take another drink. Then she'd left him again when he went on another binge. He'd had the reputation of being one of the most brilliant newspapermen in town. His paper finally dropped him because of continued drinking on the job, and he just up and died one day.

Everybody told Jake all about it. Dick and Laura had been nuts about each other. He was good-looking, brilliant, and she was beautiful and just as brilliant. They were made for each other, and yet that guy couldn't stop drinking.

To Jake she was a wise, lovely woman with a girl's face beneath the dark hair, which was long and pulled back softly and coiled in a loose, round knot at the back of her head.

To Jake she was a lovely, gracious lady who listened to him for hours, and gave him cups of coffee. Then they began to go out on Sundays. He'd pick her up, and the dogs, and they'd drive out to the country. He'd take pictures of her in dozens of different poses, in dozens of different settings. They swam sometimes, then came in and had dinner in her studio apartment. They talked. They drank sometimes, and she'd light candles in the studio and they'd sit in front of the fireplace and stare at the burning logs. They'd play records; she had all the best of the old ones, and the new ones, too. She never talked about Dick, never.

What had happened? Exactly nothing. The first time he kissed her, she had laughed and patted his check. It was a funny, sad, little laugh, and he'd demanded, "What's the matter, why are you laughing?"

"Oh, Jack darling, you're sweet," she'd said.

He'd kissed her again, hard, but it had been like kissing something that wasn't there.

Well, after that he knew he was in love. He knew he'd go through hell for her, and everybody on the paper knew it. She knew it, too, and didn't seem to mind.

Well, what was there to say, after all? He'd loved her for ten years, and still there wasn't too much to talk about. She was fond of him, sure. She always told him that. She let him come up to the studio whenever he wanted to, which was practically every other night.

She let him kiss her whenever he wanted to. Really, she was wonderful to him. For example, his stomach always got upset for any reason whatsoever. He'd feel nauseated when he got to feeling sore about something, or those times when he loved her so hard and wanted her to marry him. Well, she was always very sweet. Fixed him stuff to drink that would stop the nausea.

Whenever he told her he loved her, she would laugh and pat his cheek. Or kiss him, very lightly. "You're a wonderful boy," she would say, and then she'd mix drinks for them.

What was there to talk about? He was just nuts about her. He'd never love anybody else, he never could. He'd just go on thinking about her.

A funny thing. Whenever he thought about her, he'd think about how beautiful she was, how smart, how wonderful, what a really brilliant woman she was. He'd never think about bed. He'd want to kiss her, yes, and be close to her. Jesus, when he didn't see her one evening it was like being lost. But he never thought about that.

He wanted to protect her, kind of. That business with Dick had been more than enough for one woman, damn it! He wanted to see to it that she never had to cry again, never had to stay awake nights worrying about anybody. He just wanted to fight the whole damn world for her. He'd kill anybody who tried to hurt her.

Funny. Funny as all hell. For about ten years. And in a funny way she loved him, too. They'd eat together a lot. He slept there often, out on the studio couch, with the two dogs on the floor close by. She gave him books for presents, and he gave her records most of the time. They saw each other every day at the office, and almost every evening. But he never understood her. He talked and talked, and she'd give him advice, she'd listen. But she hardly ever talked. It was like she just wanted to listen, like she got enough out of just the listening.

She finally left town. He remembered that, all right! Three years ago, but it might as well be today, for the way he still felt. She left to take a job in Washington, fashion editor for a plenty big-shot chain of newspapers. Why shouldn't she leave town? The *Register* was only one sheet, and here they wanted her to cover fashions for a lot of them. Who wouldn't have left?

Well, what happened, about a year after she hit Washington, she married this millionaire. A guy about sixty. Kathy told me about him. Kathy and Laura write to each other. Every time Kathy goes to Washington she sees Laura, stays in that fancy million-dollar house. Sure, she writes to me sometimes, too. Sends me Christmas and birthday presents.

Kat says she isn't happy. She's doing some free-lance writing. And she does Red Cross work a lot since the war started. She isn't especially unhappy, though, Kat says. "What's the matter?" Kat says to me whenever I ask her, "still Laura Anderson's lap dog?"

That's what some of the office people used to call me. Laura Anderson's lap dog. I knew about it, and I didn't care either. Sometimes I even felt like that, like her lap dog. I wanted to be near her all the time. When I felt rotten and I got near her and she put her hand on my head or my arm, everything was better right away. Like a kid runs to his mother, sort of. And she says a couple of words, and then everything is all right again.

Jesus, I remember the day she left. I thought I was going to die. I thought I'd never get over feeling lost, and kind of scared, and—well, absolutely alone! As if the only piece of family I ever had was leaving me for good. See, Laura was kind of like my family by that time. I loved her for all kinds of reasons, I guess. It was like I didn't need anybody else when I was near her. No mother or family or girl friend, or anybody. See, the Old Man was retired by this time, and I didn't even have him around.

I knew she was going, all right. Hell, I'd even advised her to scram. A job like that. Washington, and a chance to hit twenty, thirty papers every time she writes a column.

So she was going. So I came in to say so long. I remember

how I felt. Like the whole world was shaking. Like I'd never have anybody to hang on to again, or come close to. She was always so warm, and she smiled a lot, and she always said the right couple of words. Yeah, like I'd never be warm again. . . .

. . . When the night edition came up to the city room, and Bobbie tossed him a copy from the bunch under his arm, Jake felt more jittery than usual. He knew it was because of Laura and tried to quiet himself, but the nausea rocked him hard. For a minute, or two, he watched Bobbie race through the big room, dropping copies of the paper on all the desks. The print looked fresh-black and still wet and he stood there watching Ernie spread his copy on the city desk and start studying the look of the front page.

Then he opened his own copy and began flipping the pages rapidly, looking for his art.

Both pictures were in, and the long shot of the pier and the boats looked pretty good. They'd given him a by-line on that one. Photo by John Brown, staff photographer.

Jake's breath pushed out and he tossed the paper onto one of the desks, walked quickly into the photographer's room. Ted Pope was sitting at the one desk in the room, his young freckled face close to the sheet of paper on which he was drawing squares and rectangles.

"Hey, kiddo," Jake said, his voice quick and overly gay, "what are you around here, a photographer or a cartoonist?"

Ted look up and grinned. He was a nice kid, the youngest photographer on the staff, and he had a kind of camera crush on Jake. He would talk eagerly about the detail in Jake's pictures, and the sensitivity of one shot and the shading in another.

"I'm doing a rough layout for my show," he said. "It opens Monday."

"Swell!" Jake said quickly. He felt a burning, sliding movement in his chest. "That makes your third one-man, huh, kid? Nice going."

"It's at the museum again," Ted said. "Like I told you last week, Jack. You coming down? I'm showing a lot of that stuff I took in Mexico; you haven't seen half of it. I want your opinion."

"Who, me?" Jake laughed very deliberately. "Go on! Get a

guy like Sutton to tear your show apart. He runs the art column here. Or I'll tell you what, phone the Old Man. He'll really give you hell."

One of Ted's idolizing looks came into his eyes. "Aw, come on, Jack. What do you say? Nobody around here knows more about photography, and you know it."

"Sure, sure! Don't worry, I'll be there with bells on. You'll wish you'd never seen a camera when I open up on you." It was the familiar mixture of jealousy and panic like a burn in his chest.

"Listen, kid," he said in the same airy way, "I'm going over to Laura's office. I haven't got an assignment until two but if Ernie gets a rush call tell him I'm in there."

He meant it, Jake thought as he walked quickly through the city room. He wants my opinion. Now, for Christ sake, what makes one guy go in for shows and keeps another guy from even trying?

Afraid they'd throw it out before it got up on the walls, he thought painfully.

Laura's office was clear across the huge room, off the curving hallway that led to the elevator. He stopped for a moment to read the neat print of the sign on her door: LAURA ANDERSON, FASHION EDITOR. Then he opened the door and went in.

Laura was talking on the telephone, and when she gestured that she would be through very soon he sat on the wide window ledge, first carefully pushing away the wooden head of Shakespeare she kept there.

Jake had loved her office from the first day, the day he had come in to take some art for her. Now that he knew Debby (he had not been aware of her on that first day), he knew Laura's office reminded him of his sister. It was a room for her, and yet the gloomy, dusty living room at home was a room for her, too; the music and the lamplight, the silence punctuated by a sleepy groan from his father's bedroom, or by the half-hour and hour bongs from his father's clock, were the right setting for Debby, too, just as this roomful of books and papers and sunlight seemed to be hers.

The room was dominated by the big desk, always covered with books and magazines and clippings. The wall behind Laura's chair was solid with book shelves, the sun very bright today on the brilliant colors of dusty jackets. An electric hot plate stood on the small, squat table between the windows and the desk, where she could easily flick the current on and off.

Jake's eyes moved slowly around the room and paused at the opposite wall, which was covered with framed photographs of Laura's two dachshunds. He had shot them in every conceivable pose, with and without Laura, singly and together. His eyes moved haltingly from picture to picture; each stood for an hour or a day or an evening with Laura.

Lighting a cigarette, he listened to Laura's voice. His lips twitched at the patient, cool inflection. Suddenly he remembered why she had so attracted him (a million years ago!). That cool, wise voice of hers.

"For heaven's sake, Hal," Laura said with some irritation into the phone, "what do you think I am, a maker of destinies? Tell that artist of yours I'm only a lousy fashion editor. I can't fix up his perspective, all I can do is call it bad!"

Jake watched her. She had tranquil blue eyes and a girl's skin, but the rare and wonderful thing about her was that wise, water-cool way she had. It made his chest hurt just to see it.

The telephone snapped down. She wrinkled her forehead at him. "Never be a fashion editor, Jack. Promise me."

"Hello, you maker of destinies," he told her glumly.

"Stay away from drawing, too. Do you want some coffee?"

"Not right now." He came over to the desk and sat on the edge of it while she poured herself a cup. He mashed out his cigarette in the bronze ashtray. "How are the mutts?"

Her eyes swung toward the wall. "Fine! Karl found a rat out in the yard this morning and Rudy was so jealous he wouldn't even say good-by to me."

Jake watched her drink. He had never mentioned the word Jew to her, never, not even casually. He swung one leg, began to twist the freshly sharpened pencils lying in the glass tray.

"Come on, come on," she said softly. "It's not the end of the world. I'll come visit. You'll fly up to Washington."

"Nuts," he said bitterly. "Who the hell wants to see you for a half hour at a throw? Or maybe never."

"Uh-uh," she said softly but warningly. "I'm going, you know. It's all set, Jack, remember? Let's not start any of that pro and con stuff, please."

He flushed, slid off the desk and walked over to examine one of the photographs.

After a moment, his back still turned, he said roughly, "Do you know Ted Pope's show opens Monday night? Flying back for it?"

"Aren't you getting a little tired of sitting in Ted's shadow?" Her voice sounded cold.

He whirled, wanting to hate her. "That isn't fair, Laura! You know damn well my stuff isn't good enough for a one-man show."

He stared at her dark, rich-looking hair, felt walls trembling inside him.

"What's the matter with you?" she said, her eyes puzzled. "What the hell are you afraid of, Jack?"

His hands were shaking, and he lit a cigarette quickly, fussing with the match and then with the ashtray. He had never had the guts to talk about it; and yet, the knowledge that not even she knew somehow had used to fortify him. Now that she was going, still unaware of what lay in his blood and in his family, he felt weak and dizzy. Tomorrow he would not have her warmth to come close to, nor her laughing casual ways, nor the well of her into which to talk, the dark, warm, sympathetic well which held him and all his words so completely, so effortlessly, so naturally.

"You said it once or twice," he said, his voice hard with misery. "You called it a feeling of insecurity, didn't you? Are you looking for another reason?"

"Oh, for pete's sake, Jack! You're like a kid sometimes!"

He wanted to hurt her, to leave some kind of a mark on that chiseled, fresh face. "A guy who waits for the paper every day to see whether they've thrown out his stuff."

But he was hurting only himself, he thought as he felt his cheeks stiffen.

"Don't be so proud of it," she said. "Don't hang on to it so hard. Get yourself some other excuse."

"What the hell are you talking about?" he demanded mechanically. It was a moment when her warmth seemed to have disappeared. Her mouth looked petulant, not sympathetic, and the eyes were just cold. The dark and warm listening quality seemed gone.

"Listen," he told her, still mechanically, calling up the old and familiar words with which he had sheathed himself for so long, "feature me on a Washington paper, will you? No, take a squint at me in the army. Waiting for my prints to come back from the second looey with a—a demerit, or whatever they pin on you in the army."

It was the first time he had consciously thought the word army, and for a minute he went on to think with the most intense longing of the anonymous kind of life he could live in the army. Everybody the same, no one squinting at you to see if you had a different way of eating or talking. No one examining your face or your name to find something different. Everybody the same, the same uniform, the same food and orders, the same reason for being there; you and the thousands of other guys in the army.

Laura had pushed her chair back and walked to the window. As she stood there, looking out, he watched her back.

Sure, he thought miserably, take that to Washington with you. How my stomach turns to wet sand when I have to stack up against other guys. Even Ted. For example, what's a kid like Ted got to be ashamed about?

He talked to her back. "You can't monkey with a guy's perspective and make him an artist, can you, Laura?"

She turned around very quickly. Her eyes stunned him, they were so full of pity. It seemed to him he had never seen them so patient, so unloverlike, so wisely sympathetic.

"Poor little boy," she said, her voice like a pat on his head. "Darling, haven't you anything to feel proud about?"

"Nothing," he cried, blindly furious at those wise, old eyes. "Not a damn thing." He slammed out of her office.

He had his first drink on the way to his two o'clock job, a regular assignment. It consisted of getting art of the straggling groups of drafted men, groups which recently had become a novel sight on downtown streets. Usually he got his art in the railroad terminal, one semilong shot of that day's quota and a close-up or two of the rare enlisted father. He always asked the father to hold the child in his arms, and there was always a small crowd of men and women to watch him take the picture; behind him, as he got his flash bulbs ready, he could hear the murmured words of sympathy about the child and its father.

He always wished he could get that half-audible sound of gentle sorrow into the picture. (Detail, detail, kid! he could remember at such times. You got to feel the thing!) He knew that the brooding sound of the crowd was part of the feel of the pictures he was taking, but he knew that even the Old Man could not get that detail in the shots.

At the station today, he did his usual careful, quick posing and shooting, then jotted down names and addresses to go with the close-ups, talking all the time in the fast, bright voice he had trained into himself that first year after the Old Man had got him transferred from the city room.

As he worked, his eyes wandered, picked out face after face in the crowd for possible pictures of his own.

"O.K., thanks," he shouted brightly above the confusion and talk.

As the small crowd broke up, he walked away, his camera clutched against his chest, the zippered case full of extra bulbs and films slung by the leather straps over one shoulder and bumping his hips as he walked. He threaded his way around the loosely drawn, curved edge of the crowd. On this slow, step-by-step way out of the station, he stopped now and again to take some of what he called "his own" pictures.

These were the shots which reached out at him invariably wherever he went. It was as if his eyes were always peering for possible pictures of this kind. They always made themselves for him, as if clicked out by a small, fast-moving signal in his mind. They pushed out at him from a crowd of people, or from a back yard, or from among small, leaning houses in a narrow street. These pictures all had an odd similarity about them, as if the same kind of blood ran through them and provided a tenuous, delicate tie. Each picture was marked somehow, as if a name had been branded into it, with a kind of hunger, a gaunt and unappeased quality which came up from underneath faces, or from the stoop of bodies, or from the way the picture had caught the death of a house.

Jake had been taking such pictures for a long time. He had never shown them to anyone, but kept a file of prints in the bottom drawer of the big, old-fashioned desk in the office morgue. He had typed out a slip of paper—BROWN, PRIVATE—

and pasted it on the drawer. The negatives he kept filed, by date, in his darkroom cabinet.

Now, in the terminal, he stopped twice; once to snap an old, shawled woman in black, whose look of anguish was carved into an earthen, peasant face, and the second time, to catch the stern mouths and the gripped hands of two men who were shaking hands harshly and almost automatically. And NOW IT WILL BE GOOD-BY; a caption for the pictures clicked in Jake's mind.

All the while he was thinking of Laura.

On the way back to the office, he stopped his car in front of the Negro housing project on Hillside Avenue. Five children were playing a silent, secret, close-grouped game on the new grass of the project grounds, and he came out of the car very quickly, his steps almost as secret as theirs. It took him a few minutes, and he concentrated hard on the look in their eyes, the marvelous, carved lines of their small bodies where the heads and throats were molded into them.

I could call it ONCE SLUMS, he thought when he was back in the car and driving again; and all the while he was thinking of Laura. She had called it insecurity. But Jesus Christ! Ted Pope was secure, eh? Well, what the hell did Ted Pope have pulling at his brain, pulling him away from the pure and simple business of just getting a picture?

With a sick feeling, Jake remembered Ted's mother coming up to the office about a week ago. They were lunching together, Ted had told him; it was his mother's birthday. She was a tall, well-dressed woman who had smiled at everyone, who had said in a soft voice (in perfect English, of course!), "Oh, how do you do, Mr. Brown. Ted's said so many nice things about you."

Jake's lips pinched together. Once he had said, oh, very casually, "Ma, when's your birthday?"

"In the winter," she'd said.

"What do you mean?" he'd asked, startled. "What month, what day?"

In her mind it had been so simple, but to him it was tragic, more of the wretched difference that hung over their whole family.

"How do I know when my birthday comes?" she'd said.

"My mother always told me it was cold when I was born. A blizzard. The whole town was covered with snow."

She had smiled then. "Jake, in Russia they don't have birth papers. You're born, so you're born. It's enough that you know what time of the year it was when you came."

He yanked at the steering wheel. Imagine Ma coming down to the office. Imagine her saying, "How do you do." (What would she say? "Glad to meet you." This is my mother, Mrs. Brown. Well, as a matter of fact, my brother changed our name a long time ago. Yeah, he was smart enough to do that.)

"Jake is my youngest boy," Ma might say, once she got over her shyness. "He's still single, can you imagine? He's supporting us. Him and Debby. My husband is old, sick. My other son? Well, his job is no good. But once! I'll tell you, once the other one brought in plenty to the house! Jake was only a baby in those days. What does a baby know from money?"

And then he would lead her past Ernie and Wally at the desk, past that bastard Dave Adler in his special little corner (look, Adler, we're Jews, too!), past Kathy's desk, past the editorial offices, out into the hallway. He'd knock on the door, his knuckles landing on the wood underneath that sign. The door would swing open. Ah there, Miss Anderson, this is my mother. Ma, I want you to meet the woman I love.

"A gentile?" He could hear her shy, soft voice. Maybe she would giggle, if she felt very nervous. "Jake, she's a gentile?"

He pressed down savagely on the gas pedal, tried to lock his mind.

Between his last two assignments, he developed his own three pictures. They were good. Expressions were sharp; almost, he had achieved the etched look of some of the Old Man's art. The picture of the Negro children was particularly good. He had caught them in a look brave and new, and yet retaining a shabby gauntness. No, he thought, I'd better call it STILL SLUMS.

Studying the pictures, he felt depressed. His own pictures never worried him; it was only the art he took for the desk that made him sweat. Was that because no one saw his own shots, no one had the chance to criticize?

The curtains to the darkroom came apart as Ted stuck his head in. Jake quickly turned over the picture he was holding, but Ted disappeared as soon as he said, "Hey Jack, you in there? Laura's been looking for you. Twice."

The depressed feeling thickened. He'd see her at the train, he in the midst of the whole gang. And to hell with anything else.

At six-thirty, he was still sitting in the morgue, halfway through the stocks edition. He was waiting for the Adams Steel strike to break, so that he could get some gate art and maybe a couple of shots at the temporary union headquarters they had set up in a store opposite the factory. Ernie wanted the art for tomorrow's night edition.

The phone rang. It was Dotty, the night switchboard girl. They all knew he'd be in the morgue when he was not anywhere else in the office. He had adopted the room long ago. He had liked it first because it was quiet and shabby and dark, and the corner with the desk was isolated most of the time; the files and clipping tables were at the opposite end of the long, crooked room, and people congregated at that end, almost hidden behind the tall files.

After he had taken over the bottom drawer in the cluttered desk, he liked sitting around the morgue because he could be near his pictures that way. Often, when no one was around, he would spread some of the pictures on the floor and study them for mistakes, or look through the pile of them for one shot in particular, a shot he had been thinking about for several days, for no reason at all.

"Yeah?" he said into the phone. "Brown talking."

Ernie's voice came on. "Jack? You can beat it. The strike won't break until seven tomorrow morning. You'd think those damn prima donnas were planning a picnic! Get me some art in the morning."

Jake finished the paper, then went to the darkroom. He loaded his camera and filled his case with plenty of films and bulbs. On his way out, he grabbed a final from the switchboard desk.

After he had locked the stuff into his car, he went over to the Brass Rail. It was too early for anybody to be there, and he sat on one of the high stools at the bar and talked to Jim about the doubleheader game.

He had four drinks, but a small niche inside of him stayed

clear and cold with Laura's name in the middle of it. He thought maybe he'd go on drinking. Laura's train didn't leave until eleven-forty that night. . . .

"You don't talk much about Katherine. She seems to have been an integral part of your life. How is it you do not say more about her?"

"What's there to say? Kat's a swell kid. We call her Kat a lot, or Kathy. She's fun to be with. Sure, fun to sleep with! Or drink with. She runs the society column. I go out on assignments with her once in a while. I'll tell you what, I always feel funny about Kat the next day. I mean, if I've been with her the night before. Depressed, kind of."

"Depressed. Tell me, has it ever occurred to you that you'd like to wait until you fall in love with a woman before you have intercourse with her?"

"Jesus Christ, Doctor, I'm in love with Laura!"

"Are you?"

"Well, but look! You mean it's wrong to go to bed with Kat if I'm not in love with her?"

"Wrong. We've discussed that word before. It's rarely wrong to do a thing you really want to do. Something you know is right for you, no matter what might be said about it. That depressed feeling you describe, why do you think you have it?"

"I don't know. I never tried to figure it out, Doctor."

"Well, suppose you do try. The next day, as you put it, do you seek out Katherine? Do you want to see her, say at the office?"

"No. In fact, I try and stay away from her."

"Let's carry it further. What other things make you feel depressed?"

"Other things? My house. My mother, I guess. The kids— Sarah's kids, I mean. Sometimes my brother Sig, or when I think of Roz. Sure, and that bastard Adler, at the office. The way he looks like he thinks he's God."

"Did Laura ever make you feel depressed?"

"Laura? Course not! . . . Well, I'll tell you. After a while it got so I couldn't even kiss her. She made me feel like a—a kid. Now look, don't get me wrong! She was wonderful to me, just

108

wonderful. Take one thing. The way she'd call me dear, or darling. My God, nobody in my house ever says a word like that!"

"What do you mean, you couldn't even kiss her?"

"How the hell can a kid kiss a woman! I told you she made
me feel like a kid sometimes! Oh sure, sometimes I wanted to
feel that way with her!"

"But you were able to kiss Katherine? She didn't make you
feel like an adolescent? Like a son?"

"What the hell do you mean! . . . Jesus Christ! . . . Why
should you say such things to me? . . . It's probably true,
though. Sure! I can see in your eyes it's probably true!"

"And if it is true, there's nothing to get excited about, you
know. That's what we're here for, to get at the truth. Remember?"

"Sure, sure, I remember!"

"Do you remember, too, that here in this office nothing is
too shameful to discuss? That nothing is too terrible to name,
to describe in actual words? Do you?"

"Yes. Yes, I remember, Doctor."

The panicky sensation had begun to seep away, and Jake
felt more relaxed than at any time since he had begun to talk
about Laura. The bitter, secretive sound of her name had come
out into the air of this room. The air was full of those moments
he had never understood, those gestures between them which
he had loved and wanted and hated and despised, and now
they were beginning to be put into words.

"She never even knew about my own pictures," he mumbled, and suddenly he was glad he had never shown them to
her. But there was an ache about it, too. How close she would
have been then. If he had shared his pictures with her. No one
would ever have been closer then, for the rest of his life.

"What are you thinking now?" the doctor asked.

"I feel sick in—in my heart." He nodded hesitantly. "All I
know is, I'm so Goddam unhappy I can't do my job right.
Every time I take a picture! Well, I'm just scared they won't like
it, that's all. Every Goddam time I take one."

Then he mumbled an amendment. "Except my own
pictures."

"Tell me, what do you mean when you say 'my own pictures'? You use that phrase all the time. Those are the pictures

109

you take for your own collection, for your own benefit; is that it? When I say 'your own benefit,' I mean that such pictures give you pleasure. Is that right?"

Jake nodded. "But there's more to it," he said slowly. "It's not easy to tell you because I don't know a hell of a lot about those pictures. I take them for my own collection, yeah, and I get a hell of a lot out of just taking them, sure."

"Yes?"

"Well see, I'm never nervous about my own pictures. It's like—like drinking a glass of water to take them. Simple! Like you're born doing it, kind of."

"Yes, I see."

Jake hitched forward eagerly, took a cigarette and lit it. "It's funny as hell," he said excitedly. "I mean, those pictures. I think about them a lot, you see. I make plans sometimes, kind of."

"What kind of plans?"

"Well, funny plans. I mean, well, I'd like to take pictures of my mother and the old man. Can you feature that? Me hating that guy the way I do, and the way I feel peculiar about my mother."

His rough mouth shook slightly with his eagerness to explain. "Think of the swell pictures I could take of them! In the kitchen there, the way they always sit at the table. They're reading the *Jewish World*, see, and I get their faces and part of the paper, the Jewish print showing. I get the *feel* of their faces."

For a moment he watched the doctor write, his eyes very alive as they followed the movements of the pen. He looked up then, into the doctor's quiet, interpreting eyes.

"I've even got captions for pictures like that. In my head," he said. "That kitchen picture I could call, AMERICANS, EVENING. How does that sound to you? They're Americans, after all. And then that Jewish newspaper. Jews, sure, but here they are in their kitchen in America."

"I like that very much," the doctor said. "It's a very fine idea and a fine caption, too."

Jake lunged on. "There's one picture I really want to get. Friday night. It isn't dark yet, but the room is full of that shadow stuff. My mother stands in front of the candles she's just lit. Her hands are over her eyes, her lips are moving. That's one I'll call, IN AMERICA THEY PRAY. How do you like that one?"

The doctor studied him for a moment. "Why don't you take that picture?" he asked. "And the other one, the 'Americans, Evening' picture. What are you waiting for?"

The brightness went out of Jake's eyes, but he had to go on looking at the doctor. The miserable, familiar feeling of confusion began licking at his chest, like a candle burning inside and the flame flickering tall and short, licking there like a hot, sharp tongue.

"How can I take pictures if I'm ashamed?" he mumbled at last. "My own pictures are—. I can't, that's all! I have to take pictures of—of people I—I want to be near. I mean, my own pictures are for me!"

"You mean that your own pictures are reserved for people and things you want to study? To keep in this collection of yours? You take these pictures out of joy, out of a desire to be close to living things. You mean that you can't bear to waste any of the joy, the craftsmanship, on your family, on people of whom you are ashamed?"

Jake shook his head. "No, that isn't it exactly. That's a little of it, yeah. But see, anything I use for one of my own shots—well, I'm not ashamed of it. I don't ever feel like hiding any of my own pictures! They're good. They're—well, they're kind of like proof that I can do one thing as good as a lot of other people can. I hate to tie that one thing up with my family. It belongs to me, nobody else knows about it, nobody can put a—a dirty hand on it."

He was breathing rather rapidly now. "Nobody can call them Jewish pictures! They're mine. Nobody knows anything about them. I don't even want my father to be in them. Or my mother either!"

"And yet," the doctor said immediately, "your parents are in your plans for future pictures?"

Jake's eyes flickered. "Yeah. Well, I told you that was the one funny thing about my own pictures. One night I almost took pictures of them, too. In the kitchen. Boy, was that a funny feeling!"

"When was that?" the doctor asked quickly.

"The night Laura went to Washington," he said, staring at the doctor. "The same night I was telling you about a while back. I was a little drunk, I guess. I wanted to take the pictures, but I didn't. I was on my bed and they were in the kitchen, and all of a sudden it was like I was dreaming that I took my camera and walked into the kitchen."

He watched the doctor's pen move.

"I didn't take 'em. I just wanted to."

"Yes, I understand. Have you wanted to take any such pictures since that evening?"

"I don't know. I guess so. I've wanted to take pictures of Debby, but I just haven't. I haven't got any captions in my head for hers, though."

"That would be difficult," the doctor agreed, smiling. "You don't understand your sister enough for captions."

"Well, do I understand the old man?" Jake demanded. "Or my mother? But I did captions for them."

"Perhaps you do understand them," the doctor said. "We'll see."

"It's like something won't let me take pictures of them," Jake tried again to explain. "Like I said. Sometimes, lately, I've wanted to do it. I've wanted it—bad. But I just couldn't."

"We'll see what can be done about that. Will you tell me about the evening when you almost took those pictures? I'd like to hear about everything that occurred that evening. I'd like as detailed a description as possible. Do you feel like talking about it?"

Jake shrugged. "Sure, why not? I remember everything. I remember that night because she was leaving town. Everything that happened. I've thought about that night a hell of a lot, it was such a funny night. I sat in the Brass Rail, talking to Jim and drinking. After a while, more people started to come in and Jim was busy. I ordered another drink and finished that one. . ."

. . . then he sat there for a while until the heaviness in his chest began to ease. It was easier, then, to pick up his folded final from the bar and stick it into his jacket pocket, leave the haven of the Brass Rail. Behind the wheel of his car, he sat and stared out through the windshield. Get some dinner somewhere? Go to a movie? He was, suddenly, too tired to figure anything out.

I'll go home, he thought, and at once a crooked, little comforting ache began in him. As he started the car and turned it toward the East Side, a childishly tearful feeling soothed him.

Yes, he would go home. They would be in the kitchen, at the table. (Would that strange, blond girl be in the other room, a book in her hands, her eyes too blue, too much to face, as they lifted in the lamplight to watch him?) The two would be sitting in the kitchen, like two little, old, puckered gargoyles holding up (with their elbows, their gnarled hands knuckled into their cheeks, their eyes on the Yiddish print) the ends of the porcelain-topped table.

And, thinking of it, the way they had always been at home only in the kitchen, so that the rest of the house was uneasy to them, he felt comforted at going home now to that kitchen.

He knew there was no reason to go home, but the feeling of comfort lingered. There was reason (but God knows what it was!) only to go home on Fridays, to eat the holiday meal. What was Friday night to him anyway, he wondered as he drove through the dark streets of the East Side. A habit maybe, one of the few things he still had out of childhood, out of the past, though Roz and Sig and Debby never ate at the same time, though he himself deliberately came either early or late that night, so that he could eat alone, his mother waiting on him silently (would she speak if he spoke?), while the old man read the paper opposite him at the table. What was Friday night to him that he had to come home to it? Maybe you know, Laura, he thought harshly, twisting the wheel at the last intersection and coasting into his street.

He stopped the car abruptly on a wistful impulse, and jumped out, crossed the street and entered the delicatessen store on the corner. He ordered two corned beef sandwiches and a dill pickle to take out. The store smelled of fresh rye bread and pickled meats, and at the round tables people were eating and laughing, talking Yiddish. There was a homelike feeling for him in the store, and he lingered as he counted out the money and pushed it across the glass top of the counter. He felt no kinship with the people but rather with the sharp and

113

pungent odors, the laughter, with the familiar language which filled the small store and seemed to enrich the air.

Back in the car, driving down the long street, the tiredness was still with him. He could smell the wrapped sandwiches and pickle next to him on the seat, and he thought vaguely that they would taste good.

Driving slowly, he remembered how his mother used to have corned beef sandwiches sometimes, but more often salami and eggs, every Saturday night for supper. All the years of growing up, Saturday night was delicatessen night; salami or hot dogs, yes most of the time corned beef was too expensive for anybody but Sig. Sometimes she would fry a batch of potato pancakes, too. Jew food. A long procession of gentile food, the meals he had eaten in downtown restaurants, clicked across his mind: ham and eggs, steak and salad and French fries, roast beef and apple pie. (She had never baked a pie that he could remember. Maybe she didn't know how. Didn't all mothers know how to bake pies?)

As Jake parked the car at the curb in front of the house, he thought wryly: Wonder if Laura ever tasted potato pancakes?

He was a little drunk, to the point of feeling depressed, his tiredness accentuated, and as he walked up the driveway he thought that he'd better drink a lot more before train time, to match the gaiety that would be floating around Laura and Kathy and the others at the station.

He walked in by way of the back door. There they were, just as he had seen them in his mind, his mother at the end of the table next to the sink and his father opposite her, near the cupboard. Each was reading a section of the *Jewish World*. And that was another hazy fillip out of childhood, looking at the pictures in this paper and thinking how queer the print looked. Sure, they had read this paper even when he was a child.

The rest of the house was dark. No Sig, no Debby; he felt an immediate relief that she was not in the living room, or his brother in the bedroom.

The kitchen was bare-looking in the glaring light of the unshaded bulb stuck in the middle of the ceiling. Maybe it was the faded wallpaper of pink flowers, the gaudy colors of the woman on the calendar, the linoleum with its worn patches near the sink and near the stove; the room seemed stark and lonely, the two people at the table tiny, hunched.

Jake did not greet them. When his mother looked up, a small shy expression like a smile came into her eyes, and her lips seemed to want to move, as if she were simply waiting for a word from him. He could not say it. Her eyes were like faded blue denim, it occurred to him. Was she afraid of him? Why didn't she ever speak first? Then maybe he could answer her.

The old man went right on reading, as if no one had come into the room.

It's all right, he thought, no harm done, none of us is insulting the other. It's just the way we are.

He remembered fleetingly, as he dropped the package of sandwiches on the table and went to put his camera and case in the bedroom, how often he and Sig would meet downtown and nod, not even stop for a word.

When he came back into the kitchen he saw that his mother had moved to the chair near the sink, and was sitting there, the section of newspaper folded across her knees. She seemed to be sitting awkwardly, poised, as if waiting for him, and he hurried past her to the table, where he unwrapped the sandwiches. He flattened out the folded oiled paper and laid the sandwiches and pickle on it as if it were a plate. As he sat down, Jake wondered if she could smell his breath.

"I'll make you a glass of tea," his mother said in her usual Yiddish, and went to light the burner under the kettle. She had dropped the paper on the sinkboard and now came to hover near the table. In her shy, fumbling way she took a fork and a spoon from the table drawer and put them near the sandwiches. She brought the sugar bowl from the cupboard. Then she went back to the stove, stood leaning against the oven door to wait for the water to boil.

The moment she had moved and he knew she would come near him, Jake lit a cigarette and surrounded himself with smoke. His face felt hot. She knew he drank, but he couldn't stand the idea of her smelling the whisky; he had the trembling, stomach-sinking fear, always, that some day her eyes would look into his and reflect a word like drunkard.

Puffing rapidly, Jake stared for a moment at his father's gray hair and the way he was absorbed by the article he was reading, his face stony and yet that little, sneering look seemed painted on the high cheekbones, the look that seemed to really center around the mustache and lower lip.

He propped his final against the sugar bowl, his eyes focused now on the jumble of words in the headlines. The usual helplessness about his mother came into his throat and he did not quite know what to do. That deep, anguished feeling he had for her seemed now to back up in him, and he wished to Christ he had not come home.

He rubbed out the cigarette in the ashtray the old man kept on the window sill. Then, from the corner of his eye, he saw the cup of tea being pushed close to the sandwiches. Without looking at her, he knew how she looked, shy, half afraid to talk to him, that little expression like a smile making her old, shapeless mouth tender for a moment.

"Thanks, Ma," he mumbled and spooned sugar into the cup.

As if his few words gave her courage, she said hurriedly, "Jake, you had to buy sandwiches? Why didn't you call up you wanted supper? I would have made you a real supper. Fish, vegetables, cutlets, anything you wanted. Why should you bring supper from a store?"

"Aw Ma," he said, embarrassment making his voice rough, "you know I like stuff like this. I like it better than cutlets and potatoes." He talked in the mixture of English and Yiddish which he and the others had always used at home.

"Well, all right," she said with a kind of patience and humbleness which hurt him.

She went back to her chair and began again to read, the folded paper held close to her face so that she could see. Her lips moved, making a small, sibilant sound; reading was difficult for her, and she had got into the habit of half whispering words so that she could grasp them more easily.

When his mother was reading, Jake could hear this sound no matter where he was in the house. The groping, struggling whisper seemed to accentuate his feeling of helplessness now, as always. Listening to it, he ate very quickly, sipping at the hot, sweet tea between bites. The food seemed tasteless, and he thought dully that he must have remembered wrong, that the memory of those wonderful Saturday night suppers must be just part of the kid sensations he clung to so hard somewhere at the back of his dumb head.

The thought of Laura came to mingle with the sound of his mother's reading, and he swallowed the last of his tea hurriedly, picked up the paper which was still folded so that the same headlines showed.

Pushing back his chair with what he wanted to be a casual air, he walked past her, past that poor, struggling sound. In his room, he closed the door three-quarters way and pulled down the shades before he snapped on the ceiling light. There was no bed light in the room, and it had never occurred to him to buy one though he loved to read in bed when Sig was not there. He would read by the glaring ceiling light, then jump out of bed to snap off the wall switch, cursing at having to do it. Several times he had fallen asleep with the light on, and Sig had turned it off after he had come home.

Jake took the bottle of bourbon down from the closet shelf and sat on his bed to have a drink.

The warmth of the whisky dripped through the heavy feeling of helplessness, and then the thrashing started again in his mind. It seemed to him at this moment that he no longer knew even the small fragments of what made up his torment, that year by year a chaotic sort of confusion had grown in him until now he did not have the strength to peer over the high fence of it to see what sharp, pronged source lay below in the fenced-off area.

He tipped up the bottle again, then sat very still with the glass of it warm and smooth between his hands. Sometimes it felt like he was existing in a small, dark, ghetto-like place, and like someone had closed the gate of the thick wall which rose between this segregated place and the rest of the world. In his confusion and fear, it was as if he could not see even the outline of the gate in that high wall.

Maybe I closed the gate myself, Jake thought suddenly as he went to put the bottle back on the shelf.

After a while, as he lay on the bed, on his back, his hands flattened under his head, he became aware of his father's voice in the kitchen. It made a steady monotone in the bedroom, his father reading a newspaper article aloud. He could distinguish the small, melancholy sounds his mother uttered from time to time, a kind of punctuation to the words.

Jake strained to hear. For some reason, the lonely room seemed warmed by the drifting kitchen voices. He thought he had stopped listening a long time ago for the sound of either of them, but tonight the mutter, hitherto a part of dingy wall and dank room, of depressing undercurrent of house, became father, became gentle and meaningful mother. In the room, he felt a warmth as of flesh and blood.

He lay there, son of them, their quiet parental hands on his brow, on his shoulder.

The Yiddish of his father's words made a nostalgic twang in his chest. The article concerned a city in Poland. It told, with mournful drama, how the Jews in that city had fought to their inevitable death, attempting to hold the walls of their ghetto as other peoples in the world attempted to hold palaces. These ghettos were home to them.

"There stood the Jews," came drifting into his room, and Jake's head dug back into the palms of his hands. "Yes, behind them and on all sides of them stood their wives and children. All shared the blood, the agony, and finally the piercing death. The words, 'God, God!' were on all dying lips. Yes, in the world Jews were once again dying, and for the old, old reason—that they were Jews."

Jake heard the soft, sad breath of his mother's sighs. "To be a Jew today," she said.

"Today, yesterday, tomorrow," his father said impatiently. "What do they want of us!"

Jake's neck felt rigid as he strained to hear that soft, mournful kitchen dialogue.

"All right, all right, I'm glad," his mother said. "I want to be a Jew. I'm glad. I'll go, a Jew, to my grave. But let my children live! Let their children!"

"They'll live, they'll live. Do you see one ghetto in America? A woman talks, as if to fools!"

And then, very suddenly, he wanted to get some pictures of them. He wanted to get the feeling of them, as if the Old Man were standing there near the bed, his fierce eyes bright, his stained finger pointing out the sunken throat of his mother and the way her faded-denim eyes peered up, and the high-cheekboned face of his father, the mustache and gray hair, the calendar on the wall near them, with the flashy girl on it, the line of his mother's back, humped a little with age and work, and the big gnarled hand of his father holding the glass of tea as he read the paper, the way the picture would get that hand with its broken, dark nails and the dirt and weather ground into the skin. AMERICA, AMERICA! (What the hell kind of a caption is that! the Old Man would yell. Feel it, dope, feel it! I'm feeling it! he'd yell back. They came here, they're talking about here, they want to die here. I said it and I mean it, the caption is going to be AMERICA, AMERICA!)

A curiously soaring emotion rushed up in him. He wanted to take their pictures. He wanted to feel them in the camera, the lens, the print, carefully and with his brain and his guts, the way he got his own pictures.

Lying there, unmoving, that which he had never identified as pain or longing or loneliness or love choked in his being. He wanted to take their pictures.

How would it be? Oh Christ, how would it be to go to them with the camera!

And, lying there, unmoving, he dreamed himself up and out of this room, into the kitchen, together with them.

He dreamed he ran to his camera and swung it up to his chest, scooped up a handful of flash bulbs, walked rapidly into the kitchen. He did not know what to say, what to feel, but he would do it all with pictures. That was his, and he would make it encompass them, too.

There they sat, one at each end of the table. His mother's face was closer to the paper lying flat on the table, her eyes peering harder at the print, and the hush-hush sound of her voice made a soft little aura about her. But at this moment, in the dream, it did not hurt in his chest to hear her!

Their heads came up at his abrupt entrance. He saw a startled look in her eyes and he said stiffly, shyly, "I want to take some pictures of you."

They stared at him and he felt icy all over, exhilarated.

"Pictures?" she asked, bewildered.

He didn't blame her. He had never made one move toward any of the family with the camera.

"What kind of pictures all of a sudden?" the old man asked hesitantly. Jake could not see a jot of a sneer, or of a brutalized, dirty look on that face, and this astounded him so that he could scarcely talk.

He looked back at them. "Just pictures," he finally managed to get out. In the dream, his throat felt cracked. "I just want to take some pictures of both of you."

His mother's hand made a shy, almost halted gesture toward her hair, to smooth it. A beginning of excitement lifted across her face, like the shadow of a wing, then Jake had to look at the old man's face. It no longer seemed stern or sly. Jake thought he saw a pleased, warm look in the eyes and he quickly looked away.

"Jake," his mother cried, "pictures? Of us?"

"Sure," he said hoarsely. "Why not?" As if he had been taking such pictures all their lives.

"Wait, wait," she cried then in a little flurry. She began to giggle and to struggle to get up from the table. "Wait five minutes. I'll go put on a good dress. I'll comb my hair."

"No you won't!" he yelled, laughing, starting to get the camera ready. "I want you just like that. Sitting at the table. Reading the paper. Pa, you too. Just like you are now."

"Just like I am?" the old man repeated, glancing down nervously at his baggy jacket, the loosely knotted, shabby tie.

Jake laughed with excitement, with the roar of warmth pulsing in him. "Come on, come on," he ordered, "just be yourselves. Be Ma and Pa, that's all I want."

They laughed, too, edged closer to the table and nervously clung to their sections of newspaper.

"Look down at the paper. Pretend you're reading. Don't laugh. Just look like you're reading an article. Come on, come on!"

Without another word, they became solemn. Almost trembling, they pretended to read, their bodies stiff.

"No, no," he said softly but very gaily. "Forget about the picture. Read the paper. Ma, read it for real!"

He snapped them once, waiting until the hush-hush sound came from his mother's lips. He had caught them and the shadows of them on the wall, the stooped, tired-looking blotches on the walls seeming to further the actuality of them.

"Wait a minute," he cried. "Don't move. Ma, just keep on reading the article. Pa, lower the paper a little bit."

Jake moved quickly, lightly, about the kitchen, feeling them in relation to the room, to the wall, to the angle of ceiling and floor. He talked continuously, and the kitchen seemed thickly warm with a jumble of Yiddish and English, with their excitement and his. He felt happy.

He took them from three angles, carefully and quickly, feeling the way their faces would be stark and peasantlike, their bodies stories of the decades and of the places on earth where they had lived and worked.

At each flash they quivered, and he said briskly, so that they nodded at the safe, authoritative tone, "It's only a bulb. Don't be nervous. That's all, only a bulb."

Then, after the third flash, he stood there and grinned at them. "O.K. That's all. Watch the *Register* tomorrow, ladies and gentlemen! Right on the front page!"

"Listen how he's joking," she said fondly, and the giggling started to gush in her like a soft little fountain.

The old man cleared his throat, a friendly sound. "You'll bring home samples?"

"Oh, sure," Jake said eagerly. He did not know exactly what it was, what had happened, but there was that feeling of soaring.

"Well, I have to go back to the office," he announced. "I've got a little job to finish up."

They nodded, and when he left the house they were sitting there at the table watching him, smiling.

"Good-by," he said.

"Good-by, good-by," they told him gravely in the dream.

At the office he bumped into Ted, who was sitting at Ernie's desk with a stack of papers and scissors.

"Hey," Ted shouted, "you drunk, or what? You're on days this week, chump!"

"Shut up," Jake yelled happily, running for the darkroom.

Then later, when the pictures were drying and he knew they were good, he went to the morgue.

So what if you can't say it in words? he said very quietly. Say it in pictures.

He switched on the lights and went to his drawer. He

spread some of the prints out on the floor, the pictures he had been taking through the years. The shawled old women, the ragged kids on street corners, the leaning houses with inches of sky like secrets between the close-jammed roofs; he leaned over the faces of people lit out of despair or torment or drunkenness by the lift of eyes or by the soft line of mouth.

On his knees, he began to sort them, his mind ticking off captions; he remembered musingly the vivid moments of taking each one.

Ted came into the room, leaned over Jake, his hands on his bowed shoulders. After a long while, he said, "Hey, Jack!"

Jake nodded absently. "Think they'd make a show, kid?"

"A show? They'd blow up the museum! Hey, pull out that big one, Jack, will you please? No, the other one, the old man with the beard."

Ted took a deep breath. "That's absolutely alive, Jack. He looks as if he'd just stepped out of the slums. No, out of one of those ghettos you read about."

Jake knelt there. He felt quiet, deeply content.

I'll work for a couple of hours, he thought. Maybe get some of them captioned. Grab some sleep later, and get the strike art first thing in the morning.

He started gathering up the prints, Ted silently handing him the ones which had pushed out of reach.

And then, Jake thought, I'll have breakfast with Laura.

Laura. The dream stopped abruptly. In the bedroom, Jake glanced at his watch, got stiffly off the bed and went to the closet.

His hands were numb, and as he stood there shaking and rubbing them, a bitter taste welled into his throat.

After a while, he took down the bottle and had a few drinks. It was time to go to the station to say good-by to Laura.

C·H·A·P·T·E·R

Four

. . . And discussion points strongly toward this same lack of identity. S' relationship with Laura is traced back to his mother need, an overwhelming one; he has never been able to identify himself as a son. S found Laura a "wise, beautiful, older" woman. Drawn to the mother in her (wisdom, warmth, sympathy, the listening quality), his confused thinking dressed her in lover's clothing. At the same time the barrier of his need and of his adolescence stood between them. The relationship could not be fulfilled because the deep need of S for a mother has never been fulfilled. Though unrecognized on part of S, this was nevertheless a withdrawal from what would have seemed to him to be an incestuous tendency.

The relationship between S and his mother has always been strained, unreal, just as the relationship between his sister Deborah and their mother was unreal. Both S and Deborah have been forced—without recognizing it—to take on the role of their father, a man who has failed obviously all his life to be either husband or father. S could not act the part, but all his thinking and way of life have been affected by his need to do what he could not.

Deborah succeeded more, through greater strength and sensitivity, and thus assumed more and more male characteristics. However, she balked at the injustice of such a role, realizing that it was unfair even though she could not recognize the implications. The struggle between her mother's need and her own need (to live her own life, not her father's) almost broke her. This barrenness of parental life and the consequent need in the children probably is the source of what S calls "difference" in all the rest of the family, too (Sigmund, Sarah, Roz), though each child seems to have expressed the need in a different way of life. *Watch.*

Like Deborah, S was almost at breaking point when he came to D. He is not, as he thought at first treatment, broken. However, Deborah brought herself to D, and S had to be brought. He thinks the need of his nephews brought him. His ego cannot recognize his own wasteland. He has seized upon his nephews as the "excuse" to come to D. He thinks it is they he wishes to save; it is really himself, his own youth and future, not theirs. By using them as the excuse, he has managed to get enough strength to come to D. Without them he could not have come. S can't face his own wasteland but must think of their waste while really meaning his own. Though he describes only atrophy and shame of his family, he claims that the youth (future) of that family must be saved, and that this is what brought him to D.

Laura seems to be an echo of "the mother I never had." Until that mother loss and the reason for it are understood by S he always will be drawn toward the mother in women; he himself always the boy, the adolescent, the weak and sensitive son who has tried (and failed) to share his father's guilt and who cannot grow past that impasse. The wasteland he has always felt in the house is the sexual and social barrenness of his mother and the emptiness of the figurehead of husband and father. Assuming a burden not his own and failing to carry this heavy, unnatural weight has given him a feeling of guilt. He feels guilty when he thinks of his mother. He feels helpless, impotent, choked with pity, unable to talk to her. He feels hatred for the man whom he senses is the reason for all of this. He cannot blame her for anything, yet the unrecognized knowledge that he has never had anything of her has colored his entire life.

Further need for identity in S is seen in changing of name. Besides being typically Jewish, that name was given him by father and mother who were never parents to him. The religion of his ancestors is a parenthood, and his parents definitely have failed him. Also, Jewishness, in the eyes of the world, has failed—as evinced by the persecution and fleeing now going on. Thus, over and over, Jewishness has failed him—in his parents, in the eyes of the world, in himself. Religion, therefore, is something of which to be ashamed.

S has felt nameless for some time, began a long time ago the search which has not yet ended—for name, for identity (as an adult, as Jew, as son and brother). He attempted to flee from the house and everyone in the house in a number of ways—by casting off love and obligation to the family, by changing his name, by living in direct opposite to this house, as far as his job and gentile friends and women were concerned. Yet, through the years, he has not been able to cast off the house. "The house" is birth, people, family ties, the loneliness of a man without a mother, without a sister or lover.

Something, S says, has kept him chained to that house. He thinks it might be his mother. He is right. Get S to clarify in his own mind the position of his mother as an unsatisfied, unfulfilled woman. He must know that the chains are an outward symbol of the mother; as soon as he understands her need and that he cannot satisfy it, the chains will start slipping. He will know that every man needs to cast off his mother. But the strength to cast her off comes only if he has had her himself, as a complete mother.

S has become drained, weak. The lack of recognition of such facts has done this. The need for parents, love, for a father's strength and a mother's warmth, has confused him, put these strange burdens of guilt and debt on him. He is physically and spiritually unable to pay off his father's debt to his mother but he cannot recognize that debt as someone else's, not his. S will not be able to break his chains until he understands both the debt and his struggle.

The resemblance of Laura to his mother was made stronger by the feeling of debt. Not only was she an older woman but she had been made unhappy by a man, her husband. The pity felt by S, the desire to keep further unhappiness from Laura, were debts to assume. At the same time Laura was everything his mother was not: fine, genteel, educated, with absolutely nothing of the peasant or Jew. This created its own fascination and confusion, a feeling he attempted to identify as love.

S has got to the temporary point of being wholly dependent on D. In talking, in "giving up" (his shame and fear of family, of thoughts) to D, he has given up the desperate kind of strength these things engendered in him. Until the new, not false, strength comes to him through understanding, he will continue to be frightened, to cling to D. In this ephemeral moment, S sees in D the image of all those people he has needed for so long: father, mother, confessor, brother, sisters. With the cessation of wrong thinking and of false debts, S must be led to assume a responsibility which is truly his own, i.e., toward Deborah, the nephews, and/or wife, Jews, his country.

S telephones D at least once a day. Says he thinks of D and treatments incessantly, that people with whom he comes into contact are unreal, that the time spent in D's office is the only reality he knows at the moment. This kind of reality comforts him. The office is the uterus momentarily, where he goes back to a protective mother, to the womb, where he is simultaneously supported by D, a male strength. He has never had such protection or strength in his house.

S knows by now that he must identify what has gone before in his life and in the lives of his family before today becomes real, and tomorrow possible. For the most part, S is fully co-operative. It is only when remembrance brings too much pain or fear that he balks at going back, at "giving up."

S seems to clarify a good part of his confusion simply by putting it into words, as if the silence of the years had muffled his thinking, or covered it over so that he could not see clearly. Often, when he describes a look or a gesture, or a scene out of childhood, just the impact of the spoken words seems to release an answer. Often, one of D's questions seems to be the switch to some understanding.

S is definitely sensitive, though in an entirely different way from his sister Deborah. She is painfully so, by instinct, a watcher of people and of herself. His watching of people is only for the sake of comparing their creativeness with his wasteland. S has a tortured, delicate, but totally inadequate sensitivity to his mother and to anything that touches on her. . . .

"What sort of a week have you had?"

"Bad, bad. I've got so damn much to think about. Sometimes I feel as if my head would burst. It's packed with too many new things to think about. Debby said not to tell her anything, to talk only to you."

"That makes sense, doesn't it? To talk only to your doctor?"

"Oh, sure. But it feels good to have her know what I'm doing. She looks at me. Well, it's like her eyes say everything will be O.K. Sometimes her eyes are just like talk."

"You slept Wednesday night, after we talked on the phone?"

"Yeah. Say, I'm sorry I was so messy on the phone. I got to thinking about Laura, see. I mean I had to think of her in an entirely different way! It—it got me, kind of."

"You can telephone me any time you need me. You know that, don't you? I meant it when I first told you that. Any time, day or night."

"I know. I felt like I wanted to die Wednesday. I tried to go to sleep. I drank a hell of a lot. Nothing did any good. Debby wasn't home, I walked around the house, didn't even want to put a light on, couldn't read or anything. Honestly, I thought I'd die. That's when I phoned you."

"And after you talked, after you told me what was worrying you, it was possible to go to sleep?"

Jake smiled crookedly. "Sure. All I needed was you telling me there wasn't anything to worry about."

He took a deep breath, sat contentedly under the doctor's steady look.

"Tell me, Jake," the doctor said very quietly, "what do you want to talk about today?"

Jake felt a terrific, fisted blow land inside of him. His face grayed as the doctor's eyes held his own; his lips felt stiff.

After a long pause, he stammered, "My name is John, Doctor!"

"John? Are you sure?"

Varying emotions broke in him; he felt reproachful, then

humiliated, then strange and unreal. And all the while, in that silent, warm, homelike room, he felt how the doctor was waiting patiently for an answer.

"I've got to get used to it!" he burst out finally. "Give me a little time! Nobody's called me that for—Jesus, for about eighteen years!"

"You have all the time in the world. It would be good to get used to your own name, wouldn't it? Do you dislike the name itself? Aside from any of the things to which it seemed to tie you?"

"I don't know," Jake said, trying to say the name to himself and to isolate it from the things to which the doctor referred. "It's just that nobody ever calls me that. I told you, I kept waiting for eighteen years for somebody to say it."

"What does your mother call you?"

"Jake," he said, his face hot. "But that isn't the same thing, damn it! You know it isn't."

"Of course. And Debby, what does she call you?"

"John. I told you that," Jake said sullenly. "Jack sometimes, when I'm drunk. I told you."

"Jake," the doctor said. His voice sounded quiet and firm, and Jake listened hard. Now that the huge, unbearable moment was over with, that moment he had dreaded so long, he listened in a different way. It was even, in a tiny odd way, a relief to have the moment here.

"Yeah, Jake," he said harshly. He kept listening to the sound it made.

"Tell me, Jake, do you like anyone at home?"

"Sure," Jake said wretchedly, "I like most of them. We just don't have anything to do with each other."

"Do you?" the quiet voice pressed him. "Any one of them?"

"Debby," Jake said after the pause. Then, almost immediately, he cried, "But I don't know why! I don't even understand her. But she's always been—."

"Yes?"

"Strong. And so damn clean! As far back as I remember. A funny little kid. Always hanging out with boys, they had a gang. She always made me feel—uncomfortable. I guess that's the word." He frowned. "You always feel funny when somebody acts different. When she's not like all the people you know. Hell, I don't care much now. I think she's pretty wonderful. But she looks more like a boy now than before. Her hair's been cut like that for years. But I don't care much. I'm not afraid of her now."

The doctor's voice pounced. "You were afraid of her? Why was that?"

Jake tried to answer, felt confused. "I don't know. I guess because I couldn't make her out. I wasn't afraid, exactly. I just didn't know what the hell she was. My sister, a girl. But she always acted like a boy."

Then some of the confusion focused. He said glowingly, "She's so smart! You know, she writes. Stories and stuff."

"Yes, I know."

Jake nodded, a little abashed. "Sure, I keep forgetting she came to you once. But I can tell you how I feel about her, at least. She's wonderful, that's how I feel. Not like me. I mean, we even like different things. She goes for that classical kind of music, and highbrow books and magazines."

He talked faster, his eyes removed from the doctor's. "I kind of got to know her when I came in drunk one night. See, it's lucky I drink sometimes! I probably wouldn't have got to be friends with her if I wasn't drunk that night. I told you I never get near people unless I've had some drinks."

Now the confusion was all around him in the room, and his voice petered out. A thousand things he remembered came to prick at his thoughts and to antagonize them.

"You kind of got to know her," the doctor prompted him after a while.

"Well, I did and I didn't!" Jake cried, his face flushed. "After that one night, when we got to be friends, all of a sudden I remembered a lot of back stuff, and I understood it a little. But not too much. Damn it, Debby bothers me too much! Even though she explained a lot of stuff that night."

"What bothers you so much about her?" the doctor asked.

"Why does she go with colored people?" Jake demanded. He felt breathless. "That's something I still can't figure out, even though she explained it that night. Why does she act the way she does? Like a man! Why does she have to make me ashamed?"

He glared across the desk.

"Have a cigarette," the doctor suggested.

Jake took one, lighted it. "She's clean, she's smart," he cried. "Why does she do those things?"

"You say she tried to explain herself the night you came home drunk?"

"Yeah. She tried," Jake said.

"You didn't understand her?"

Jake dragged on the cigarette. He tried to tell the truth. "Well, I did that night. While she was talking, everything made sense, but the next day I felt—all mixed up."

"And you feel mixed up about her now?"

Jake rubbed out his cigarette. Then, immediately, he lit another one. When he looked up from the ashtray, his eyes were puzzled.

"It's a different kind of being mixed up now," he admitted. "But I'm mixed up about why people turn out the way they do. Me, for example. But Debby! The way she turned out, Jesus. Why should people have to go through things like that!"

"You feel sorry for her?" the doctor asked.

"Sorry?" Jake's head bobbed up. "She wouldn't let anybody feel sorry for her. She's so proud. Jesus, that's another thing I'm kind of mixed up about."

"Could you talk to me about your sister Deborah, Jake? You must realize by this time how important it is that you understand her. And your reactions to her."

Jake stared at him, feeling the flush creeping into his face again. His heart was beating heavily. He felt almost frightened at the idea of understanding her.

"What is it?" the doctor asked.

"She's awfully important to me," Jake muttered. "If I find out she's—bad—. I tell you, I don't understand her! I'll talk, sure, but I won't understand it."

"We'll do as we have throughout your previous talks," the doctor said soothingly. "Ask questions, I'll answer them. I'll try to explain points you don't quite get. Things will clear up as you talk them out. They have before today. Remember?"

"Sure, sure, I remember." Jake hunched forward eagerly. "But what if I find out something—the truth—I don't know?"

"You're afraid you'll discover that your sister is—what? You called it bad. Do you mean dishonest? Are you afraid she's a thief?"

"My God, no!" Jake cried. "I didn't mean things like that. Jesus, I don't even know what I mean. She just makes me feel— well, something's wrong, that's all."

He looked straight into the doctor's eyes, his face burning, and the doctor said, "Do you feel sometimes that she is encroaching on your territory? Do you feel sometimes that she, a woman, is stealing what belongs to men?"

Jake could not answer. He kept staring into the doctor's eyes, straining toward those soft, terrible words.

"Do you feel sometimes," the doctor went on, "that she, a woman, has no decent right to another woman?"

"Goddam it," Jake cried frantically, "I never said anything like that!"

"But you thought it?"

"No! I never put it into words like that, damn it! All I said was, I felt funny about her."

The doctor remained silent until Jake's eyes lifted, then he said quietly, "Now that it is in such words, is that what you meant by your word 'bad'?"

"Maybe. I don't know, maybe," Jake muttered.

"Tell me, Jake," the doctor said, "what do you remember about your sister Deborah?"

"I remember a lot," Jake stammered. "What do you mean, everything I remember? Where do I start?"

"Start anywhere. What do you remember of her childhood, for example?"

"I don't know too much about that. I never paid a lot of attention to her when she was little."

"Tell me what you do remember," the inexorable, soft voice said. . . .

Jake remembered that when Debby was a kid, everybody on the street called her Tomboy. Some of the kids even got into the habit of calling her Tommie. They'd stand outside the house and yell at her to come out. "Hey, Tommie! You comin'?" Or they'd call her Whitey. That was because of her hair and her skin, of course. She was practically white blond, and her skin looked like it had a sun shining behind it all the time.

He didn't pay much attention to her because he was busy with his own affairs, and he was a good five years older. He knew she had a gang, and she was the leader even though she was the only girl in the gang. She wore knickers after school and over week ends. She walked like a boy, with a boy's tough walk, but she didn't look much like one. Her hair was cut Buster Brown, but she always was passing her hand through it and brushing the fringe back from her forehead. She had a soft, oval-shaped face, and he remembered that she looked solemn much of the time, that she frowned a lot, looked like she was thinking or was worried. Right now, today, she had three or four lines cut deep into her forehead, but in those days she looked like a solemn little girl with that oval face and those blue eyes that were always looking straight into yours when you talked to her or looked at her. A little girl dressed up in knickers, with that boy's tough stride.

She was the little "fixer" in the house. When a screw came off of anything, or the stove wouldn't burn right, Ma always said: "All right, Debby'll fix it." And Debby did. She always seemed to know what to do. And she seemed to get a kick out of doing such things. She'd whistle, doing them.

Dirty things, sometimes, not what a girl would want to do. Washing out the garbage can, or greasing the sewing machine, or fixing the leaking hot water faucet. All the things with which Ma worked; whenever they went wrong or needed attention, why, nobody but Debby seemed to be around.

She'd help the old man, too. Help him fix a flat tire on his truck, or hold the tool in the grease of the motor while he screwed on the part. Everybody kind of took it for granted that Debby would do all these things. And she—well, she always seemed pleased at being asked; proud, kind of.

Funny, funny combination! I mean, when she was in the house and nothing else to do, she was always reading or doing homework. The teachers would always be sending home notes to tell how smart she was, what a wonderful pupil. When Ma would ask what the notes said, Debby would read them aloud to her (the old man never gave a hoot about any of us in school or home) in a small voice, and then Ma would say, "That's good, Debby. I'm glad. You want to run over to the store and get me a bread and a bottle milk?"

Ma was glad, but I guess such things didn't mean too much to her; she had plenty to worry about. Maybe Debby understood, too, because she never yelled or acted like she was a big shot. She just went to the store, or took the broom out of Ma's hands and swept the floor.

There was that clean business she had. Too clean, like she just had to be. She was the only one of us who had her own towel. She'd hang it in the front room closet, where she kept her clothes. All the rest of us used the towels that hung in the bathroom. She'd take a bath three times a week, or more. I used to like to take a bath right after her, she left the tub so white and shining. My old man always has been a pretty dirty guy, especially in the bathroom. Scarcely ever flushed the toilet after he used it, and made the sink just black—he got pretty dirty because there for a while he dealt in the old clothes business.

Well, I remember how that kid would walk into the bathroom with a can of cleanser. Her jaw stuck way out. She'd flush the toilet three or four times, very fast. Then she'd start scrubbing. Next time I walked into the bathroom, everything would be shiny white. But it was like Ma used to say: "What's the use of cleaning? He makes it dirty five minutes afterward." That couldn't stop Debby, she went right on being clean. Dirty as he was, or we were, the house and all—she was twice as clean, it seemed like. After a while, Sig got into the habit of having his own towel, too, but in those days she was the only one.

After she got a little older, I remember how she'd try to do everything she could to keep Ma from crying or worrying. I used to wake up some nights and I'd hear Ma and Debby talking in the living room, where the girls slept. I'd listen for a while.

"Ma, just don't worry," Debby would be saying, and I knew Ma was watching out the window for Roz. "She'll be home soon. All girls go on dates, and they stay out late. Gee whiz, Ma, Roz knows what she's doing. Go to sleep, Ma."

And Ma's voice would be half crying, so soft. "She's killing me with worry. A fourteen-year-old girl should stay out half the night! What does she want from her own mother? I should die away from worry?"

I could hear the old man snoring in the next room. Maybe his clock would bong: one, two. Sig was sleeping in the other bed, and nobody in the house was worried but Ma and Debby.

I'd go to sleep as Debby's voice, kind of patient and soft, was saying: "Aw Ma, stop worrying. I know where she is. She'll be home in a half hour. She went dancing, that's all."

"With the Italians!" Ma moaned, and Jake went to sleep, half hating Roz for her sins, her dancing, her mysterious doings that made mothers cry; and half glad that Debby's patient, strong voice was there in the night with the worry and tears of Ma. He would go to sleep kind of ashamed not to be there on the scene, but awfully glad Debby was around to take care of everything.

After she got a little older, those blue, tender, straightforward eyes changed somewhat. Jake scarcely knew how. There was a hurt look to them sometimes. He remembered how Debby would be sitting in the kitchen with a book. It was evening. Ma would start, in a low voice, to ask the old man something. The old man laughed silently, went on reading. Ma's voice grew louder. The old man looked annoyed, his eyes kept moving on the Yiddish print.

Finally he would look up from the newspaper he was reading. "What do you want from me?" he'd demand in a loud voice. "What do you think, I'm made of money?"

Eventually Ma would start to cry, that helpless terrible sound, her hands going up to cover her eyes. She'd run out of the kitchen into a bedroom, and the muffled terrible sound would come into the kitchen.

He remembered Debby at those times. Her face would turn white. She'd go on reading, then when Ma would run out of the kitchen, her eyes would swing up from the book and she'd look at the old man. She'd look at him for a long time as he sat there, reading, not knowing she was looking. Then she'd look at Jake. Her eyes had that look as if something inside of her was hurting terribly. Her face was so white, her eyes were so awful with that look, that he was forced to look away.

She grew older. Maybe she was fifteen or so when she started to shout. He remembered the first time. Ma asked for money—for herself, for a change. Usually she was asking for money to pay for food, or the gas bill, or shoes for Debby or him. This time she asked for it because she needed a dress. A cousin was going to be married.

"I'll be ashamed to go to the wedding," she said in her hesitant way. "We haven't seen them for years, and now Joe is getting married already. I remember when he was born. They're making a wedding in a hall. If I could get a dress."

The old man went on reading.

"Joseph," Ma said again. "I can't go to the wedding if I don't have a dress. It'll be shameful to go in my old clothes. In a hall, Joseph. The whole family will be there. I can't go and be a shame on the wedding."

"So don't go," he said, his eyes moving over the print.

Jake watched Debby's face go dead white. She was watching the old man, and she looked crouched in the chair.

Ma couldn't talk any more. Her mouth twisted, and just then Debby jumped up and her book smashed on the floor. The old man looked up at the sound, and Ma stared at Debby's face, which was all distorted and scarlet now.

"Leave her alone," Debby yelled at the old man. Her voice was hoarse and loud, as if it were tearing out of her throat. "You son of a bitch, why don't you ever give her anything? Why don't you ever act like a—a husband!"

The old man stared at her as if she had gone crazy.

"Sh," Ma said. "Debby, shah!"

Debby turned toward Ma. She was yelling in English, not the half Yiddish, half English all of them used in talking to their parents.

"Why is he like that?" she demanded of Ma. "I'm ashamed that he's my father! I hate him! I wish he wasn't my father, I tell you!"

The old man started to yell then. "Shut up! Who are you to talk like that? Shut up, I say! Don't talk like that to me. I am your father."

"You're not, you're not!" Debby shouted back at him. She was shaking all over, and Jake saw the veins standing out in her neck. "I don't want you for my father! You're a dirty, stingy man and you'd better be careful how you treat her. You hear me? I'll kill you if you make her cry. I'll kill you!"

Then she started to cry terribly hard, shaking all over, her fists all balled up, as if she wanted to punch. Everybody stared at her because Debby never, never cried. Then she ran out of the house, the door slamming behind her.

Jake felt breathless. He squeezed back against the wall, remembering Debby's eyes as she had yelled.

"Since when does a child talk like that to a father?" the old man said.

Ma didn't say anything. She looked scared and as if she didn't know what to do, then she walked out of the kitchen and into the bedroom. Jake heard the springs of the bed as she lay down. The old man shrugged after a moment, and went back to the paper.

Debby must have been about fifteen when that happened. After that, Jake noticed, she never helped the old man with the truck or anything. When he came into the kitchen, sooner or later she left the room. Every once in a while, when he tried anything funny with Ma, Debby would shout at him to leave her alone. When that happened, Jake saw that her eyes and mouth became spread over with a look of hatred, but she never cried after that first time.

Ma always said, "Sh, sh. Debby, please, don't holler. Sh."

Then Debby would walk out of the house, fast, as if unable to remain near anyone at all. He would always remember her tortured, hating look at such times. . . .

"What was your feeling toward Deborah when she shouted at your father?"

"I was a little scared of what might happen, but I—wished I had done it, I think. It never occurred to me to do anything but hate him. And here she was, really doing something."

"You envied her. Did you feel jealous?"

"You could call it that, yeah."

"And when she helped your mother so much, in all those little ways, what was your feeling?"

"Well, what do you mean, Doctor? I never wanted to do those things. Or help the old man with his lousy old truck.

Why, she even used to wind that clock of his sometimes, when it started to strike slowly as if it were running down. He was pretty careful to wind it, but sometimes he forgot."

"You didn't want to do those things, yet you resented her doing them? You were jealous of her place in the family?"

"What do you mean, I resented her?"

"Try to be honest, Jake. You were jealous of her, weren't you? Jealous that she was able to take on the position of—let's call it the little son of the family. Weren't you?"

"How the hell do I know!"

"You were jealous of her because she had taken your place in the family. She had not usurped that place; it was empty, wasn't it? The oldest son was busy, first at school and then at work. That left you, but you couldn't be the son to help your mother, or, occasionally, that man you disliked. You couldn't fill that empty place yourself, and yet when Deborah did try to fill it, try to help your mother in everything possible, you were jealous. You felt guilty at having forced her into that position. She was taking the place which should have been yours. . . . Isn't that right, Jake? . . . Isn't it?"

"I—don't know."

"Is that why you were afraid of Deborah? Were you afraid that she would take more and more of what was yours? Were you afraid, or did you feel guilty?"

"I don't know, Doctor!"

"But now you do know. Now you are beginning to understand. Did you resent her strength in taking that place you could not fill? Did you resent your own weakness next to that strength? Your own carelessness next to her cleanliness? Your own poor marks next to her extremely high school standards? Your own cowardice next to her stand against your father? Did you feel guilty because you had put yourself in this position and forced Deborah into hers?"

"For God's sake, Doctor!"

"But it's the truth you want here, Jake. You want to understand yourself, and your family, and what has gone into making you what you are. Isn't that so? . . . Isn't it?"

"Yeah."

"Are you afraid of your sister's honesty? You say she acts like a man, that she acted like a boy as far back as you remember. Isn't that honesty on her part? She was pushed into the role of son all her life, was she not? Into the role of strongest one? Was your father stronger than she? Was your brother? Were you?"

"No. But nobody pushed her! Nobody pushed any of us. She just went ahead and did all those things."

"You helped push her. But do you know of any greater strength than the kind that helped her accept such a burden? She was sensitive enough to the emptiness in that house. She was strong enough to know that somebody had to do something about it, and that she was the only one. You didn't help. Your father didn't, nor your brother. Does that make sense?"

"Go on, Doctor! Please go on!"

"In your family all the men were weak. I call it weakness that your father thought only of himself, and that your brother went his own way, and that you felt squeezed against a wall. Your sister Roz escaped into the street, into dancing and boys. Your mother asked for help, of anyone in the family. It's customary for women to ask help of men, their husbands, their sons. She got that help from Deborah. And only from Deborah. Is that correct?"

"She got money from Sig. Then from me, after I started to work."

"Did she get love from anyone? Did she get companionship, help in the small drudgeries of household jobs? Did she cry only because of the lack of money? From whom did she get help?"

"All right, from Debby! All right!"

"Does Deborah begin to make sense to you? Are you still afraid that what you say will prove her to be 'bad'?"

"Listen, Doctor! Don't get me wrong, for God's sake! I just don't know about her. All I know is, she's different from the people I know. I told you I think she's wonderful. I told you that!"

"But you're afraid of what she is, what she must be. She's different, you say. She acts like a man, she looks like a man. I call her honest. All her life, she was forced to be as strong as a man, inside and out. Or else she would have broken. She did not want to break. To die. When I use the word die, I mean it as decadence, as spiritual defeat, you understand. You agree to that, to the fact that she was forced to be stronger than the

138

daughter, harder than the youngest girl in that family. She was forced to be stronger and better and cleaner than any man she knew closely. In other words, the men of her family."

"Jesus, Jesus!"

"Of all in your family, she was the one to hold up your mother. She was the one to be insistently clean, in an attempt to clean up her entire dirty world. She was the one who fought for the right of your mother not to weep. All things which should have been done by her father, or by her brothers. Your family was on its way to defeat as a family, or a unit, but her insistence, her strength, fought for the life of it. She, not you, fought. She, not your father, and not your brother. Why do you wonder that she looks and acts like a man? She had to, all her life. She had to throw off all weakness and softness, all femininity. She had to, or she would have crashed. If she had despaired, or wept, or been soft—as a girl might have—the whole family would have crashed with her."

"Jesus, Jesus!"

"What else do you remember about your sister Deborah, Jake? Anything less beautiful than her childhood?"

Jake remembered when his father went on relief. He did not know too much about that because neither his father nor his mother had told him until after it was over, until after the food tickets had started coming to the house. Even then they had not told him. Debby had told him.

He had stared at her, feeling a kind of horror, feeling that some last support was sliding and oozing away from under his body.

"Jesus Christ," he'd finally whispered, "why'd they do that? Relief! My God, what if they find out at the office?"

She had stared back at him very steadily. He didn't know her very well, and he knew Ma and the old man were in the kitchen, listening; a thick silence seemed to seep out of the kitchen and all the way into the living room, where he and Debby, this sister whom he did not know very well, were talking.

They were standing face to face, and he looked at her, at her strangeness, the short hair, the knickers, the grave, steady eyes, and he felt like crying and crawling on the floor. He kept thinking of Laura, of Wally and Bill, of Katherine, of what they would say, how they would look at him if they found out. He felt smothered by a nauseous, frightening blanket of shame.

"They can't get along without it," Deborah said to him in a low voice. "Sarah and Max are on relief, too."

"But I give Ma money," he said, still dazed, his whole body hot with that shame.

"It isn't enough," Deborah said. "Your money pays for the rent. We have to eat, too. We have gas and light bills to pay."

As he stared into her unblinking, grave eyes a terrible mixture of emotions boiled up in him, a mixture at once of helplessness and rage and that hot, smothering shame.

"I can't afford to give her any more," he shouted. His voice was shrill and uncontrolled, and as he went on, it became louder and louder. "I have to live too, don't I! There are others in this family, aren't there? Why does it always have to be me for everything? They've got me in a trap, Goddam it! I'll never get loose, never! And now they go on relief. They had to do that to me yet! I might as well be dead now!"

"Take it easy, will you?" Deborah said. He noticed how pale she was, but her eyes still had that calm, grave look. "You're not in this. I saw the relief people when they came. I talked to them. I told them you don't live here, you come home once in a while and you give Ma money sometimes."

"Did you tell them where I work?" he cried desperately.

"I had to tell them the truth about that. I lied about you not living here." Her face glistened white in the lamplight. "Don't worry, they won't come see you. I told them you had to support yourself, that's why you couldn't give us more."

His stomach quivered. He began to cry in a low, strangled way. "Oh Jesus, Jesus," he said brokenly, "why did he have to do that to me?"

Deborah's voice became more urgent, quicker, but it was still as steady. "Listen, John, please don't feel too bad. We're not gypping anybody. We really need it. Honestly we do. Sig hasn't worked—well, you know how long it's been. I can't get a job. I wish I could, John, I wish I could help out. Roz left Izzie—I don't know if Ma told you. She just got herself a job. She's making enough just for herself; she has to pay the rent in that place where she's living. She used to give Ma money when she and Izzie were still together. We just can't help it, John."

"I'm getting out of here!" he cried then. "Damn it, I'll never come back!"

He ran out of the house. He got drunk that night, at Laura's, without saying a word to her. But he came back home the following night, late.

Then that specter haunted him for two years. When would the office find out his family was on relief? When would Laura find out? He himself did all he could to ease the horror that had hit out at him. He came home to eat only on Friday nights. He slept at Laura's or at Katherine's two and three times a week. He talked less than ever in the house. He didn't see Sig for weeks at a time, and when he passed the aging, dull-eyed man in the bedroom or living room once in a while, he rarely spoke.

He suspected what Debby was going through. A few times, on his days off, he ran into direct evidence. He'd sleep late, then take a bath and get dressed, and while wandering from bedroom to bathroom he would hear Debby and his mother talking.

He gathered that his mother had never once gone to the store for relief groceries. The old man did most of the shopping, at stores not too close to the house.

This one morning he heard his mother say, "He went somewhere, who knows where? To play cards! He knows we haven't got anything in the house. What will I do now? I won't go myself. I will die rather than go. I wouldn't be able to look anybody in the eyes again. Never again!"

He heard Debby's voice, flat, expressionless. "I'm going to go, Ma. Don't worry. Give me the paper."

"Where will you go?" his mother's anxious voice asked.

"Don't worry, don't worry, I won't go to our own grocery. I'll walk over to a Towers store, or an A & P. Stop worrying, Ma. What do you need? I'll make a list."

"As long as you don't go to Levine's. Oh, I should only live to see the day when we don't need it any more! When we can buy with our own money. So get milk, bread, a can of salmon—."

Jake turned the water on full force in the bathtub. His face was hot; he was thinking of Debby and the tone of her voice.

One morning of a day off, he had left the house and was

driving slowly up the street toward the corner. It was a warm morning, the sun bright on the just-beginning green of grass and trees and bushes, and women and kids were in the street, a lot of babies in their carriages. He was on his way downtown. Maybe he would lunch with Laura, or see an early movie.

Then he saw Debby walking home from the corner. She was in slacks, a short shabby jacket buttoned around her, and hatless, as usual. The sun had whitened her hair even more than usual, and she was walking fast, with that long stride of hers, a heavy, full bag of groceries hugged to her.

When his car rolled up closer to her, he noticed that she was pale and that her eyes were cast down toward the sidewalk. She looked very stern and young, and he had a sudden feeling of pity for her, a feeling so strong that tears came to his eyes.

At that moment, just as his car rolled past her, he noticed a group of four women standing on the walk a short distance behind her. One of them was pointing at her, and all of them had turned from their babies and were laughing. He stepped on the accelerator, hard, and whizzed past their laughter.

His tears had stopped instantly, as if the hot, awful breath of their jeers had dried them. Why shouldn't they laugh? he fumed. Look at her! They wonder what kind of a thing she is, and they laugh. My God, what if I were walking with her? Her brother, and they started to laugh! How can she stand it? My God, how could I stand to walk with somebody people laugh at like that?

And then Debby had taken a WPA job, and the relief had stopped, but what was the difference anyway? Everybody knew what people thought of the WPA. The cracks at the office; and then the new-old specter had started to meet him around corners. What if they knew his sister worked on this ludicrous, comical WPA?

He'd never known too much about that phase of Debby's life either.

One morning his mother had told him a little. "They wanted Sig should take a WPA job," she said.

"Who wanted?"

"The relief." She peered anxiously at him for fear he would shout, or become irritated. "They said he's the son. They said Pa is too old, he's got that sciatica, and he can't write English anyway so good, so they said Sig should take it. I was scared he shouldn't take it. I was scared they would take away the relief. So I told him."

"What did he say?" Jake said bitterly.

His mother looked at him sadly. "He said he'll rather starve, he'll rather go from the house."

"Let him go!"

"Jake," his mother said, her voice intensely and deeply quiet, "where will he go?"

"Aw, nuts!" Jake said, his teeth gritting.

"Jake, he's a man. He's the oldest son in this house. You would be ashamed to take such a job, too, wouldn't you?"

Jake did not answer.

"So Debby said she'll take a WPA job," his mother said. "She's working three months already. You know Debby; she keeps only what she needs to eat, to spend for carfare, and the rest of the money she gives to me. I made her she should buy a pair of shoes and a blouse. She was in rags."

"What does she do there?" he asked, curious despite himself.

"She is on a writer's job," Ma said. "She got one raise already. She makes ninety-three dollars and fifty cents a month already."

"Does she like it?" he said grudgingly.

Ma shrugged. "How should I know?" she said in a small voice. "Last week she says to me, 'Ma, I'm *working* for the money. We're not taking it for nothing. Don't ever forget that.' She doesn't talk to me that she likes it or she doesn't like it. She just gives me money twice a month. In the WPA they pay you twice a month."

"Yeah," he mumbled.

"She's got friends there." His mother's voice, small and humble as it was, sounded pleased. "Such things she talks about to me. Friends, gentile ladies, supervisors and bosses. They take her to eat in fancy restaurants, they take her to their houses. You know how Debby is, how smart, how she can work. Right away people like her. Like when she was in school, the best one in the whole school. You know Debby."

But he didn't know Debby. When he bumped into her sometimes in the house, he did not know her. And when he thought about her, he did not know her.

All of a sudden she had sold a story, but he still did not know her. That strange girl with the grave, intent eyes; and now the music was in that living room where she read and where she slept and wrote, that music low and solemn and strange as she was, and when he read the story, and then the next story, he felt that he would never know her. Of Negroes, of strong sharp protest, of a feeling sad and depressed enough to make the reader feel awful. What kind of stories were those, to be written by a girl, by a sister, to be shown off to one's friends? They made him uncomfortable, just as she did. When at last one of the family had done something halfway decent, the thing was full of such peculiar business that he could not even boast about it!

She was like a secret in his mind, a rankling, mysterious thing that he had to keep locked away not only from his friends but from his own self. And yet, constantly, painfully, he fumbled at the lock. . . .

Jake remembered Debby's friends. She was the only one of the family to bring friends into the house. Oh, Roz had used to bring an occasional girl friend home with her once in a while, to wait in the living room while she dressed; then they'd both beat it on a date. She'd never brought boy friends. But of course Roz had been gone for a long time now. She had married that cheap little racketeer and had lived with him, then divorced him, and now she was living in her own apartment.

Debby's friends. Not the kid friends, the boys from the gang; he didn't mean those kind. He meant the friends she had made within the last ten years, up through the WPA days.

No, he didn't know too much about them, except that they made him feel hot in the face. He asked his mother about them once in a while. Why? How the hell did he know why! except that maybe he thought they might explain Debby.

No, they didn't explain her. They just went right along with her strangeness, with the shame and discomfort of her.

She didn't have any men or boy friends, that sister of his. Of course not! That would mean being too much like other people; she had to be so different in all ways, in every Goddam way there could possibly be!

There was this colored girl. Her name was Jean, and she was a social worker. (Ma had told him; she had said to him, "You know what a social worker is? Debby explained to me. You see that black girl? She is a real fancy person. She went to college, her sisters are schoolteachers, her father is dead but he was a lawyer. Can you imagine such a high-class colored person?")

All he knew was, this girl had a bitter, brilliant look on her face, and when Debby had introduced her on that Saturday night he had come home earlyish, she had looked at him as if she knew what went on inside of him. She had sat there, looking up, and had said in a soft, deep voice with a kind of bitter music in it, "How do you do, Mr. Brown?"

There was the woman Debby had introduced as Barbara Something-or-other. A slight, lovely woman of about thirty-five, curly black hair, a tired face but just beautiful. ("It's her boss on that writer's job, that WPA job," Ma had told him when he had asked. "She's real crazy about Debby. She told me Debby's the smartest one in the whole place. A gentile, sure. Isn't she pretty?")

Yes, she was pretty, and his scalp prickled as he wondered, his heart banged hard as he tried to think of something else. What was that pretty woman doing in this house on a Saturday night, laughing softly in a corner of the couch, listening to that damn classical music, looking at the solemn, strange, golden boy's head his sister made in the lamplight?

Looking at Debby, smiling at that colored woman, taking a light for her cigarette from the match held by Toby. ("She's studying to be a lawyer," Ma had told him. "She likes to make jokes and to cook. One night she baked a cake for the girls. I ate a piece, it was wonderful. Chocolate, you'd think it came straight from a bakery! Sure, she's a gentile, too.")

But it was Fran who really made him feel—. Well, Jesus, the way she looked at Debby. She was Jewish, and good-looking in a dark, thin, unsmiling way. ("Fran?" his mother had told him. "She's Debby's best friend. They go everywhere together. I know her mother good. Her father has a pawnshop down there where the niggers live, and she works in it. They're not poor people like us. They own property, even the house where they live. Debby says she's very smart. Sure she's Jewish, I know her mother real good, I see her in the grocery store every day. Her father goes to the same *shule* with Pa.")

And it seemed strange and yet right, somehow, that this girl should be Jewish, among all the gentile friends, and from a neighboring family, a family that went to the same temple and grocery as his family. Leave it to Debby, he sneered to himself, to pick a Jew. And yet he never put it into words; he never got beyond the sneer, nor the shock at the lovely, womanly Barbara being there. He never called it jealousy, or fear. The drum he hammered at in his mind was the shame of Debby associating with Negroes, the shame of her look and walk, accentuated by the sound of that colored girl's laugh booming through the house and that short-haired, red-headed girl's gesture of leaning forward and lighting the lovely one's cigarette.

One night he had lain on his bed, his door ajar to hear them; and that low music came through the night, that music which was tied up with Debby in his tired mind. The words had come, too, as if borne on the music, words about a book, poetry, Negroes and jobs, a play they had all seen and liked. Then they had all gone into the kitchen and he'd heard them fussing with dishes, he'd smelled coffee. (Ma and Pa in bed, Sig somewhere, only he to hear, to listen.) Now the words were clearer. Jews, persecution, the source of hatred. And he had lain there in the darkness of his bedroom, his mind buzzing with the secret, mysterious, anguished import of his sister.

Sure, he was ashamed. What was she if not the symbol of all the strange and distorted aspects of their family?

Other fellows had sisters; he had seen them, feminine, dressed smartly, smiling, their hands carelessly and fondly on their brothers' shoulders. These fellows brought their sisters to the office, introduced them to people. They took their sisters to movies, into bars for a drink and conversation with people.

Jesus! what if he was walking downtown some day with friends, and Debby came along? They'd look at her, all right (would they laugh? examine him closely in that minute to look for any sameness? walk away from the two, Jake and Deborah, as quickly as possible, so that the world wouldn't see them in any kind of association with such queerness?). "This is my sister Deborah."

His insides cringed away from even the possibility. . . .

And Jake remembered the night he and Debby had really, finally met.

It was not quite midnight; he knew that definitely because when he let himself into the living room, that music of hers was coming from the radio, very low, very sad, and he knew by now that it was a program of recordings that went off the air every night at midnight. (He had listened to the program several times recently, in his car, trying to figure out what she loved about this music, and why it was so much like her. He could not figure it out, but he kept listening anyway, to the fascination of that unknown quality.)

Debby was sitting in the big chair, the lamplight coming down on her yellow head, on the open book in her lap. She was in pajamas and bathrobe, and one leg was curled under her; the light shone on the bare ankle of the other one and on the brown, shabby house shoe she was wearing.

He noticed, in that first look, that the couch had been turned into a bed for the night, one corner of the blanket and sheet turned down neatly, no pillow, the white of sheets seeming extra white in the shadowy room. He stumbled as he passed her chair, and her eyes went quickly back to the book as he passed. He took with him into the dining room that look of steady, calm blue, and when he draped his coat over the chair in the dark room and tossed his hat on the table, the music came from behind him and stood with him leaning over the table. It turned with him fuzzily and softly as he faced the living room, and hesitated with him as he stood wanting suddenly to go to the liveness and warmth of her corner in the house.

The old man's clock began to bong, the slow, long strokes coming from the bedroom, and then the music whispered into silence and he heard Debby snap off the radio, and then only the slowness of the clock strokes was left.

He went to her, sank into the other chair, which stood almost opposite her, and closed his eyes. The clock strokes seemed heavy, went on and on though he was sure they had long ago struck twelve. "Why doesn't he wind it?" he mumbled, his eyes closed, his head back on the chair. "It takes so long to stop striking, for Chris' sake."

"I'll wind it tomorrow," Debby said. Her voice seemed soft and soothing, his eyes shut that way, as if a friendly woman sat opposite him. He kept his eyes closed, and that soft, womanly voice went on talking. "Sometimes it's as if the clock is Pa. Like his voice in the house, or the sound of him walking in another room."

He didn't want to open his eyes, he didn't want the soothe and caress of that voice to disappear. "I don't like that clock."

"Oh, I like it. It's like a father in the house, Jack, really. An old, respectable sound. You'd miss it if it weren't here. Really."

Jake opened his eyes. For a moment, she swam a little in that soft and golden light, then she steadied as his eyes focused on the oval, smiling face, the firm, white look of her throat as it rose from the blue stuff of the bathrobe. She seemed entirely different tonight. Her face seemed girlish and smiling; and then he suddenly noticed the beautifully shaped, soft, woman's mouth. He was deeply touched, so that his heart lunged a little.

"What's the matter, Jack?" She closed the book over one finger of a hand, and then he noticed in a sharp, excited way the look of her hands, strong and rather square, the skin white and soft, the little hairs gleaming yellow in the light; and it was like talking to a woman, and yet the hands were stronger than that, and the soft, curved mouth had an insistence to it, a strength, a definitive shape and form which seemed to haunt the youth and softness of the face.

"What do you do, call the clock Pa?" he said, almost a bitterness to the question.

"Not in so many words." She smiled again, and again the face was so much a woman's that his heart dipped down.

Then she questioned him. "Do you hate him so much?"

"Don't you?" he shot back.

She shook her head. "No. I used to, but I don't any more. Sometimes I feel sorry for him, but mostly I just don't think about him."

It suddenly hit him that Debby and he were actually talking, and that the room was warm and yellow; he was together with someone in a friendly way, with words, and he leaned eagerly toward her, toward the woman and family and friend of her.

"It's wonderful to talk," he stammered. "Come home and find somebody in the house to talk to. Sit around this way."

"Yes," she said. "It's nice, isn't it?"

The chair and she began to swim very slowly again, but he knew she was there, the soft and womanly listening of her, and the words gushed out of him to her, to that new, wonderful receptiveness.

"It's hard for me to talk to people. It's funny! I try like hell, but I just close right up. Get into a roomful of people, and I start to blush, I don't know how to talk to them. It's funny as hell, Deborah! But I'll take a couple of drinks and then it's easy. Then I can talk."

She swam with the chair, and she was nodding, her eyes were deep and sympathetic, and she was nodding at him in a half-sorrowful, half-gentle way, so that he felt wonderfully close to her. It was as if she were older, with a look of wisdom and gentle strength in her eyes, and he felt that he must lean on her, he must tell her all the things he did not know, and she would know, she would support him, soothe him.

"Jesus!" he stammered, leaning toward her, so close he could touch her, he could look into those sister eyes. "Doesn't it get you? This house, Jesus! The old man, Ma, and then you go downtown, you get together with people, and you have to worry about—everything! What to say. How to act."

Watching her eagerly, it seemed to him that she shrank back into the chair, that her eyes were like she was going to cry; and, almost frantically, before she could disappear, he clutched at the warmth of her hand, felt the soft but firm reality of it, hung on as tightly as he could.

"Listen," he said, the words coming out so fast they stumbled over one another, "all I want to know is, what's it all about? Maybe you know, maybe you'll tell me. I tried to find out. I read all the time, I go to movies and hang around with people. I just don't sit around and want to die! I don't! I'm telling you I try, I just don't sit down and die the way I feel like doing!"

He stared at her, and the blue eyes swam a little but he could see how they were deep and full of wanting to cry, and he said hoarsely, "Nothing means anything, that's all. I come home every night, but what for? The old man? Ma? I go to the office—. Hell, I love my job! I'm good, I do a good job, but I'm telling you I don't know why I'm doing anything. I feel trapped here, Jesus! just trapped! But where would I go? Why would I go? Why would I do anything? It's like I've got a hole in me."

Her hand was motionless in his, warm, firm, the livest thing he'd ever touched, and he squeezed it tighter and tighter, trying to extract from it some of that strength, the woman and friend of her, the insistence of her tread and the proud poise of her head, the way, surely, her heart must be quiet.

"You feel empty. Lonesome." Her voice was musing, far away, as though she were describing somebody else to him. "There's nobody around. There's no reason to come home, but you do, and then there's nobody here for you. The house is dirty. Pa is like one of the dirty, silent walls. Ma doesn't know what you're feeling, what you want. You don't know what you want."

He stared wildly at her, cluching at her hand as she swam with the chair. "Listen!" he pleaded with her, and then he began to cry, harshly and bitterly and yet softly so that his chest and sides ached. He cried, remembering the aimless nights and the lostness of Laura and the emptiness of this house, the peering anxiety of Ma, the meaningless nights with Katherine; and now there was this sudden softness of Deborah after all the years of her strange, harsh boy-girl accusation in this house. He was unable to stop, unable to move from his fixed, crouched position, and he felt the tears dropping on his hands and knew they were wet on her hand between his.

Then he felt how her other hand was holding his shoulder, pressing it, touching him with sympathy and harshness, with a touch like herself that was at once womanly sweet, and yet it was brother-or-friend insistence on helping him, too.

He began to be aware of her low voice. "Come on, Jack. That's all right now. It's going to be all right. Come on now, come on."

And when he looked up, she was not swimming with the chair. He was very close to her, and he could see how pale her face was, how much darker blue her eyes seemed, how steady and grave they were.

"That a boy," she told him softly, and he released her hand and watched her rub it with the other one. When he looked up, her eyes were still there and with the same steady look.

Her book was on the floor. He took out his handkerchief and wiped his eyes, and he wanted to pick up the book and hand it to her, but he couldn't.

"Listen," he said urgently, "will you have a drink with me? Will you?"

"Sure," she said.

His tongue felt thick, and the words had come out blurred. He felt abashed for the first time as he got up and quickly walked into the dining room to his coat. There was half a bottle of bourbon in his inside pocket, and when his hand touched it he had a swift, prodding picture of what Katherine's face had looked like when he left her apartment so abruptly. They had started in the Brass Rail, then drunk half the bottle in her place. Her face; what had been in her eyes to make him get up that way and beat it? Empty eyes.

Quickly, he went back to Debby with the bottle. Again he sat opposite her, unscrewed the top of the bottle and tilted it to drink.

When his head came down and the whisky was warm in his chest and stomach, his eyes went to hers and he suddenly said, "I don't drink this way all the time!"

"I know," she told him gravely, and put her hand out for the bottle.

He gave it to her. Her eyes were friendly, and yet he had to go on. "All of us drink once in a while. The whole bunch of us."

"Of course. I know. Especially in newspaper work." He watched her wipe the top of the bottle with her handkerchief, then she tipped it and drank. The bottle came down and she was smiling at him, her mouth untouched, her eyes the same.

"That's good whisky," she said and put the bottle on the floor, near the foot of her chair. "Have a cigarette?"

He took one from the package she held out, and she lit it, then lit her own. Leaning back, he felt steadier, and the heavy bar had gone miraculously from his chest.

151

She pushed an ashtray closer to him on the small table, and he took a deep drag, peering at her sideways to see what she was feeling about his crying jag. She was blowing smoke out of her mouth, looking intently at the burning tip of the cigarette.

Just then the clock struck one, and she smiled at him. "A word from our father."

He smiled back, his mouth crooked and a little tremulous. Her eyes sobered then, and she said gently, "I know how you feel, Jack. I used to feel a lot like that. Maybe worse." She smoked for a while, then her eyes came back to his. "I couldn't understand why. Why I was even living."

He nodded quickly, and she went on. "I know. That's the main thing, isn't it? Trying to figure out what's the point of living this way. With everything as rotten as it seems. No meaning to anything." She hesitated. "It's because you don't understand."

"Jesus, what's there to understand?" he mumbled, putting out his cigarette.

"Us," she said softly. "Ma and Pa. What's going on in our house. What's going on in the world, and what connection we have with it. Me." Again she hesitated, then she said, "Wouldn't you like to understand me?"

He flushed, his eyes flying to hers in a startled way.

"I'd advise you to go to a psychiatrist," she told him, her voice very quiet.

He was horrified. "You think I'm nuts?"

She shook her head. "No, I think you're confused. I think you're fighting stuff you don't know the name of, and you can't figure out why that kind of stuff should be in you."

"Why the hell should I go to a head doctor?" he cried.

She rubbed out her cigarette. When her eyes came back to his, they were very sympathetic.

"I went," she said. "I wasn't insane, I just didn't see any reason for living. I'd been feeling that way for years. When I couldn't stand feeling that way any more, I went to a psychiatrist."

"You went?" It seemed impossible to him. This girl whose strength and strangeness always had seemed like a whip in her hand, this sister of his whose head was high enough so that shame could not get anywhere near her; it was impossible to visualize it.

She lit another cigarette, inhaled deeply. "I was sick. I needed a doctor. I had some kind of poison in my head, instead of in my blood or my lungs. Like germs. So I went to a doctor. Wouldn't you go to a doctor if you had flu?"

He nodded, his face red.

"You know," she said, "a psychiatrist is a doctor."

She was silent until he looked up at her, until she had made the point with her eyes, then she went on.

"Why was I sick? I hated my father. It seemed to me that my mother was not really a mother, just an old woman who needed my help—and yet I needed her help. My brothers, my sisters—I didn't even know them. I, myself—."

After a while he said to her softly, "Don't stop."

Her eyes seemed very tired, but deeply aware of him as a person. The last of his drunkenness had gone, and now it seemed to him that Deborah and he were the same age, of the same blood and bone, almost like twins sitting in a close, warm-breathing place from which everyone but them was barred. And he felt, vaguely, that if he could enter this twin of his he would find the same torment he had known, the same anxiety, the same choked and dark pleading for love, for help, for living touch; and at the same time he felt, in the same vague way, and without resentment, that this twin had gone beyond him, that she had struggled with more intelligence, with greater sentience, with deeper understanding.

"I?" she said. "I knew how sick I must be, because every moment of the day I felt ashamed. Not only of my family and our way of living, but of myself. I felt isolated, part of a tiny minority of people who did not dare lift their eyes to the level of the rest of the world. No matter how clean I kept myself. No matter if I loved beautiful music and beautiful words. No matter if I tried myself to write such words. Wherever I went, I felt that people must be looking at me with repugnance and with laughter."

Jake felt unreal. He felt so close to her that every word she said to him was familiar, almost echoed, as if he had heard such words before; and yet, sitting across from her, that short space between them, he saw her as if through a haze, her head so young and boyish, the yellow, clean hair so short, and yet her mouth so girlish and soft, the curve of it a little twisted now with what she was saying.

She offered him her pack of cigarettes, then lighted the one he took.

"I never thought I'd be telling you any of this," she went on, and he knew she was watching him, waiting for him to say something. "I think I've known for a long time that you were suffering—inside of you. There wasn't any way to get near you. Even if I had known you wanted me to. I couldn't be talking this way to you now if I hadn't been to a psychiatrist. I know you feel odd about me, Jack."

"Well, Jesus!" he blurted out, but then he did not know what to say.

"I'm sorry," she told him quickly. "Don't feel badly about it. I don't. It's better if I say it out loud. Really it is. You see, I never said it out loud even to myself until I went to a doctor. I used to think it, and feel it. That I was like—a cripple. Something for people to draw away from. Terribly ashamed."

He put out his cigarette, kept looking at his hands as the silence grew. Finally she asked him softly, "Do you want me to stop? Do you want to go to bed?"

"No, don't stop." He looked up at her, and there were tears in his eyes.

"I'm sorry!" she cried. "I didn't want to make you feel rotten, Jack."

"No," he said, his throat aching. "It's all right. Just don't stop."

He loved her intensely at that moment, feeling her years and her torture through those years like clubs in him; he felt that she had shadowed him through all those years, and he her, and yet always there had been hands between the twins, pushing each away from the other, away and back one from the other.

There was a silence around them, and Jake shoved his head back against the chair. He felt relaxed, his eyes open and musing on the shadowy ceiling. He thought quietly of his mother and the old man, asleep in the back bedroom, and that

Sig would come in soon, that it would be morning next and he would go downtown to the office, Debby would go to her job.

Debby. He and she, he felt then, must have been talking in this way all their lives, she having gone ahead and tasted the quick, tormenting years, and he coming along later, anticipating them, asking questions now about the stumbling, dragging walk, about the sweating and the weeping, how it felt when they came, and about the weight, the feel of the cut across the shoulders and the agonizing, growing weight on neck and back.

"I always wondered why you hung out with colored people," he said quietly. "That friend of yours. I suppose you have other colored friends, too."

"Yes, I have." Her voice, too, was relaxed, and the room seemed closed about both of them warmly. "I went to them first because they seemed—yes, wounded. I felt that way, too. Wounded. What I called, after a while, people with social wounds."

His head came down, and now they were looking at one another, talking in low tones, nodding their heads.

"I guess," she said, "I had to go to them so that I could feel stronger. By feeling not so alone. My doctor helped me figure that out. In those days, I thought of myself as part of any group that was persecuted or looked down on. Any group of people wounded by the world. Jews, Negroes, cripples of any sort. I pitied them, I wanted to help them, I wanted to protect them and push them up to where the rest of the world was living."

She smiled. "It was myself I was pitying. It was my own crippled look I was protecting. That was how it started. After a while, I knew I was part of these people because they were part of the world. But not of a special world, you understand. The ordinary world, the whole world. Just as I was part of that world. Nobody had any right to keep that world from me."

"Jews, too," he said very softly.

She nodded. "You too."

He winced, and she smiled gently. "And Ma. Roz. The old man, whom I hated so and did not even want to understand. Jews. But besides the Jews, there were all the others who were hated and laughed at. The world belonged to all of them, as

155

well as to me. All the odd ones, the queer and different ones. They were people. I was people. After a while, I knew I had to hang out with them. I was them."

"Why?" he asked, watching her intently. "You mean, your hair? The way you look?"

He saw her flush, her mouth twist for a second, but she did not look away. "The way I am," she said. Her voice shook for just a moment, then deepened and steadied. "The way I am inside. It's the way I've got to be. I'm a person in the world. There's got to be room for me, too."

She rubbed her cheek, and he studied the square, strong hand for a moment.

"I'd like to tell you exactly how I feel about it," she said after a while. The short, deep lines sprang out in her forehead and some of the youthful, boyish look seemed gone from her face. "It's hard to put into words. I hate that business of intolerance. They hurt me with it all the time. But I'll tell you, feeling it, I can feel how they hurt the others with the same thing. I can feel how I'm part of a person they call nigger, or dirty Jew, or cripple. Maybe it takes hurt to understand hurt, I don't know. But it's like I can understand all kinds of hurt now. Every kind there is."

He sat quietly under the monologue, feeling the closeness between them.

"If you went to my doctor," she said, her forehead wrinkled deeper. "If you talked to him, asked him questions. It's like being sick and needing medicine, is all."

When he did not answer, she went on. "Before I went, I used to feel that awful shame. Of what I was. So ashamed I couldn't see straight, or even think. I'd be so hurt all the time, so ashamed of being different, that finally I just couldn't make sense of anything. Everything I touched—it was like I was in a dark room all the time. Sick. Sort of—empty. Do you know what I felt like? Like I was being wasted. My brain and—and my heart, and everything decent I had ever wanted to do. I felt like a—a desert."

"I know how you felt," he broke in eagerly.

"After I went to the doctor, after I didn't feel ashamed, it was so different."

His eagerness mounted. "You weren't afraid after that!"

"It wasn't fear, exactly. I just didn't believe in myself. I think that's what it was." Then she laughed. "But that's a kind of fear, too, isn't it?"

He did not have to answer. After a while their father's clock struck two. The strokes seemed never-ending, and he seemed to hear their sound old, tired, like the house. He looked up to Deborah's small smile, and this time he smiled back.

"Tired?" she said. "It's pretty late. Don't you want to go to bed?"

He shook his head. "I feel like we just got started," he told her.

"I do, too."

He took his pack of cigarettes out and offered her one, then struck a match.

They smoked silently for a time. He liked watching her now. Her clean look reminded him of sunlight on yellow. The deep, blue color of her eyes was another vividness, and he remembered wryly how much that insistent look had used to disturb him. He saw now, in another of the first and startling glimpses of the evening, how gracefully she held her cigarette, with what fresh and eager gestures she passed her right hand through her hair when she became engrossed in a thought, and how her words flowed intensely and smoothly, like a beautifully written story, when she wanted to describe a thing.

Jesus, Jesus, he thought warmly, she's in the family, too.

"Listen, Jack," she said after a while, "I want to talk about Sarah's kids."

"Sarah's kids?" He was startled.

"Bernie and Allen," she said. "Our nephews. Do you ever remember that we have nephews?"

And then she told him about the waste of their sister's children.

Five

The doctor smiled at Jake. "Today we are enemies, aren't we?"

Jake looked back sullenly.

"Aren't we?"

"I don't like you today, that's right," Jake said. "If that's what you mean."

"Why not? Do you have anything definite on which to pin your dislike? Or is it a cloak for your dislike of someone else? Or perhaps yourself?"

"Nuts!" Jake burst out. "I'm so damn sick of all this cloak talk. This escape and stuff! It's like being in—a movie, for Christ sake!"

One of those silences came then to nip at him. Gradually, the heat and choked weight seeped out of him and the silence became quiet.

After a while, the doctor said softly, "What's the matter? What happened?"

Jake shook his head hard. "My Goddam father, that's what! He's such a cheap bastard."

"What's he done?"

"Nothing special." Jake lit a cigarette, his eyes narrowed and miserable in the smoke. "I just don't know how to treat him. How to—feel about him. I can't go on hating him."

"Why not? What's changed you?"

Jake's head flung up, his eyes sullen again as they met the doctor's. "I'm not changed! After all, I don't understand the guy, so how can I go on hating him? But last night he gets that sly kind of a smile on his face, and he asks me if I've got an extra pint of whisky I don't need."

"What makes you so furious?" the doctor asked quietly.

"He's got enough money for whisky! Debby and I pay the rent, all the bills. Sig helps, a little. That cheap bastard doesn't put out a penny for anything in the house. We even pay for his food. And his tea, that he guzzles all day and night!"

"What really made you angry?" the doctor said insistently. "You've known all these things about your father. What happened last night? It was one of your Friday nights, wasn't it?"

"Yeah." Jake smoked in silence for a few moments, then he said, "It was nice. Debby and I ate together. Roz came later, about the same time as Sig. I was telling Debby and my mother about how I took the mayor's picture."

"The mayor."

"Oh, sure," Jake said. "I'm always snapping the big shots. The mayor calls me Jack. He likes me. Well, my mother was tickled. Her eyes were all big, and she was excited. Debby wanted to hear, too. I could see in her eyes how she wanted to hear about it."

"And then your father burst into your moment of glory and cheapened the whole thing. Was that it?"

Jake swallowed. Finally he said in a very low voice, "That's about it, I guess. I hadn't really figured it out."

He lingered for a time over putting out the cigarette, his fingers pushing the dead end around the ashtray. "I was sore at him to start with," he admitted. "I'd been thinking about what he did to Debby when she was a kid. I was thinking how she'd had to make up for the way he was, never giving a damn about Ma or the rest of us. He was really responsible for putting Debby on WPA."

"Look here," the doctor said rather suddenly, "isn't it time you saw this WPA bugbear for what it really was?"

"What do you mean?" Jake said.

"I mean, exactly what was the shame of being on WPA?"

"Exactly what! Look at the way people laughed at it. It was just a fancy alphabetical name for charity, wasn't it?"

"Was it?" the doctor asked gently. "You talk about wasteland a lot. Try to look at WPA in the light of wasteland. It strikes me our government, in putting millions of men and women to work, used WPA to put an end to wasteland. Not only the wasteland of people, but of forests and cities, and of literature and theater, too. If you recall, you'll remember that WPA workers put on plays, wrote books, replanted forests, repaired streets and public buildings. Do you recall?"

Jake flushed. "I used to read about that, yeah."

"Now look at that. This WPA you think was so shameful. It was a product created expressly against a nation's wasteland. It was given to your family to help them climb up out of their own wasteland. Do you see that at all? Forget the way people laughed. Understand it. The people who laughed never did understand it."

Jake's breath puffed out. "Jesus, a guy can be dumb!"

"A guy can find it difficult simply to understand," the doctor said. "He's ashamed of too much, to begin with; and then there's all that laughter. Too many people want to jeer at a thing. It's easy for him to listen to all those people."

Jake groped, his mouth loose and rough as he tried to figure it out. "But even so, the old man wasn't anybody to like. He was weak, wasn't he? He just went along and did everything his mother told him, everything but the one big thing of getting married."

"Where did you get that?" the doctor asked very quickly. "You haven't mentioned your grandmother."

Jake looked confused. "Well, I never knew too much about her. I never really cared." He lit another cigarette. Red-faced, he mumbled, "I got the story from Debby. All about my father and mother when they were—young."

The voice coming over the desk was soft again. "What made you ask her?"

"I don't know. All of a sudden I wanted to know about them. All of them." Suddenly he asked, a tiny lunge of fear in his voice, "Why did I want to know, all of a sudden?"

"You're looking for the roots of your life. Of your self. You've never before wanted to find the source of anything, have you? Not even the source of yourself."

"No," Jake said eagerly. "But, Jesus, it's interesting stuff! I knew Debby would know. She and my mother always talk a lot. I asked her Monday night. I'd had a couple of drinks, came home late. She—well, you know! Reading, sure. That music was coming from the radio. Her kind of music. It was nice in the room."

He looked up, his eyes humble and grateful. "So nice," he said in a choked voice. "All of a sudden, I wanted to know about how it was before I was born. I asked her."

"And she told you. She knew."

"Yeah, she knew, all right." His rough mouth shook slightly. "She knew all about my mother. How she felt, all those things she went through. My God, I get all mixed up when I think about it! That lousy father of mine!"

"Now you feel more ashamed?"

"No. It's funny, but I don't." Jake pressed at his lower lip, his forehead creasing as he tried to figure it out. "I was just sore. I felt so damn sorry for my mother. But I wasn't ashamed."

He looked across the tranquil plain of the big desk, at the small smile in the doctor's eyes.

"You know," he said abruptly, "it's funny. The first time Debby saw me drunk I felt bad. Ashamed. But she made it O.K. She made it so I didn't have to feel ashamed."

"That was the evening she asked you to see a psychiatrist."

"Yeah. And Monday night, it was the same way. See, I was kind of drunk then, too. When I asked her about Europe and the old man. But I wasn't ashamed."

"Is it still so much easier for you to talk when you've had something to drink?"

Jake said, very slowly, "I don't have to be drunk to talk to you."

"But you feel that you have to drink in order to talk to Deborah?"

"Well, I thought so," Jake said dubiously. "It helps. I wasn't stinko Monday night. Just enough to talk easy. I came in, and there she was, in the living room. I told you, she sleeps there. She never had a bedroom. There wasn't ever enough room in the house."

"It's always been that way, hasn't it? A bedroom for the boys. None for the girls. Men are the important members of your family."

"Yeah." Jake's jaw clenched.

"What happened Monday night?" the doctor calmly reminded him.

"We had a drink together. I didn't think she would—again. It made me feel—well, I wasn't ashamed of drinking when she acted so free about it. After that one drink, I didn't even want any more. We sat around, talked about little things."

His eyes softened. "Then I asked her if she knew anything about Ma and Pa before we were born."

"Yes?"

"You know, it seemed to tickle her that I wanted to know. She looked happy about it. She said, 'Oh Jack, I'm so glad you want to know about us.'"

"Do you know what she meant?" the doctor asked.

"Not exactly. But I sure am glad I know about them now."

"Why?"

"Why, why!" Jake cried nervously. "You're always asking me why. Maybe now I know a little more why things happened the way they did in our house! Maybe that's why I'm glad!"

"Good," the voice said gently. "I'm glad you know why you asked your sister to tell you. You didn't ask her out of a clear sky, did you? You very much wanted an answer, didn't you?"

"Yeah. Guess I did." Then, after a while, Jake said, "Sorry I yelled that way."

"That's quite all right, Jake."

"Jake," he said slowly after the doctor. "It still sounds funny."

"It won't after a while, you know. And the story Deborah told you?"

"Stories. Little bits of this and that. Most of them were about my mother." His forehead wrinkled. "She went through a lot of hell. Practically from the start. She married him in Russia. They were both born there. It was Russia then. Now it's Poland."

His voice was very soft. "Her name is Esther, did I tell you? His is Joseph. They're cousins; second, or maybe third, cousins. She was very pretty when she was a girl. Debby saw a picture of her at our aunt's house. A lot of men were crazy about her, but she wasn't in love with anyone." . . .

She was not in love with anyone, certainly not with her cousin Joseph. At twenty-one, life was quite exciting. She was strong and healthy, and not bad looking (the *Mima* had told her that, and the eyes of the men in town had told her, too). Having passed her apprenticeship, she was now an expert seamstress, with plenty of work. And in the evenings there were the promenades at the railroad station, arm in arm with her best friends. The daily promenade meant giggling and gossip, watching the trains puff in, and giggling again as they passed the clumps of young men with eager eyes.

But then, not a half hour would pass when Riva would nudge her and whisper, "Well, there he comes." And there would be Joseph, his book under his arm, trudging across the fields toward the station.

She had left him at home, in the corner, his book open. When she had put on her coat, the *Mima* had whispered anxiously, "Where are you going? He came to see you."

She had tossed her head, whispered back, "He came to read! I am going to promenade, what do you think? Let him read if he wants to!"

But then, not a half hour would pass and he was there, still with the book, a soft-voiced, blond young man full of silences, who had somehow fallen in love with her.

Of course, it was most flattering, even though she did not love him. He was practically engaged to another girl, a girl whose father had promised a wonderful dowry. It was the talk of the town, that dowry. He was the oldest son, the best educated, of the Widow Braunovitz, the well-to-do owner of the only bakery in the Jewish quarter. Why he had ever become interested in her nobody could understand.

A poor girl, Esther would not have even a small dowry to bring him. Her father was as poor as he was stern, a grinder of flour who had taken a second wife when Esther's mother had died in childbirth. That was the *Mima,* a little, hunchbacked woman who was called *Mamele* by all the poor Jews—"Little Mother." A woman who was so kind, so generous, so sweet, that she wept when she heard of starvation or sickness. Esther's father could not abide people, and stayed away from them, kept them away from his house. But when he went to synagogue Saturday morning, the *Mima* would tie a big apron around Esther, fill its held-up skirt with the tiny loaves of bread she had baked the day before, and whisper: "Quick, Esther, before the father comes home! Quick, run and give half to the poor widow, Rachel, and half to Cousin Sophie, who is so sick she can't move on her bed. Quick, before he comes home! Even the poor and the sick should eat on the Sabbath."

It was most flattering. He was really one of the catches of the town. Of course he never said a word, he just hung around, always with a book in his hands. He was one of the most boring people she knew. God knows why she married him. She loved to dance, for instance, but Joseph could not dance a step. She loved to talk, to be with people, but that silent man loved nothing better than to open a book, or to play an occasional game of cards. God knows why she had married him.

The *Mima* had said gently, anxiously, "You're almost twenty-two, Esther. When will you get married?"

Her father, a man with a white beard, cold eyes, a booming hoarse voice, had said, "Well, I hear a scholar is looking at you. Why, I can't even imagine! No dowry, a seamstress, a girl with a poor miller for a father. Why you're so lucky, I can't imagine." But Joseph had never said a word.

She had gone promenading that evening, had had a wonderful time, then when she had got home the candles were burning in the house. Around the table sat her father, the *Mima*, and Joseph's mother! They were all drinking tea. They were all in their good clothes.

His mother looked at Esther. She was afraid of his mother. A tall, well-built woman, always in a black silk dress, she was the talk of all the Jews. When her husband had died, she had taken over the bakery, the hiring, the supervision of the stoves, the selling. Instead of marrying again, she had proceeded to make herself wealthy, to raise five sons and a daughter, to wear silk every day. Esther was afraid of her. She wore a smooth, brown wig and her eyes were cold and blue, piercing you to the heart. She talked like a man, her voice strong and very sure, and her eyes made you feel like nothing at all.

That evening, her eyes looked you up and down. She did

165

not talk to you, but to your father. The gentle little *Mima* sat there, so tiny and crooked next to this tall, sure woman, her shy face all pinched with listening.

"Young men get strange notions," his mother said to Esther's father. "He was engaged, it was all settled. I assure you, this girl's dowry is enough to give a couple a start in life! No, all of a sudden, he does not love her! He loves Esther. He knows I do not approve. He knows, but he insists. He is my oldest son, I don't have to mention his education! He has never before said no to me, but this time it is life and death to him, he says. This is the only thing he wants. This is the only time he has ever gone against his mother's wishes. He is not marrying a dowry, he says to me. He is marrying for—love."

Esther sat in a corner. When this woman said the word love, her voice became edged like a saw. She was afraid of her. She was too strong, too sure. Esther took a deep breath. How would it be to marry that precious son of hers, right from under her nose! This woman with money and assurance, this woman in silk, with a gold watch pinned to her bosom.

"He has learned a trade," Joseph's mother said, sipping her glass of tea. "A carpenter. He will be able to support a family. He is educated, as befits the eldest son. She, can she even write her name?"

In the corner, Esther listened. No, she could not even write her name. She could dance, she could laugh, sew a fine seam, bake braided bread just like the *Mima's*, but she could not write her name.

She married him.

Within three months, she knew what her life would be. Bitter, bone poor, a matter of bed and work. Within three months, she knew Joseph. He was not gentle but weak as water. He had fought his mother for her, but having won in one thing he wanted nothing more. A wretched carpenter, he read more than he hammered. The occasional card games turned into a passion, and when he was not reading his book in a corner of their one-room house, he was off playing cards with other young men. She discovered why he did not talk to her. There was nothing small enough to say to her; he was a scholar, she an ignoramus. What language could they possibly share?

Their one common ground would always be the physical touch he needed and wanted of her. She herself got no pleasure from their bed, and expected none.

She was a strong, simple girl for all her timidity. Life was something one had to maintain, bitter or tragic as it might turn out to be. If the man could not make the daily bread, then the woman must do it.

Her sewing machine became the focal point of their one room. Two apprentices came every day to help her with her orders. In the morning, Joseph cleared out, to wherever he went, then the day became bright and busy. Within an hour she had the room scoured and scrubbed, the floor sanded. Then she pushed the big bed toward the wall, the sewing machine into the middle of the room. Then the two young, gay girls arrived, and all three settled down in the midst of the piles of new, clean-scented goods. The sewing machine chattered as Esther pumped at it with one strong foot. The young voices chattered with the machine, and she herself laughed and gossiped with the apprentices. The daily bread.

Sometimes the *Mima* came to see her, her apron full of bread, or a dish of hot food in her hands. They never discussed the marriage. She told the *Mima* when she knew she was pregnant, and the old, gentle, twisted woman burst into glad tears and kissed her all over the face and eyes. "A little child! New life!"

Yes, she was glad, too. A child would be hers, a voice in the house, a living and laughing life of her own. Her child would know how to laugh, talk; every minute of the day the baby would talk and laugh. Yes, a baby would stand between her and Joseph's mother.

For, as she soon discovered, Joseph was only a feather to be blown about by the wind of his mother's breath. Joseph was a poor imitation of that woman; poor, because though he had her cold blue eyes and her miserliness, he did not have her strength, her canniness, her knowledge of ways to make money. Her sneering laugh he had, and her cold disdain of kissing in love or in friendship, her pride in self, her way of looking at people as if they were dregs of humanity.

But even the baby was born at the beck and call of Joseph's

mother. The new little life came into a strange world far from the *Mima* and from the good and familiar things of her own life simply because that black-clad woman pointed a finger. Whatever they did, wherever they went, it was at the look and will of that wigged, man-strong mother of his. . . .

Her finger began to point after the great fire in the village. It was during this fire that Esther had her first glimpse of a Joseph she could have loved.

It was Saturday morning. Joseph was in *shule*. Esther, alone in the room, was thinking about the baby. Of course, it was months from being born, but she was thinking of it anyway. She wanted a girl, someone like herself, someone to name Sarah, after her dead mother. Suddenly, she found herself thinking of that mother. The *Mima* had known her. The *Mima* said she had been lovely, that mythical Sarah, a tall and slender girl with a soft way of laughing, a frail girl.

Then, with an abruptness that seemed to shatter the room, the whole world outside became full of shouting and confusion. Esther's heart drummed high; how could Saturday, a day of prayer, be so noisy? Then voices began to materialize out of the wild racket: "Fire, fire!"

She ran. The street flowed with running, screaming, weeping people. Over all, over everything, was the smoke, thick and black, and the smoke was coming from the direction of the slaughterhouses, at the other end of the town. Over the roofs, in the distance, she saw flames.

She ran toward the fire. She joined the crowds of mesmerized people who were watching. The fire companies were there, with their horses and wagons, and were working feverishly, but nothing could stop the fire. Esther watched one house after another catch; first the roof, then downward, sucking through the whole house.

She heard the older people whisper, "It is the devil. Look, like devil hands."

It was summertime, not a breath of wind, yet something seemed to be pulling that fire straight through the poor section of the city, the Jewish section.

Suddenly the spell was broken. People tore themselves

away, to run in the opposite direction. For a moment Esther continued to stare, listening to the screams: "My house! My furniture! My fine pillows, my dowry!" Then she caught the germ of panic, too.

"My house!" she screamed, and ran, ran straight to the one-room house. One end of the roof was burning. In she ran, to her sewing machine. That was the only thing she could think of, the only thing she wanted close to her. She swung it up on her back, the heavy machine, the bread not only for her but for the baby, swung it up without feeling the weight, and ran into the nightmare of the street.

She ran for blocks, and then when she lifted the machine to the street and leaned against it to rest, she saw the fire crawling to overtake her. Again she slung her treasure up, staggered on. She rested next in the *shule* yard, but then within minutes she felt the heat of the fire reaching into the yard after her. It was a race for life, and she knew she had to have that life just as she had to have her sewing machine. She lurched on.

She rested once more before she reached the railroad station at the other end of town, the stone station where the fire could not reach. In that moment of rest, when she had to stop until her heart could quiet, she saw Joseph running down the next street. For all her fear, it was a dream of some kind, for she saw him in that narrow street like a beautiful, godlike creature, running between the torches of houses enclosing him. He shone all over in the reflection of those torches, his hair and mustache a silvery color. She had never seen a more beautiful sight.

At that moment, he almost fell over a child who was lying in the street, screaming like a feeble, shrill whistle. Like an angel in that hell-fire, Joseph stooped, plucked the burning child up and again began to run between those lanes of fire. As he ran, he smothered the child against him, beating at the tongues of fire in the child's clothing with one hand. Then, like a silver dream, man and child disappeared.

She herself began again to run in a dazed way from the fire crawling toward her. All she knew was that the sewing machine must be taken to a safe, cool place of earth.

The city burned for two days, and the ashes smoldered for

169

almost a week, and during all that time she thought of Joseph in that silvery, heavenly light, and the way he had plucked up the burning child.

She went out into the ruins after the first fierceness of the fire had gone. She walked into the yard of Reb Israel, a teacher of Hebrew to young children, and there beheld the bitterness of life. The house was in ashes, and in the front yard, laid out neatly and sweetly, was the class he had had in his house the first morning of the fire. The bearded man lay there, and next to him the ten children of his class, all of them looking as if they were asleep. They had been stifled by the smoke. But she thought of silvery, godlike Joseph and felt comforted.

In the next yard lay a man wrapped in his prayer shawl. He had been talking to God even as the fire crawled over him, but Esther, shivering, remembered silvery Joseph running before the flames.

She went back to the Jewish cemetery, where all the homeless had gone for shelter. She sat on a tombstone, the sewing machine next to her, and all around her people sat or slept on the stones. Men wandered among these stones, calling the names of their wives, their children. Through the night, she sat on her stone, listening to the heartbreaking sound of women calling the names of their children over and over.

In the morning, Joseph found her. His hands had been burned black, he was no longer the silvery god of the fire. "Come," he said brusquely, "we'll go to my mother. She has food. She is at the stone of her father, and she wants all of us to assemble there."

He was no longer the fire god, and she followed him to the tombstone of his grandfather, the sewing machine again on her back. It was a comforting, familiar weight. . . .

It happened only two months later. Esther was now big with the child, and the city had sprung to life again, little government shacks having been built for the people.

"We are going to a place called South America," Joseph told her. "All my brothers and my sister. We are going, too."

"But why?" she cried to him.

"My mother has planned it," he said, and his eyes seemed full of misery.

170

"Our child," she said to him.

"We will be rich," he replied. "Our child, too. My mother says so. She says this is an opportunity we must not miss."

It was all very vague, very muddled and terrible to Esther. It seems that a Baron Hirsch owned all this land in a country across the world. He was offering the land for nothing to all families who desired to work the land. He was offering free journeys across the seas to such families.

What was there to do? The little *Mima* said, weeping over her as if she were already dead, "A woman goes where her husband goes."

That was true, of course. But does a man go where his mother goes?

Sarah was born in a place called the Argentine, a place where snakes came up through the earth of the kitchen floor, a place where Joseph rode on a huge, white horse, and where, gradually, after the first lost and terrible year had gone by, life assumed an idyllic wonder.

Joseph was a real carpenter in that country, riding, on the white horse, to all the little villages near by to do repair work and to build houses for the gentile people. These people were friendly, the warm sun making them laugh all the time. She herself sewed clothes for them, and was paid well for it, and in the sun little Sarah turned brown and fat. Joseph's brother Isaac was a cobbler, and made good money repairing the shoes of the gentiles. The other brothers, his sister Anna, worked Baron Hirsch's land. His mother ran the house. People laughed all the time. Joseph had a fine look in his eyes sometimes, especially when he got up on that horse. The months went by in sunlight and laughter.

Then the finger pointed again. They were going back to Russia.

"But why?" Esther asked.

"She says we have to," Joseph said. "She says we are turning into gentiles here. There is no rabbi, no kosher slaughtering. She says she cannot be responsible to God for our turning into gentiles."

They left the sun, and the little houses which finally had turned so homey and gay, and they left the prosperous carpentry and cobbling, the fertile land.

In Russia, the *Mima* kissed her home, the *Mima's* eyes became tearful and joyous over the little Sarah, but the houses were dark, the streets narrow. The sewing machine clattered again, and she had two new little giggling apprentices. Again Joseph played cards, or read silently in corners of the room. A boy, Sigmund, was born. Laughter was something she remembered after the day's work. Life became a drab, dark, narrow dream of some kind, in which she had lost one baby between Sarah and Sig, and another one after Sig. The little baby Sarah had become a pretty girl in a shabby dress, her long blond hair like Joseph's, her eyes green and mysterious and full of the laughter of that long-ago idyll. Again, Esther was pregnant.

And then the finger pointed again.

"I am going to America," Joseph told her. "My mother and Isaac, and I."

"And I?" she asked.

"I will send for you. There is money now for only three. As soon as I get work, as soon as I have money, I will send for you and the children."

He went away with the tall, wigged woman who still wore a black silk dress, the gold watch pinned to her bosom. She never seemed to change; her face seemed sterner, perhaps, but not older, not ever softer.

The dream continued. It was a dream in which she scarcely missed him; Sarah, the sewing machine, the *Mima*, these were more real in the dream than he.

In six months, the money came. "There is enough for you and the boy," the letter said. "Leave the girl with my sister. I will send money for their passage when I have saved it. Reb Joseph will get tickets for you and the boy and will make all arrangements. Here is my address. When you get to Castle Garden, show it to the officials and they will inform me you have arrived. Come as quickly as possible. A wife's place is with her husband."

She went to America; the finger was pointing to her now. Only Sarah saw her weep, and when the little girl cried, "Ma, Ma!" she kissed her and said sternly, "You will come very soon with Tante Anna. I will have candies for you, and all kinds of presents."

She left as sternly, and when the gentle, crooked little

Mima clung to her, crying, and she knew she would never see her again, her sternness deepened. Her sternness took her to the ship, kept her alive across the ocean in the throes of such sickness that she never wanted to lift her head again, took her to a place called Brooklyn, to a basement in a narrow alley called Amboy Street.

The wigged, tall woman in silk lived across the dark hallway. From the moment Esther arrived in America, she nagged Joseph. Day and night, she nagged him to send money back for their daughter. Day and night she, who had never demurred about anything, cried and talked and shouted for one thing. Then, when Sarah had come at last, she could turn to face this America.

It was like Russia, only worse. There was less money, less food, less air, less from Joseph. His mother supported them. Every morning, in silence, Esther watched the tall woman, in the dress which was shabby now, go out into the streets with her pushcart. It was heaped high with dry goods, and she pushed the heavy cart out of sight each morning except Saturday, and at dark came back with money. Even on Sunday, the American holiday, she worked. She never tired, never kissed, never smiled at a child. She brought the food into the house herself, and put it on the table, then went to wash and pray. For as long as she lived, Esther liked only one thing about the woman, her almost fantastic cleanliness. . . .

America became the real, Russia the dream, the almost forgotten childhood. America became the years of shifting scenes, the bare and bone-poor years, one flowing into the next until children were born and grew taller, older, until evening merged with day and still the work went on, until the finger pointed again, and they went from the place called Brooklyn toward the West. By that time there were three more children, and one had died soon after birth, and one she had never seen after the miscarriage. . . .

Certain years of the American life she remembered more vividly than others. They were sharp as teeth in her remembrance, sharp as the Argentinian idyll, as the fire in her home village, as those long evening promenades before the eager eyes of young men.

She remembered the first American depression through which she lived, the year Jake had been born, the same year when she had come to this America.

Depression. It was a word she learned in America; the flat, mourning, horribly meaningful English word became another tooth to bite into her memories. In Russia there had been hunger, yes, and occasional pogrom; but there had been the fields, the mill, the sewing machine, the *Mima*. In America there were the cold, stark streets, the joblessness, the grocery store where one could run up a bill, yes, but the bill of shame in facing the grocer's pitying eyes sometimes was too high to pay.

In America one had a place to live in the basement because one had taken over the job of janitor. In America one washed the hallways and stairs, three flights up, after midnight. There were two reasons for this midnight stealthy, weary scrubbing. First, one was ashamed to do such work before the families who rented the apartments, and second, at that time, no hundred feet, hundred muddy shoes, tracked dirt in even as one washed.

And he? During a depression he played cards more of the time, spoke less, read more books. An occasional job of carpentry came his way, and then he became garrulous for a brief time. He was becoming a man she not only did not love, but disliked intensely. Sometimes she even despised him; but all of it in silence, letting him embrace her in bed and not one word out of her. This was one of the things she despised most, the brief change in him when he could jangle money in his pocket; how, at such times, he boasted, how he played the man with property, how he smoked a cigar, instead of those wretched, hand-rolled cigarettes of ordinary days. But even on such days he went to the library, came back with the heavy books, the novels, the marks of a scholar, the free library books of America in their red and green bindings.

All of it she felt in silence, sometimes even a feeling of hatred for him. Vaguely, for she was a simple woman who had never thought deeply, she knew he was a failure; as a man, a husband, a father. This she never put into words. She did not know such words, even as she did not know that a woman could possibly leave her husband.

And she, his mother? Sig and Sarah now called her the *Buba*—"The Grandmother." Each day she went into the streets of New York with her pushcart. Still without love, still the stern, clean one who could tell them all what to do, who prayed before each meal, who went each Saturday morning to temple, to sit upstairs with the other wigged, old women in their black dresses. Still without a gesture, a look, a step, of love—even for her grandchildren.

Esther's day came, and her hour. She was not frightened; the coming of children had never frightened her. They came easily, and she had always gone on working to the hour, and the following day she had taken up the work where she had left it for the actual birth pangs.

This baby was coming in a different way, and she felt sad and uneasy. This baby was part of that ugly, flat word called Depression. For this baby she had not even one diaper, not one little dress. The house was clean, but not even a loaf of bread was in the box; the *Buba* would bring bread that evening, when she came back from the market of the streets, pushing the half-empty cart ahead of her with those arms and hands which had never been anything but strong. For this baby she had no midwife, not even the *Mima*, the crooked, little woman with the anxious and tender eyes.

Mrs. Greenberg, next door, Mrs. Perlman, on the floor below, both had urged her to go to a hospital to have the baby. She had not even answered them, only shaken her head. Imagine going to a hospital of one's free will, that place where they did bad things to one, from which one never came back alive!

This baby, which was coming in America, on Amboy Street, poor little baby, it did not have even one diaper. Its father was over in New York, playing pinochle with other jobless men. Its *Buba* was selling from a pushcart. And its mother?

Esther turned and looked at Sarah. The girl's quiet, mature, greenish eyes were watching her.

"Sarah," she said, feeling very tired suddenly, "go and find Pa. He's playing at Uncle Isaac's coal place on Delancey Street. Go tell him to come home, the baby is coming."

Sarah looked frightened, then she said in a very low voice, "Ma, how will I find Uncle Isaac's coal place?"

Esther dug in her shabby pocketbook, finally found the coin she had been saving. "Oh my," she cried softly, desperately, "I forgot you're a little greenie yet. Sarah, please run, please. Take the subway that's going to New York, then ask the subway man to let you off on Delancey Street. Sarah, so go already!"

Sarah ran. At the door, her mother's faint voice stopped her: "Sarah, call Mrs. Greenberg first."

And in the subway, Sarah rode to New York on a long, rumbling train of hatred. (Long after, when she was grown, she told her mother about that ride of hate. And she told her little sister Debby, too, repeating it in never-slackening hatred.) On the streets of the East Side, stumbling along among the hordes of people, stopping to ask where the coal cellar was, every step was another pang of hatred. And when she found him, when she cried breathlessly that the baby was coming, the cry was of hatred, too. By that time the baby was all mixed up with how this man had sent money for only her mother and Sig, how he had written from America: "Take the boy, leave the girl." And all the way home, perched on the seat next to him in the rushing, swaying car, watching him out of the corner of her eyes as he sat and read the Yiddish newspaper, his face stern and unmoved as usual, she hated him.

When they got home, down the steps and into the basement flat, Jake had been born. The rooms were full of smiling, loud-talking women. On the table was food, lots and lots of it; Sarah caught the look of the jammed table as she fled past it into the little dark bedroom and threw herself down on her knees next to the bed.

"Ma!" she cried.

Esther smiled at her. "He's here," she said. "Look, he's here. They brought me everything for him, diapers, little clothes from their own babies. Sarah, go find Siggie and give him something to eat. Did you see what they brought, Mrs. Greenberg, Mrs. Perlman, all our neighbors? They haven't got for themselves, but they brought us rolls, a whole chicken!"

Sarah stared at the baby, at the little, odd-looking baby. Behind her, her father came into the room, followed by the gay cries of "*Mazeltov, Mazeltov,* a boy!"

Her mother's voice, tender, happy, soft, lapped at her as she stared at the baby: "People. How wonderful people can be. It's just as my *Mima* said all her life, nothing is as wonderful as people. Look what they can do for a neighbor in such times. Look, Sarah."

Kneeling there, Sarah thought bitterly, For me it will be different. I will have a man's love and money, and my children will have clothes when they are born.

She heard her mother say in that tender, dreamy way, "Well, Joseph, we have another boy."

And years afterward, after her own children had been born, Sarah told her mother how full of hatred she had been that day, kneeling at the side of the new baby. . . .

Other things Esther remembered, but not as sharply toothed as some things. The word Depression faded from the American air, but in her it would never fade completely, she knew that. Sometimes there was a little money, and then she did not have to be a janitor any more. Sometimes there was no money, and then again the *Buba* walked into the house with packages of food, the silent, black-gowned woman whose face was beginning to line, but whose silence was deeper, whose eyes were sterner, who had taken now to sitting in the rocker and moving her lips in prayer most of the time. The scrubbed, strong hands looked splotched in the black, silken lap, but they did not shake. The face looked like wintry earth, lines cracking the strong, brown surface.

Other things Esther remembered. The baby between Jake and Roz died a month after it was born, and for the first time she was sick. She remembered with what terror she went at last to Jewish Hospital when Roz was coming, knowing she must die there, that living people would never see her again; and then the relief, the ease, the gaiety, of her stay there after the baby had come. And she remembered when Debby was born; this time she had gone so willingly to the hospital. A little, fat thing with hair like milk; and all of a sudden the plump cheek had moved, and Sarah had cried: "Ma, she smiles!"

She remembered how, three years after Debby had been born, the old, strong, splotched finger had pointed again.

"But why should we go to a place we don't know anything about?" Esther cried to her husband. "Here are our friends, our neighbors. Here is our home."

"Isaac is there a year already," Joseph said. "My mother says we should all go, it's like a new land there. Jobs for anybody in the building trade. A healthier air, trees."

"So let her go!"

"She says we should all go," he said, his eyes evading Esther's. "She says a family should be together. She went for the visit to Isaac just to see with her own eyes. There's no work here for me."

"And there?" Esther said, flushing deeply.

He shrugged. "She says there is plenty of carpentry there. She says it's like a new land."

She remembered, but gently now, as in an old dream, the tears of neighbors, the packing of cheap, sparse belongings, the lost feeling in her breast when at last the train pulled out. Beyond the windows, wherever her eyes looked, there was strangeness and lostness. In the seat opposite hers sat the old, erect woman, her lips moving soundlessly, the gold watch pinned to the bosom of the black silk dress, the wigged head high. Many more lines ran across the wintry, earthen skin that day, but strength and insistence were in the cheekbones, in the cold, blue, stern eyes.

She remembered the new city in America, the bad days, the good, the subtle yet swift growing of the children, until suddenly they were no longer children. And then there were the grandchildren, Sarah's own children; and suddenly Sig was forty, Jake was thirty-five, Roz was divorced, Debby was thirty. Debby, the baby!

But there was to remember, too, how the old, stern one had done the most inexplicable of all the strange things she had done in her lifetime. The pushcart days were long over, and the splotched hands shook now, and the wigged head shook as she sat silently moving her lips; yes, she was old now in the fullest sense of the word, but never a look of love, never a kiss, a tender move of the shaking hand, never a little present to a grandchild, a dime, a penny, of all the money she had saved. To her grandchildren she was a dark, silent, old woman who came to sit in the kitchen some days. Never did she beckon one of them to come to her, not even Debby, the baby.

And then, one day, she was gone. She packed her down comforter and pillows, her few clothes. She said good-bye in the same stern, insistent way in which she had lived, and left. Esther still remembered the feel of skin like leather, the claw-like, brief touch of hand, as the old lady offered a cheek to her, and then her hand.

"But why?" she asked Joseph. "She's so old, her sons are here, her daughter. Why?"

"She wants to die in Palestine," Joseph said. "She says it is the real home of the Jews, the only home." He was pale, his eyes red, his voice strangely muffled. "Do you know anybody who can stop her from doing anything?"

For many nights Esther dreamed of her, on the boat, alone in a chair, the lips moving, the icy eyes staring out at the water. In the dream Esther saw her sitting erect, the wigged head shaking, the splotched, immaculate hands shaking in the silken lap.

She was gone out of their lives, the finger pointing no longer, but it did not matter now. She might have been sitting still in the kitchen, or walking slowly from synagogue to house on a Saturday, or sitting opposite her son at the kitchen table, both of them sipping the dark, unsweetened tea from the thin glasses. She was gone, but her icy look remained in Joseph's eyes, her silence lay in his throat, her stinginess with money and with love clotted his veins.

Word came within a year that she had died, and Joseph went to *shule*. When he came home his eyes were red, and he looked old, and she noticed suddenly that his hair was quite gray; and then, of course, always after that, he lit the year-time candle in memory of her death. But not one grandchild mourned her, for not one had ever known her, or could remember a kiss or a caressing word.

And, gradually, Esther stopped thinking of her, though the tooth of memory remained, the sharp and bitter thing of memory to come out and bite sometimes when Joseph laughed, or when he turned his back, or that time when Debby had screamed out at him. That was a time for the tooth to bite! When Debby had screamed she didn't want such a father, then had run crying from the house; then, at that moment, she had thought of the old woman. So clear, as if she stood in the kitchen, her stern eyes on all of them, her silence and icy coldness wrapping them like a shroud! . . .

She remembered the time when the word Depression came out of the air again, out of her heart where she had hid it so long ago. The flat, terrible American word; and now the children were grown, she was old and tired, Joseph was sick. Again came that American word, and soon she learned other flat, stark words to go with it, words like eviction, relief, WPA.

Never would she forget that one night when all of the harsh and meaningless years came up in a wave out of the American sea to drown her. Yes, she was a dumb woman, as Joseph said so often, but would a smart woman, or man for that matter, find it possible to explain such a thing? Explain the bitterness and futility of life, and how the culmination was simply more bitterness, saltier tears, a futility so empty that one was left absolutely alone in the heart? Husband, children, memories, all were washed away by that wave, and one was left in a corner of the deepest, darkest shore of life, flung and lost there, more alone in this moment than at any time in the lonely years.

Yes, that night would always bite in the memory, not like a tooth but like a small, terrible animal.

It must have been close to midnight when the knocking came. Somebody was on the front porch, a heavy hand crashing on the door, behind the hand the weight of a heavy body.

Esther woke out of the deep and troubled sleep in which she had hid an hour or so earlier, to hear that awful sound. In that moment of waking, she thought for a terrible instant of the word pogrom, like a nightmare catapulting of her senses into childhood.

She called out, her terror automatically focusing on the familiar name, "Debby, Debby! What's the matter there? It's so late, Debby, what is happening?"

From the living room, where she slept on the couch, Debby called back soothingly, "Nothing, Ma. I'm going. It's nothing, I tell you. Stay in bed, Ma."

Then Esther heard Debby stumbling about in the dark, muttering, "Goddam, Goddam."

She can't even turn on the light, Esther thought painfully, suddenly remembering.

Joseph groaned from the other bed, awakening. (Yes, she had finally prevailed upon him to bring in two beds, for which he had paid practically nothing. "You will be more comfortable with your sciatica," she had told him. He had bought them with a load of old clothes. Yes, and now she could sleep alone!)

"Esther, what is it?" he wanted to know. "What's happening?"

The bedsprings, under his thrashing body, were like a sound of wind blowing upon rust. For years now he had slept noisily, groaning in his sleep, awakening with a half moan on his lips. It must be that he dreamed bad things, she thought.

"Sh, sh," she said as automatically as she had called Debby. "Maybe it is the city doctor to examine you. He was so busy yesterday and today, they said; maybe he finally came."

She struggled out of the bed, her backache immediately recalling her to the daily feelings of life. The floor was icy, and a long list of things immediately wrote themselves on her awakening mind: almost out of coal, they turned off the electricity and if it's the relief doctor how will I look in his eyes for shame, my dear God I hope Sig and Jake aren't home yet, Jake'll holler after the doctor goes, he always hollers when there's trouble, my dear God how cold it is, Jake doesn't know yet that the company turned off the lights, I was afraid to ask him for more money, what will he say?

In the darkness, she ran to the closet, groped for the first thing she could reach. It was a coat of some kind, and she wrapped it around her, found her old bedroom slippers. As she hurried into the hallway and toward the kitchen for a candle, she heard Debby unlock and open the front door.

"Just a minute," Debby shouted, and then the bangs stopped.

Esther scurried into the chill of the living room, her left hand cupped round the candle flame. There was a heavy, tramping sound on the porch just outside the door, and the thin channel of yellow from a flashlight, the feel of snow, the sound of it, crunching and thick-fallen, beneath a man's heavy boots.

She peered around the corner of the small hallway in which Debby stood, heard her stammer, "What is it? What do you want?"

The man on the porch was dressed in a heavy coat, galoshes, gloves, a thick cap pulled over his face. Behind him, off the porch, the snow fell soft and thick as feathers upon the street and upon the man's automobile, which stood at the curb, its motor running, its lamps making two roadways in which the snow looked yellow.

The flashlight came up in his hand, and the thin, yellow light came into Debby's face.

"Special delivery," the man said. "Hey, you know your bell don't work." He had a warm, cheerful voice, and the whole thing—bundled man, thick snow falling, the soft, muffled night outside the door—reminded Esther of the Russian winter.

"Special delivery for Joseph Brown and Esther Brown. Sign here, please."

Debby said, "All right, you'd better come into the hall here. It's pretty cold." Her voice sounded frozen and stiff, as if she were angry, and Esther began to shiver, as if the snow were falling on her.

The man came into the little hallway. Esther noticed then that Debby's feet were bare, that she was wearing one of Jake's old coats.

"Yes, ma'am," the man said pleasantly, "it sure is cold. Paper says it'll be eight below by morning. My car froze up twice a couple of hours back. It's not so cold now though, started to snow a while back."

Ah, why are you talking so much? Esther thought in an agony. Leave her alone, she wants to cry, you can tell when she sounds angry Debby wants to cry.

Behind her, a ghost voice in the house, Joseph called dismally, "Who is it? Esther, Debby, you'll tell me what's the matter!"

"It's my father," Debby's frozen voice said, and then she turned and smiled at Esther, standing shivering behind the candle.

"Debby," Esther said hesitantly.

"It's only a special delivery, Ma," Debby said, and she smiled, smoothing the shaking hand that held the candle. She took the candle into her own hand.

"Debby, Esther! You won't tell me what's the matter?" He was a ghost lying in a back bedroom, his legs stiff. She herself was a ghost, mouth and cheeks fallen in, an infant ghost; she felt like Debby must be her mother at this moment, mother to her and to that squalling man back there in the bedroom.

"Quick," Debby said, thrusting the candle between the man and herself. "Let me sign. Quick, it's so cold."

"Haven't you got a light in the hall?" he said. "You can't hardly see where to sign. Here, can you see by the flash?"

Esther took a deep breath, a hand squeezed her heart at the mention of the lights, but then Debby said coldly, "I can see, all right. Give me the pencil, will you?"

Leave us alone, Esther thought painfully.

"All right," Debby said quickly. "Thank you very much. Good-by."

She took the two white, long envelopes, and the man said cheerfully, "Well, good-by."

"Good-by," Esther said gently. In America, she thought, everything is done with a smile, with a please, with a thank you.

Debby shut and locked the door, turned to face her mother. In the candlelight, she looked like a slim, tall, gentile boy in a borrowed coat. Her eyes were very bright, and Esther shrank back.

"It's so cold," she said softly to that bright look. "Maybe the relief will send another ton of coal soon. We have only two or three lumps left. But they're big lumps."

Debby did not say a word. She marched through the rooms into the kitchen, and Esther padded after the candlelight.

"Well," Joseph demanded from his bed as he heard their steps, "who is it? Maybe the relief sent me the doctor they promised? Twelve o'clock at night!"

"It's from the bank," Debby said, her voice very low. She was making the candle stand in a saucer, dropping hot wax first and then pressing the candle on the melted wax.

"The bank," Esther said faintly.

"The bank!" Joseph shouted. "So, at last! Twelve o'clock at night the bank sends us special deliveries! Robbers, murderers! So this is big business, hah?"

Esther heard him thrashing about in the bed, and soon he came hobbling into the candlelight, his face gray, his white hair awry. One hand clutched the beltless trousers to his thin belly, the other hand attempted to light the thick cigarette he had rolled for himself.

He saw the letters, picked them up as if they were poison laid out fresh on the table. In the candlelight, his eyes squinted and his lips moved. "Mr.—Joseph—Brown. Ha, me! Mister, just like a real person. Hah! This is what comes of owning property in America. With your wife you own a house! Something happens, you can't pay taxes, and you have to leave your property to them. Special deliveries! In America, they send you special deliveries to tell you it is not your property any more!"

He glared at his daughter, his thin, shrunken face twitching. His mustache seemed too large for his face suddenly, and Esther saw how Debby was staring at nothing, nothing at all.

"Thirty-two years in America," he said, and Esther saw Debby's fists clench. "I used to make sixty dollars a week. A better carpenter was hard to find in the whole city. When the union wanted a carpenter, Gold would go down on his knees to me. I didn't have enough hands for the jobs they wanted me to do."

He sighed, his body sagged. "Thirty-two years in America."

Esther began to weep softly, her hands over her face. She heard Debby rustling the letters.

"Well?" Joseph said. "Read them already!"

"They're both the same," Debby said, in that queer, frozen voice. "You are hereby notified that you must vacate said premises by Monday, December fifteenth, or—."

"Or, or!" Joseph shouted. "Or your furniture will lie on the sidewalk like corpses. Hah? That's what it says? They should do this to people, God in heaven! How can it be?"

"Ten years we lived in our own house," Esther whispered. Nothing was real. The candle was burnt halfway down. Debby stood like a white, frozen little boy. Joseph leaned against the table, a man who looked like his own father.

Nothing was real, only the sadness, the tears, the bewilderment of life. Russia was the dream of childhood and young, strong womanhood, Argentina the brief dream of sun and laughter, the white horses galloping by, bearing young, laughing men.

What was real? Sig, the eldest son? Was it real that he was old, balding, his forehead lined with worry, jobless, he who had supported the house for so many years? Was Jake real, the silent son who smelled of whisky sometimes, who hollered sometimes, who so rarely came home? Was Roz real? Roz, of whom she was sometimes afraid to think because of that life she led? Sarah and her family; that was realness, eh? How Sarah was sunk in poorness, how Max cared about nothing these days, dressed like a bum, not even shaving, how the children cursed and fought, and Sarah and Max cursed them in turn. Debby, was she real? A strange one, different from all of them, as if she had wandered into this house, with her books, with her pencils and paper. To be a little afraid of, but to cling to, the strange, strange Debby who always knew what to do.

Joseph? One does not even think of him. What does he know? Just his own self, his own glass of tea, his own little bit of food on a plate, how to put an extra dollar in his pocket and not take it out if one died for it. A man who was a faded replica of his mother. Turn the coin: on one side, the stern, unsmiling face of the *Buba*, on the other side the cold, selfish resemblance of his face, but faded dim, a shadow of her face.

"Debby," Esther said hesitantly again.

Debby took up the candle. "Let's go to bed," she said quietly. "We'll figure it out tomorrow. Let's go to sleep now. There's nothing we can do now anyway. Come on."

Esther followed Joseph to the bedroom. Debby walked them to the door, holding the candle up high so that they could see.

When Esther turned, at the bedroom door, there was a little crooked smile on Debby's face. "We'll fix it up tomorrow, Ma," she said. "You go to sleep, hear me?"

"I hear you," Esther said, and went to her bed.

From the other bed, Joseph muttered, "This is what they do to people."

Esther buried her face in the pillow. Only the cold was real. Only the aching, bloodcurdling cold; nothing else was real. . . .

185

Jake opened his eyes, looked dazedly at the doctor. "I'd like to have taken pictures of those people. They'd make real art. That grandmother of mine, my God. The old man riding that white horse. My mother getting off the ship with Sig, looking around at the new country, scared to death but not showing it."

Across the desk, the quiet eyes watched him.

"My mother washing those steps after midnight," Jake said uneasily. "Some picture! And what about all those neighbors who brought the diapers for me? A whole chicken, rolls. I'd take the picture way back of the bed, shoot into the room where they were all laughing and gabbing. Get one of the bed and my mother and the baby, too, the old man walking in. They would have made some pictures, all right."

"You'd take pictures of your father? Hating him the way you do?"

Jake flushed. "Hating him? He's kind of a pitiful guy, isn't he? It's like he never got used to anything, being married, or coming to this country, or—us. Us kids, I mean. For all I know, he never got used to my mother. Whatever the old lady said, he did. He's somebody you can feel kind of sorry for."

The doctor tapped his pen lightly against the notebook. "One doesn't hate anyone for whom he feels sorry."

"Well, I mean," Jake stumbled on, "you hate somebody who makes trouble deliberately. That poor sap just didn't know how to do anything. He was so busy following his mother's finger he couldn't see his own wife, or his kids. See what I mean?"

"No," the doctor said. "Can you make it a little clearer?"

Jake hunched up at the edge of his chair. The words came with difficulty. "Well look, the old man—and my mother—they were sort of a wasteland, too. She married him even though she didn't love him. They went to South America just because the *Buba* said it was a good idea. Then they went back for the same reason. Then, when she wanted it, he went to America. I mean, he never did anything because he thought it was a good idea. Neither did my mother."

"They were directed by others," the doctor said. "Is that what you mean? Everything they did was forced on them, either by a strong person or by economic necessity. Everything?"

"He married her," Jake said slowly. "Guess that was the only thing."

"You call their lives a wasteland," the doctor said. "Do you see anything at all admirable in those lives?"

"Admirable?"

"Yes. For example, did it take courage for those people to go to a strange land, to uproot all their ties, to leave friends and family? Did it take courage and faith for your mother to follow your father to one strange land after another?"

"Faith," Jake said in a low voice.

"Wouldn't you call it faith? In her husband, perhaps in the future, in life?"

"You could call it that, maybe." Jake's forehead wrinkled. "I was thinking. I keep wondering if our Seders would've been any different if the *Buba* had been there."

"Different?"

"Yeah. I mean, if she had sat across the table from my father. Maybe those Seders wouldn't have been so—meaningless. She was such a strong old dame. Anything she wanted, she got."

"So strong that she would have strengthened Judaism for you?" the doctor asked softly. "So strong that she would have made you forget that you despise your father, your name, your ancestors, your race?"

Jake looked up quickly, fiercely. "She was stronger than my father! She wasn't a failure. She even died where she wanted to, even if she had to die alone. Catch the old man doing that! He calls himself a Jew, but if he had a chance to make money on Saturday he'd do it like a shot—if nobody saw him doing it."

"She was honest about her belief, is that it?"

"Sure. She might have been an old witch about a lot of things, but you never saw her being a hypocrite about her religion."

"Do you feel better able to be a Jew because she was?" the doctor asked. "She was a strong, dominant woman, not a failure. Does knowing that make you feel better about your family?"

"Nuts," Jake said. "Look what she did to my mother. To him. She took their whole lives."

"And the lives of her grandchildren? Her great-grandchildren?"

"Well, she probably helped!" Jake said defiantly.

"And is it your fault that she made life miserable for your mother? That she helped make a weakling out of your father?"

"My fault!"

"Do you have to pay your grandmother's debt to your mother, as well as your father's debt to her?" the doctor continued smoothly.

"I don't get it."

"Your grandmother was a material reason for your mother's unfulfilled life, wasn't she? She was another wall between your mother and social and sexual satisfaction, wasn't she? She herself, in addition to her constant influence over your father. In other words, she took from your mother, she owed your mother much that she never repaid. Are you attempting to pay that debt to your mother?"

Jake lit a cigarette, his hands trembling. "I hadn't thought of that."

"Then do think of it. Is there any need for you to assume such debts?"

"No."

"Could you, simply by assuming them, ever hope to pay them?"

"No." He began to cry softly, sitting hunched over his cigarette.

"What is it?" the doctor asked after a few moments.

"How a guy gets tangled up inside," Jake muttered. He smashed out the cigarette, blew his nose. "Even if I wanted to make up for all those years, I couldn't give them back to her."

"Your mother?"

"Yeah. Every time I think of her scrubbing those steps, so terribly ashamed, afraid somebody would come into the hall and see her!"

"Jake Brown's sin?"

"No, no! I know it wasn't my fault! But Jesus, I can't stand to think of it. I want to go back there and scrub those steps myself—instead of her doing it."

"But you can't, can you? What can you do instead?"

Jake stared at him through reddened eyes.

"Can you try to understand?" the doctor prompted him softly. "Can you try to understand her need through the years, why it was not answered, why it is you can never hope to answer it now?"

"Yeah," Jake said doubtfully.

"Your father's failure is not yours, is it?"

"No," Jake said uneasily.

"What's bothering you? Do you want to tell me about it?" The doctor pushed the cigarette box closer to him.

Jake lit a cigarette, squinted a look of misery across the broad desk. "I was wondering if—. You know, my birthday this year is the same day as the first Seder."

"Yes?" the doctor prompted.

"I was wondering if I should come home for it."

"For your birthday?"

"For the Seder!" He dragged on the cigarette. "I told you, for the last five years I haven't been coming home for the Seder."

"What made you stop?"

"I don't know. Maybe I got sick and tired of just sitting there."

"That's fine," the doctor said casually. "Then it doesn't bother you any more, I suppose."

"But it does," Jake cried quickly. In an odd way, he felt betrayed. "You know it bothers me," he shouted. "It's not only that I swore I'd never eat with them. Hell, I came back to the Seder a few times after I swore not to—not that it meant anything."

"It meant nothing?"

"I just sat there. Like I was pretending not to be there. Sometimes it worked."

He reached for another cigarette, lit it with a sharp, restless motion from the end of the one he had been smoking. "I'll tell you something. For the last five years, every first Seder night I've gone out and got drunk. Stinking drunk."

He took several quick, deep drags at the cigarette. "I feel bad that night. There's no reason to go home, yet I keep thinking it's Seder time." His voice lowered. "Time to ask the questions. So I get drunk."

"What was that Seder like?" the doctor asked. "The last one at which you asked the questions. Do you remember it clearly?"

Jake's lips tightened. "I'll say I remember it! Debby, mostly. I keep remembering her eyes. Jesus, I never wanted to go back to that table and sit across from her eyes again."

He rubbed his forehead, shaded his eyes as he hunched deeper into the chair. "Let's see, when was that? Last five years I didn't even go home. To hear it, or smell it."

He looked up, his eyes wistful. "You know, you can smell Passover in the house. It's a good smell. Clean, different. It reminds you spring is coming. Everything's been washed, everything smells new."

Again he rubbed his forehead, the skin wrinkling into anxious lines under his fingers. "Yeah, I remember. Six years ago, I came home pretty soused. I stayed in my room that night and got drunker. The year before that, Sig asked the questions."

"You stayed away that year?"

Jake's eyes were full of misery. "No," he said slowly. "I came home early and ate right away, before the rest of them got there. I meant to leave, but I just stayed in my room. I—I heard Sig ask the questions. After that, after I heard him, I just had to beat it. I told them I had to go back to work. Guess they believed me. Nobody said anything."

He sat back in the chair, smoking, a bemused look on his face as he remembered.

"Guess I was almost twenty-eight last time I sat at the table and asked the questions," he said at last. "I haven't thought about that night for a long time. Not till today."

"Would you like to tell me about it?" the doctor asked.

"Yeah, I think I would," Jake said. "You see, I sat there and told myself I was bored. I told myself there'd be a good supper, so I might as well sit through the Seder business and then eat. I'd brought a final home with me. . ."

. . . and he sat there in his usual place, reading the folded paper. The *Haggadah* was open at the questions, and lay on the table ready for the moment of asking.

He had nodded at Roz when she came in, had mumbled to Deborah when she arrived from work. Sig had not come home.

"He's invited for the Seder to a friend's house," his mother had told Jake with a smile. "He told me yesterday. This friend lives in the Heights. It'll be a real fancy Seder."

Not like here, Jake thought coldly, with a small pang of fury. She means, fancy not like here. That fancy brother of mine!

He sat opposite Deborah and read the sports page, seeing out of the corner of one eye the big, shabby book open in front of his father. The room was full of the old man's chanting, mournful voice as it half sang page after page of the Hebrew. The sound seemed vague to Jake, a comfortable background; and now and again he heard his mother and Roz whispering at the far end of the table.

The odor of the wine hovered on this background of chant, and Jake idly lifted his glass every once in a while to sip from it. In this same idle way, it occurred to him that he was drinking out of turn, that heretofore he had always watched his father carefully and had sipped when he did, cast out the symbolical plagues by flicking his smallest finger over the glass when his father dipped his finger.

So what? he thought casually; and, surreptitiously, he watched Deborah's hand tip the wine bottle and fill his glass each time it was half empty.

Go ahead, go ahead, he thought with a tinge of amusement. Pretend like we're all doing the right thing. I know the glasses are supposed to be kept filled, but if you think I'm going to wait till he drinks, you're just crazy.

He broke off and munched bits of a matzoth out of turn, too, washing down the dry crumbs with wine. He had finished the sports page, and had turned the paper, with quite a crackle of pages, to the amusement section, when his father said: "All right, Jake, it's time to ask."

Dropping the paper to the floor, Jake picked up the *Haggadah*. He read quickly, with no expression, slurring over the words.

"Wherefore is this night distinguished from all other nights? Any other night we may eat either leavened or unleavened bread, but on this night only unleavened bread; all other nights we may eat any species of herbs, but this night only bitter herbs; all other nights we do not dip even once, but on this night twice; all other nights we eat and drink either sitting or reclined, but on this night we all of us recline."

Having flung out the words, he closed the *Haggadah* and tossed it to the table. Then, as his father's voice again took up the Hebrew, Jake looked across the table. The look in Deborah's eyes slapped his face. He met her eyes for only a moment, then looked at his wineglass, and for the next ten minutes or so kept his eyes fastened on the red color, but the moment had been enough.

Choked and flushed, he tried to figure out what her look had meant. It was troubled, her eyes very grave and inquiring. For some reason, which he fought hotly, he felt as if she were condemning him. But for what, damn it? Does she expect me to sit here like a good Jewish son, swallowing all this hypocritical gush the old man is praying?

He wanted very much to look up again, to see if her eyes were still the same, but he could not. Finally he turned his head stiffly and looked toward Roz and his mother.

Roz was turning her wineglass slowly with one hand. The electric lights above the table sparkled on her rings and jeweled wrist watch, and on her dark-red fingernails. He stared at her expertly made-up face, her elaborate hair style. She was looking dreamily into the wineglass as she turned it, and he was surprised at the soft look of her mouth, the absent smile in her eyes.

Looking back at his own wineglass, he thought confusedly, Maybe the Seder means something to her.

His father's voice seemed to rise, swell. No longer was it a vague, comfortable background upon which he could loll; a note of threat, dark, mournful, foreboding, seemed now to ring through it. He wanted to look up; he knew Deborah's eyes would be like that, the blue dark and mournful, the look of a finger pointing straight at him. His insides quavered.

Suddenly he mumbled, "Be right back," and fled to his bedroom. Quickly he got the bottle off the closet shelf, drank two long gulps, then leaned breathlessly against the wall.

Into the room came his father's voice, dark and sad as tears, the singing, foreboding prayers and the accusation of Deborah's eyes. He could not go back to those eyes.

After a while, he did not know how long after he had drunk, his mother called, "Jake. Jake, we're going to eat now."

"I'll be right there," he called back, and quickly took one more drink.

Then he went back to the table. Inside, he felt as if he were crawling.

. . . and though alcoholism has been an escape mechanism for S on several counts, he has begun to say: "I used to have to take a couple of drinks before I could do it, but guess I don't have to now."

192

Just as he can talk now without first having to blot out shame by drinking, S will soon be able to face "the look in Debby's eyes" without first having to be fortified by drink.

Not only is he jealous of Deborah but, and this is much stronger, he has a deep feeling of guilt where she is concerned. He has failed her as a brother. He has not been the strong older brother to a young sister. This failure identifies him with his father; it is another masculine failure within the family.

Not only does Deborah steal from him what belongs to men but he has, all along, stolen from her what belongs to her—the possibility of being a girl, a daughter, a sister. He has forced her into the position of son. This makes up a great part of his feeling of guilt; he has helped make her a Lesbian.

The shrinking of S from Katherine is part of this masculine failure he feels. In his mind, he has failed all women, having failed his mother and then his sister. He hasn't the right morally to lie with Katherine, just as he hadn't the right to be Laura's lover, because his relationship with his mother is not normal. S is still tied with the umbilical cord; normal intercourse with women will be impossible until he cuts the cord.

His unwillingness to face the significance of the Passover and Seder ritual, an ever-recurring pattern, also has forced an escape. This pattern is tied in his mind to the pattern of his family, each generation repeating itself (like the yearly Seder) in a new generation of wasteland.

At the same time, S is unable to leave these traditions in his mind, even after he has left them physically, because he feels a strong, groping urge for roots, for the stable cultural, racial, social roots of a people. He is eager to ally himself with the Jews, a people with so strong and permanent a past that surely their future will hew to the same lines.

His sister Deborah had the same fierce clinging to tradition, the same nostalgic desire to observe holidays "just like all other Jews do." Deborah's attempts to cling to the faith and strength of her ancestors (within the hostile, unstable world she knew) were even deeper than these attempts of S now. She would never have children, never be able to perpetuate herself in them; her pepetuation would have to be through association rather than through blood: her association with her undying people, with their capacity to live despite persecution and

193

hardship, with their capacity to live in the troublous present and into the mysterious future; ergo, she, as part of such a people, would live on, too.

S thinks he does not want children. His present struggle to establish his identity, however, is deeper and more honest because of the unacknowledged possibility of progeny. His own suffering, preceding the similar experiences of his nephews, makes him unwilling to face the idea of progeny. He is afraid of the continued perpetuation of "wasteland," and yet he now tries courageously to discover the truth of that condition, the source of it, perhaps the cure. . . .

Six

The walls of Saturday moved in on him with a combined pressure of fear and relief, the walls of a confessional. And yet these walls were different, too, pressing as they did ever closer toward him. Instead of the soft voice of humility and forgiveness, there were the eyes of the doctor wherever he looked; from wall, from ceiling, from floor, came that patient, impersonal, yet merciless glance. Instead of a voice: "I forgive you, my son," there were the eyes which never spoke of forgiveness, nor the need of it, only of honesty, only of truth without shame, admittance without fear. And though always he was afraid before the actual moment came to uncover, to bring out the choked, clogged emotions and hidden thoughts, always the feeling of relief afterward was like the hour after sickness, like the moment after the horrifying dream has ended.

Within these walls today, the doctor asked, "What would you like to talk about?"

The fear began to bang in Jake's breast, and a hundred flying, crafty tangents caught on his tongue to obscure the one thing about which he should talk today. He felt excited and afraid at once, a feeling similar to the ones he had experienced many times in childhood when he had lied to his father or had fled from the kitchen silently, leaving his mother there with the job he should have done.

"I was thinking of that wasteland business," he said, his eyes on the cigarette box. "How it started way back in Russia, and then hit us here, and how it's working on the kids now. What do you call that, the sins of the fathers, or something?"

"Do you ever read the Bible?" the doctor asked.

Jake looked up, startled, and found the friendly, impersonal smile at the end of the desk "Me? Of course not. Why should I read the Bible?"

"Some people read it for the beauty of the words," the doctor said quietly, "if not for the religious content."

A bitter thought twisted Jake's mouth. "Yeah! My sister reads it sometimes. She's got one. One of those soft leather things."

"You know what books she owns?"

Jake reddened. "She's so damn brainy! I used to look over her books to see what kind of books a person like that reads."

"You mention the sins of the fathers. Did you ever open her Bible, read a few pages?"

Jake clutched at the cigarette box. The doctor struck a match, held it for him, and as Jake lit his cigarette he looked up into the obdurate eyes.

"What do you want me to say?" he muttered savagely.

"Whatever you need to say."

"Why should Debby have a Bible?" Jake burst out, the crafty plans at concealment falling from his mind and leaving him naked again. "Why should a person like that read the Bible? It's like she—she's trying to kid the world!"

"Kid the world? In what way?"

"What do you mean, in what way! Who reads Bibles, anyway? Religious people. Normal, decent people. Good people." Jake tried to smoke, but his lips were shaking so hard he could not grip the end of the cigarette. "She doesn't have to try and kid me! She's full of that wasteland stuff, too. She's no different than the rest of us."

He managed to take a deep drag of the cigarette, then he pressed it against the ashtray.

"What has Deborah done to you?" the doctor said. "Do you want to talk about it?"

"She hasn't done anything special. It's just that she needn't think she's so much better than the rest of us. Just because of that music and writing of hers. A Bible. Does she think reading a Bible and writing stories are going to make her life any better than ours?"

"What has she done to you?" the doctor repeated quietly.

Jake flushed again. "She stole from me, that's what! At least the rest of the family doesn't steal. Maybe the kids do. I don't know! But the rest of us—. Hell, we're dirty, we're low-down Jews, we monkey around in night clubs and get drunk, we're— failures, all right! But we don't steal."

"What did she steal from you?"

"The questions. She took them away from me."

"The what?"

"The questions. The Seder questions. You want to know so much about the Passover and me. Well, I haven't told you that yet!"

The accusation died out of his eyes suddenly, and the fear took over. He felt as if he had done something wrong, shameful, and that the watching eyes were unmasking him.

"You don't like it that Deborah stole," the doctor said. "The one person who was clean and brave in the house of wasteland. Is that it? The one person in the family who was decent, and now you have to put into words the fact that she is a thief. Is that it?"

Jake stared at him.

The soft, steady voice went on, pinning him down to not the obscure fear, the hidden shame, but the words he had known he would have to say sooner or later.

"You don't want her to be a thief, do you? You don't want that clean, intelligent sister of yours to be connected with the family wasteland. How can you stand it, you ask yourself, if the only good part of the family turns out to be—bad. How can the family be dragged out of wasteland, you ask yourself, if their only hope, their only strength, turns out to be half buried in the same wasteland. Is that it?"

Jake's eyes, straining toward the doctor's, burned. A confused, struggling babble of voices, remnants of words, flowed through him, as if, inside himself, he were trying at once to absorb the doctor's words and answer them.

197

"She pushed me away from the table," he said sullenly. Then his voice rose. "She took what belonged to me. A girl. Jesus, what kind of a man am I that a girl can take my place at the Seder! Those questions should be asked by the youngest son present that night! The Goddam *Haggadah* says so. Jesus, it's like the Bible says so, isn't it? And all of a sudden she's reading the questions!"

"A girl takes the place of the son," the doctor said. "She steals the place of the son in the family. How can the son trust her? Ask her for help? Already, he is weaker than she, even without this latest insult. He knows how weak his own father is, too, and now he himself is unable to be anything but weak. What shall he do? Must he hate this sister? Must he be jealous of her, afraid of her? She could help him. With her strength, with her poetry and music, but how can he go to her after she has stolen from him? What if she steals the last remaining bits of maleness from him? Then what would happen? Must he always hate her now?"

Jake mumbled, "Hate. Maybe it's just jealousy. I don't want to hate her. She's so wonderful. She's all we've got in the house."

When he looked up, his eyes were filled with tears. "She got me to come to you. She helps me. When I think of her sometimes, it helps me. Just thinking of her. But she'd done that to me! It's hard for me to be with her because I keep thinking of how she stole that from me. I've tried to forget it. Sometimes I don't think of it. But now I've got to. You've made it so I've got to think of all those things. What am I supposed to do?"

"You're supposed to get it out of your mind, out into the open where you can examine it. Now, when did it happen? When did she steal from you?"

"Five years ago. I never came home for the Seder after that. How the hell could any man come back after a thing like that!"

"Did you sit at the table that night?"

"No," Jake said, his voice uneasy. "I came home drunk. I ate early and went right to my bedroom. I didn't go out to the table for the Seder."

"What made you get drunk?"

Jake looked at him indignantly. "I knew the Seder would be lousy. You know why I got drunk! I didn't want to sit there listening to the old man go through that rigamarole. And watch Sig and Roz just sit there."

"Did you want particularly to face Deborah at the table?" the doctor asked.

"I didn't think about Deborah when I got drunk," Jake asserted.

"You didn't? You had forgotten so completely the Seder of the year before, when her eyes made you leave the table?"

"I'm sure I wasn't thinking of her," Jake insisted.

"Well then, you got drunk. But you went home anyway. Why was that? Why haven't you gone home these past five years for the Seder?"

"She's kept me away! Ever since that night when she stole the questions. How could anybody expect me to go back? She took my place, didn't she?"

"But why did you go home that night?" the doctor asked again.

"Because of her," Jake admitted reluctantly. "I kept drinking and drinking, but I kept thinking of her along with every drink."

"Of Deborah?"

"Yeah. Of how her eyes get sometimes. When you can't stand looking into them, they're so—well, you feel as if you're acting lowdown, not like a person should be acting."

"That was the way her eyes looked at the Seder when you left the table," the doctor reminded him softly. "The Seder you described last Saturday."

Jake looked at him.

"So you drank more and more in order not to go home for the Seder," the doctor went on, "but all the time you kept remembering the way Deborah had looked at you during the ceremony the preceding year. So you went home after all?"

"Yeah," Jake said, his eyes dazed. "Sig didn't come home at all that evening. I figured maybe he wouldn't. I ate right away when I came home. Told my mother I was hungry. She didn't even ask me if I wanted to wait for the Seder."

"That hurt you?"

"Oh hell, I didn't care! But she might have just mentioned it!"

"She was not in the habit of questioning your actions, was she? Why should she have asked you that time?"

"Because it was Passover, that's why! She's my mother, isn't she? She acted as if she didn't even care whether I did or not."

He was silent at that.

After a moment, the doctor said, "You know that's not so."

"Yeah, I know it," Jake muttered.

After another moment, the doctor's voice reached out at him. "You ate as soon as you got home."

"Yeah. The whole works, the whole Seder supper, only I ate it alone in the kitchen. Fish, chicken, soup, matzoth, stewed fruit. I even drank three glasses of wine." He went on doggedly, miserably. "Everything was clean. My mother had her good dress on, an apron over it. She didn't say a word, just served me. I didn't talk to her either once I'd said I was hungry. Everything tasted wonderful. The worse I felt, the better each course seemed to taste. It had been a year since I'd had matzoth. I remember the dishes, white with a red-and-blue flower. I hadn't seen them since last Passover, when my mother had packed them away after the holiday ended. . ."

. . . and they'd been on the top shelves of the cupboard all year, but now they had been taken down for the days of the holiday. Seeing them, he felt a fresh spurt of nostalgia, sad and yearning, to go with the Passover odors in the house, to go with the empty, lost desire for birthday, for spring, for the sharing with many people of the laughter and hope which were so many thousands of years old and strong.

Jake stared at the matzoth crumbs on the white tablecloth, at the empty wineglass, then pushed his chair back and walked out of the kitchen. His mother was standing in the shadows near the stove, and neither of them had switched on the light, so that the kitchen was full of the dusk seeping in through the two windows. He walked slowly and stiffly, in order not to stagger, and he wondered if she had smelled his breath when she had stooped over the table to serve him. But this usual small fear was not as strong as his resentment. Why didn't she ask me? he thought. Doesn't she even want me at the Seder?

As he walked into the hallway that led to the bedrooms, he caught a glimpse of the dining room table. It was set, and in the shadowy room he saw the wineglass at each place, the pillow on the old man's chair, the dish with the herbs, the egg, the bone. A *Haggadah* had been placed at the chair in which he usually sat.

He wanted to cry as he turned from the table and stumbled down the hallway. It was too lonely. Everything was too lonely. They filled a glass for the Messiah at the table, and at one point they opened the door and invited him in to drink the wine, but their own son, they kept him from the table.

In his room, he went immediately to the closet and took down the bottle. He left the door ajar; he knew that he wanted to hear every word, every footstep, he wanted things to come mournfully and bitterly into this room.

Sitting on the edge of the bed, he drank from the bottle, his ears straining for the first holiday sounds. He heard them between gulps, on the blurred back of the hot wave of drunkenness washing over him again. Roz came, and he heard the exchanged laughter and words, the rattle of dishes, the new note of excitement Roz always brought to his mother's voice.

The old man came, and his deep, monotonous voice joined the quick, shrill voices. Sig did not come. Deborah came home from work. The water ran in the bathroom. Roz's high heels made a quick, feminine clatter on the kitchen floor, and Deborah's voice, slow, tired, mobile, sauntered into the bedroom and up to the bed, and Jake flipped the bottle up and drank hurriedly again.

And then the chanting began, the Seder began. Into the room seeped the mournful prayers with song in them he had been waiting to hear, and Jake sank down on the bed, lay flung there, his body sprawled under that sound, his eyes staring up.

Into the room, to wash over him, came his father's voice chanting the Passover story, and little sounds rode on the chant: his mother's giggle, Roz saying something to her, and the answering Yiddish of the reply.

Had Deborah asked for him? He thought of her eyes, the blue look, and the ache in his chest grew deeper. What was she thinking, as she sat at the crippled table? Sure, it was crippled; the sons weren't there, not even one son. The old man sat surrounded by women, and by God it was Debby's fault that not one deep, male voice was there to back up the head of the table. Not one man, by God, and what the hell kind of a Seder could you have without a man?

He lay tense, waiting for the moment. He had come home for that moment, and all evening he had been waiting for it, his entire being stiff with a suspense like agony. In his blurred mind, he had not gone beyond the moment, only up to it, and there hovered.

There was a small pause as the chanting stopped. Then, into the room, came the terrible sound of Deborah's voice, quiet but clear, the words uttered solemnly and with almost a tenderness to each one.

"Wherefore is this night distinguished from all other nights?"

Jake made a move to get up, to run from this room into the other, into that festive one. A terrible struggling feeling, full of pain and fright, tightened across his chest and almost stopped his breathing.

He had expected it. He had known she would ask the questions. And yet, now, when she had shaped the actual words, he was incredibly shocked.

He slipped back, his hands covered his face in the dark room, and he began soundlessly to cry, his body shaking violently. All the while he was listening to her quiet, solemn voice, which seemed to be in the room, close to the bed.

"Any other night we may eat either leavened or unleavened bread, but on this night only unleavened bread; all other nights we may eat any species of herbs, but this night only bitter herbs. . . ."

She had done it. She had stolen even this last thing from him, his place at the Seder table, the place bequeathed to him by all the years of tradition. The youngest son. First she had taken his place at the side of Ma. Then she had taken the place of scholar, of clean and dependable one in the family. Through the years she had walked with an ever wider stride, she had worn trousers, she had cut her hair short as a man's, she had borne their mother across the swollen rivers of relief and shame, she had stood up to their father, she had dared to aspire to intellectual heights through the writing of stories. And, with each step that she took closer to the powerful male, to the place occupied by men, he had taken a step backwards; as she strode onward, as she gained masculinity and strength, he stepped backwards, he crawled toward weakness. Through the years, then, had she not taken his masculinity from him and used it for her own? Had he not become weaker and weaker as she had grown in strength? Through the years, had she not stolen from him all the masculine traits she now exhibited? And tonight! Was not tonight the culmination of all those years, the grossest stealing of all? In the eyes of their family, in the eyes of all the Jewish gods and traditions, had she not taken what was right-fully his?

". . . all other nights we do not dip even once, but on this night twice; all other nights we eat and drink either sitting or reclined, but on this night we all of us recline."

Then his father's chant came into the room once more, a sound suddenly weary as well as mournful, sung with the thousands of years behind it, with the thousands of weary, endlessly walking exiles behind it, and Jake could not stop crying.

It's true, it's true, he thought as he wept. She's better than a son. She's always been better. She deserves it, even though she stole it.

And all around his bed, thick in the room as a living chorus affirming and reaffirming his thoughts, was his father's yearly chant of the Passover. . . .

"You say she stole your place. Think about that word, stole. The Seder was in progress, you were not at your customary seat, the time for the questions had come. If the questions had not been asked, the ritual would have broken down. Is that right? The Seder would have been a failure."

"It was a failure anyway! Sig wasn't there, I wasn't there. The person whose place it was to ask wasn't there, anyway."

"But some part of the family was there. Wasn't it Deborah's duty to go on with the ritual? Put yourself in her place. Isn't it more than duty? Would you, in her place, have wanted to see the ritual destroyed? Perhaps in her mind, as it is in yours, that ritual is synonymous with family, with herself as a living mem-ber of the family. Would you have wanted to sit there and watch the family be destroyed? Or would you have asked those ques-tions had you been Deborah?"

"You think it wasn't stealing?"

"Or was it the impact on your conscience? Was it stealing, in reverse? Did you remember, way down inside yourself, all the things you've stolen from her through the years? And in that moment of remembering, did you accuse her of stealing?"

"What did I steal from her!"

"Who helped steal her right to be soft and delicate? Who helped steal her right to be a girl, a baby sister, the one to be protected, not to protect?"

"Did I mean to do things like that!"

"Yes, but let's keep it honest in the mind, Jake. Whether you meant it or not, did it happen?"

"Yes, it happened! All right, it happened! Don't think I'm sorry to know the truth. I didn't want her to be a thief! When I thought of how she asked the questions, I couldn't stand it. I told you that! I need her. I need her all the time. I told you that! You can't figure somebody is a thief and yet go on needing her at the same time."

"You hated her that evening? You were jealous of her?"

"No. I thought she'd pushed me away from the table. That she'd stolen the right to ask the questions. I thought she'd put herself in my place of youngest son. What made me think all that—my feeling of guilt?"

"Yes."

"And when I was afraid because I thought she'd stolen enough from me to be more of a son than I'd ever been, I was really trying to hide the fact that—that I'd helped push her into being like a boy?"

"Yes."

"So, to tell the truth, I helped make her the way she is? Not only my father helped, and my mother—but I, too?"

"Did you?"

"Yeah, I guess. . . . I want to tell you something, Doctor. Something very—odd. The way Debby is now. That way I used to hate so much, and be afraid of—."

"Yes?"

"Is it such a terrible way to be? Just because she isn't like most women?"

"You tell me, Jake. Is it such a terrible way to be?"

"I mean, I used to think it was like being crippled, or sick! But it isn't. And she used to feel that way about herself! But it's Debby, it's her, the way she is. And Debby is—. Jesus, what's wrong with her? Anything, really?"

204

"You mean you feel that she's fine, sensitive? She's as worth while as all so-called normal people?"

"I mean—. Sure! I know a lot of people, and she's as good as any of them. Better than a lot of them. I mean, damn it, I don't want anybody laughing at her! Or making cracks. Don't think I'm nuts, please. I mean, the way I rip into her, and then the next minute I say she's wonderful. That's just the way I feel! Exactly!"

"You want to protect her?"

"I want—. It's like I want to give her things. I want everybody to know she's wonderful. Now that I—. Oh hell, I don't know how to say it!"

"Now that you've recognized her? Is that what you mean? Now that you're proud of her, proud she's your sister, that you are both in the same family? Is that it, Jake?"

"I—think so. But it's more, too. Maybe I'll know what it is after a while. . . . I haven't told you yet, but I took pictures of Debby the other night."

"What made you do that?"

"We were talking. I spent the whole evening with her, in the living room. We even started to read together. It sure was— funny!"

"Were you drunk?"

"Kind of. At first. But it wore off after a while, and then— well, then it was like we'd been sitting there and reading, talking, for a long time. We had coffee later. She made it, and we sat in the kitchen and drank it. It was—. I tell you, you've no idea how wonderful it felt to be able to do that. Sit around and talk to your sister."

"Yes, I know."

"She's got so many good ideas. She never laughs at you. I mean, well, what if I told things to most people? I couldn't even tell them to Laura! What if she'd laughed? And my mother— she wouldn't know what I was talking about."

"And Deborah?"

"She knew, all right! Funny thing, I wasn't going to talk about photography at all. I was just going to sit there. Near her. Read something, maybe. I've got such mixed-up feelings about her. Sometimes I like her, sure, like that night. Yeah, and some-times I can't trust her because she—well, I just can't under-

205

stand her! When I came in that night, it was still early. She was reading. It looked—kind of homey. She looked up and said hello. I had my camera, and she said, 'Do you have to work tonight?' I told her I had a six-thirty assignment next morning and I'd go straight from home. She nodded. You see, she looked—interested. After I took off my coat, I came back into the living room. Left my camera on the dining room table. I walked around the room. She didn't bother me, just kept on reading. . ."

. . . and finally he asked, "Say, got anything good to read?"

She looked up. "Magazine? Or do you feel like a book?"

"Oh, anything good."

She reached out toward the table near her chair and took a book from the pile lying there. "These are good," she said. "Short stories. Modern stuff. Most of them are pretty short, too. I don't suppose you want to start anything too long tonight."

He sat in the chair opposite her and began turning pages at random. She had begun to read again, and quickly, before she could get too far away, he said, "Ma home?"

"In the kitchen," Deborah said, her eyes on the page of her book.

"The old man?"

She looked up. "He's there, too. I guess they're reading. I haven't heard a peep out of them."

She smiled, and he got a whiff of tenderness, gentle amusement. "Don't feel much like reading, do you?"

He flushed, licked his rough lips. "Sometimes it's nice to just talk," he muttered.

"Oh, sure!" Her eyes lit up, seemed to become intensely blue in the lamplight. She held up the book she had been reading. "Have you read this novel yet? It's really something to talk about."

He peered at the cover, shook his head. "No. You mean it's that good?"

She offered him her pack of cigarettes, lit his and then her own. "It's good, yes," she said, slowly exhaling. "But that isn't what I mean. It's about people we know. You don't run into books like this often. Not novels, anyway. Do you remember the people on Hillside Avenue?"

"You mean where we used to live?"

"Yes. Do you remember them at all? On one street, we had Jews like ourselves, and Italians—."

"And colored people," he broke in eagerly.

"That's right. Do you remember what happened?"

"Not very well," he said.

"People started moving. Escaping. First, the Jews. We were among the last of the Jews left, and I remember the Italians started getting out next, and more Negroes started moving in. I remember how worried Ma was, and a few of the other Jewish families. See, here were the Negroes coming, and we couldn't get out. We couldn't escape them."

"Well, we finally moved," he said. His drunkenness was leaving him.

"Do you think we escaped?" she asked quietly.

"Well, sure we did," he said, leaning toward her, forgetting the danger of his breath. "We moved out of there."

"But did we escape?"

He stared into her thoughtful eyes.

"Any idea what we were trying to escape from?" she asked softly. "Was it really the Negroes? Or was it fear; and of course we pinned the word Negro to the fear, didn't we? Did we really think the Negro would contaminate us, or was it some old, secret nightmare we could name nigger now? And run from? It's easier to run away from something with a name, isn't it?"

As he stared, she smiled and tapped the book. "That's what the novel is about," she said, and placed it on the table. "I'd like to have written it."

Smoking, he felt a happy excitement, a shyness, a wonderful moment of warmth and intimacy.

"What kind of stuff do you like to write about, Debby?" He thought of his camera, felt himself reddening, and glanced quickly at her to see if she would answer.

She was putting out her cigarette. When she looked back at him, her eyes were good to see, thoughtful and clear and full of meaning.

"I'll tell you," she said, "I've always wanted to write only about certain kinds of people." She hesitated a moment, then she said quickly, "Excuse it if I sound too dramatic, but there's only one way to say it. I write about unfortunates, the people who have wandered off into odd alleys. Physical, mental, or spiritual alleys, I mean. The strange people, the ones who are despised, or condemned, or lost."

His eyes dropped, as if she had said "people like me." She went on, her voice very alive and vibrant, with an urgent quality that excited him.

"It's the strangest thing. I walk along a street, or I'm in a room with people, or I bump into them on the job, and all of a sudden inside of me something says, 'There. That's someone to write about.' It's sort of as if your heart picks them out of a crowd, or out of a lonely street. All of a sudden, as if a switch clicked on. And all the crowds of other people don't mean a thing for a story. I mean, I can see thousands of them and nothing happens, and then one, or a small group of them, will just reach out and grab me."

His heart was beating fast, and he glared at her out of the mixture of happy, shocked confusion he was feeling.

"Listen," he cried, "that's just like me with my camera! Only certain kinds of people, certain kinds of streets or things. Like something inside of me recognized them. Only I never put it into words. Just what you said. That's the kind of stuff I shoot for my own pictures."

She smiled at his incredulous look. "That's very nice. I had no idea you were interested in such things. What do you mean when you say your own pictures?"

His eyes looked oddly frightened, and immediately she said, "It's all right. I don't have to know if you don't want—."

But he broke in on that. "No, it's all right, Debby. I just haven't ever told anybody. Just—the doctor."

"Oh, don't tell me," she said. He saw the red come into her face.

"But I want to," he said eagerly. "It's just like your writing. You aren't ashamed to talk about that, are you?"

"No, of course not."

He lit another cigarette. "They're pictures I take for myself. Aside from the art I get for the paper. I look at them a lot. Nights sometimes, when I'm in the office and nobody's around. I've got captions for them."

Her eyes seemed very bright. "You might have a show some day," she said. "Are they good?"

"Some of them," he admitted. "Pretty good. They're not like the stuff I take for the paper. Nothing at all like that. They're—queer. You know what I mean?"

She nodded, her eyes so excited that he felt happy and shy.

"I take them with the same camera. A speed graphic. That's my favorite camera, see. Some people don't like it for anything but news stuff, but I like it for anything. The Old Man used to use one all the time, too, and Jesus, you should see the kind of stuff he took."

"Who?"

He grinned. "Not Pa. The Old Man. His name is Pete, only nobody ever calls him that. He's retired. Used to be head photographer on the paper. Wonderful guy, just wonderful. He's the one who showed me how to use a camera. Broke me in. He took the best shots I've ever seen. You know, background and details. He knew all about that, like he'd been born with it in his head."

She nodded, her mouth tender. "I know. I had some teachers like that. They told me I could write. They showed me my rotten, terrible sentences, but they talked about the few good ones, too."

After a second, she said thoughtfully, "Are any of your pictures as good as his?"

The color flared into his face and neck, but he answered honestly. "Some of them. Maybe ten or twelve, all in all. But they're a different kind of picture."

"Would he like them?"

"I don't know," he said, his hands fumbling at the ashtray. "I was always kind of nervous about showing him anything. He—he's not a Jew."

"What's that got to do with it?"

He searched painfully for the right words. "I always called them—Jewish pictures when I was thinking about them. I don't know why. It was like they went with this house. With Ma and Pa." He stopped, abruptly.

"And with me," she added gently.

"Yeah. With the whole bunch of us. Roz and Sig, too. There was something queer about every picture I took. Like—well, like it had some of our family in it. Do you know what I mean?"

"Yes, I think I do." She studied him. He liked the little lines at the corners of her eyes when she smiled. "I've never called it Jewish, but that's the tone of my stories, too. It's not Jewish, I don't think. It's us, how we've lived, what we've gone through. It's the *Buba*, and Pa and Ma, and all the streets we've lived in. Sure, it's the Jew of us, too. But not only that."

He listened eagerly, feeling a kind of ache, but he could not answer her or add to the words in any way.

"Look, Jack," she went on, "anything creative has so much in it. Of the person who is trying to create the thing."

Looking into his eager, half-hurt eyes, she pushed her hand impatiently through her hair. "I know that doesn't make much sense to you. I mean, I know you don't use a word like creative, or put a hell of a lot of stock in such things. But it's your word, anyway. And when you create, you shove into your work—oh Lord, everything you've got! Naturally! But so much more. Everything that's ever touched you. Everybody who's ever come near you. That's why honest creative work is so wonderful!"

"Yeah, that sounds good," he said slowly.

"Aren't you planning an exhibit, or a show of some sort?" she asked eagerly. "I know a lot of people who would give their eyeteeth to see some of those pictures."

"No," he said quickly, automatically. Then, seeing her eyes, he stammered, "I hate to—. They're my own pictures, Debby!"

"Of course they are," she said after a moment or two. She took a cigarette out of the pack on the table, and lit it.

"The way I feel about things I write," she said then. Her eyes were on the cigarette she was holding, and she talked in a casual way. "I write something. Sometimes it seems good, sometimes it seems as if I didn't get anywhere near what I'd wanted to say. The good pieces—it's an odd thing. Even those good stories, they don't seem to—what I call come alive, until I see them in print. Some magazine takes one, and prints it, and then a lot of people are reading that story. Things are different suddenly. That story isn't just a bunch of words. It's something people are reading, maybe thinking about. Maybe some feeling comes to them as they read it. They want to laugh, or cry. Or swear. Maybe they want to do something, change something. Just because they read that story of mine."

Her eyes swung up to his, clear and very quiet. "The way I

think, a person writes for people, not for herself. For as many people as there are, and she hopes all of them will read the story. She hopes they'll get out of that story something—of what she put into it when she was writing it. Herself, and her parents, maybe. Maybe, the sound of crying she heard next door ten years ago."

His voice was very low, he said, "What do you think if I took a few pictures of Ma and the old man? You know, in the kitchen. Think they'd think I was nuts?"

"No," she said, her own voice low. "I think they'd be puzzled, but they'd love it."

"They would?"

"People love to be in pictures. It's fun. It's flattering. Especially when your own son, a professional, bothers to want to snap you." She smiled, as if the words had been half a joke.

After a while he smiled back, and her smile deepened into a grin.

"Listen," he said abruptly, his voice excited and full of the smiling, "could I take a few shots of you?"

"Sure," she said. "I'd love it. Do you want to do it now?"

"Say, do you mean it?" he cried.

"Of course I do." She was still smiling, but her voice was serious. "What caption would you use?"

He jumped up and ran into the dining room. In a moment he was back with his camera and the zippered case of films and bulbs. He sat in the chair again, but this time crouched at the edge, and studied her in the lamplight.

She sat quietly, watching his eyes whip over her features, the chair, the table.

"You could keep sitting right there," he said. The finger of one hand tapped the camera, then the hand fiddled with the flash gun. "Would you hold some paper and a pencil, Debby?"

She reached for the hard-backed notebook and opened it to a page half filled with scrawled words. Then she placed it against her drawn-up knee, and poised the pencil over it. "How's that?"

"That's good."

"Are the slacks O.K.?" she asked casually. "Or do you want me to put on a dress, or a suit?" She didn't look at him.

"Just the way you are." His voice was a little shy, blurred

with it, but underneath was the excitement. "Caption, huh? I'd call it YOUNG WRITER, Debby. Maybe a series of four or five pictures. What do you think?"

He was on his feet now, walking around, peering into the camera, then moving to another position.

"I like it," she said, smiling down at her notebook. "I like it very much."

He came close to the chair and pushed the notebook down an inch. "Lean back," he said, his voice crisp now. "No, don't look up. As if you'd stopped for a second. You're kind of tired. You're thinking of exactly the right thing to say. It'll come to you in a minute, but right now you have to look for it—and you're pretty tired. You kind of wonder if you'll get the exact thing you want. That's right! Don't move now. But don't get stiff. Think of what you're writing, Debby. That crying you heard somewhere, ten years ago; you can't exactly get it into words."

Looking down at her, he saw the oval face tilted, the lips tender and drooped a little with tiredness, the golden, clipped hair shining in the lamplight. The hand flat at the top of the notebook looked very square, with fine, slightly ridged lines running under the skin, the lines glinting blue under the softness of the skin. The pencil was lifted an inch or so from the last line of words on the page.

"Here we go," he said, almost whispering, tightening the bulb a last time. He was thinking, as he squinted into the camera, My handwriting looks just like hers.

. . . so that, for the past five years, S has been unable even to enter the house on that night. Up until that moment, though the Seder made him uneasy, unhappy, he was able to be near it, even to sit at the table. The terrible implication of that evening was the final blow. Deborah had committed the ultimate sin; she had taken away from him the place assigned to him by religion, by his forefathers: the place of youngest male in the family. For years before that night, she had been coming closer and closer to male; she had taken on more and more of the attributes of son, the strength, the protective demeanor, the clean and scholarly mien. This was the last, the most secretive thing, she could possess. It was a thing which had always been his. In his mind, the asking of the questions was invested with the sacred and binding vows of the Bible, the synagogue, the God of the Jews. When Deborah asked the questions that night five years ago, S felt the final defeat. He had been cast off completely, at last, and in his place sat a woman.

His feeling of guilt could not stretch further than this. The breaking point had been reached; if ever he went back to the Seder table, he felt that he must go as a broken man. He told himself she had stolen the right to ask the questions. He could not face the fact that his weakness had given her the right to— not steal, but protect, the questions. His guilt at having helped force her into maleness was now complete: it was she who now asked the questions, she who now occupied the male seat given him by tradition and ritual. Now he was deeply and basically proved guilty—by the last Word, by the terrible, shining truth of God. How could he, from this moment on, dare enter his home on the night of spiritual disinheritance? How could he do anything that night but get drunk, so that he might not have to remember the actual moment of being disowned?

The Passover, with its undertones of birthday and symbolic spring, the time of hope and fertility, will be the critical period for S in the future, as it has been in the past. It was at the Seder that S first was catapulted into conscious thinking of family and self. It was at the Seder that he felt the final step of his guilt and weakness, the final degradation of being cast out of the family, his place filled by a woman who already was stronger than he.

It will be at the Seder, probably, that S will feel the actual moment of release. Symbolically, it is the most important time of the year for him. That time, during the traditional and symbolical ceremonies, must be the moment of freedom for him. . . .

Seven

Jake was sitting in the living room when Roz came home, and then Debby, about ten minutes later. He was reading the final, and he heard the dishes rattle in the kitchen, and knew they were eating what he already had eaten, fish, chicken, soup with noodles, stewed prunes, thick slices of their mother's fresh-baked bread. He knew the old man was eating silently at his corner of the table, Ma snatching little bites in between serving Roz and Debby. Roz's laughter came, full-bodied and slow, into the living room, and he thought that with gentiles it would be church every Sunday, but with him it was Friday night, the fish and chicken and soup as meaningful as wafer and wine. (Kathy went to mass sometimes, but Laura had never mentioned either church or God.)

The phone shrilled at his thoughts. It was Sig. "John? Tell Ma I won't be home for supper. I'm eating at a friend's."

Turning from the phone, he saw the candles burning in their sticks, which Ma set on the dining room buffet every Friday.

"Ma," he called toward the kitchenful of conversation and laughter and odors, "Sig is eating supper at some friend's house."

"He just called?"

"Yeah." He went back to the newspaper, sat there thinking of Sig. His only feeling was one of curiosity. How did Sig make out inside himself? How did he stay so well dressed, smoking such good cigars?

He put up the paper quickly as Roz came to the phone in the dining room and dialed a number.

"Johnnie?" she said. "I'll be late. I'm going to stop at the hospital and see Claire. Yeah, I ordered flowers. I wrote they're from all the girls on the card. Sure."

From the open doorway leading into the dining room, Deborah said, "John."

He put the paper down, and she was smiling at him. She had changed to slacks and a sweater, and her hands were in her pockets, the ceiling light in the room very yellow on her brushed-back hair.

"Do you want to drive Ma and me over to Sarah's?"

His mouth went dry. "Roz takes her on Fridays, doesn't she?" he managed to say.

"But Roz hasn't the time tonight," Deborah said, still smiling. "I thought it would be a good chance for you to come up and see the kids."

He saw Roz's face, startled, as she lit a cigarette. Ma came in from the kitchen, drying her hands on a towel. Her peering eyes looked a little frightened.

"I'll go on the streetcar," she said hesitantly.

"Don't be silly," Jake said stiffly. "Certainly I'll take her. You say you're going, too?"

"Of course," Deborah told him, her smile very quiet. "Let's go now."

Roz got into her fur-trimmed coat. "Swell," she said lightly. "That'll give me plenty of time. Ma, did I leave enough money for the phone, too? I don't remember, and it's my turn to pay for it."

"Plenty, plenty." The bowed, thickened back disappeared after Roz into the kitchen. "Roz, don't forget the little loaf I baked for you."

Deborah looked at him. "Don't you want to?" she asked softly.

He nodded, his mouth still parched. He tossed the paper

to the other side of the couch, rose. "Only I wasn't exactly expecting it tonight," he mumbled, coming toward her. She was standing next to the chair over which his coat was draped.

As he got into the coat, he gave her a sideways look, and she said, "We won't stay long."

He felt confused, anxious. He listened closely as Deborah called, "Ma, we're ready. Here's your coat."

As they left the house, walking through the kitchen, he noticed the old man staring after them, and he flushed.

In the car, Debby sat next to him, their mother next to the door. It was the first time either of them had been in his car, he thought suddenly as he swung out from the curb.

"Nice car," Debby said. "Doesn't it ride smoothly, Ma?"

"Beautiful, beautiful." Ma's voice was nervous, impressed, and Jake's jaw ached as his lips came together.

"Debby," Ma said softly then, "maybe we should've telephoned Sarah we were coming?"

"Oh no," Debby said, her voice casual. "Turn left here, John. It's the third apartment. That's right."

She led the way, her hand on their mother's arm. He followed them in, then up two flights of stairs in a close, musty hall. He began to hear the shouting and cursing halfway up the second flight, and Debby said, "Sounds like a fight." Her voice was still deliberately casual.

"It's Bernie," their mother said angrily. "Listen to that! It's a shame for the neighbors, that's all. You can hear such things all over the street, but what do they care for people?"

Jake's stomach quivered. He wanted to run back down the steps, into the safety of his clean, new car. He could be downtown in twenty-five minutes, inside the Brass Rail, sitting at the long, circular bar, talking with half a dozen people.

Debby and the peering, anxious woman were waiting for him outside a door at the head of the stairs. He noticed that Yiddish newspapers were spread over the landing, and his mind clicked: Somebody washed the steps, and spread the papers to keep them clean for a few hours. Ma used to wash such steps late at night.

The quarreling was very near, behind the door. Jake heard a woman's anguished voice crying in Yiddish: "Just take him away from me, that's all! All my suffering comes from him!"

217

Then Bernie's voice shouted, "That little son of a bitch thinks he can get away with anything. Why the hell should I let him hit me?"

"Shut up!" somebody cried sharply.

That's Leah, Jake thought, and he looked up at Debby, whose hand was on the doorknob; but she did not open the door. Her eyes glanced down at him, as he stood five or six steps down, and he thought, She wants me to hear enough before we go in and stop it. Goddam it, she wants me to really get a bellyful!

A boy's lisping voice cried, "You leave me alone, damn you. Ma, you kick him out of here."

Then Bernie's voice mimicked the lisp: "Ma, you kick him out of here!"

A man's thick, heavy voice cried furiously, "Bernie, you want the strap?"

Then a horn began outside the apartment, and Jake thought, My God, let me out of here. Before I have to see them. What does she want me to do?

The horn continued, three blasts, a small pause, then three blasts again. Deborah, with a smile, stepped back from the door just as it opened and Leah came running out into the hall.

She stopped for an instant, her eyes jumping from Deborah to Jake. "Oh, Debby!" she said breathlessly, and the voices and cries died down behind her, then the horn started again and she cried, "That's for me. Good-by!"

She clattered down the steps, her high heels sharp as thin drums, and the hall door slammed. Sarah's fleshy face, the eyes puffed and tearful, appeared at the door. Her eyes looked frightened as she saw Jake.

"Ma?" she cried.

Debby said, very gaily, "John drove us over, Sarah. Wasn't that nice of him? He hasn't seen all of you for such a long time."

Then they were inside the flat, the door closed behind them. Jake saw a tiny living room, a gray ceiling pressing down on too many pieces of shabby furniture.

Almost at once, his eyes flew to a familiar object, Debby's high school graduation picture. The round face, the smiling eyes, were framed on the low, narrow mantel which rose above a small, gas-burning stove. In the picture, Debby's hair was parted on one side, and was down to her ears.

She looks much better with her hair short, he thought in amazement; I didn't even remember that she used to wear it as long as that.

He stared back at the grave smile in the picture, and then, from a corner, Max's voice boomed, "Well, well, if it isn't Jake. Hello, stranger."

Jake turned. Max was sitting in front of the radio, a Yiddish newspaper folded on his lap. He had become very fat, and some of his front teeth had been extracted. He seemed much heavier and shorter, much darker, than Jake remembered.

"Well, how are you?" he said, his face reddening painfully.

"Pretty good, pretty good." Max spoke with a heavy Yiddish accent. "What do you think of the war, huh? I'll bet you never thought there'd be another war, huh?"

Jake became aware of the kids; Allen, a skinny, tall boy with very quick, sly eyes, Bernie sullen, bigger somehow than he remembered, his face badly pimpled. His eyes, which would not meet Jake's, seemed odd. In his confusion, Jake could not figure out what was wrong with them.

The next hour passed very slowly, in unreal fashion. Jake found himself in a cluttered kitchen, sitting at a table like the one at home. Sarah served tea to him and to Debby, cut uneven slabs of a spongecake for the two of them.

Ma had said, "I just finished supper. Not for me, Sarah."

Max had not stirred from the radio, and in the living room now a loud, monotonous voice talked about the war.

Debby and he sipped tea from their cups. Allen stood in the doorway, staring at them, but Bernie was not to be seen. It was as unreal as anything Jake had ever read. He was aware of Sarah's suspicious, red-rimmed eyes. She had grown huge since last he'd seen her, folds of flesh obscuring her neck, and her upper arms and bosom immense. He did not know what to say; only the sense of unreality was real, and Debby's eyes.

"Where's Bernie?" she said.

"Where do you think?" Allen said, giggling. "He ran away. He's afraid of you."

"He is?" Debby asked with a smile.

"Sure! Ma always says she'll tell Debby when he does something bad. He doesn't want you to holler at him. He wants you to like him." He spoke very quickly and eagerly, one word slurring over the other, and the lisp running like water over the entire swift pattern.

"What happened tonight, Sarah?" Debby asked.

Allen cried, "He took Leah's magazine and—."

"Wait a minute," Debby said immediately. "I'm talking to your mother, Allen."

Jake saw the kid bite off his sentence, lean eagerly toward Debby as she spoke to Sarah. The unreality thickened as he watched all of them turn to Debby, like bitter, complaining children, Sarah, his mother, and the boy.

"What happened?" Debby repeated. "What was that horrible business when we walked in?"

"What, what!" Sarah cried. "It's always Bernie. You don't even have to ask. He's the one. He makes my whole life black, that's all!"

The familiar Yiddish crowded into the unreality. His mother's worried voice added to the tale. "She's right. Whatever happens, it's always Bernie."

"He fights with everybody," Sarah said. "Like he has a devil in him. Nobody is too old, too big. His father, his sister! Everybody's property is his."

Allen could no longer stay out of the conversation. "He and Leah were fighting," he said. "Hey Debby, and I laughed at him, so he turned around and smacked me. Hey Debby, what he does all the time, he makes fun of the way I talk, that's what." His little eager face leaned closer to her, the slyness suddenly gone from his eyes.

"What did you call him?" Debby asked quietly.

Allen shrank back. "I didn't! Ma and Leah, they called him cockeyed. So he slaps me!"

"After you laughed at him?"

Jake lit a cigarette. The more they shouted, the more quiet Debby became.

"Debby," his mother said solemnly, "he acts like a half-wit, like a boy of the streets."

"He is, he is." Max's voice came to them above the radio voice. "I've seen half-wits before. He is the best one I've seen. A No. 1! And who made him one? Ask her, ask her!"

The thick feeling of unreality grew. Jake lit cigarettes help-lessly, smoked them fast, his eyes jumping from one strange face to another; even his mother's, in that cluttered, small, hot room, looked unfamiliar. She sat nodding, her nearsighted eyes peering at Debby, at him, at Sarah. The hot dual gush of Yiddish and English flowed at him.

Eventually, Debby stood up. "I'm tired," she said, and her voice was still blessedly quiet. "Ma, you're tired, too. Let's go home."

Jake slid some coins into Allen's little wet hand, held the eager, moist eyes for a split second, then he followed Debby into the living room. He put on his coat, stood helplessly at the door.

"Sarah," Debby was saying in a low voice, "give the kid a chance, will you? If all of you would only quit tormenting him."

"I torment him!" Sarah cried. "What does he do to me!"

And then, after a long time, Jake was behind the wheel of his car again, Debby next to him, their mother silent near the door. He had rolled the window down, and the cool night air rushed in as he pressed down on the gas pedal. The clean, swirling wind said over and over: Wasteland, wasteland.

Halfway home, Jake said brusquely, "For Christ sake, what's the matter with his eyes? He never looks at you!"

"Would you look at anyone if you were cross-eyed?" Debby said steadily.

"They call him cockeyed, don't they?" he said, remembering.

His mother cried an answer so eagerly that he felt an ache. "But he calls them names! His own mother, he calls her fat pig. What kind of talk is that? And his own sister he calls a bum. A child should know such words!"

They rode the rest of the way in silence.

In the kitchen, the old man was sipping tea from his thin glass, a bowlful of lump sugar on the table, the newspaper spread close to it. He did not look up as they came in, and Jake walked into the dining room, tossed his coat over the chair. The candles had burned down to stubs, and a secret, wavering light hovered above them. He walked quickly into his bedroom, lay face downward on the bed. In the kitchen, his mother said, "Sig didn't come home yet?"

He felt intensely depressed, more helpless than he had felt

for a long, long time. It was an empty, impotent kind of sensation, no tears to it, just a dark and heavy weight in his chest.

Then his mind reached out, clutched at the idea of the doctor. The darkness within him took on substance, shape; suddenly he could name it, face it, because it was no longer a nameless, vaporous thing to encompass the world.

He got off the bed, brushed his hair in the darkness, went quietly toward the living room. Passing the kitchen, he saw them at either end of the table, reading, saw the timeless, motionless pose of hunched bodies over a section of the newspaper they had divided between them.

Debby looked up from the book. Her eyes pitied him. "I have a hunch Bernie ran off to the movies," she said. "He goes often, you know."

Jake lit a cigarette, sat in the chair opposite hers.

"I imagine," she went on, "the poor kid feels that a lot of people are laughing at him. Maybe because of his eyes. That's a good reason for feeling different."

Her voice deepened with the pity. "Maybe he's ashamed of his parents."

Jake winced.

"That's a pretty tough suit of armor he's put on himself," she went on. "It's liable to be hard to crack."

He sat slumped, smoking.

After a while, he said, almost absently, "Debby, do you think Ma and Pa would mind if I took their pictures?"

He reached for the ashtray, not looking at her, knowing what her eyes would be like, without looking.

After a pause, she said warmly, "I still think they'd love it."

He did not look up. "I'd like to get Ma at the candles," he said, his voice still absent.

"You will. Next time. Just before sundown, remember?"

Then he looked up. She was smiling, her eyes affectionate. "Want some help?"

"Not right away," he said carefully. "You can come in after I once tell them. While I'm taking the pictures."

He went to his room for the camera. Standing at the threshold of the kitchen, a wave of shyness rose in him. Watching their old bodies hunched over the newspapers, the thick, short shadows flickering on the wall, he felt as though he were re-peating motions and steps made familiar by a dream, each motion already made, each step taken a long time ago.

"Ma," he said. "You, too, Pa."

They looked up, the old man's eyes curious, his mother's startled, a small glint of anxiety piercing the blunted, peering glance which, for a long time now, had made him think of blind people.

He walked toward them, the camera in one hand, steps well dreamed, coming closer and closer to the faces and eyes out of that same dream.

"I want to take pictures of you," he said shyly. . . .

The evening caught up with him after he had gone to bed. It was Sarah, not Bernie, who sat on the edge of the bed and stared down at him in the darkness. Her great bulk loomed whitely in the room, and her reddened, suspicious eyes stared out of the folds of flesh encasing her face.

After a long time, Sig came home. Jake heard him in the bathroom, in the kitchen, then watched him through slitted eyes as he undressed and got into the other bed without putting on the light, as he sometimes did. All the while, Sarah sat on the edge of the bed, staring down at him.

For a long time he tried, lying there, to touch the idea of the doctor. Nothing but the formless, terrible miasma moved under the fingers of his mind. Little, flicking tongues of things came and went: Bernie's sullen eyes, which would not look at anyone for more than an instant, and his pimpled skin, the beginning of mustache above his rough mouth, Allen's skinny eager face, his tumbling, cascading words. Goddam you, leave me alone! Listen, you cockeyed little bastard, you better watch who you're hitting. Aw, you're only a big, fat pig, that's what! Get out already, get out, before I die away from you!

Sig groaned in his sleep, then his heavy breathing began again. The old man's clock struck three, and Jake sat up, the twin fear and depression unbearable, seeming to race in his mind like two joined animals, the race growing more intense each moment.

He got out of bed, swung his arms blindly into his bathrobe, and left the room. He did not know what to do, and stood for a moment outside the door he had carefully closed. The door to his parents' room was tight shut; he tried it, then stood in the dark hallway, shivering. Whatever happened, their door was shut, Ma would not hear him walk through the house.

The figure of Sarah had disappeared, but he was still frightened. The idea of the doctor was as unreal as the night in which he stood immersed. Only one person was alive in that night. He ran toward the living room.

"Debby!"

She was awake immediately to his frantic whisper. In an instant she was off the couch and had put on her bathrobe, then she snapped on the dimmest light of the reading lamp.

"Sit down, Jack," she said, and then they were both sitting in the big chairs, and she had given him a cigarette, had lit it and taken one for herself.

It was better as soon as the light was on and he could see the clean, sharp lines of her head and face. He knew she could see his hand shaking on the cigarette now, but, in an odd way, it was a relief to have her know.

"Do you want a drink?" she asked.

"A drink?" It had not even occurred to him. "I don't know what's the matter with me," he cried frantically. "I'm scared, or something. I can't forget that—that house. You didn't tell me it was like that."

"Yes, I did." She held his eyes steadily. "Why should you forget it? It belongs to you, too."

"My God," he said desperately, "what do you expect me to do? What's the use, if people are like that? Did you see Sarah? What the hell good can anybody do her?"

"Her children, not her." Debby's eyes suddenly were stern. "I never asked you to do anything for Sarah. But let me tell you something, Jack! Help Bernie, help Allen, and you'll be helping her, too. She lives for them."

"She!" he cried, remembering the mountainous body, the shrill cries she had made.

"Yes, she. If they turn out decently, she'll be happy."

"If they turn out! Why doesn't she do something about it? Why does she let herself look like that? So fat! Her teeth. Why, they're all rotten at the front of her mouth!"

Debby's eyes crashed into his with that iced, wrathful blueness he had almost forgotten.

"Listen, sonny." Her voice slapped at him. "Let me remind you that Sarah comes from this house, too. The old man is her father, too. The *Buba* was her grandmother, too. Let me remind you that she's the oldest, she's had a bigger bellyful than you ever will. Did you see that awful man she's married to? He also happens to be the father of her children!"

"Wait a minute, Debby," he begged.

"No, I won't!" she cried softly. "I won't have you sitting in this house and talking like a smug fool about somebody who knew this house before you were born! Every dirty, lonely inch of it!"

"Why does she scream and curse that way?"

"Maybe because life is a rotten, lousy trap for her! Maybe she's scared, and tired, and lonely. You want to run away to the army. She screams, instead."

"Jesus," he whispered, his hands going up to cover his face.

After a while, she said, "I'm sorry, Jack. I had no right to say that about you and the army." Her voice sounded tired.

He heard her strike a match.

"It isn't just running away," he said, his heart beating fast.

"What?"

He looked up. The anger had gone from her eyes.

"Listen, Debby," he said very eagerly, "that army business. I feel different about it now. I just didn't know. It isn't only to get away."

He flushed under the watchful eyes. "I haven't got it all straight yet, that's why I'm talking like a dub. It's the war, too. I mean, I want to get into this war, Debby. I've got a right to be in it."

The blueness warmed. "Yes, you have."

She offered him another cigarette. Miraculously, the fear had gone entirely.

"Tell me," she said after a minute, "do you remember what Sarah looked like when she married Max?"

"Sure I do. She was pretty. Tall. She had long, blond hair fixed in cute dips, the way the women wore their hair then."

Debby nodded. "I don't remember too well. But I've seen her wedding picture. She was very pretty. Her eyes, especially.

225

They were sort of eager. I always remember her eyes when I look at her now. Do you know how old she was when she was married?"

"Twenty-five or six, wasn't she?"

"What Ma and Pa called an old maid," Debby said. "You know the way they think, how their minds work. After twenty-one a woman's an old maid if she hasn't married. Somebody brought Max over to the house to meet Sarah. Ma's told me the story. So has Sarah."

She smiled. "Sarah likes me. She's often told me never to get married."

He flushed, and she said quickly, "After all, she's never seen too many decent men. Pa. Max."

"Sig, me," he finished in a low voice.

She shook her head, her smile gone, but she did not touch on his words.

"Max fell for her. He wasn't a bad-looking guy. Ma says he was very different in those days."

Her eyes shadowed. "Life sort of gets people down, doesn't it? I understand Max was a soft-spoken guy, crazy about children and of course about Sarah. He had quite a bit of money, too. I mean, he seemed like a swell guy in all respects. I imagine Sarah thought it might be wonderful to have her own home, be away from the old man. Not to be an old maid any more—in the eyes of her relatives and friends. So she married him. . ."

. . . and for a long time she was glad to be married. He was a war veteran. He had been wounded twice in action, and after a while, when they were going "steady," he showed her the two medals, the framed citation signed by Pershing. He still had his uniform, too, and a picture of himself in it. It all seemed very romantic.

He had enlisted with his brother Bernard, who had died at camp during the flu epidemic. The insurance policy of ten thousand dollars had been made out to Max, so he had plenty of money coming to him. And a good trade; he was a cabinet-maker.

It was easy to imagine herself in love with him. He was shorter than she, but slender and handsome in a dark, ardent way. They talked Yiddish most of the time—his English was heavily accented, while her only accent was the New York tinge that colored her words—but she did not mind after a while because everybody was so excited about him.

She did not mind either that he was so different. He did not care for shows, especially the musical comedies and dramas she adored. Nor did he care to dance, or to listen to the records she had bought for the phonograph at home; the Caruso records, and "Beautiful Ohio," and the Strauss waltzes she loved. The way he sent her American Beauty roses once a week was enough, and the way he brought candy for Ma and cigars for Pa when he came to take her out, and pressed money on Roz and Debby and Jake.

She married him, and it was as wonderful as she had hoped it would be. They spent their honeymoon at a Jewish farm two hundred miles away, that Max had located, and then they came back and found an apartment on Woodlawn Road, a district where many Jews were moving from the streets like the one where Ma and Pa lived.

They both picked out the furniture, beautiful showy pieces, and added to the silverware and dishes and linens they had received as wedding presents. Her silver was initialed. Ma would pick up a spoon or a fork, her eyes would widen, and she would say: "It's got your name. I never had a complete set of silver, or a dinner set, and you have twelve of a kind, with your name on each one!"

Every morning, after breakfast and after Max had gone to his job, she cleaned the house until it could not take another dab of rag. Then she got supper ready, or shopped for two or three days' food. By noon she was free. Usually, she'd take the streetcar down to Ma's and spend several hours there. Or she'd ride all the way downtown and shop, see a movie.

On these streetcar rides, she would remember Brooklyn. How she had worked in suits and cloaks, as a button sewer. The Winter Garden had been her favorite spot, and she'd gone there with Tillie and Rose, her best friends. She had always been tall and blond, with plenty of dates, but she'd never been interested in any one man. She'd been proud of her clothes, proud of wanting to take in an occasional opera, the best shows.

When she had met Max, here in this city, she had still been in suits and cloaks. She thought, with a smile, of the beautiful dinner set her boss, Mr. Stein, and the girls had sent Max and her for a wedding present. Her boss had liked her. Indeed, all the girls swore he'd always been sweet on her, and Max had kidded her about it.

She was happy. On Sundays, Ma and Pa and Debby, sometimes Jake and Roz, too, would ride up to this fine place in which she lived, and she would make a wonderful dinner for them; things Ma never made, hot potato salad, steak and onions, pie. It made her happy when they stared at her clean, lovely place, when Pa looked impressed at her possessions, at the heavily laden table. She still hated Pa, but it was a feeling softened now by her happiness.

She still remembered how he had written to Ma: "Leave the girl, bring the boy." And the way she had felt, alone in Russia, while Ma was in America. She still rememberd how he had jeered at the idea of further schooling for her, had plagued her until she'd quit school and got a job. Yes, she still remembered the time when her shop had gone out on strike and Pa had said, after three days of it, "When a person doesn't work, a person doesn't eat." She had gone to Tillie's house for the remaining week of the strike, hating him, glorying in her ability to walk out of his house, away from his sparse table. Only the thought of Ma had brought her back to that house.

Time passed so quickly when one was happy. Leah was born, and Max became more ardent, more wonderful. He brought home candies and cakes, presents. It was beautiful to have a baby; each day was packed with the thousand things to do for the child. She kept Leah scrupulously clean, dressed like a small doll. When she went walking with her, and people stared, or stopped to talk, she felt that life could offer nothing more.

It was particularly wonderful to show off her possessions to Ma, whose eyes grew big and moist when she sat in Sarah's house, or when little Leah came to climb up in her lap. Ma did not say much, but Sarah knew that she was happy.

Time passed, and where the mistakes first were made nobody knew—they crept up and grew so slowly and so gradually. Max and Pa bought the house in partnership, the house on Woodlawn where Bernie and Allen were born. Max used some of the insurance money for that, and the remainder of the money went to lawyers, because suddenly there was a mysterious law suit about the insurance. She never did understand that; something to do with Max's relatives in New York, whom she had never seen and about whom he never spoke. It was at this time that, for safety, the ownership of the house was put in the names of Ma and Pa.

Yes, time passed, and the mistakes of life were starting to crowd in on them. Leah was six, and Bernie was born, and somehow Max was changed. He was now crazy about the baby, with no eyes for Leah, or for that matter, for her. He had lost his job, and had suddenly become a carpenter. He had begun to put on weight and to have trouble with his teeth. He had developed a habit of sneering at people, especially at her family, who lived downstairs. Yes, he was changing all the time. The ardency was gone, the neatness. He never brought presents home any more. Having spoiled Leah, he was now giving way to every whim of Bernie's.

One recently acquired quality in Max bothered her more than anything else. He was lazy, or maybe it was that he just didn't care about anything: things like cutting grass, or emptying the rubbish cans, or putting on a good suit on Sundays, perhaps going for a ride or to the park or to the movies. It was becoming more and more difficult to stand firm against that laziness, or indifference, or whatever it was. She was surprised to discover that she found it difficult even to keep the house clean in the face of those habits of his. It was easier to feel nervous and irritable, to give way to strong impulses to shout at the children and at Max himself, to weep.

She never admitted it to herself, but she hated to get into the big double bed. Max rarely bathed these days, and unless she fussed at him he never changed the suits of thick underwear he wore, and in which he slept. His embrace in bed came often, was fierce and animal-like, and over in a few minutes; she had had pleasure from it only in the first half year of their married life, had almost forgotten the sensation of gratification in her constant feeling of distaste for intercourse now.

229

Yes, she thought often, time passes and we do not know where the mistakes first happened, nor how. All we know is that life is not good any more.

Suddenly, too, there was a depression, and absolutely no money except the veteran's check Max received from the government once each month. Suddenly the bank had foreclosed on them, and the house was no longer theirs, and Allen had been born. Suddenly, one day, she looked into the mirror and saw a stranger there, a tall, fat woman with bad teeth and skin, with faded, ill-kept hair. Only the light eyes looked familiar, for all their sadness.

What happens to people? she asked the stranger in the mirror.

She was changing, each day, into more and more of that mirrored woman. When one of the children was hurt or ill, she went to pieces immediately, screaming and weeping. It was because she loved them so terribly, she told herself, they were the only things she had in the world. And yet when they exasperated her, or worried her, she screamed and cursed at them, feeling a strange, terrible satisfaction in the sound of the curses as she uttered them. They were elaborate and deadly phrases, curses she had heard years ago in Russia, and on the streets of New York, and never realized she knew until they gushed from her.

And now Max had changed completely, as if to match the change in her. He had taken to jeering at her, insulting her with smiling, hard eyes. He had favorite words for her in Yiddish: gossip, neurotic, half-mad one, spoiler of children. And he called her these things in front of the children, in front of Ma, in front of Debby. Of course, when Debby was around she ordered him to hush up; and he did, too. But, for the most part, it was really unbearable. A woman could not bear to keep the house clean, to see people, to go to a movie or to a park. What was the use, after all, of trying to do the things civilized people did? She and Max were of the lowest of the low, acting this way, and the children were growing up to match.

She wept often, several times a day usually, her crying touched off by any small, unpleasant thing. Sometimes she wept even when she was sitting on the front porch in the afternoon, with Ma in the other old rocker.

"Why are you crying?" Ma would ask in her soft, gentle Yiddish, and Sarah would murmur: "I'm tired. Life is unbearable."

Ma would nod, a sad look in her eyes. "Yes, life is hard," she would murmur back, and the melancholy creak of the rocker mingled with the words. "A man could make it easier, but what man ever does?"

Then the kids would come home from school, Max would come home from wherever he had been; all the shouting and anger and irritation would begin again.

Often she thanked God for Ma. Their relationship had become a close, odd one from the moment they had bought the house and moved into it, one family upstairs and the other down. They went everywhere together, shopping, downtown, and to the Saturday poker games which were their one social event. These games occurred at a sort of family party and get-together, held each Saturday evening at a different aunt's or cousin's house. After a gala supper, all settled down to the cards, which they played for money in dead earnestness, until an early hour of the following morning.

They were more like sisters than mother and daughter, and though Ma was a good twenty years older, often she seemed to look more like an older sister of Sarah's than a mother. It was an odd relationship, yes. After the house had been lost and they moved apart, she felt lonely if she did not see Ma each day. And yet she was jealous of Ma, and often bitter toward her. If Ma grew fond of a neighbor, or of one of the children in the street, Sarah would say some sharp, cutting thing like, "Oh, you like these strangers better than you do your own grandchildren, your own family!"

Sometimes, at a poker game, Ma would have a winning streak, though she was a wretched player and half blind to boot, and Sarah, who was one of the experts in the family, would lose consistently. Then, in front of all the aunts and cousins, Sarah would make an insulting remark, and then she and Ma would not speak for—oh, sometimes a full week. Not until Debby made one of her fancy speeches to both of them, and shamed one or the other into patching up the quarrel.

Debby could make her do almost anything; Debby, with her fancy, writer's way of talking, and the way her eyes made you feel ashamed and hopeful at once. Debby was the only one of them who was worth a dime. Roz was really a bum; there was no way of getting around that fact. Sig was a man who thought so highly of himself and so little of his family that he had nothing to do with them. God knows why he lived home; it must be because he did not have enough money to live for himself! As for Jake, with his classy job and his newspaper friends and his mayor friends, he was also too stuck up to have anything to do with his own family. John! What kind of a name was that to take for a Jewish boy!

The only one who was really, truly fancy was Debby. She talked to every one of them. She tried to help. She gave advice in those words which always sounded like they came out of a book or a movie. How many times had she sat up all night next to Bernie's bed, or Allen's, when they were sick—so that Sarah could sleep a little? How many times had she come, with her calm eyes and quiet words, between Max and Bernie, and, for that matter, between Bernie and herself? How many times had she come upstairs and sat, smoking in silence, at the kitchen table? Then, after a while, that voice out of a book had said: "There's no reason to cry, Sarah. Really. Try to take it easy. Things aren't really so bad, are they? We're all healthy. We're eating, the kids are going to school."

Even during the relief days, the WPA days, when Max was hammering on one of those projects and her shame was so terrible that she couldn't bear even to go shopping; even in those days, Debby could comfort her. Debby even shopped for her when Max wasn't around to do the shameful thing. She read to the kids, told her sharply not to be so nervous, told her harshly that Leah would be all right, that she was an intelligent girl, not the bum that Max called her.

Yes, even when she, the mother, saw Leah going the way Roz had gone, and in her heart a terrible fear grew like a fungus, even then Debby's book-and-movie words could quiet her, make her hopeful for a few hours.

She knew it would not do any good, but she called Debby to talk to Leah and to Bernie anyway. She was the only one to whom they would listen, and they did listen while Debby was talking, even though they sprang, like pieces of steel, back into their inflexible ways the moment she left the house.

Yes, they lost the house. She moved to one street and Ma

232

to another. Leah graduated from high school and began to work as a clerk. Bernie failed classes, brought home stern notes from teachers, but Allen started school and was smart, brought home report cards like the ones Debby had used to bring home, only not quite so good. Yes, she felt weak and tired, and ate too much all the time, getting a queer little comfort out of all the eating. The poker games went on, and Max called his own daughter a street girl, and beat Bernie or called him a half-wit, and Bernie swore back, Bernie laughed at everybody, and her teeth ached most of the time, but there was not money enough and courage enough to go to a dentist, and then her body took to aching, too, especially in the middle of the night, when she was lying next to Max and worrying about everything.

What happens to people? Where are the first mistakes made, and how do such mistakes crawl, like an ever-deepening night, over people until there is no identifying them any longer?

She did not care for herself; it was too late for her. But what about the children? What was going to happen to them? At night, lying in bed, her body hurting all over, a mother feels how she is going mad with that question. Her own flesh and bone, her only excuse for living; and suddenly, she is watching how that flesh and bone is drifting toward God knows what. Today Bernie fails in school, today he curses, he fights with everybody, he calls his sister a bum and makes his baby brother cry, today he turns and screams at his mother: "Leave me alone! All you know how to do is eat and play cards. Go on, why don't you eat another whole bread?" Tomorrow, what will this same Bernie do?

All right, there was another war now, plenty of work, Max with a factory job, enough money for food, for clothes for the children, even an occasional dress for herself. She could remember Pa's words: *Gelt iss duh welt.* Yes, she had believed in such words, too. Money is the world. But what did money have to do with the terror of facing a tomorrow for Bernie? For Allen, Leah? Yes, but especially for Bernie. Somehow, he seemed to symbolize the sullen, shouting, cursing, inexplicable days of life.

Mama, *Mamele!* she pleaded in the darkness of that small, close room where she slept.

Once she had thought that maybe Debby would save them

all, drag them with her on her way to some high, shining star of life. She knew that Debby's hand would always be out to them, but now she was desperately afraid that Debby's hand was inviolate; it could touch, it could soothe, but just as she could not be changed by any of them so could she not change them. Debby's hand was like Debby, strong, wonderful, but steadily fading from all their lives; and one day that hand would be gone with her, out of their lives, only the remembered, wonderful imprint of it left.

Mamele, Mamele, she thought despairingly as she lay in the hot, dark room; let me at least sleep! . . .

". . . and after Debby told me all those things about Sarah, I felt better." Jake's voice was still excited. His fingers seemed to prickle as they touched the package lying on his thighs.

"That's when you phoned me?" the doctor asked. As he put his pen down for a moment, and rubbed the fingers of his right hand, Jake saw the fine, closely spaced sentences he had written in the notebook.

"Yeah, that's when I phoned you. It was like I believed in you again, but I had to hear you to make sure." His head jerked up. "Jesus, how I felt before Debby gave me hell! I just didn't believe in anything. Not you, either, I don't think."

"And today?"

"Today is Saturday," Jake said slowly. "You're real today, all right."

"But that was only last night, early this morning," the doctor said just as pointedly.

"Yeah, but I had a reason then, didn't I? It was the first time I'd been to Sarah's in years. The first time I'd seen such—."

The doctor helped him. "Such wasteland? At first hand?"

Jake nodded, his eyes somber. "I was scared. It seemed too late to do a damn thing about anything."

"And today? This minute?"

Jake reached for a cigarette. "I feel like a dope," he said, lighting it. His left hand dropped quickly back to the package. "The fact is, I'd like to get sort of better acquainted with those kids. Bernie, especially." His eyes narrowed. "I'm acting pretty funny, huh?"

"No, I don't think it's odd. You understand Sarah much better since Deborah's explanation. You can trace some of her reasons for her behavior."

"Yeah. I feel plenty sorry for her today. And that kid, Bernie!"

"Do you have any plans for that kid, Bernie?"

Jake hesitated. "No, not yet. I'll have to figure out something really good. You see, he's such a tough kid. I mean, the way he looks at you. You can tell he doesn't trust anybody." Quickly, he added, "Hell, I don't blame him! You know, that kid doesn't even have a room of his own. He sleeps on a folding bed, in the living room. A hell of a small room, too."

"Like Deborah, eh?" the doctor asked softly.

Jake started, but his eyes held straight. "But Debby knows things. She's grown up. She knows reasons for things. He doesn't. He's just a kid. With nobody to trust."

"Nobody to tell him," the doctor said, as softly as before. "Maybe he'd like to trust somebody. You?"

"Maybe he'd take it from me," Jake said gravely, putting out his cigarette. "It didn't work when Debby tried. Maybe he needs a man to do it."

"And Deborah is not a man, eh?" the doctor said.

"No," Jake said, then he started again, caught the doctor's smiling eyes. "No," he repeated, his eyes soft, "she isn't."

His hands fiddled with the string around the package. "Say," he said abruptly, "I brought you something to see."

He snapped the thin string, pushed back the brown wrapping paper, and took several photographs from the pile disclosed. None of them was framed. Silently, he slid them across the desk toward the doctor.

After a moment or two, the doctor said, "You took these last night?" He turned one toward Jake. "This is remarkably good."

"Think so? I'm calling it AMERICANS IN KITCHEN, EVENING. Do you really think it's good?"

"Very." The doctor turned another print toward him. "And what are you calling this one?"

"That's the one I was telling you about," Jake said fondly. "YOUNG WRITER. Do you like that one?"

"That's a fine picture. Of a very fine-looking young woman."

"Debby takes a swell picture," Jake said. "I'm going to take plenty more of her. Notice the way her hands show up?"

"You know," the doctor said, his eyes still on the picture, "I'm glad you didn't title this differently."

"What do you mean? What other thing could I have called it?"

"Oh, any number of things. YOUNG LESBIAN, for example. Or, PORTRAIT OF A DEGENERATE."

Jake stared at him, his eyes blank.

"You might have used such words not too long ago," the doctor said, picking up another print. "If you had taken the picture at all."

Jake swallowed. "You mean if I'd titled it truthfully, the way I really felt?"

"Yes, that's what I mean."

"But that's the way I think of her now," Jake said painfully. "As a writer. As Debby. I don't think, she's a man, or she's a woman, or what in hell is she?"

"The way you used to?"

"That's right, the way I used to." Jake swallowed again. "That title is the truth, Doctor. I—I don't lie about my own pictures. Not in captions for them."

"I wanted to be sure you knew that," the doctor said, his eyes kind. He turned around the print he had picked up. "This one is exceptional, too, I think."

"Ma. Yeah, that's good." Jake rubbed his nose, squinted at the picture. "The Old Man would like that one, I guess. Notice how the shadow points up the way she sits when she reads? The way the shadow leans?"

"Thinking of showing these pictures to the Old Man?" the doctor asked casually.

"I was kind of thinking about it," Jake said, scowling at the pack of prints he was thumbing through. "I don't know which I'll show him. I wanted you to see some of these first."

"Oh," the doctor said, as casually as before, "have you brought some from your drawer at the office?"

"Yeah. I went to the morgue this morning after I developed the stuff I took last night. There wasn't too much doing at the office today. I picked out a few things I thought you'd be interested in."

He slid several prints along the desk.

"What's this one?" the doctor asked.

"I took that on Hillside Avenue. Near where they've put up a housing project."

"I didn't think you'd be too interested in photographing Negroes."

"Oh, sure. They make marvelous shots. Notice that kid in the middle? He looks a lot like Bernie. His expression, especially. I just noticed that."

"Going to photograph your nephews?" the doctor asked softly, shuffling the prints.

"I guess. One of these days, sure," Jake said absently, selecting a print from near the bottom of the pile. "Here, how do you like this one? I want the Old Man to see this for sure. He'd go for the background. Notice the way that sign works right in with the action?"

"Excellent, excellent," the doctor said. He picked up the portrait of Deborah again, studied it closely.

Jake watched for an instant, then he reached slowly into the inside pocket of his jacket and drew out a five-by-seven print, which he slid over to the doctor.

When the gentle eyes looked up questioningly from the picture, Jake said, "See any difference between that and the others?"

"Yes. It seems different. Almost as if another photographer had taken it."

"I took it, all right," Jake said, his mouth tight. "What do you mean, different?"

"A different mood, perhaps. But then, it's as if she's of an entirely different type, or, let's say, class of people than these others. No, it might be just the mood of the picture."

"That's just not one of my own pictures," Jake said, his voice hoarse. "I took it, and I tried to do a good portrait, too."

"It is a good portrait," the doctor insisted. "It seems a little—thin. The others seem warm, I would say rich-blooded, in comparison."

"That's Laura. I've taken plenty of shots of her, but not one ever looked like one of my own. It used to worry me. I had plenty of feeling for her, plenty! But when I'd print the damn pictures they all looked—sure, what you call thin. Like water. Like a damn shadow! Jesus, it sure used to worry me!"

"Does it still?"

"No." Jake leaned over the desk and took the picture of Deborah from the doctor. He set it down, carefully placed the portrait of Laura next to it, hung over them with squinted eyes.

"No, it doesn't worry me any more. Some people are for me, some aren't, I guess." His head turned. He smiled at the doctor. "I used to wonder what a picture of Debby would look like. Maybe I was afraid it wouldn't look right. Because I didn't know what right was, for her."

His eyes turned back, became tender. "Does it look right, Doctor?"

"Yes, Jake. That's a truthful picture. As well as an artistic one."

. . . and this break into fear and doubt may be likened to the crisis in his illness. The nightmare turned into sense when Deborah told the few simple details of Sarah's life, tied that life to the same source of unhappiness he knows so well. S always has reacted well to truth, to known facts. From the beginning, only when he could not fathom the why and what of things did he give way to depression and doubt. Attitude of S at today's visit signifies that he is leaving behind the period where D was substituting for his father. Idea of showing D his pictures (and pointed emphasis on Laura's picture) was his own decision, not D's suggestion.

Last night's sharp doubt came with S' first actual touch of the wasteland he had known heretofore only in his mind. The fact that he permitted himself to go close enough to touch the secret fear is evidence of strength. It will not be fear next time, even if he feels he cannot do anything about the problem. The visit was Deborah's suggestion, but S realizes he was eager for the suggestion.

His "own pictures," as S calls those special photographs he takes, are a strong symbol of his identity, as well as a longing to fulfill his creative instincts. S has made of these pictures a powerful mental and spiritual drive, and at the same time has attempted to close this creative room to his family, his people, to his own emotions. Instead of permitting his art to portray his inner self, his freedom, his identity as Jew as well as artist, S attempted to keep his ego under lock and key.

He hid these pictures in what is known, in newspaper terminology, as the morgue. He kept them a secret from his lover, from his "father" (the Old Man), and from his family. He tried hard to keep his family from creeping into the subject matter of his art, and he tried as hard to make his lover a part of it. Both attempts were failures because of his deep need for truth. His family became a part of his creative life because they are a part of him; Laura never was, and inside of him he knew it.

The fear and doubt which have kept him from any kind of adjustment have muffled his creative powers as well. The pictures are fine, showing great talent, but he does not believe in them. He locks them in a dark place that is known as death. In his mind, as well as in the morgue drawer, his creative talent is not alive.

S has tried to keep from these pictures any "stigma" of family, Jews, self. He has tried to keep these photographs "untainted," untouched by the emotions which have tortured him. Yet their great talent, their sensitiveness and art, lie in the fact that into these pictures have seeped his hunger and shame, his tormented family relationships, his "name." The power and beauty of the pictures come from the very things which he has tried to bar from them. The pictures, all along, have been a more truthful mirror of his identity than any physical act or gesture on his part.

For years, S has had an unrecognized longing to photograph his family. The longing has engendered more fear in him. He has had a similar longing to come close to them, been afraid of that, too. His pictures, like his feelings for family and for Jews, have been stifled by his shame, by his fear of the potential and actual evil inherent in that family. His feelings and his pictures must be released at the same time; the two are synonymous in him. In giving his pictures to his family, that is, to an undistorted reality of his family, S will release his creative drive, achieve identity, avoid the wasteland of which he has been so afraid. He will, in this way, bring a free creative ability to the world, achieve his rightful place and identity in that world.

S has begun to take his pictures out of the dark corner of the morgue, has shown them to D (person of authority, symbol of the world). S has begun to take pictures of his family, made the first attempts to include his family (religious origin, name, self) in his creative self. Not only has he taken pictures of his mother and father, of Deborah (who disturbed him most of all), but he has lost most of the furtive, ashamed, frightened attitude toward such photographic subjects. His attitude is almost casual; he evinces interest in the artistic possibilities of these subjects, speaks of future pictures not only of these three but of his nephews, whose situation furnished him his first acceptable excuse for psychiatric assistance.

Attitude of S toward Deborah has been clarified to great extent. The picture he has taken of her is a sensitive, warm portrait of a poet, a woman. . . .

Eight

Now, almost suddenly, the room had become a peaceful place, to which one could always come back, every week. It had been a long time since he had felt frightened sitting here, or so it seemed, a long and far time back when the ghosts of people he had known came to stand around this chair and peer at him. Were there any ghosts left in the world?

Jake swerved into words. "I had two drinks before I came up here. Not that I wanted them. I just wanted to try them out. Know what I mean?"

"Deliberate drinks."

Jake smiled back briefly. "I guess you could call them that, Doctor."

He could not stop thinking of the word ghosts.

"Did the drinks do anything in particular?"

Jake looked uncomfortable. "No. It isn't as if I sat there drinking them down. You know, six or seven of them."

"How did they taste?"

Jake watched him carefully. "They tasted good."

The doctor smiled. "Why didn't you go on drinking?"

"I didn't want any more." Jake kept watching, felt a little breathless. "Besides, I had an appointment with you."

"Ever break an appointment?"

"Yeah." The word ghosts wafted softly and slowly about the room, poised itself like a dark bird on the broad desk. "I didn't want to break this one."

"You didn't want another drink," the doctor said again. "You'd had two, and you didn't care for another."

"Yeah," Jake said stolidly. "That's the truth."

He took a cigarette from the box on the desk, lit it. As he leaned back, he felt the soft, reiterated impact of the word flying dark and slow as a bat in the room. Let him bring it up, he thought, waiting for the voice.

"You've learned quite a bit about yourself, Jake. And about your family. Has it made very much difference in the way you think?"

Jake stared at the doctor. He had expected something else, felt a sudden rush of air as if the word he had anticipated and dreaded had flown swiftly out of the room.

"The way I think?" he stammered.

For a few moments, he sat motionless, his mind absolutely empty, and watched the bright end of his cigarette. Then an image of the doctor rose into the blankness, an outline of a man, something white and impersonal as a surgeon's jacket, and out of this anonymous picture a pair of gentle but impersonal eyes looked at him. Rising directly after this image, another face, another pair of eyes, seemed to be created in his mind. Debby; and the eyes, the mouth, of this second image were warm and urgent.

He looked up, across the desk. "Yes, I feel sort of different," he said slowly, but this time it was a hesitancy of earnestness, of slow thoughts pushing at him. "In my work, mostly. When I take pictures now, I—well, it's sort of hard to explain, Doctor! It's like I don't have to hold back any more!"

At that, his face reddened. He waited for a question, a comment of some sort, but the doctor's eyes seemed unchanged, remained calmly upon his, the head and face in shadow so that Jake could catch nothing but that grave, unhurried air of expectancy.

He labored on then, trying to find words to match the eagerness to explain. Debby could say it, he thought, and the push of her name in his mind again made words.

"I feel as if I don't have to be afraid to go the limit. Do you know what I mean? I used to be afraid of what I'd find. I mean, if I ever took pictures the way I really wanted to."

The words petered out; they had not sounded right. He peered across the desk into the shadowy face.

"What do you mean, go the limit?" the doctor asked.

"Photograph way down," Jake said quickly. "Into people's eyes, the way they're really feeling and thinking. Photograph their—what Debby calls their soul. I never had the guts to do that. Jesus, how I always wanted to!"

He paused. Very moved, he muttered, "I've started to do it that way. It's a wonderful sensation, Doctor! You've no idea! You feel—free. Not to have to be afraid you'll uncover something hidden, something you'd have to be ashamed to face."

"But you've done that all along," the doctor said. "In your own pictures."

"Yes," Jake cried, "but I never *felt* free about it! And now I can do it in any picture I take, maybe! Any shot for the paper, even!"

He hitched forward excitedly. "It's a wonderful feeling. All of a sudden, not to be scared of what you might get with your camera. What you might uncover. Jesus, I don't care who sees those pictures now. Maybe three out of five are good!"

He began to stammer again. "Honestly, I just can't tell you. I used to feel how I was wasting a hundred shots a day. Just because I was afraid to—to let go."

The doctor was smiling gravely. "So we come back to that word wasteland, don't we?"

Jake's eyes dulled. "Yeah," he said. "That's some word, isn't it?"

He lit a cigarette, his gestures cramped and closed suddenly. He heard the word ghosts again; it was in the room again, fluttering heavy and soft, with a kind of blind flopping, all around his head.

The gentle voice came across the expanse of desk. "What are you thinking, Jake? Care to tell me?"

"About Sarah," Jake said in a low voice. "Her wasteland. How it came from Ma and Pa. How it got together with Max. With his wasteland. How it starts up in Sarah's and Max's kids. Jesus, what a word. Wasteland. It makes me sick to just say it."

243

He dragged roughly on the cigarette, looked up, his violent glance crossing the broad desk.

"It's enough to scare you. The way waste like that goes on and on. Bernie and Allen grow up. They get married. Maybe their kids get born into the middle of that same wasteland."

The quiet voice caught at him. "Do you really think it's as inevitable as that? What if Bernie and Allen are stopped now? Their lives directed? Someone dominant enough to push them in another direction, away from this wasteland toward which they seem to be so steadily moving?"

"I don't know. Where will they get that push?" Then Jake cried hoarsely, feeling the words an old, not quite forgotten reiteration in him, "Debby can't push all of us!"

"What about you?" That voice never swerved from the quietness. "We've discussed it before, but things have changed, haven't they? Could you do the pushing now?"

Jake put out his cigarette. For a long time, his hand kept mashing the dead end into the ashtray. When finally he looked up, his eyes were full of tears.

"What is it?" the doctor asked. "Do you want to tell me?"

"Sure, sure!" Jake reached into his inside pocket, brought out a folded piece of paper. Big, sprawling, penciled words covered both sides of the paper.

"It's a composition," Jake said fiercely, wiping his eyes with the back of one hand. "The teacher gave them a subject. 'My Ideal.' They should write a composition on it."

"Bernie?"

"Allen, for Christ sake! That little, skinny thing. He got an A on it. Sarah showed it to Debby. Well, Debby thought I ought to see it." He glared at the doctor. "I said to Debby, 'For Christ sake, why should a kid write lies like that?' And she tells me even a kid like that has a right to dream!"

" 'My Ideal', eh?"

"Yeah! Listen to what that kid wrote." Jake read in a low, savage voice: " 'My ideal is my Uncle Jack. He is a photographer for the *Register*, and I admire the way he got to the place he is now. When he was a small boy he started selling papers in front of the *Register* building and because he worked so hard and was so cheerful they asked him if he wanted to be a copy boy in the office. He was only fourteen then.' "

Jake looked up. "How do you like that! I suppose Sarah told him that one."

He went on. " 'By the time he was eighteen he was a cub reporter. When a big hospital burned he was the only one who dared to go inside the burning building with a gas mask and take pictures.' "

He made a helpless gesture. "I wasn't the only one, for Christ sake!"

"Please go on," the doctor said.

" 'This brave thing he did gave him a promotion. My uncle took pictures of all the big events in our city and even went with our ball team every spring when they took their training in Florida. He has been to Chicago, Cleveland, and St. Louis. Every summer he goes to Mexico and takes pictures of the people and the country. They are all very beautiful. When he comes home we are always eager to see him because he tells us stories of his trip and he always has some presents for us. He brought home little sombreros, clay ashtrays, jumping beans and straw horses for all of us.' "

When Jake looked up, there were tears in his eyes again. "I never brought them a thing. I never discussed Mexico or anything else with anyone but Debby. Jesus, and listen to this!"

He read, " 'When he is home in the summertime he takes pictures of our family with his camera. I have a picture he took of me when I was one year old. He put me in his suitcase and only my head stuck out.' "

The tearful eyes looked up for an instant. "Dreams, Debby calls it! And it gets dreamier. Listen. 'Whenever we go to his office in the *Register* building we see his darkroom where he develops his pictures and we meet all his friends who like him very much. I think anyone who is so well liked is someone I would want for my ideal.' "

Jake's voice faltered.

"Would you rather not finish reading it?" the doctor said, pushing the box of cigarettes closer.

Jake gulped. "I'll finish it. I know it almost by heart, anyway."

He lit a cigarette, dragged deeply for a few moments.

"I just can't get over it," he said thickly. "When they come up to the darkroom! When they meet all my friends!"

"Terrible prospect?" the quiet voice asked.

"That's not it! The kid writes as if it all happened. I keep wondering what Bernie thinks, if this is what Allen thinks. Allen's practically a baby."

"Bernie probably doesn't dream this way at all," the doctor said. "Perhaps he did, when he was as young as Allen."

"Yeah," Jake muttered. "Maybe he did. Let's finish this damn thing. It gets better and better!"

He turned the sheet, peered at the other side of it. "'I want to be like him because I think he is very smart and he is very good and kind to my brother and me. He always gets us passes for the circus, baseball games and other things we want to see.'"

Jake cleared his throat, did not look up. "'It is his brave ways and his kindness that makes me admire him and I hope that I can be just like him when I grow up. That is why my Uncle Jack is my ideal. By Allen Radin.'"

He could not raise his eyes. He felt desperately ashamed, and yet excited, too. It was the same feeling he had had when first he'd read the paper, when he had looked up from it and into Debby's eyes.

"You're pleased, aren't you?" the doctor said.

"What?" Jake cried, looking up at last.

"Because this isn't wasteland," the doctor went on gravely. "Your nephew is full of a very creative imagination, isn't he? And he is very fond of you, isn't he?"

"Yeah," Jake stammered. "He'd write little lies like that because he likes me, wouldn't he? He and Bernie—they want all those things from me, don't they? Sure, I'm pleased!" His excitement was focused now. "Who wouldn't be? I just didn't know they liked me. Kind and brave, my God!"

Carefully, he folded the paper and thrust it back into his pocket.

"I've got to figure out some way of getting along with them," he said, almost to himself. "Not scare them away. It would probably be easy to scare them off."

"Your sister gets along with them, doesn't she?" the doctor asked.

"Who, Roz?" Jake said fiercely. "She gives them money, but that's all."

"I meant your sister Deborah," the doctor said quietly.

Jake's face burned. The idea of ghosts had trapped him, after all, he thought wryly. He'll know I've been thinking of Roz ever since I got here, he thought, and began to play with the cigarette box.

"Do you dislike her so much?" the doctor went on, as quietly.

"That isn't it!" Jake cried immediately. "Wouldn't you be ashamed of a sister who served drinks in a joint like the Glens?"

"No, I don't think so."

Jake stared across the desk.

"Is she earning her living by waiting on people?"

"Sure, she's earning it. She pays for her apartment and clothes. She bought her own car. Sure, sure!"

"Do you think she has relations with men? Of what are you ashamed, exactly?"

"She's probably sleeping with every guy on the Avenue!" Jake flung across the desk, and then the word came flying softly and heavily out of the air, and he knew he was stuck, he knew he would have to face Roz now, as he had faced Debby, and Ma and the old man. Then that'll leave Sig, he thought with a feeling of dread.

"Have you any proof of that?" the doctor asked. "Are you certain of it?"

"No," Jake muttered. "But it stands to reason, doesn't it?"

"Just as it stood to reason," the doctor said coolly, "that Deborah was a strange, degenerate creature. That your mother was deliberately withholding love and care from you. That your father was an evil man whose actions were deliberately calculated to torment all of you."

Jake stared at him with a helpless look.

"Look at your sister, won't you?" the impersonal voice said. "Are you ashamed of such seeming relationships, or are you afraid of her wasteland, too? Is it wasteland?"

"She's wasted her whole life," Jake cried. "What else would you call it but wasteland? I suppose Bernie is proud of an aunt who serves drinks in a night spot!"

"Did you ever ask Bernie if he is ashamed of her?"

Jake's mouth sagged.

"Has Deborah ever spoken of being ashamed of Roz? And Deborah is a sensitive enough judge of most things, isn't she?"

Jake shook his head, a dazed look in his eyes. Finally, he said, "I've just been afraid to think about her. I've been waiting for you to ask about her."

At that, and at the look in the doctor's eyes, he felt uncomfortable again. "I knew I'd be talking about her sooner or later," he protested. "Maybe I wasn't ready to talk about Roz. Not until now."

"Maybe not," the doctor said calmly. "You do want to talk about her now?"

"Yeah," Jake said heavily, "I guess. Maybe I can figure it out if I talk about it. The way I did with Debby and my mother. And the old man. I don't see Roz much. Only on Friday nights, when she comes home to eat. I never go to the Glens. Sure, it's a popular spot, and the newspaper gang hangs out there a lot, but I stay away. I figure, what's the point? Let well enough alone. This one particular night I couldn't help myself. This night I keep thinking about. I was with Katherine and Wally Lowell—he used to be my boss when I was on the sports desk, and we've been real pals for about twelve years. We had Carol Armstrong along, too. She's a model for one of the stores, a swell-looking girl, hangs out with Kathy a lot. Well, we got pretty tanked up at Kathy's place, then Wally wanted to go out and do the town. I didn't care about anything by that time. Kathy and Carol had both been talking about Laura, ripping her to pieces."

"Exactly how?"

Jake nodded in that heavy way. "Oh, about the way she used everybody. Kathy brought out a scrapbook and showed us how Laura'd used part of other people's articles in her fashion columns. You know, New York columnists and magazine writers. Then Kathy said Laura had never really given a damn about anybody but her husband. I got pretty drunk after that. Then we piled into Wally's car and he drove us around to a couple of places. We kept drinking. Then we ended up at this joint that was jammed to the rafters. We sat there for about ten minutes before we could get a drink, and Kathy kept talking. . ."

. . . kept insisting, "All right, tell me that one thing. Then I'll lay off. Do you agree that she played you for a sucker?"

"Leave him alone," Wally growled. "She played everybody for a sucker, but everybody loved it. Let's have a drink. Where in hell is that waitress?"

"Yes, but everybody else knew it," Kathy went on. "Jack didn't. Jack thought she was in love with him. All I want is for him to admit it. That's all."

"Oh, for the love of God," Carol said, "let's cut it out. Here we are, in the Glens, and we haven't even got a drink to show for it."

The Glens. Jake's eyes lifted from the spot on the table he had been studying. A feeling of fear came whimpering out of the noisy air and settled on his chest. He stared about him so wildly that Kathy leaned close to him and cried, "Jack, what's the matter? Are you sick? Jack!"

He pulled his eyes away from one of the tables. "Who's playing?" he said. "That's marvelous music."

"Cody Anderson's outfit. They started Wednesday, right out of New York. I told you about them last week. Don't you remember?"

"Yeah, sure." His eyes went back to the table, and he felt a rotten, bitter taste in his throat. Sig was sitting there, with about ten others, men and women dressed to kill.

"Where the hell's our drinks?" he said.

Sig and his Jewish doctor friends, and lawyer pals. Who in hell paid the bill at a time like this, in a joint like this? Sig? Or did he chisel his drinks, too? The way he chiseled his food and bed at home? No, nobody at home knew Sig went to the Glens, the way guys with plenty of dough went. No, everybody at home felt sorry for poor Sig. No money, no decent job, poor Sig, let's pay the house expenses, let's not bother poor Sig with money problems, he's got a tough enough time of it as it is.

"Bastard," he murmured. "Keeping up with the big shots, sure."

"What?" Kathy said.

He looked around, into her concerned eyes.

"Jack," Wally broke in with a laugh, "what are you drinking? The waitress finally condescended to see us."

It was Roz. Of course. Naturally! Of all the waitresses in the jammed, casual, noisy room it had to be Roz.

His head felt swimming and hot. He could not take his

eyes from her. He felt glued toward her, not only his eyes but his entire rocking, hot being, and he sat there staring at her, waiting for her to greet him, to tell that she was his sister. He could not move an inch from her, the green, beautifully fitting slacks, an orange sheer blouse, the narrowed eyes in a smiling face, the big, artificial, white flower pinned at the side of her head.

"Hey, Jack," Wally bellowed. "What's the matter, you drunk already? Tell this beautiful gal what you're drinking, for Chris' sake!"

"Scotch and water," he said, looking directly into her eyes. He could not make out their color, and this bothered him a lot; he had forgotten what color her eyes were.

"Scotch and water," Roz repeated, writing it on a pad she held, and turned to the others.

Jake shrank back, fumblingly lit a cigarette. She wasn't going to let on! Had Sig said hello to her? In front of all those classy friends of his? Hell, no! What if she said, with that cold smile, "Well, well, if it isn't my brother Jakey"? What should he do? Leave? Laugh? Call her a liar?

He watched carefully, without appearing to watch, her swaying hips and provoking walk as she moved toward the bar. With a kind of anguish, he heard Wally say, "Some stuff! I've been telling you, Carol, the Glens has the best looking waitresses in town. Did you take a good squint at that one?"

Then he had to wait, with every inch of him stiff and cold, until she brought the drinks. What would happen if I just nodded at her and said hello? Wally would want to know who and how. Kathy would make a crack, maybe. Yeah, but is she going to say anything to me?

"How long we staying here?" he mumbled.

"But we just got here," Kathy said. "Why so restless, Jack?"

Then the drinks were on the table, and Roz had disappeared. He couldn't find her in the room, and people were dancing, and he had gulped his drink down, and at the other table Sig was laughing and talking to a Jewish-looking girl. She was looking up at him as if she were nuts about him.

"Laura Anderson always had one thing," Kathy said. "Nerve. Just plain, unadulterated gall. She's still using art by

Jack Brown. But would she give him a credit line? Hell, no!"

"What d'ya mean?" Wally said, drinking.

"She's doing a syndicated fashion column. So she's still using that marvelous shot of Jack's. The one she used in her column here. Without ever using his name under it!"

"So what?" Wally said.

"She might give him a line, or mention it, or something."

"Aw, Kat," Jake mumbled. He felt bone-tired.

Carol and Wally were looking at somebody and giggling, and Kathy bent close to Jake, her eyes tender. "Darling," she whispered, "why the hell have you got such an inferiority complex? I thought after Laura left you'd snap out of it."

He shook his empty glass, peered miserably into it.

"In a joint like this," Kathy whispered, and when he looked up her eyes were blurred and anxious. "Nobody here is better than you, Jack!"

He shook his head vaguely, drank the last drops out of his glass. To hell with Kat, too! And with the whole bunch of them. The way everybody took it for granted he had an inferiority complex. Everybody. Wonder if Sig has one? And Roz, what about her?

"Here, have some of mine," Kathy said, pushing her drink toward him, and Wally put up two fingers and bellowed, "Hey, four of the same, cutey!"

Then the green-and-orange colors were back, the blurred, huge white flower, and when he looked up Roz's cold, smiling face swam before him for a moment, her eyes seeming to study him. He wanted to cry to her, "Did you wait on Sig, too? Did he tell those people you're his sister? Did he!"

Her eyes seemed full of dislike, and he thought confusedly, What, is she ashamed of me? She looks as if she doesn't want anything to do with me!

Then the provocative walk disappeared again, and he drank, peering over the rim of the glass for a flash of the orange-and-green, the silken hips.

Carol and Wally were dancing. When Jake looked again, Sig and his party had gone, and the room seemed full of undulating, separate waves of orange and green, one wave shimmering into the next. That was the last thing he saw, one wave after another, slow and provoking and endless, before he passed out. . . .

"I didn't have the nerve to say she was my sister. In front of my best friends."

"Why was that, do you think?"

"I was ashamed of her. What she was doing. How she was dressed. The way Wally looked at her."

"You were ashamed of her, you say. Was there any shame of yourself mixed into your emotions?"

"Of myself! Why should I be ashamed of myself in connection with Roz?"

"You've always acted toward Roz in the traditional, older-brother way?"

"What? I never had anything to do with her. She went her own way. She was out in the streets when she was only twelve. Running after every dago and bum she could see. I told you that."

"Running away from a lovely, comfortable home? A home to which she could invite her friends, boys and girls both? Parents who would welcome her friends, laugh with them, serve cookies to them, ask them to come again?"

"What?"

"Running away from her brothers, who were friendly, who gave her advice, who laughed with her or talked with her evenings, who perhaps helped her with homework?"

"But Doctor, you don't understand! She never wanted that. She rushed out of the house every night. Like a clock, my mother used to say. Like a clock, every night Roz gets dressed up and goes to the street. And comes home twelve, one, two—with my mother worrying about rape and babies, and the whole Goddam smear. Crying, walking around the rooms till Roz got home."

"Out she went every night, for no reason whatsoever, to escape from a gay, laughter-filled house, eh?"

"All right, it was dark and dirty there! It was my mother crying for money and the old man laughing his no to her! All right, but why didn't Debby run to the bums? Why didn't Sig and I run to bright lights and music? Why only Roz? . . . Hell,

252

I'm sorry. That's a pretty dopey thing to say, isn't it? Debby goes one way, I go another, Roz goes a third. People are different, O.K. People go after different things. What was I supposed to do about it, for Christ sake? I'm only three years older than Roz. Was I supposed to act like her father!"

"Are you asking me, or yourself?"

"Sure, I could have said to her, 'Roz, I'm your brother. Let me help you.' But I had my own troubles, didn't I? I was a kid. All I knew was, I was ashamed of the whole bunch, including me. How the hell was I supposed to understand what was eating on Roz?"

"But you're not a kid now, are you?"

"Now?"

"You're not ashamed of them now, are you? Now that you understand them a little better? Deborah, your mother and father. Are you?"

"No."

"But you continue to be ashamed of Roz? . . . Is it Roz you're ashamed of? You have difficulty facing her at the Friday night suppers. You cannot call her sister before friends. You see in her the ultimate in wasteland, a woman who is wasting her body and her mind, a woman with no hope for any decent kind of life, marriage and a home, children."

"That's it! What kind of a guy would marry her?"

"This life of hers, this woman she has turned out to be, did she pick it all by herself? Did she make herself with her own hands?"

"What do you mean?"

"Did anyone help her? Did anyone try to keep her from being pushed into her kind of life?"

"Help her? I don't know."

"Did you?"

"Me? What did I have to do with it?"

"You are proud of the influence you have had on your sister? Of the way you have helped her?"

"Proud? No, I'm not proud."

"What are you?"

"Please, Doctor!"

"But you want to know what this feeling of shame is, don't

you? There must be a specific reason for your shame. Just as there was with Deborah. It may be unpleasant to face, but you'll have to bring it out—look at it. Can you think of the reason you feel this way about Roz?"

"Yes, yes! Yes, I know what it was. I know, all right! It's just hard to say, that's all. Sure, I'm ashamed. I'm so ashamed I can't look at her. Sure, I helped do it to her! Like I helped do it to Debby. I didn't make a single move to stop her. Why shouldn't she have run away from that lousy, hard cot she slept on?" . . .

. . . in the living room, the cot set up in the middle of the living room floor; but always there was the comfort of Debby sleeping on the couch, so close that she could wake her up when she was scared in the middle of the night.

Debby always woke up fast, quiet, ready to soothe the very second her eyes opened.

"What's the matter?" she whispered immediately. "Don't be scared, Roz. What are you scared of?"

"I don't know. Ghosts, maybe. I saw a terrible movie tonight, Debby. I was so scared. I told Ross let's not go, but he laughed at me so we went."

"But you're here now. I'm here. Nobody can do anything to you."

The room filled with comfort, and Debby had come to sit on the edge of the cot, her hard little hand so strong, her face thin and steady in the half light, her face and hand absolutely unafraid of anything.

"I'm scared to go to sleep, Debby."

The room filled with hot, comforting whisper, with Debby saying, "Go on, go to sleep. I'm going to sit here until I hear you snore. Honest, Roz, I'm right here. Go on, go to sleep."

She had always been afraid when she was alone. At night one was most alone, and at night, in the darkness, she had always been most afraid. But when the night was all full of glaring lights and music that pounded the stillness out of life, full of boys' bodies that pressed close and danced or boys' mouths that kissed the loneliness away, then she was not afraid; then she loved the night. It would be wonderful to sleep during the day. Then, when the first darkness came, she could wake up, get all dressed in beautiful clothes, put on rouge and lipstick, and then all night long the music and the lights would be there, exciting, full of laughter and dancing, nobody ever crying, nobody ever lonesome or sad or needing money.

Little things stood out glaringly in her life, and she remembered them years later, amidst the blur of ordinary hours. The way Sarah kept talking about things like Pa writing Ma to bring Sig but not Sarah to America with her, and the way he had said to Sarah once: "When we don't work, we don't eat" (the old tightwad!). That was the way her own little remembered things kept popping into her head, in exactly the way that Sarah kept talking about the things she remembered. Only she didn't talk about them the way Sarah did, she just remembered them to herself. Except for the times she had talked to Debby. But that was different; in a way, that was like talking to herself, sort of.

For instance, there was the diary she had kept for almost a year when she had first started going out on dates. She'd been twelve at the time. A funny thing to keep remembering through the years, but somehow the diary had stuck in her mind, and every once in a while, out of a clear sky, she'd think of it. That time she'd had the abortion, when she was stretched out on the white table in that lousy office, all of a sudden she'd thought of the diary, kept thinking of it for a long time, and then the doctor had said, "All right, that's that, Mrs. Stern. I'll want to see you in three days. If anything goes wrong, call me immediately."

Dear Diary (she had written on the second page of the ten-cent notebook; on the first page she'd written her name and, under it, she'd printed in big letters: PRIVATE): I want to write in here only about nighttime. I don't like daytime. In the daytime everybody can see my skin, how my face is so terrible and broken out. I don't know why God did that to me, my face should be so full of pimples and blackheads, and I pray all the time it should go away. Sometimes I feel so ashamed I can't hardly stand it to go to school. But at night they can't see my face too good, and that's one reason I wish I could live only at night. People are different at night. When I go away from the house on a date at night, or just walking on Hillside Avenue with Rose or Jennie, everything and all the people too are so wonderful and so different. It's like boys' eyes when they look at you. And the way they dance. And kiss! That's at night, and there's music and dancing, and then the kissing starts.

She kept the diary hidden in the living room closet, on the shelf, in back of Sig's old straw hat that he didn't wear any more and that Ma didn't want to throw away.

Dear Diary (she had written, sitting cramped in the bathroom, with the door locked): Last night I went out to a dance with Ross Giordino. He's tall and dark. He's Italian but nicer than any Jewish boy in school. He dances so romantic, just like a movie star. On the way home he kissed me! That was like a movie, too. Then we didn't want to go home. We kissed a lot. It's wonderful to kiss. You don't have to be afraid of anything. I wonder if he noticed my skin. Could he feel it with his lips? Would he say anything if he felt anything? It was terrible when I got home. It was one o'clock and Ma was waiting on the front porch. She hollered a lot, but Debby made her go to sleep.

She got through that semester just by the skin of her teeth, and sitting in class was like a continuation of the diary, except that she dreamed it instead of writing it.

Dear Diary: Should I do my homework tonight, or go out? Rose told me in study hall today that she's got a double date for us. One is Jewish, too, but Rose says she wants the Jewish one. I don't care. Should I go? It would be dark before I met Rose on the corner and that new make-up I bought yesterday hides my skin real good. There's a test tomorrow, Diary! But I'm going with Rose, I'll bet you!

The school nurse called it something mysterious, acne, and said something about proper diet for the skin, but Roz kept going home to the fried cutlet and potato pancakes, the delicious potato pudding baked in deep fat, marinated herring, French fried potatoes; and, right after supper, while Ma and Debby did the dishes, she locked herself in the bathroom and wrote.

Dear Diary: I met a boy named Joe Rini! He knows Ross, but he's nicer than Ross. He's older. He works after school in the Southern Pool Room and he spends money, gee whiz and how! He took me to the show and held my hand all the way through the picture. He wants me to meet him every night. After the show we went and drank beer in his brother's restaurant. He doesn't like ice cream. He says it's time I drank a beer. That's what he calls it, a beer. I don't like it, but he says I will when I get used to it. He kisses a lot better than Ross. Oh Diary, it was so wonderful! I want to meet him every night. He calls me good-looking and I'll bet he didn't notice my skin. He wouldn't have kissed me so much if he'd noticed, would he? I got home real late. I don't even know what time it was, and Ma was crying in the front room, and Debby told her it was all right but she didn't stop crying for a long time. I guess I'd better stay home a couple of nights. Debby hollered at me after Ma went to bed.

One evening she came home about nine o'clock. She had been walking with Rose and suddenly she had started to worry about her homework. She had not done any all week, and tomorrow was hand-in day.

The house was empty. Not even Debby was home. For a while she sat in the kitchen, trying to write a composition. Then, very suddenly, she felt a cold breath on the back of her neck. When she turned quickly, there was nothing back there, and again she started to write. Then she began to hear a hundred creaking sounds, footsteps, wavy undulating noises like air moving coldly, and then Pa's clock struck the half hour and in a panic she ran into the living room and snapped on the lights, cowered in the big chair.

Years passed her by as she sat with closed eyes, and all the cold, secretive things of dread swished around her, and she was afraid now to open her eyes, or to move, or to run out of the house.

Then the kitchen door opened and she jumped up, ran toward the living noise, sobbing.

"Jake!" she cried, the tears feeling hot on her face. "Oh Jake, I'm so glad you came! I was so scared. Nobody's home, Jake!"

He looked at her coldly, and she caught her breath.

"Nuts," he said. "You weren't scared last night. Stay out all night, Ma walking around the house like crazy. That don't scare you, huh?"

He turned toward the sink.

"The house gets full of footsteps," she tried to tell him. "It's so scary."

When he turned, she saw how red his face had become. His fists were clenched.

"Why don't you call Ross? Or Joe? Or one of those lousy dagoes? If you're so Goddam scared!"

She stared at him, the tears suddenly gone.

"How do they like your pimples?" he snarled.

"Oh, you dirty, dirty rat," she whispered. "You dirty crook!"

He banged into the bedroom where he and Sig slept, and her heart had simply stopped beating, she just kept staring at the closed door.

That was when she started to hate Jake. Until that moment he had been just a brother, somebody who paid no attention to her, who was silent around the house for the most part. Now he was somebody with a man's look in his eyes, somebody who had stolen her biggest secret from her. That night, long after she had torn the diary to bits, when she lay on the cot too afraid to sleep, she finally woke up Debby and told her what Jake had done, crying softly and bitterly as she told it.

She had never liked Pa either, but she did not start hating him until she was in her first year of high school and he began to nag at her to quit school and go to work. She did not care a lot one way or the other, but Sig said she had to graduate. She wasn't very good at typing and shorthand, but Sig said she'd get a better job if she finished, so she decided she'd better get her diploma.

"All right," Pa said, and he had that laugh on his face, that look that wasn't a real laugh at all. "So go to school!"

Well, he just never gave Ma enough money to buy her any decent clothes, and she was the worst dressed girl in school. That, on top of her skin, was enough to make her want to die. She cried practically every day.

The real hell was when Pa refused to give any money for a graduation ring and a white dress. All the girls were wearing the same kind of dresses, ordered and fitted at the Carp Company, downtown, just as the fellows were all wearing the same kind of dark jackets and white trousers. It was terrible. She knew she would die of shame because everybody had a ring, and a lot of the girls were wearing theirs and asked her where hers was, and she said she'd ordered it, but she could not keep saying that forever. And she knew she would not go to graduation if she had to be the only girl in her class in a different dress. She wanted to die, that's what, and she hated him, absolutely hated him.

Well, Debby asked Sig for the money for the dress and the ring. She told Sig she'd pay him back as soon as she got a job. Roz heard her say it to him, and she cried soundlessly, listening. Sig gave Debby the money for the ring and the dress (in those days he had money), and it was like not having to die any more.

Pa didn't come to commencement. She knew he wouldn't, and she was terribly glad he didn't anyway, because he was somebody you had to be ashamed of, the way he couldn't talk decent English and the way he looked like a bum except on Jewish holidays when he went to *shule*.

Ma and Sarah and Debby came to commencement, and Debby had got some money somewhere and had bought some beautiful roses, just as beautiful as any flowers the girls were carrying. Ma cried a little, and Debby smiled so that her face looked like it had sunshine on it, and Sarah said: "I wanted to graduate from high school, too, but he didn't let me." And that evening her skin didn't look too terrible either, and she introduced her teachers to Ma and Sarah, saying, "My dad's sick and couldn't come." Ma nodding and beaming, not saying much because she was ashamed not to talk real good English, but Sarah talked real fancy, and she looked fancy in those days, too.

Those were things to remember through all the years; things that popped into her head at the oddest times. When she was serving drinks to a big party, too busy to even breathe, or when she was out with a guy on her night off, and she was three-quarters drunk, the guy smiling at her; suddenly, one of those little remembered things would flash into her head. A thing like Izzie, whom she had not seen for years, and who (she'd heard by the grapevine) was now in North Africa. The army had made him a quartermaster—what a laugh!—just because he had written in the army papers that he'd owned a couple of restaurants as his occupation. Yeah, a couple of beer joints! but now he was a quartermaster somewhere in North Africa, my God! life sure was funny. He'd probably get a medal too, that cheap, penny racketeer.

She had married him, sure. He was cute, and nuts about her, and a swell dancer. He had seemed to be rolling in money, too. Everybody else had thought he was rich, too, not only she. The kind of clothes he wore, the way he threw money around. And he was Jewish, too.

They drove to Kentucky secretly one night, with only Rose and Joe along, in the back seat of Izzie's Buick. All during the brief ceremony, she told herself they'd get married by a rabbi as soon as they could, just to make Ma feel good about it. She knew she'd feel better about it, too, if they got married in Jewish, as well as by a justice of the peace. Though Izzie was the kind of Jew who didn't understand or speak a word of Yiddish.

They never did get round to a rabbi, and after a while she was intensely glad they hadn't. Sarah told her that a man and woman were not really, truly considered married if they were Jews unless a rabbi did it. After a while she was glad the marriage was not binding as a rabbi would have made it.

She stuck to Izzie for five years. They were years filled with cops, and no money sometimes and a little money other times, and a lot of borrowing in between. The company took away his Buick, and he borrowed enough to get a Ford. When the Ford was taken, he bought something else, using her name for credit. Once he used Debby's name; she didn't like the idea, but she let him use her name anyway because of Roz. He always had a car, and good clothes, and always saw to it that she had as many clothes as she wanted. They always ate well. Izzie loved to eat; though he didn't like the Jewish food she did, the potato pancakes or *gefüllte* fish, or even chicken soup with matzoth balls floating in it.

He was a weak, namby-pamby guy who had never really grown up, just as he had never worked honestly in his life. He talked a lot about his mother and father and brothers, who all lived in Denver. He was always saying they'd go there on a visit, but nothing ever happened. She never expected it to.

Their marriage lasted five years, and she learned a lot and she learned fast. One year of it she sat out while he went to jail. She could not leave him at that time because you couldn't walk out on a guy when he was down and out; it just was not done, even if the guy was a little, jealous, no-good punk like Izzie. She planned to leave him as soon as he got out, but of course she didn't.

That was the year when Ma cried a lot; the cops had even come out to Ma's and Pa's one night, to ask about Izzie, standing on the front porch so that any of the neighbors could see the police uniforms. That was the year when Max made nasty cracks until she just stopped going to Sarah's house, and Sig and Jake (it was John now!) didn't even talk to her. But Debby— sure, Debby even drove out to the can with her to visit Izzie and to bring him cigarettes (you couldn't just forget all about a guy who was shut up that way, for Christ sake; it wouldn't have been nice). She never did know why he went to the can. He hedged all around the subject when she asked him, just the way he hedged about everything.

And that was the year when she got her first job in a night club, serving drinks, and knew what it was to make money fast, just by smiling the right way; the year she learned to know all the real big shots, not punks like Izzie; learned to know them like friends, so that the whole night club beat in town respected her and liked her but never made a pass at her. That had been a really tough job, but she had done it. They called her the smartest gal in town, and they really liked her, on top of respecting her. She could walk into any night club in town, after her own job was over with for the night, or on her night off, and walk in alone, even in the toughest cheating spot, and not a guy got funny. It was Roz this, and Roz that, and "Hey Roz, come and sit with us and have a drink," but nothing funny, ever. She was the only girl in town who could travel alone and get away with it.

She knew every boss and big shot on the night club beat, and they knew damn well she wasn't like the other waitresses, or the hostesses, or like any of the cheap floozies floating around town. She was the only Jewish waitress on the beat, and that added to the respect, too. Half the big boys were Jewish themselves, but even the dagoes respected her. She used to make little remarks in Yiddish, and the big boys would answer in Yiddish, and it was like a big family, like they were her brothers or cousins or something like that.

Finally, Izzie came out of the can. She quit working for others and went to work for him, in one lousy joint after another. He'd own them for a few months at a time, sometimes close to a year, until the debts caught up with him. The Black Cat, Jonesey's, the Apple Cart; not one of them panned out, even when he hired a swell cook once to make the barbecued chicken and ribs.

They had an apartment, and she insisted on buying some swell furniture, on time, let him worry about the bills and the rent. He started monkeying with a cheap, hazardous racket in song sheets, and the cops were on his tail most of the time, but somehow he managed to keep doing a sneak on them. Once it was so close that they arrested his printer; it was something big, something that was a Federal offense, to do with copyrights, but he hadn't given the printer his right name and he even got away with it then.

It was year after year of quarreling about money, about sex, years of his jealousy and separations every six months or so, Izzie begging her to come back, threatening to kill himself until she did come back; and all the time she kept learning plenty, knew enough to keep up the old loyal contacts of respect and liking she'd made.

She got caught once, and that was when she had the abortion. She was terribly frightened at having it done, went into the doctor's office with her teeth gritted and her lip bitten, but she knew she had to do it. She didn't know why, but she knew damn well she didn't want to have a baby of Izzie's, she knew she didn't want that at all, even if she died for it. Nobody knew about the abortion but Debby and Izzie. Debby waited for her in the outer office, and then drove her home to the apartment. Debby stayed with her for a week, going home each evening to eat supper at home. She told Ma she was staying at Roz's place so that she could write a very special story. It was a relief to have her around, too. She made coffee and things to eat, and never talked until you wanted her to. She'd never said one word about the abortion or about Izzie's way of doing things, or anything else. It was hard to feel scared with Debby around.

Once, when she left Izzie, she was broke enough to have

to go home, to the cot, to the dark smelly house where Pa snapped off electric lights as soon as anyone left a room for a second, where the air was depressing and stale and like a kind of death. She went back to Izzie after a week of it. He had that weak, silly grin on his face when she came back, and she said to herself, Not for long, you cheap punk, not for long.

When she divorced him he let her keep the furniture. For a while he kept hanging around the club where she worked, and sometimes she'd have dinner with him because he looked so lonesome, but she was through with him and they both knew it. She had her own car within a month, and paid for it completely in six months.

And that was when her life really began, when she paid for everything herself, the Negro woman who came three times a week and kept the apartment as clean as she had always wanted a house to be, the closets full of clothes, the expensive wrist watch and jewelry, the huge purses and handbags, the silver compacts, the little glass horses and cigarette boxes and figures strewn all over the living room.

She kept learning; how to buy "hot" clothes and jewelry and stockings at one-third the price she would have had to pay in the stores; how to identify that point of drunkenness in a patron at which the bill could be jacked up, the surplus divided between the bartender and herself; how to maneuver it so that the big guys and their parties would sit at a table in her station, so that the ten-dollar tips could go to her; how to go out with a guy and drink all night long and then say: "Wonderful time, look me up again," and get into her own car, drive to her own apartment alone in the early-morning light which made her feel so washed out and tired. How to sleep alone; the way she'd always known she had to.

There were the periods of blues sometimes, the lonely and bitter times, and sometimes she had to cry. But she did not permit herself these depressed moments for long; within an hour, of even the loneliest of times, she would bathe very quickly, put on her best outfit, her most subtle make-up, and run off to a movie. Or to the expensive, downtown gym she frequented. The business of reducing took care of a large part of her life; every time she thought of Sarah she shuddered, did ten minutes of extra exercises every morning before she fell wearily into bed. She knew damn well she'd get fat as a house if she let herself go; she was plump enough as it was, what with the occasional drinking and the way she kept eating bits and snacks all through the night. She did love to eat.

There were men through the years, some good-looking, some not, all of them plucked from the same cheap night stuff that was her life. Some were Jewish, some not; one had been Italian, but she could not stomach that for long, though he'd been a swell guy, generous and warmhearted and absolutely nuts about her. She'd kept thinking of Ma and how upset she'd be if she knew. Ma would cry: "An Italian? Roz, Roz, an Italian!" So she'd got rid of him after a few weeks, taken up with Mort. He was a Jew, all right, but the kind that Izzie had been, didn't understand one word of Yiddish. He was in what she called a "legitimate racket," something to do with manufacturing juke boxes. Mort had been very vague about the whole thing. He was a good-looking guy, big, not a shrimp like Izzie, but he acted like a spoiled baby plenty of times.

When the army got him she felt a little relieved; they'll make a man out of him, she said to herself, and when everybody at the club acted like she and Mort were engaged, she shrugged her shoulders about it, wrote him a two-page letter every other day. She kept going out with other guys, though, and she never thought of the definite day when she'd marry him. Another thing about Mort, he came in very handy when she was trying to keep a guy from getting too troublesome. "What's the matter?" she'd say indignantly. "Trying to make me cheat on my boy friend? Just because he's overseas?"

One Friday night she had told Debby about him, while Ma was getting ready to go over to Sarah's with her.

"Do you love him?" Debby had said, out of a clear sky.

Roz looked at her, shrugged her shoulders. "He's a lot of fun. I'm not getting any younger, am I?"

Her eyes narrowed. "Why? Do you believe in love?"

After a minute Debby's slow, kind of tired voice had said, "Yes, sometimes. For some people. Do you like this man?"

"Oh, sure." Looking up, she had seen in Debby's eyes that she knew Roz did, too, believe in love. She had probably seen, she was so smart, the years and years of waiting Roz had been doing, waiting for nothing but that love.

Then Ma had come out of the bathroom. She had changed to a good dress. "Well, are we going?" she had cried gaily.

Roz had smiled back. Ma, who didn't know what the word love meant. Ma, who always felt good when she was around. It wasn't only that she brought Ma presents, one of her huge, expensive handbags, only slightly worn, or a pair of nylons without even one run, a handsome jeweled pin she had got tired of, or the money she was always giving her.

She'd never known exactly what it was, why she made Ma feel so swell; she'd just felt it. Then, one Friday night, Debby had said it in words.

"It's as if you're bringing part of your life into the house, Roz. The night life, the music and the sound of all those people laughing, out having fun. When you're around, she senses the way people enjoy themselves. It's as if you bring the world into this house, a world she reads about in the papers, or sees in the movies sometimes. You yourself, Roz. Perfumed, divorced and yet unbroken in the least by it. You're dressed like the fancy movie people. You walk across Ma's path, and she gets the smell and sound of the kind of life she never had. Sophisticated, glamorous stuff. You bring life to her."

"I do?" Roz had said. It made her feel good to hear it. It made her feel kind of like a big shot. If Debby said it, then it was true. Debby was the smartest person she knew.

When Roz wanted to make an impression on some extra big guy, one of those out-of-town guys with plenty of money and class both, she always told about her sister, who was a writer. Sometimes she mentioned Jack too, how he was a photographer on a paper and knew everybody in town. But mostly she talked about Debby. A writer, with stories in magazines, my sister. She was the smartest person in school. She was going to be really famous some day, maybe write for the movies, live in Hollywood. Not that you'd think it to look at me, but this sister of mine always has a book in her hands.

She had finally told Debby about how she used her sometimes, when there was a big guy she really wanted to impress. Debby had smiled.

"But you should see how it gets them!" Roz had cried. "They say, 'You? You got a writer for a sister? Honest?' And they take a third look at me. Then, after a while, they always say, 'What's a girl like you doing in a joint like this?' Honest, Debby, it never fails. They always say the same thing."

Debby had smiled, such a funny, little, soft kind of smile. "Help yourself," she had said. "Use me any time you like. . . ."

When he came home from school, Bernie climbed the two flights of steps and turned the knob of the door. When the door remained shut, he knelt in the dim light of the hall to lift the mat and grope under it for the key. He cursed softly as his fingers gritted over dirt.

As he let himself in, he thought uneasily, Yeah, wait'll she hears about math and English. Boy, will she holler!

In his mind he had an instantaneous but fast-fading picture of his mother, a tall fat woman with bad teeth, whose voice was shrill and anxious most of the time. He wished she weren't so fat; none of the other guys' mothers were as fat as that. She didn't hit him much but she hollered a lot. He wished sometimes she'd hit him instead of hollering. Whenever anything happened, right away she started to holler. She cried a lot, too.

He kept himself from thinking of his father, a short, dark man who was always bringing home bags of stuff to eat. Bernie thought for a hard moment of how his father never paid any attention to anybody, except sometimes to Allen, until something happened and his mother started to holler, then he'd take off his belt and go after Bernie, all the time calling Ma crazy, calling her curse names in Yiddish. Or else he turned on the radio, way up, and sat there listening to the war news. He always acted like such a Goddam big shot, like he knew all about the war—just because he'd been in that other war. Or else the telephone would ring, and most of the time it was for Leah. Then, after about fifteen minutes of her talking so sweet to the guy on the phone, his father would start making cracks, right there near the radio. Sure, Allen and he would laugh, real loud, at the cracks. Leah got sore as hell, and after she was through with the phone, she'd holler at their father but he didn't pay any attention to her, just went on making cracks. Sometimes Leah would finally start to cry and run into a bedroom, then their father would stop talking and pay attention to the radio again.

Bernie went directly to the icebox. There was always part of a salami in there because his father kept bringing home whole salamis. He took out the chunk of sausage and cut off a thick wedge, then he cut a jagged slab of rye bread from the loaf on the table. For close to a half hour, he sat hunched over the table, eating, drinking a bottle of cherry soda he had found in the box, reading the new comic book Jerry had given him at school in exchange for one of his. It was a fifteen-center, and a beaut.

He sat there until he had finished the book, then he threw the remaining piece of salami back into the icebox. He did not touch the table, cluttered with crumbs and with bits of the translucent, oily skin he had peeled from the salami.

At this point, he felt a little unreal, the bright pictures of the book vivid in his mind, more alive than the dingy, cramped rooms of the apartment. He wandered about the living room dreamily for a few moments. The radio story he was following did not go on the air until five-thirty.

He tried drawing a new, free-hand picture of a guy he had made up, Bill O'Brien, the Greatest Athlete in the World. He liked to draw. One of these days he was going to draw a comic strip about Bill O'Brien. Then he'd be famous and rich, just like those guys who'd made up Superman. Right now, though, the drawing wasn't any good. It was too hard for him to sit still. He crumpled the paper, left it on the dining room table.

For an uneasy moment, he toyed with the idea of doing his math homework. But what the hell was the use? He didn't even know what the teacher was talking about, half the time. He knew damn well she'd laugh at him if he asked her to explain. Everybody else in the class always seemed to know. They never asked. He sure must be a dummy. Then, too, if he stood up to ask a question, she'd notice his eyes. Maybe she'd say something. Boy, what if a teacher ever made a crack about his eyes! What would he do! Kill her, that's what!

Where was the hell was his mother? And Allen. Usually

they were home when he came from school. Usually she was there, hollering for him to change his clothes, to eat, to stop giving Allen hell. As if Allen didn't start it! But she wasn't here today.

The small, thick, familiar fury began to swell in his chest. He stood near the electric light switch in the dining room and snapped it up and down, faster and faster, his breath coming faster, too, in the momentary garish flashes which seemed quick and dangerous as heat lightning in the room. Suddenly, he turned and ran out into the hall. Viciously he turned the key in the lock, threw it under the mat.

Outside it was not so hot, and as soon as he stepped from the hallway into the street he stopped running, stopped pounding and cursing inside. He swaggered slowly, hands in his pockets, to the lamppost, where some of the guys were standing around and doing nothing.

"What do you know?" he said sourly to Joey Goodman.

"Hey, Bernie," Martin broke in eagerly, "we're going up to the Colonial tonight and sneak in the back way. There's a swell war picture."

Bernie turned to Jerry Adler. "You going?" he demanded.

"Naw." Jerry tried to act nonchalant, but everybody knew he didn't have the nerve to go because of his mother and father, who made a fuss about such things.

"What's the matter," Bernie said, "scared?"

"Aw, who wants to sneak in the Colonial?" Jerry said bitterly. "That lousy show! I could go to a downtown show any time I want to. My mother and father take me all the time, all the way downtown, too. They take me any time I want to go. I don't have to sneak into a two-by-four show."

The small, tight ball of fury in Bernie's chest exploded, and he hit Jerry as hard as he could, even though Jerry was his best friend.

Everybody watched the fight gravely, in silence, knowing that Jerry had insulted Bernie because Bernie's mother and father never took him anywhere like a downtown show. Most of them went places with their parents, but Bernie never did; they all knew that, Jerry knew it too.

Jerry finally started to cry, then Bernie stopped punching him and just stood there until Jerry turned around and ran home.

"Nuts," Bernie said, breathing hard.

They all watched Jerry until he turned into his yard.

"What he have to start making cracks for?" Joey said.

"Yeah," Martin said, "he's all the time acting like a big shot. Downtown shows."

Bernie glared at them. The fury had not abated. It pressed at his chest, and now there was a bleak and heavy weight there, too. He felt so lonesome suddenly that he knew he was going to cry unless he did something fast.

"Aw, nuts," he said again, and swaggered off. He walked slowly, his hands sweating in his pockets, until he got inside the hall, then he pounded up the steps, crashing his feet down on each step to match the thunder and drums in his heart. He felt his cheeks shiver and his mouth shake, and he felt like a ghost pursuing an unknown, lonely thing up the two flights of steps.

The door to the apartment was ajar, Leah must be home from work. Bernie stopped on the landing and tried to tie up his heart and body. When finally he walked into the living room his mouth was twisted into a sneer, the kind he had learned within the last year.

Holy cat, she was on the telephone already! He clumped past his sister, where she sat on the window seat.

Yeah, listen to her! he raged. Sweet as sugar as long as it's a guy! They should hear her yell when she was home with just the family. Yeah, she looked just like Roz, with all that lipstick and the same kind of clothes that stuck to her shape that way. Sure, Leah would probably start working in a saloon soon, too, just the way his father said she would. "Just like Roz, look at her," his father said all the time. "Soon we'll have two saloonkeepers in the family."

In the kitchen, the dark close feel of the apartment accosted him and he felt as if he were fighting one of the boys in the street, his muscles tense, his heart wheeling all over the inside of his chest.

He opened the icebox door, then almost immediately slammed it. He began a shrill whistle and marched through the dining room, past Leah and her slow, soft talk. In the living room, he snapped on the radio, whistling and staring dully at the wedding picture of his father and mother on the table. They were slim, young strangers and they didn't look like his mother and father at all, at all! He kept his eyes from the picture of Debby on the mantel.

A rush of music came into the room and he kept it high. Leah's voice disappeared.

She came at him within a minute, her face red, her voice pitched above the music.

"You little rat," she shouted, "what's the big idea? You did that on purpose!"

She snapped off the radio. He glared at her. Just like their mother! All the time hollering, calling names. He'd rather get hit with a strap, that's what! All they did was holler at him.

He snapped on the radio. "I got a story to hear," he shouted. His face was like chalky stone in the dim room.

"You have not! You're doing it on purpose, you dummy. Just because I was on the telephone." She turned off the music again. "Where's Ma, for God's sake? And Allen? Better go wash your filthy face before supper, that's what you'd better do."

The huge, dark, wheeling thing in his chest swooped and plunged. He turned the radio knob, feeling his hand hot and tense against the wood.

Before the music could start, Leah had pushed his hand from the knob and snapped the radio off again. "Listen, cock-eyed," she cried, her voice threatening him.

As they faced each other fully, the dark thing plunged and plunged.

"Aw, you're nothing but a lousy bum," Bernie ground out at her. "Who the hell do you think you are, Roz?"

She flushed, stepped back. Suddenly, she was conscious of his eyes. She saw the faint, dark growth on his upper lip and the sneering mouth, and her heart sank.

It took her a moment to down the feeling of panic, then her hand flew up and she slapped Bernie's face with all her strength.

His eyes showed no surprise. He turned quietly and opened the door, walked out of the apartment.

270

She heard him all the way down the two flights, his steps unfamiliar and slow, heavy as a man's. . . .

"How is it you know so much about Roz?"

"I don't know too much. Most of that stuff Debby told me. Some of it I figured out. Just now. While I was talking."

"Did Deborah tell you the incident between Bernie and his sister, too?"

"Yeah, Leah told her about it. She was pretty disturbed, so she asked Bernie what he had to say. I don't know why, but he told Debby his side of it. Usually he won't talk, but this time he did. It's funny—."

"What is?"

"All those things Debby told me. When she was talking about them, I was sore, and kind of scared. Some of it I didn't get. Then I start talking here. You ask me a few questions, you say a word here and a word there, I go on talking. And all of a sudden it's like I understand those things!"

"Do you really think it's so odd that you understand them now?"

"No, not really. But sometimes it hits me all over again. It's so easy to understand those things. Here, I mean. The same things I used to break my head about. Jesus, I remember one Seder! How I wanted to kill Roz, just kill her. She hadn't done anything. Or said anything. She was just sitting there, that's all."

"Just sitting there, and you wanted to kill her?"

"Well, you don't understand! She was all made up, dressed to kill in those fancy things she wears. And sitting there, at a— a holy thing like the Seder. It was like a—."

"Yes?"

"Like a—a whore in a church! I just couldn't stand the idea. It was like looking at a —well, a doll sitting there. An empty doll. I don't know."

"Empty?"

"Yeah. Somebody wasted. Kind of like all her life had been wasted. The thing is, she was sitting at the Seder, looking like that. It was the Seder that—well, that showed her up."

"You were sitting opposite her at the table?"

"Oh, no! I didn't go to the table that year. I wasn't even going to come home that night, but—I don't know. I'd been thinking about it all day, figuring that I'd grab some food downtown and go to a movie. But it kept bothering me . . ."

. . . and throughout the day it seemed to him that he could smell the wonderful odors of the Seder. Now and again he would think of the house, how this evening it would be so clean, and the Passover dishes would be down from the top shelf, the dishes which always looked new. He knew how the matzoth would sound, cracking under his fingers, and how the wine was poured to the very brim of each glass. And he would be twenty-nine that year, birthday and Seder time mingled in his senses sweet as Passover wine and bitter as the herbs at once.

He would go home just to eat, he told himself, just to catch one glimpse of the Seder table. Maybe—well, who could ever tell?—maybe things would be different this year.

So he came home early, and in the clean kitchen, fragrant with the scents of chicken and fish, the newness and spring of the season, his mother served him silently. He ate, the final propped against the open pasteboard box of matzoth, the headlines flaring in the dim light of the room. He broke the square matzoth, the sharp cracking sound a kind of music, and chewed the ragged piece with a wonderful, secret relish. First time this year, first matzoth this year! the secret song went inside him, the Passover and birthday song.

"I better eat right away," he had told his mother. "I've got to go back to work. There's some kind of a meeting downtown, they want pictures."

"By them it's no holiday," she had said, nodding, taking his words so for granted that he felt a twinge of disappointment.

As he ate the chicken, the soup with the yellow, feathery-light matzoth balls floating in it, he watched her moving about from one last-minute job to another, her eyes peering at the hard-boiled eggs she was cooling under the cold water tap, her lumpy hands quick on the jar of horseradish and beets, which made a beautiful blotch of color in the kitchen. She seemed to carry an air of gladness and swiftness about with her, on her face, on the short stumpy body clad now in a holiday dress with a clean apron over it.

In despair, he pushed the scarcely tasted soup from him and escaped to his bedroom, there to sit on the bed and listen to the holiday sounds as they started all over again with each bang of the kitchen door.

When Sig came into the room, Jake was buttoning the clean shirt he had put on. He caught his brother's tired, rather jaded-looking eyes in the mirror, nodded.

"What's the matter," Sig said, "aren't you hanging around for the Seder?"

"I've got an assignment," Jake said carelessly, and Sig left the bedroom, and then Jake could hear Debby and Roz in the kitchen, and the deep voice of the old man calling from the dining room, "Where are the herbs?"

"Ma," Debby said then, "come and sit down. We're ready to start."

The first praying half song, familiar as all the years of the house, came into the bedroom, and Jake poured himself a drink, sat with it on the bed, pinned there by the prick and torment of the old, wonderful sound of the prayers. *Blessed art thou, O Eternal, our God, King of the Universe, Creator of the fruit of the vine.* He could remember how the words looked in the English column of the *Haggadah*, with the mysterious Hebrew in the other column, and pictures to fascinate him as he waited for his own ceremonial moment to come.

Yes, Sig would be fingering the *Haggadah* now, the first of the four cups of wine was poured, the old man was clearing his throat as he sat on the pillow, and it was springtime again, birthday time again. What the hell was he doing here? Why, for Christ sake, had he come home!

He bit his lip; Sig was asking the questions. Jake sat hunched over the glass in his hand, and listened to the amused tone of voice, the fast, light flick of words as Sig rattled them off.

"Wherefore is this night distinguished from all other nights?"

He gulped down the drink, went quickly to put the glass on the dresser, to comb his fingers through his hair, to see in the shadowy mirror the set jaw, the angry eyes; and Sig's voice, with a kind of smile under it, came into the room.

". . . all other nights we eat and drink either sitting or reclined, but on this night we all of us recline."

Jake walked out of the bedroom quickly and softly, and now his father's voice had taken up the story, and, standing in the narrow hallway, he felt the impact of the chanting, sorrowful, plaint-like praying. He wanted to get out of the house, but he had to see them first, the table with them round it, the wine and the herbs, the stack of matzoth, his brother and sisters, his mother, his own place at that table.

Softly, he stepped to the doorway, stood leaning on the wall just outside the room. He was immediately aware of Roz. She sat facing the doorway, and she was powdering her face, peering into the round mirror of her compact.

Debby and his mother were talking in whispers, Sig was cracking bits of matzoth and popping them into his mouth, his eyes staring off toward the living room as he chewed, his face almost slack-looking.

A feeling of intense anger swirled in Jake, rising thickly in back of his eyes like smoke. He struggled against the words flashing so absurdly into his mind: whore of Babylon at God's table, creature of the night who has crawled into this house of sanctity; as if he were reading a distorted, shaking leaf of the *Haggadah*.

At that moment he suddenly remembered Roz's diary, how he had found it when he had gone to look for some gloves, and had taken it into the basement to read, how the shivers had crawled up and down his back as he had read.

His father's voice rose. A barrage of the somber, singing words came at him as he stood in the doorway, and then Roz's eyes lifted from the mirror and she saw him. For an instant their eyes meshed, as all around them the chanted words solemnized the air, and Jake wanted to shout at her to take her Goddam lipstick and her night club look away from that table, to take her lousy wasted life and get it the hell out of this holiday house.

Looking at her, he felt that he could kill her if she didn't get away from that table, with her sex look, with her powder and lipstick in the midst of the wine and the prayers; and yet, a strange thing happened at that moment to confuse him.

Roz held his eyes for that instant, then her face reddened and an almost sad expression blurred her eyes as if with tears; her glance fell to the table. As he turned and walked softly out of the house, he felt suddenly shaken and weak.

In the car, driving toward the corner, he thought for a vague moment that it had been almost as if Roz had known what he was thinking, that she had recognized and agreed with his thoughts, yes, and that the recognition had been so sad.

He felt lonely, and for that moment his loneliness seemed to encompass her, too, as if both of them stood on the same high, perilous crag with nothing about them but empty sky and space.

Jesus, he thought despairingly, I better stay away from the Seder! I better never go near the house that night. Or I'll just go nuts!

She stayed with him all evening, through the movie, and then when he went up to Katherine's for a drink she was there, too. Late in the night, when he was drunk, she still walked in his mind; but it was the waste of her he saw, not the lipstick and the smile.

Now he seemed to know; not that night, but now, looking back and suddenly seeing that night the way it really had been. Now he knew how his anger had burned all around the emptiness of her that night, and maybe it had burned at his own emptiness, too, his own guilt at never having put out a hand to her, never, just the memory of a stolen diary with scrawled names and the first small sins between them.

. . . and articulate, clear discussion of S about the sister, who, until now, has been the symbol of sexual waste and promiscuity, points to further adjustment.

When told that treatments will be scheduled now for every other Saturday, S accepted new, promising status quietly and with satisfaction.

S has not discussed war or plans for enlistment for some time, except to inform D he has talked briefly to Deborah about it. He has been too engrossed in clearing up questions on family. His decision to enlist may come as end result, not as means to escape adjustment to family and society. He has not mentioned feeling of shame recently; guilt feeling has been clarified to great extent.

All details of the Seder and Passover difficulty seem freed. Questions today show he has accepted the importance of the ritual but that the holiday is no longer the fantastically important thing it was before treatments began. The Seder ceremony will continue to be of significance to him, but will assume real perspective when he makes the proper place within it for himself. That perspective has almost been attained. . . .

Nine

"Parents and friends," he began, speaking out into the darkened auditorium where the blur of faces hung. He knew all the eyes were watching only him, not the rest of the class behind him, or the principal, sitting near the ribboned box of diplomas, or the superintendent of schools, next to the principal, who was going to make the speech; only him, as he stood at ease, well dressed, well poised, on the stage.

"As president of this graduating class of Roosevelt High School, I am honored to welcome you to our commencement, to the most important night of all our years of school."

Behind him, the class moved restlessly; he could hear an occasional muffled clearing of a throat, a shuffling of new shoes. But maybe he was aware only of Helen, back there in the class. She was watching him. She was listening to him.

"As we stand before the slowly opening door of the world this evening, we feel deeply the solemn promise which we make to ourselves now, the promise to do our share as citizens of this world just opening to us."

Maybe he was thinking of how he had not even been born in America. In Russia, a country most Americans would laugh at; and how he had come here, a greenie, as people had called him, green as grass, fresh out of the peasant Russian fields.

And now, by God, now he was president of his class. This moment! Well, what other moment in the future could ever be as wonderful, as full of a feeling of power and freedom, of ambition?

"It is only fitting and right that we give our humble thanks at this time to you, our parents. It is you who have taken us, with care and with love, past the perils and difficulties of childhood. It is you who have led us to this new branch of the road to life."

Maybe he was thinking of his handwriting. How at first he couldn't even write English, that fabulous language of the fabulous new country. How he had practiced, how in his mind he had wanted to write so beautifully that people would look at the paper and gasp with delight, how he had sat for hours practicing arm movement, capital letters, how at last his penmanship teacher had said, "Well, Sigmund, I'm proud to say you've been the best student in the history of my class." On a piece of paper that name, Sigmund Brown, looked like the signature of a great banker, a distinguished businessman, a millionaire.

"Whatever we do in life, wherever we go, our families will go with us, in friendship and respect and love."

Maybe he was thinking that Ma and Sarah and Jake were here this evening, sitting in the darkened auditorium of the school, and that afterward they would meet him downstairs, in the gym, the way all the families would meet their graduating sons and daughters. (Helen's mother and father would be there!) Thank God, Pa wasn't there, maybe he was thinking. Wonderful impression Pa would make on the teachers, on the parents assembled there in their best clothes! Wonder if he'd have to introduce Ma and Sarah. Ma probably wouldn't open her mouth, she was so shy.

"Yes, this is the hour when youth and ambition stand side by side! This is the hour when all our dreams are noble ones, and the world is ours if we put out our hands."

Maybe he was thinking that he had a steady job at the Hornsby Company, starting Monday, a job he had been doing part time, on Saturdays, for the past two years. If he really worked, if he really wanted it, there was the job of head bookkeeper some day. And maybe he was thinking of how he had insisted on graduating, not quitting to work full time the way Pa had wanted. His own money had paid for books and clothes. Yes, he was wearing flannels and a navy jacket tonight, like all the fellows in class, because he had paid for them himself, and to hell with Pa. He had showed Pa that you didn't have to stay a greenie just because you were born one!

"We promise you, dear parents, dear friends, that we will justify your faith in us. We will take our rightful place in life and become good citizens, solid members of the world. This promise we solemnly make, both to you and to ourselves in this solemn hour. Thank you."

The auditorium filled with applause. As he bowed, as he went back to his seat, maybe he felt on the wonderful brink of that life he had been describing to them, filled with an excitement so sweet, so poignant, that he trembled.

Then the principal spoke, and the superintendent made his stolid, dull speech, and then each graduate rose and walked down toward the footlights to receive the diploma, and as each named was called, a small excited burst of applause popped in a corner of the auditorium. When the principal read his name, there was a lot of applause. Then Helen's name, and he watched her walk down, so gracefully, so beautifully, and she smiled; he could see her lips move as she told Mr. Watson thank you, and, when she turned to come back to her chair, Sig could see her curls, her round face and the solemn, little-girl eyes. He had been in love with her for two years. They were going out tonight, after commencement exercises. It even hurt to take a breath when he thought of her.

And then the stage part of the evening was over, and the whole class rushed down to the gym, the back way, to meet their families.

It took him a second to spot Ma and Sarah and Jake, standing in a queer little isolated group. Ma was wearing that rusty dark hat, and she looked funny and scared. Sarah looked O.K., but Jake looked like a poor skinny kid in somebody's thrown-away suit, except his face was very excited and his eyes kept flashing around at everything and everybody.

Sig shook hands stiffly with Sarah, and Ma giggled. "Gee, that was some speech," Jake cried, and Sarah nodded.

"It made me want to cry," she said. "It made me remember

how bad I wanted to graduate from high school." Her eyes were moist, and he turned away from the look on her face.

Maybe he was impatient, burning with restlessness and that wonderful sense of power. Maybe all of him was on guard against the possibility of bumping into Helen and her family, of the dread chance of having to introduce Ma and Sarah to her parents.

He stood there with them for about ten minutes, his back to the roomful of talk and laughter. Several of his teachers came up to the group, and he had to introduce them to the three, and then there were the few stiff words, Ma's nervous giggle, Jake's excited, dilated eyes; and then suddenly he was free, he had told them he had a date, and Ma's eyes had looked relieved. In her half whisper, she said in Yiddish, "Well, Sarah, let's go home. He's going to go out and have a good time with a girl. So let's go."

His family had gone. Maybe he had turned then, and walked directly to Helen, where she was standing with her parents and a lot of people. She was wearing a wonderful corsage of roses, and she was too beautiful to look at, but her eyes were glad to see him all the same.

Maybe there were the confused, flushed moments of looking into her mother's shrewd and watchful eyes, of shaking hands with her father, who looked like a good egg, of saying, "How do you do" to a lot of relatives. Then he and Helen had left everybody and they were walking in the dark street, and maybe he could feel her arm against him, maybe her flowers filled the air with a wonderful mixture of nostalgia and joy and pain.

They had made plans to go to the dance, which was being held downtown, at the Congress Ballroom. They waited on the corner for a streetcar, and suddenly maybe he said, "Helen, let's not. Let's go to the lake instead."

"Oh Sig," she cried, "that's a wonderful idea!"

Maybe they took a taxi, because Sig must have been saving money for this evening for a long time. It was June, and maybe they walked slowly along the dark, murmurous edge of the lake, and then maybe they sat on one of the green benches which dot that part of the park, he spreading his big white handkerchief for her to sit on, and then maybe they sat in silence, looking out into the huge, dark feeling of water, hearing the small waves break so regularly against the shore.

Maybe he turned to her then, his breath choked, turned to her and said, "My God, Helen, it's so wonderful to be here with you. Tonight. Commencement, and all that. My God, Helen, I can't tell you, I just can't."

Maybe they talked about the past four years at school then, the future, their hopes. Maybe she told him how much she liked him. But maybe she told him at once, without the past and future talk to soften it, without the hope and ambition talk to sweeten it.

"It's my mother, Sig," she might have told him. "She wants me to marry a professional man. A lawyer, or a doctor. She—. Oh Sig, she doesn't want me to go with you! Maybe she'll get over it," Helen might have gone on, her eyes shadowed, her hand pressing his gently. "Maybe after a while she'll stop thinking of such things. If we wait a while and don't see each other, Sig."

And he might have sat there, in the June night which had been so totally his only a few moments before, silent, hearing in the murmurous, hushed tones of the water a kind of doom, seeming to hear words to silence him forever at a time like this: Well, you can't blame her, look at Pa, sure, and Ma, a guy who was born in Europe, poor and low as niggers almost, a doctor or a lawyer! well, can you blame her? Look how beautiful Helen is, she deserves that, not me, a bookkeeper, with a family like mine, a house like mine, would I bring her to my house, introduce her? Helen, this is my father!

They might have sat there for a while, and she might have said, "Oh Sig, I'm sorry!" They might have kissed for the last time, and in his heart he might have heard the sound, the words, of that doom. Then they might have left the lake, he seeing her to the door of her parents' house and then going home to his own family, lying sleepless in the room, listening to Jake's restless twisting and turning on the other bed.

Then, three or four years later, he may have seen that announcement and picture in the magazine section of the Sunday paper. She had married a rich, young physician. She was the newly elected president of the Junior Council of Jewish Women. In the picture she was lovely, mature-looking, a little plumper.

Maybe his heart sank even more. Maybe, after reading the paper, he walked into the living room, saw Debby sitting there, engrossed in the eternal book. Maybe he shuddered, thought, Sure, why not? How would Helen like her for a sister!

Maybe that was why Sig had started to study at night college, after work, attending three evening classes a week. Maybe he thought he had to be a professional man, too. . . .

It was New Year's Eve again, time for Sig to come home with the hired tux and spread it on the bed, the white starched shirt draped over a chair, on the dresser the studs, the pins, the black tie; and the whole house moving around him in a small fury of excitement.

In Jake's mind, that hired tuxedo each New Year's Eve was symbolical of Sig, and of Sig's position both in the house and in the world. It was a shining, exotic thing, bringing with it restless dreams of the world he did not know. And how the house rode on wheels that night!—around Sig, around that tux, around the whole identification of his older brother.

The tank had been lit in early afternoon, so that plenty of steamy hot water was ready for Sig's bath by the time he came home. Ma had bought a quarter of a pound of corned beef, the most expensive of all the delicatessen meats. Sig was very fond of it. So was Jake, but of course it was Sig's money that paid for such delicacies, and there was no reason for anyone else in the family to eat such expensive things. Sometimes there was a half slice left on the table after Sig had finished, and a thin strip of dill pickle; then Ma told him to eat what was left.

As Sig bathed, then came out to dress in the bedroom, as he basked in Ma's and Debby's and Roz's dazzled eyes, Jake sat in a corner of the living room and watched bitterly. Sig was now head of his department at the company, had been what Jake secretly called "a big shot" for eleven years. Jake sat in his corner and bitterly sniffed at the wonderful scents of talcum powder and after-shaving lotion which seemed to fill the house.

The way Ma ran around so excitedly for Sig made him a

little sick with envy; the way Pa talked so soft, so respectful. Of course it was Sig's dough that kept the house going, sure. The old man never shelled out a dime unless he just had to, for an occasional light or gas bill. The way Sig scarcely ever talked to anybody; he had a way of acting and looking like a big shot, and God knows how much he used to spend on suits and shoes and shirts, silk underwear, and there were about three hundred ties hanging on the back of the closet door. Ma used to iron them all once every two weeks; or sometimes Debby would. And Pa used to walk into the bedroom in that soft, sneaking way he had, when Sig wasn't around, and help himself to any tie he liked. But not Jake! He'd rather wear a rope than one of Sig's ties.

For eleven years; and Sig had dropped night college after a year, but he kept right on hanging out with a lot of Jewish lawyers and dentists and even one doctor. Jake always listened closely to Sig's phone conversations, and after a while he got so he could piece together a lot of things. All these guys were married, but Sig wasn't. Jake wondered if he ever thought of that girl Helen he'd been so nuts about at high school. He'd pieced together that part of Sig's life, too.

For eleven years; and all that time Sig was what Ma called the breadwinner of the house. Riding high, hardly ever home evenings, hardly ever talking to anybody in the house; and then, within the last few years, Jake started to bump into him evenings, at a hockey game he was covering for the paper—and there was Sig and a bunch of guys and girls—or at one of the bars around town, Sig always with a bunch of laughing, drinking, high-spending people.

Not that Jake ever went over to him. Hell, why should he take a chance at being snubbed! If Sig wanted him to meet any of his friends, he'd come over and say so, wouldn't he? But he never did, not once, and it happened often in those last few years before the Depression—the meeting at this place and that.

What didn't Sig like about his kid brother? Jake never could figure it out. Was it his careless dress, his not having finished high school, his way of talking, his non-Jewish look? What in hell was it? He could never figure out whether Sig was ashamed of him or just didn't give a damn.

283

And all those years he was riding high, Jake sort of hated him and envied him at the same time; hated his supercilious look and his position in the house, envied him the women and the way he dressed and the friends always surrounding him and telephoning him, the way he held a cigar, the little neat mustache that looked so right at all times.

And when the Depression came—Christ, he'd never admitted this even to himself before now!—he was glad Sig started getting slugged below the belt. Even when it went on too long for a man to stand, he didn't feel sorry, he just felt disdainful of the way Sig kept acting like such a weak guy who didn't know what to do. Like he'd turned to water, all the sneering, fine ways of him; like he'd started to waste his days and nights, and then finally his whole life; yes, he felt a kind of fierce satisfaction when life finally turned around and slapped Sig in the face.

The day Jake gave Ma some money for Sig—sure, she'd asked him for the money!—that was a day that was triumphant and bitter at once. A hell of a day. His brother, the big shot, the guy who'd never had a good word to say for anybody; his brother was now (in a way) begging money from the poor, snotty kid who'd never been good enough for him. Christ, what a day that had been for Jake! . . .

"You see, I never figured Sig had a hell of a lot to do with me. He went his way and I went mine. I used to think I hated him."

"You used to think?"

"Well, I don't really hate him. I used to think so, when he was the dressed-up big shot around the house. Even his handwriting. Mine is all scratchy, big, like a kid's. His is like—a teacher's."

"And now?"

"Now. Well, I'll tell you something funny! Do you know what changed that handwriting bug of mine? Seeing Debby's writing. It's a lot like mine. Terrible! She laughs about it; can you imagine! Calls it 'illiterate stuff' and laughs. I don't know, all of a sudden I can see how dumb I was. Hating a guy because his writing was so beautiful! Recently, I got to thinking, maybe all the other feelings I'd had about him were just as dumb. How

I quit school before graduating. Just because I wanted to be a big shot. He was! Wonderful clothes, all those fancy girls and friends. How I wanted to show him I wasn't as dumb a slob as he thought I was. Ah, the poor guy!"

"Why do you say that?"

"I was thinking. Of when he lost his job. His company merged with a larger one. They closed down his department; he had forty girls working for him when it happened. The new company kicked out all the Jews."

"Your brother told you that?"

"Sure. It was true, too. Three of his friends, Jews too, got it in the next six months. I remember when he told us, Ma and Debby and me, and I thought, Jesus, what's the matter with us anyway! What is there about being a Jew, for Christ sake!"

"He is employed now, you say?"

"Yeah. One of his friends got him this job. Selling. It's a good job, he's making pretty good money, I think. It's way beneath him, though. I mean, it isn't a big-shot job. I feel sorry for him. He's not getting any younger. But at least it's a job. Jesus, there for a while, a couple of years of it, he couldn't get anything to do."

"That was the time when you felt happy about all his hard knocks. Is that what you said?"

"Yeah. But I'll tell you, I had some damn good reasons for feeling like that! How about when he let Debby take that WPA job? After all, in those days we were all ashamed of a thing like WPA. Every one of us thought it was the lowest thing that could happen to a person. He should have taken the job. He was the oldest child. He was a man."

"Would you have taken a WPA job?"

"I? But I had a job. There wasn't any reason for me to go on WPA!"

"Yes, but if the misfortune had been yours. If you had been in his place, without a job, would you have assumed what you felt was 'the shame and degradation' of a relief job? Would you have taken the burden from Deborah? Just because you were the oldest male child?"

". . . No, I guess not. . . . But look at the way he just sank down, and wouldn't come up again. For years. He took money from my mother, from me. There were a lot of jobs he could have had, if he really wanted to work. A laborer's job, even! Was that beneath him, or what? He was too good for certain jobs!"

"Perhaps he had nothing left within himself but that one desire to hang on to his professional place in the world. Did you think of that? Perhaps if he had accepted menial work, a last fortification, a last way of strength, would have been taken from him. Perhaps he would have broken."

"Oh sure, you can say that in your quiet doctor's way!"

"Tell me, Jake, what else did he have to strengthen him? A family and home life?"

"A family? No, he didn't have that. None of us did."

"A wife? A lover?"

"He was always rushing around with women, wasn't he? A wife? A good-looking guy like that, and even when he had that manager's job, he never got married. No girl was good enough, I suppose! Even in those days, when he was riding high, he never moved away from that house of ours. I always used to wonder why. All right, maybe he didn't have anything to hang on to."

"You never found it possible to move away from the house either, did you?"

"Yeah, maybe we're alike in a couple of things, after all! Who'd ever have thought it? Debby told me about a certain night when he came in late and they talked. He never used to pay any attention to her, but maybe that night he kind of thought she'd save the whole family, too. Sure, don't I know how he must have felt! Came in the front door, and there she was, sitting with a notebook and pencil in her hands. The radio on, and that music of hers coming out low into the room. . ."

. . . and for some reason, after he put his hat on the dining room table, that other room drew him back. He and Deborah had not exchanged words when he had come in. Often he had found her in this room, still awake, when he had come in. They never spoke. After a while, she never even looked up when he came in, and he preferred this, he preferred slipping past this queer girl, this sister whom he could not understand.

Now she was on WPA. Taking his place. When he woke

mornings, she was gone, to the WPA job. Sometimes, on Sundays, she was around when he woke. Sometimes she prepared breakfast for Jake and for him on Sundays. It was nice when she did. The table was always set then, and things were served nicely, with a paper napkin at each place. Ma always served any which way, her eyes peering anxiously to see if he'd finished the fruit so that she could break the egg.

Now he wandered into the living room, stood near the mantel, listened to the soft, disturbing music. She disturbed him, too. There was something so alien strong about her. Sometimes, meeting those blue, steady eyes even by accident, he felt as if he had to flinch, to cringe. His eyes had to drop, as if that strength, that mannishness, had shamed him.

"How are you doing, Debby?" he asked abruptly.

She looked up, smiled. "Fine."

She was in the lamplight, he in the shadows. That music disturbed him very much tonight. It made him restless. He would not ask about the job!

"You know what, Sig," she said then. Her eyes seemed very bright in the light. "I sold a short story last week."

He was startled. "You did? What magazine?"

"*New Masses.*" She laughed. "Bet you never heard of it."

"No, I never did. How much did you get for it?" His thoughts must have flicked fast; a warmth must have gone all through his chest. Stories? All that book reading, all the hours she had spent in this chair, sunk in a book or in a notebook; maybe it was all starting to pay off now. Well, why not? Maybe she was the one destined to lift up this horrible, hard-luck family of theirs. Maybe this queer, not-to-be understood girl was finally the one to do it. Not he, with his college pretensions, nor Jake, with his marvelous job. Neither of them had succeeded, maybe she would.

"They don't pay anything," Deborah told him, and grinned.

"But plenty of magazines do," he said quickly. He began to walk up and down the room, his heart beating fast. He lit a cigar, puffed at it, began to talk to this kid in a patient, kindly, philosophical way.

"That's the only way to get anywhere. Don't give up. Keep plugging. One story today, maybe in the next few months another one. Maybe the next one will pay. I hear some magazines pay hundreds of dollars for one story. Just don't get discouraged. That's the important thing. Who knows; in ten years you may be a famous writer."

He talked that way for fully fifteen minutes, puffing excitedly on his cigar. When his eyes met hers on occasion, she nodded to show she was listening. Maybe he felt warm and good for the first time in months. Maybe, for a few moments, he even permitted himself a small glimpse of a possible tomorrow, Deborah famous and rich, all of them with her—in New York, in Hollywood, who knows where?

When finally he went to bed, he left the bedroom door ajar, so that he could hear the low murmur of her music. Jake was not home yet; from the other room came the sound of Pa snoring.

Maybe Sig felt old, tired, broken, the way he felt every night when he finally crawled into bed. But that music, that girl. What queer, little sort of hope had she put into him, so that her music came soothingly into the room now, lulling after a fashion, telling him sleep, sleep, tomorrow she may sell another story. And next year—who knows! The Jews had a saying of hope. When life was blackest, hardest, they could still say: "Next year, in another land!" Tonight, he could say such a thing to himself because of Deborah. . . .

Jake got in long after midnight. Maybe Sig heard the car drive in, and the door slam, then the house key in the door. Then the small lamp on the bedroom dresser went on under Jake's groping fingers, and he tilted the speckled-blue shade so that the light would not wake Sig.

Maybe Sig was pretending to be asleep, timing his breathing into regular and sustained sounds. He was clever at it, even managing a gurgle on about every third breath, almost a snore.

From the bed on the left side of the room, maybe he was watching Jake through slitted eyes. Thinking, He's got a few drinks under his belt, little Jakey! Must have spent at least a five spot this evening, dinner for two, maybe a movie, then on to a nice little night spot, maybe the Glens, and how is our little Roz tonight?

Jake eased out of his jacket and vest, slid the necktie loose enough to lift over his rumpled, dirty-blond hair. He saw his flushed face in the mirror, a little vacuous smile on it, the hair damp at the temples.

And maybe Sig was thinking: Oh, the punk had a woman tonight, all right! It's smeared all over him. Oh, he likes himself tonight, does Jakey! He likes life, all right, the son of a bitch. He has everything.

Sig was watching him from the bed. He knew damn well he was watching him. He knew damn well Sig had put himself into Jake's boots a long time ago. The job. Well, he didn't know much about a speed graphic, but Jake knew Sig could very well see himself running around with one under his arm, fast, efficient, like on that evening he had seen Jake snapping hockey pictures at the Arena.

Jake had left the two hockey passes on the dresser, and they had disappeared. Maybe Sig had taken a girl. "Look," maybe he'd said airily and casually, "there's my kid brother out there with his camera. The blond chap, with the belted coat."

Jake took his shirt off, then his undershirt and trousers. He rubbed his chest and under his arms, and across his tight, tough stomach where the band of his shorts lay. Maybe Sig was thinking: Not an inch of fat on the punk. He keeps hard by drinking! he and those other smart-alecky newspapermen who think they own the world. Give him ten years.

Jake stretched, a movement relaxed and pleasurable and free, and maybe Sig, in the bed behind him, felt a bitterly jealous flood of feeling, yes, bitter as gall, because of the young, relaxed body.

Now what was Sig thinking? Oh, the son of a bitch, he probably was whispering to himself. Just because he has a job. Sure, the whole Goddam world is his. I'm only seven years older. Feels like a hundred, like the Grand Canyon. The snot is only thirty-four, or is it thirty-three? And he's got a job. King of the Goddam world. But what if there's a war? Who goes first? You, my fine, pink-faced brother. How will Ma like that? Who'll support the family then? Maybe I will. The way I used to.

Jake's face was close to the mirror. He was squeezing a blackhead from the skin at the corner of his nose, close to the nostril. The little, vacuous smile seemed to be lingering at the edges of his mouth, and his eyes seemed to be dreaming something sly and half shamed into their mirrored look. Could Sig see Kathy in the mirror? Could he see a gentile woman?

The lamp went off. The bed creaked. Jake was in. What was Sig thinking now? He would simulate sleep, then Sig could try and imagine what he was dreaming. Did he want Jake to lose his job? Was he that jealous? Jesus, was Sig as scared as he looked? He was only forty or so. Life begins at forty, doesn't it?

Maybe Sig was crying there, without any sound. (Christ, remember how he looked the first time you saw him cry? In the living room. You'd both been sitting there, reading, you on the couch, he in the biggest chair. Debby in the kitchen. All of a sudden you looked up, and he was crying. His face wet with it, no sound. Debby was standing there too, all of a sudden, in the dining room, where she could see. When you looked at her eyes, you felt how you wanted to crawl with pity and shame. It was like his crying got itself a name in her eyes. You didn't know what to do. Debby said in a low voice, "Oh Sig, please don't." And Sig said in a terrible voice, "Why does everything have to happen to me! What did I ever do to anybody?" Then, still crying like that, he went into the bedroom. Debby went back to the kitchen. Jake sat there, crawling inside like a man on his knees.)

What was Sig thinking about? Where did he go every night, until twelve, one, two? Was it cards, women? Did he ever want to get married? Had he ever slept with a gentile woman? What was it like to go with a Jewish woman? Did he blame Jake for any of his tough luck? Did he think he should have the job instead of Jake? Well, Jesus, he left money for Sig. All the time. With Ma, or on the dresser. What in hell else could a brother do? He couldn't pull Sig out of that empty hole of his and carry him around on his back, could he?

Yeah, but what was Sig really thinking, lying there and listening to Jake's pretend breathing? Why hadn't Sig ever moved away from here? In the good days, when he had plenty of dough? Was he trapped in this house, too? A guy like that, dressed in the best, a pal of big-shot lawyers and dentists, a guy who went with Jewish women. It was impossible, but did he have anything like an inferiority complex? Who'd tied him to this house? What had wasted him, for Christ sake? Whose fault was it that Sig had turned out to be a guy who could sit there and cry, his face wet with tears?

Maybe Sig was thinking: Why doesn't Jake do something for me? What about when Jake was a snotnose in school and I was bringing home all the dough? Ten bucks a week just for Ma. She used to rush around for the breadwinner then. She'd have corned beef sandwiches ready for the few times he came home to eat. On Friday night, he was the one to be served first. Jake? Hell, give Jake a whisky and soda, and he'd be satisfied. But Ma used to really fuss about Sig because she knew he was different, he could appreciate food. A drink was just a drink to him; he could take it or leave it alone.

Jake fell asleep. When the alarm went off at seven, he clamped it shut quickly, looked at the other bed. Sig hadn't awakened. He rarely heard the alarm.

In ten minutes Jake was out of the house, silently walking past the old man, who sat sipping coffee in the dim kitchen. All the way downtown, driving quickly, Jake thought of how it would be when Sig woke up. All the way downtown, he inked in details, neatly and painfully sketched in finishing touches on the scene.

Sig would awake around ten, and the first miserable consciousness would come down heavy as iron across his forehead as he sat up. The room was dark, the shades drawn to the sills of the two windows.

He staggered as he stepped heavily from the bed to the floor, put on his bathrobe. At the dresser he snapped on the lamp, automatically looking into the mirror. His eyes were pouched dark in his face, his thin, darkish hair flared up from his head. He noticed the small roll of flabby flesh under his chin, and drew up the collar of the robe, looked away from the glass.

When he reached for his brush, he noticed the five-dollar bill which Jake had clamped neatly to the top of the dresser with the brush.

Fingering the bill, he felt a thick, desperate kind of hatred rise like blood to his head.

Oh, the bastard, he said to himself. Oh, the son of a bitching guy with his job and his women and his money.

With all his strength, he threw the crumpled bill at the reflection of his face in the mirror. He felt the tears starting to come, and he gave way to them, leaning with both hands on the edge of the dresser. And maybe he was thinking: It'll last me two weeks if I'm careful what I spend for lunches.

But maybe not, Jake thought as he parked his car outside the office and went into the Greek's next door for breakfast. Maybe that's only the way I would think if I were in his boots. Yeah, and what would I want from him if I were in his boots, and he in mine? . . .

"Maybe I'd want a few words of conversation," Jake said to the doctor, finishing the story. "I just thought of that. Maybe, way back then, a couple of evenings a week we could've talked. I don't know."

He looked across the broad desk, looked hard for a moment. "But why did I think I hated him? I mean, I knew damn well that I'd have to say I hated him, once I started talking about him."

"You hadn't really given him words inside yourself," the doctor suggested. "Any sort of perspective, or identity."

"Sure." Jake nodded quickly. "I remembered his handwriting!"

He lit a cigarette, shook his head abruptly as he exhaled. "The poor guy smashed up anyway, didn't he? Even if he did keep up that front of his. Silk underwear, my friend Dr. This, my friend Lawyer That!"

He took another quick drag, more excited. "And every time things got worse he talked less at home! Every time he got another kick below the belt, he sneered more at other people. Poor guy!"

"Ever call him poor guy before?" the doctor asked.

Jake looked at him. "Yeah," he finally said. "Last Sunday. To myself, but without really saying it in words, even to myself."

The doctor looked pleased. "Did anything happen?"

Jake put out his cigarette. "Yeah. I took pictures of him."

"Good pictures?" the doctor asked gently after a while.

Jake nodded, swallowed. "Pretty good. Yeah. He liked my doing it."

He watched the hands on the notebook, the pen moving.

"How does your back feel these days?" the doctor asked rather suddenly.

"My back?"

"Yes. When you first came in, your back ached considerably. It was difficult for you to straighten your shoulders."

Jake's forehead wrinkled. "I just haven't thought about it." He pushed back against the chair, moved his shoulders. "I don't feel any pain. Guess I haven't for some time."

"Good. Tell me, Jake," the doctor went on casually, "did the two weeks between treatments seem very long?"

"Well, I felt kind of funny. Especially last Saturday, at three o'clock."

"What were you doing at that time?"

"I took Kathy out to lunch. We were still eating at three. I looked at my watch, so I know." He took a deep breath. "It was a nice lunch. We talked about Laura."

"And how was that?" the quick voice said.

"It didn't make me feel bad. I'll tell you, it was easier to talk about her. Kathy knew her real well, all right. Laura's still married to that millionaire. She isn't writing much any more, a fashion column twice a week. Kat says she never really wanted to write. She liked the prestige that went with the column. Well, I can see that. Like I told Kat, it's all right to feel like that."

He grinned. "Kat said, 'Sure, it's all right. As long as you see her for what she was, young man!' Well, I went home and changed, read for a while. Kat and I went to a movie, then we ended up at a bar."

"The Glens?" the doctor said casually.

Jake looked startled. "No!" He thought about it then, lighting a cigarette, his eyes going back to the doctor's. "Though I could have. Couldn't I?"

"Yes," the doctor said. "Now you can."

"You know, Laura doesn't seem very important now." Jake flushed. "I mean, there are so many other things to think about."

"What did you think about in these past two weeks?"

Jake watched the pen move quietly across a leaf of the notebook. "My family. The whole bunch of them. Backwards and forwards."

"And about yourself, too?"

"Myself?"

"Yes, yourself. Jake Brown."

Jake shook his head. His forehead wrinkled again. "Mostly, it's as if I have to think about them. All the time."

"And then, perhaps, you think of yourself in the shadow of them? If they were—let's use one of your phrases—fixed up, perhaps you could go ahead and make plans for yourself? Is it something like that?"

Jake's eyes were very bright. "You know, that's the way it is! You'd be surprised; after I took those pictures Sunday I felt pretty good. They got such a kick out of my doing it. And it was such an easy way to give people a kick."

"People? In addition to your brother?"

"Oh," Jake said sheepishly, "I took some pictures of the kids, too."

"In a suitcase?" the doctor said, his eyes crinkling at the corners.

Jake laughed. "They're a little too big, or maybe I would have." He grew solemn again almost immediately. "I got a lot out of Sunday, Doctor. I still don't know exactly why I did it. Maybe it's because I was thinking of you, and of here. The way I'd skipped a week and it was all right to skip it, too. When I woke up Sunday, around eleven, Sig was dressed and in the living room, reading the Sunday paper. Debby was just making herself a cup of coffee. She'd eaten early and I guess she'd worked on a story all morning and wanted coffee again. . ."

. . . and in the living room, the radio was playing that classical music of hers. You could hear it, low, in the bedroom and then in the bathroom, and in the kitchen, too.

When he walked into the kitchen, she was squeezing orange juice. "I heard you get up," she said, smiling. "I'm cook today. Ma slept at Sarah's last night. How about some eggs, too? It's after eleven."

And it was swell. She sat opposite you at the table, sipping her coffee, and she had warmed the rolls, something Ma just wouldn't have thought to do. When you looked up from the plate you could see her scrubbed look, the eyes very blue in the sunlight coming through the windows, more gold than ever in her hair. She was wearing slacks and a blue, pull-over sweater that showed her small breasts, and she looked a lot like a tall, slim boy but you knew she was a woman all right, and your sister.

"What's the radio playing?" he said.

"It's Mozart now. It was Beethoven ten minutes ago."

Jake pulled a wry face. "Your brother's a lowbrow!"

"It's all right by me," she said, delighted with his rare mood.

Just when he had started thinking of Sig he did not know. Now, sitting at the breakfast table, it seemed to him he was full in the midst of the thinking, as if it had begun in him a long time ago.

"Sig reading the paper?" he asked casually. And then he remembered that he probably was going to talk about Sig the next time he saw the doctor; maybe thinking about Sig now was like getting ready for the doctor, and for the office, the chair, the anonymous walls.

Debby nodded. "He ate about a half hour before you woke."

His voice was low, to fit hers. "Is he still with that same company?"

Again she nodded. "That's the company car out front. They let him use it whenever he wants to."

"That's good," he said gravely.

He felt close to her, and that was natural to him, yes, but why suddenly should he want the closeness to include Sig?

Quietly, he drank the last of his coffee, offered his package of cigarettes to Debby. He lit hers and then his own, and now he was really thinking of the doctor, of the still reaches of the office and of the feeling of space and whiteness he had at the beginning of each visit, before the talk started, before the room began to breathe and move with the people of whom he talked each time.

He did not know when the impulse had come to him, all he knew was that now, at this moment, he was full in the midst of it. "Debby, do you think Sig would like it if I took pictures of him?"

Her eyes blinked once, then steadied. "I sure do," the low voice said, and her eyes had a look that made him flush with pleasure.

He mashed out his cigarette and stood up quickly. "Coming?" he asked her.

"I'm going to wash the dishes," she said, not stirring. He nodded. She was right, of course.

He did it quickly, before he could lose his nerve, or whatever it was that was pumping him full of a cool, dry air that made him feel mountain high. His camera and case were in the bedroom, and he got them and walked briskly into the living room.

Sig glanced up, a dead cigar in his mouth. His eyes looked absolutely empty. "Hello," he said listlessly, and started to light the cigar. The Sunday paper was scattered over the floor, part of it on the couch next to Sig.

He reads the funnies, Jake thought with almost a tenderness.

"Say, how about if I took a few pictures?" He had the camera open and was fiddling with the flash gun, his eyes on his hands.

"Of me?"

"Sure." Jake decided he'd better look up. "Why not?"

Sig's hand went to his tie. He looked bewildered, rather pleased.

"All set?" Jake asked, lifting the camera.

"Wait a minute!" Sig leaped up and ran toward the back rooms. Jake studied the room for angles, got three films and some bulbs ready. When Sig came back he was wearing his suit jacket, and his hair was brushed.

"Say, this is swell," he said. "Where do you want me?"

"On the couch," Jake said. "Let's take you with the cigar, because you smoke cigars all the time."

When he squinted at Sig and saw the eyes alert, the cigar held firmly and gracefully in the hand which had seemed so flaccid a short time before, his heart began to beat rapidly with a secret pleasure.

That's when you knew, and yet did not know in so many words, the power of which man is capable, the secret source of smile and joy, the infinitely painstaking capacity of the heart when once it is released. When Sig finally left the house, his hat jaunty, his eyes quick and bright; when Debby studied you for a while, and then said, "What made you do that?"

"I don't know," you said to her and you felt how pale you must be now, how your breath was hard to take now that it was over, but inside you felt the secret, scarcely understood horizons of the heart, how limitless they can be, what a depthless, endless source must be there in the heart.

"I don't know," you say again, "but I wanted to." You fuss with the camera. "I want to do something else, too."

"What?"

"Take the kids."

She knows what you mean. You don't have to say it, even if you possibly had the words in which to say it; she knows.

Debby went with him to Sarah's. In the backyard, they passed the old man. He stared at them. As Jake backed the car out of the drive, the old man kept staring, and Debby laughed. It was a joyous sound that needed absolutely no words to go with it.

At Sarah's it turned out just as easy. When he came in with Debby, they all stared. Max and Sarah, Ma, the two kids.

Ma, her eyes flickering for a moment with a kind of fear, said to Debby, "What are you doing here, all of a sudden!"

For a split minute he could not say a word, his mouth felt dry as dust. And then Debby, carelessly, so carelessly, Debby said, "Oh, Jack wanted to take some practice pictures. So we came up here."

"Well, well," Max said. He was sitting on the couch, a Yiddish newspaper on his knees. He kept staring at Jake with what seemed like a friendly look.

Then Bernie broke it up, with a bang. "Pictures," he cried in his deep voice. "Hot dogs! Come on, Allen!"

He took a family group first, Ma in the middle, Max and Sarah on either side of her, the kids kneeling. Squinting, he was reminded of newspaper pictures he had seen of peasant family groups in Russia, in Italy. Stiff, dark faces, the shaggy heads of kids, breath held for a tense minute; he looked quickly at Debby to see if she had noticed. He wanted to tell her how this kind of stiffness was just right for the picture.

"Want me in it?" she asked as their eyes caught.

"Come on," he said, his voice almost pleading.

She stood behind their mother, a full head taller, her hand on Ma's bowed shoulder, her scrubbed look so different from the look of the others that she seemed a complete stranger.

He took one of Ma and her grandchildren, then one of Ma and Sarah and Debby. Then he took one of Sarah and Max.

"Leah out?" he asked as he dug down into his case for more bulbs.

"She didn't sleep home," Sarah said. "That's why there was room for Ma to sleep here last night. Oh, she'll be so sorry. She loves to take her picture."

You see, quite suddenly, certain delicate things about people. The way Bernie keeps looking down, so that his bad eye won't show in the picture. The grave, posed look of Sarah, the way she holds her chin up, her lips firmly pressed so that the decayed teeth won't show. Allen's forced, stilted smile and the way his fists are clenched with excitement. Max's red-faced look, his attempt to look at ease. You see how straight Ma sits, her gnarled hands clasped in her lap, her peering eyes nervous and yet solemn with the gravity of the moment.

You remember how Bernie's uneasy giggle was gone suddenly, how, after he had forgotten about his eyes, he looked straight at the camera, his face set in mannish lines, his hand placed possessively on Sarah's shoulder. You are left with the memory of Debby's eyes looking at you, liking you.

And then, afterward, Sarah said, "Stay and have dinner with us here. I've got plenty. It's after one o'clock already. Debby, you too."

It was easy then, too, easy to say things without offending anyone. "I've got to work," he said. "That's why I had my camera with me overnight. Debby, you staying?"

"I've got a date," she said. "We'll come some other time, Sarah. Both of us. O.K.?"

"Sig is still home?" Ma said then.

"He went away," Debby said, patting her arm. "He ate a good breakfast, Ma."

Max cleared his throat. "Well, you'll show us the pictures maybe?" he said. One pudgy hand whipped a section of the newspaper up and down.

"Oh, sure," Jake said. "I'll make lots of them. For you, and for us at home, too."

"Boy," Bernie cried, "I'll bet I came out terrible. I'll bet I broke the camera!" He had a small dimple near his chin when he laughed.

Then Debby and he were in the car again, driving slowly toward home.

And you remember how tired you felt, but good. How scared, now that it was over, your heart really pounding now. You remember how slowly you drove, feeling almost a nostalgia, as though already you had been away from the home of it too long. How good you felt, how marvelous you felt.

You remember Debby starting to talk quietly, about Max's job in a war plant, and how that, plus his war pension, would bring them more money than they'd seen in a long time. Maybe, Debby said, Sarah would see to it that things would be nice, now that the worry about just bread and rent would be over for a while.

You said to Debby, "But will Sarah think of the right kind of things? For those kids? Bernie? Jesus, he's big!"

"I doubt it," Debby said. "She wants to do the right thing. She really wants to, she loves those kids very much. But some people just don't know what the right things are."

You drove on for a while, you remember, thinking of the expression on Bernie's face after he had forgotten to be self-conscious. You remember Debby saying, after a while, "Somebody will have to do something about the kids."

You remember how that word echoed and echoed inside of you all the way home. Somebody.

All the way home, the word said itself in you like a squeezing fist. Somebody.

Ten

"So now I really know my family."

"Do you?"

"You say that so quietly. You don't answer, you ask me to answer. And everything in that quiet, quiet way."

"Tell me something, Jake. Now that you know your family, how much of it is worth saving? From that wasteland you hate so."

"How much of it?"

"Yes. Whom would you save, if you could? The two children?"

"Bernie and Allen, sure!"

"Deborah?"

"Oh, but she saved herself!"

"Anyone else?"

"You—you can't really hate any of them! After you really know how they are. It isn't their fault. Any of them."

"What do you mean, fault?"

"That they were caught in the middle of that wasteland. They didn't want to be. I didn't. Why can't we all be saved?"

"Is there any reason all of you can't be?"

"No! No, I guess not."

"That's a good smile, Jake. What are you thinking?"

"I'm thinking I feel good. Gosh, I haven't felt as good as this—. Well, I just don't remember when I did. Maybe at a Seder—before Seders went sour on me, I mean."

"No feeling of waste these days, Jake? How did the past two weeks go?"

"Fine. Oh, swell, really! Let me tell you what I did the other evening. With Debby. It was her idea. She asked me to go to the Red Cross with her and donate blood."

"Blood?"

"Yeah. You know, for plasma. For wounded soldiers."

"That's very interesting. How did you feel about it?"

"When she asked me to go? Well, I'd never thought of doing it. I'd been down to the Red Cross to take pictures of people doing it. It makes swell art. But it never occurred to me to do it myself."

"Then Deborah asked you to go with her."

"Yeah. She asked me if I'd go, and then I felt—well, awfully glad!"

"Why?"

"Why! Because—. Well, Jesus, it's something a lot of people are doing! All over the country. Maybe all over the world, too. You give your blood. You couldn't give anything better. Why say, they couldn't take anything from you—that you give them on your own—that's more valuable. That's more you. Know what I mean?"

"Yes, I know. When did you go?"

"Tuesday. Our appointments were for eight o'clock. Evening. Debby and I went the same time. We were on cots right next to each other."

"You didn't telephone me."

"No. I was plenty nervous, but I wanted to see if I could go through with it. By myself."

"And you did."

"Don't smile! I almost passed out while I was doing it. But I got through, all right. Wasn't it all right that I did it?"

"Well, was it? How do you feel about it?"

"Good. Very good. It was swell to be in on something like that with Debby. The way she talks. I mean, some of the things she says are so swell. Things I never really thought about. But inside of me, I know damn well that's the way I feel. And the way she looked that night. She'd had a shower, and when she was through in the bathroom. . ."

. . . she came directly to where Jake was sitting in the living room, reading his copy of *Time*. She looked fresh and clean, her hair a little streaked with water and the dry part almost startlingly golden in comparison.

She was wearing a green dress, of thin flannel, with buttons running all the way down the front, the neck of the dress V-shaped, and the skin of her throat, next to that color, looked almost as golden as her hair. She looked taller, somehow.

He felt warmed. She seemed very girlish, very sisterly, her hair not like a boy's but just short, free looking, and her features were soft, her mouth the softest of all.

"Ready?" she said to him.

He was not ready. He was pretty damn nervous. Did she know it?

Yes, she did. Yes, she knew a lot about him.

"Do you think it'll be all right?" he asked.

"Yes," she said. She nodded very hard, and he got that safe, strong impression beneath the softness and sisterliness. "Come on, Jack, let's go out and join the war."

In the kitchen, their mother looked up from the *Jewish World*. Sitting at the table that way, she looked little and humped, like a gnome, and for a moment she peered at them with that expression of surprise which could flow, so quickly, into one of alarm.

Debby chuckled. "Guess what, Ma?" she cried. "Jack and I are going to a movie."

"To a movie? Where, all the way downtown?" Ma said. She looked very pleased, and inside of Jake something thudded softly, like wings. "Take a coat, Debby."

"I've got a heater in the car, Ma," Jake said quickly.

The old man came out of the bathroom, carrying a section of the newspaper. He put the teakettle on, turned to stare at them, and all the way out to the car Jake thought of the way his face would show up at that moment in a picture. With the stove behind him, and the calendar against the faded wallpaper to the side of the stove. His hair looked very gray tonight, the lines in his face deeper on either side of the gray-and-dark mustache.

Behind the wheel, he said, "Pa looks older tonight."

"His sciatica is acting up," Debby said. "Ma says he's had a lot of pain this week."

But the word pain meant almost nothing when it was pinned to the old man in his mind. The old man was a stranger who wandered about the house, brewing himself a glass of tea. He was no one to hate, or to love. It was inconceivable that the old man could himself love anyone, or touch in love. Remember when you hated him? When he was a Jew whose English offended you? When he was your father and you had no father? When he was her husband and she could bear no strong, insensate embrace from such a man? He's an old man who hurts, who sips his tea at night and his hands shake, who stares with mild surprise, a shrug, at the sudden togetherness of his son and daughter. What does he think when he sees Debby?

They were on the corner now, the car headed toward town, and Debby was smoking. He flipped open the ashtray on the dashboard.

"Want one?" she asked.

"Not yet."

"You remembered not to eat dinner, didn't you?" she said casually. "Nothing for four hours before the donation?"

He smiled. "I remembered. Are you going to let me take you to dinner afterward?"

She laughed, pleased. "I thought we'd pick up some stuff and take it home, talk and eat. Corned beef? Or salami, and a little cut-up cucumber and tomatoes? Coffee?"

"Say, that's swell!" She was remembering how he liked corned beef. Who had ever remembered such things for him? He kept thinking, with a kind of wonder, of the word sister.

After a while, Debby said, "Still jittery?"

"Not so much. A little."

She went on talking in that quiet way, and as they rode along it seemed to him they were in a small, warm room, very close together.

"This is my fourth time," she said, and opened the window

quickly to flip away the cigarette end, then she rolled up the glass again. "I remember how I felt the first time. Awfully jittery. To give a pint of your blood to—. Well, to the world! I wondered if it would do something to me. My reactions, you know?"

She laughed. "I've always been so damned interested in my reactions. I remember afterward. On the way home. I went with a friend of mine, and she kept pretty quiet. I could think as hard as I wanted to as she drove us home. I felt—. I don't want to sound dramatic or anything, Jack, but I felt at one with everybody. Know what I mean? Just *like* everybody."

"The way I want to feel," he mumbled. "Jesus, Debby, is that really the way it feels?"

She nodded so strongly he could feel the stir of air in the car. "It's not only giving blood. To our country, our war. That part is fine. What I'm talking about is, it's *our* giving. I mean, we take something like blood and we offer it to something very big. Something that wants it and needs it. Our blood, Jack. What's really wonderful is that ten thousand people are doing the same thing, everywhere in America."

Bells of echo in him: "Is that why you wanted me to go with you?"

"Why?" she said softly.

He felt breathless, wonderful, on absolutely common ground with her. "Because of how I want to be like any guy in America? Jesus, how I want to be like that! Nothing different about me. I'll bet you know that."

"Yes." Her voice was very low. "I know how it is to feel different, Jack."

He felt a small sinking sensation at that, but almost immediately she went on. "That's almost over with, isn't it? The way we've considered ourselves—low. Our family. Not as good as other people. Oh really, Jack, I've felt that way, too! The way Pa has always been. Our house. Low people, low peasant Jew. I got over it."

"I'm getting over it," he told her, his voice low and hoarse.

"But this blood business," she cried. "Really, Jack, I wanted you to do it, too. And feel the way I did. Not low. Not different. Really, you just can't feel anything but good, doing it. You'll see."

They rode along in the small, warm room, and outside the windows the night batted against the glass, and it was a time for closeness, for brother and sister togetherness. He felt as if he were at home, not in the house which he and Debby called home, but in the place of heart he had always wanted, a place of comfort and relaxed stillness.

He knew she would talk about her own self; this must be a moment of home for her, too. And then she did say it, and he was glad, almost with a kind of pride, to have her say it to him.

"It's a funny thing," she said softly, having lit two cigarettes and passed him one. "When I give blood I feel as if I'm giving it for Jews, too. Jews like Ma, who never had a break. Never. And I'm giving the pint for Negroes."

Her voice dipped even lower. "For people like me. There are so many. It's like giving your blood against any kind of segregation there is in the world. Anybody who is slapped in the face, laughed at. Pushed into a corner of—of society. They can have my blood. Sometimes, when you're giving that pint of blood, when you're lying there, it's like you hear a sound of crying. Really."

He thought tremulously, And I'll give my blood against wasteland. That's like segregation.

She went on. "You know, where we're going now they keep Negro and white blood separate. Isn't it amazing? They make little ghettos for a thing like blood. When I give my pint, Jack, it's against that, too. Dead against it. Some day they'll know they can't do a thing like that. Part of my blood will show them that some day."

He hardly understood her now, but murmured to show her he was listening. It was his own blood, and hers, which excited him. Not the blood of all these faraway, persecuted people she listed so lovingly.

When he parked the car and turned off the ignition, she put her hand on his shoulder for an instant. "O.K., here we are."

He felt the comfort of her hand there for a long time, through all the preliminary steps of questions and blood pressure and temperature and hemoglobin test. They went through together, and once when he looked around the Red Cross rooms, one leading into the next, and saw all the men and women sitting there, each quietly holding the big, white card full of details, his eyes came back to Debby's. She was sitting next to him, and they were waiting for the nurse to take their blood pressure. She nodded, as if to say that she had seen all the people, too, and that she felt just as wonderful about it.

He swallowed, looked down at his card, at his signature. He wanted to show it to Debby. He wanted to show her how he had written Jake Brown on the card.

Debby was talking to the nurse. "He's my brother. Could we have adjoining cots?" she said with a laugh.

He grinned stiffly as the nurse pushed up his shirt sleeve. "My sister's blood pressure O.K.?" he said.

"Absolutely," the nurse told him, adjusting the rubber on his arm.

Sitting there, he had a strange feeling. His blood would merge anonymously with the city's, the country's, then with the world's, blood. With society's blood, as Debby would say. A powerful sensation, like a shudder, went through him as he rose and followed Debby and another nurse into the room full of cots.

When the needle was pushed into his arm he felt faint, and a sudden feeling of fear at that piercing of his flesh made him want to rear up and run. His head jerked, he looked wildly about him to see where he could go, but then, across the narrow aisle between cots, there was Debby, her eyes watching him, smiling. She nodded slowly two or three times, and then he didn't want to run away any more.

"How does that feel?" It was a short, dark man, a doctor.

"Fine, fine." Jake kept watching Debby, the way the narrow rubber tubing extended from the needle in her arm into the pint flask standing on the ledge directly below the cot. It was wonderful to watch Debby's flask, the way it filled very, very slowly. Her blood was a beautiful color, and it was like watching something with a life of its own, and then when he looked up she was lying on her back, her eyes on the ceiling and a quiet smile on her face.

And I give my blood for people like me, she had said. Any kind of segregation. Negroes, Jews. And my kind, too.

His flask was filled first. "Your sister has very small veins," the nurse told him cheerfully. "It'll take her longer. Do you feel all right now?"

"I almost passed out, didn't I?" he said in a low voice.

She nodded, patted the small, square piece of adhesive in place. "Sit up, Mr. Brown, but don't move for a while."

He sat up, his back to Debby, and watched the nurse coil the tubing and lift his flask. There was a card attached to the neck of the flask, and he could see his name there. The nurse took the bottle into an inner room, but he remembered the rich color of his blood, the flared look of his name in blue ink on the white card.

Then, behind him, Debby said, "Well, that didn't take long, Jack, did it?"

The nurse led them to the last room, a canteen, and they sat on wicker chairs and drank the coffee a uniformed, smiling woman brought them.

He thought Debby looked pale. Her hands, on the coffee cup, were quite steady, however, and when he looked up at her face again she was smiling at him. "Here comes your reward," she said.

The uniformed woman came back to them. "Is this your first donation?" she asked Jake.

She gave him a stamped card and a small button wrapped in cellophane. "Bronze the first two times," she said. "Silver for your third donation."

When Debby offered her the card with its triple stamped line, the woman said, "Oh, how nice!" and stamped it again. "Do have more coffee," she urged. "And aren't you going to sample our cookies?"

She left them after a few moments of this, and Jake said, "Where's your silver button?"

"Home," Debby said. "I don't really need to wear it any more. I wore the first one I got for a long time. Then I didn't have to any more."

She offered him a cigarette and lit it, then held the match to her own. "Did you drink that glass of water?" He nodded. "We're supposed to start right away to put the blood back. Drink your coffee, Jack."

He tilted the cup. "How do you feel?" she asked gravely.

"Shaky."

"You'll get over that. How do you really feel?"

He looked at her. "Very good. Like—the way you said you did your first time."

"One with the world?" she said with a smile, and he nodded, feeling shy and a little tremulous.

"That's good, Jack."

He dragged on his cigarette, felt himself beginning to flush, but he had to say it. "Debby—. Do me a favor?"

"Sure." Her eyes seemed extra blue again, like they looked sometimes.

"Call me Jake from now on, will you, please?"

"Jake?" As she studied him, he felt his face crimson more, and then she picked up her coffee cup. "Sure, Jake."

She drank, and he lit another cigarette, his hands damp. When he looked at her again, her eyes were casual. "Oh, I didn't tell you," she said. "I've sold another story. To a tiny little magazine, for twelve whole dollars. What they call a literary magazine, Jake!"

She laughed, her eyes amazingly happy. The way she called him Jake, so easily, so naturally, the way her face looked so glad, warmed him through and through.

"That's swell," he told her. "That's really swell. The hell with the twelve bucks."

"That's right. The hell with it. But I'll bet it's twelve bucks full of confidence." They grinned at one another. "What do you say? Let's go, Jake."

In the car, riding again in the small, close room of intimacy, she suddenly began to talk about Bernie.

"What about getting a social worker to talk to him?" she said. "This friend of mine works for the Jewish Welfare. I mean, it's the kind of organization that might even be able to approach Sarah, get her to maybe understand the situation."

That made him feel odd. "A social worker? What good would that do?"

"Well, they're trained, Jake. They've had experience with kids of Bernie's age, kids with similar backgrounds. They know about—well, camps and clubs, say. They'd know the kind of thing that's best for a kid like that."

"He's not a bad kid," Jake said. He felt a stubborn, tight wedge back of his eyes.

"Not yet, no," Debby said. "Lord, I hope he never does hit that stage."

After a silence, she said, "What's the matter, Jake? You don't care for the social worker idea at all, do you?"

"No, I don't," he cried.

He felt confused. When she had first mentioned it, he felt relieved. Bernie would get some help. Bernie would be off his mind, and he would not have to worry about doing anything about him. He probably would not have known what to do anyway. Then that tight, awful feeling had knocked him flat.

He groped, trying to get it out right. "Look, Debby, I want to do it. I don't know how to say it, but he's my nephew. Look, all I know is I want to try and do something for him. I don't want it to be a social worker. I want it to be me. I just don't want to leave him to somebody else!"

He glared out through the windshield, driving fast, his hands tight on the wheel. The way you were left to somebody else! his thoughts ground out. And Roz, too. But mostly you!

After a while her voice, gentle and very pleased, said, "I'm even sort of glad you feel that way. Look, here's a store. Let me run out and get us something to eat, Jake."

And then they were home, the car pulled into the yard, and they walked into the dark house.

Debby snapped on the kitchen light. "It's after ten," she said. "Can you feature it? Ma and Pa have gone to bed."

For some reason, it was something to grin about, they alone in the kitchen, which belonged to their parents. She unwrapped packages, and he came to the table to sniff.

"Corned beef," he said.

She was making coffee. "Please notice the dill pickles, mister!"

Then they were eating, sitting at either end of the table, like their mother and the old man did most of the time, and she had put a paper napkin at each place and poured the top cream from the milk for his coffee.

Jake kept pressing the small lump of bandage on his arm, under the material of his jacket, feeling each time the same strong sensation of happiness. When he brought out his pack of cigarettes, Debby filled their coffee cups again, accepted a light from him.

He was in the midst of one of those tranquil, relaxed feelings he often had experienced in the doctor's office, after having talked for an hour or more.

He told Debby he wanted to enlist. Did she understand that at all? And the way he was worried about Ma, too. About who would support her if he ever got crazy enough to do such a thing. Could she see his point at all?

He looked across the table, thinking for a split second that he might be looking across the broad desk now, but the gentle, anonymous eyes were not there. Debby was there. Her eyes were very keen, and yet quiet, too.

"Why don't you do it?" she said. "If you really want to, Jake. I'll promise you something. Sig and I will support Ma. And Roz will come across, I know that. What's more, we'll make Pa shell out for gas and light bills all the time, not only when he feels like it. I can make him, you know I can. It just never seemed worth the effort. He's working a lot these days, you know. Because of the war. Even a bum carpenter like Pa."

He stared at her, and she leaned toward him, her elbows on the table. Her eyes seemed to crackle. "Jake, I promise you! If you do go, when they see you're really going, they'll have to shell out. That's a promise."

His chest hurt, as if it had a rope around it. "My God, Debby. I didn't think I'd ever be able to do it. Leave the house that way. Free to go. I didn't, I tell you!"

Looking at her eyes, at the way her jaw and cheekbones stood out tight and clean-cut, was to know that her insistence could be echoed in him. It wasn't that she pushed him, it was only that she said these things out loud, and inside of him he recognized the truth of them.

"And when you come back," she said, "things will be different. Do you realize that?"

"Different?"

"Yes. Think about it, Jake. You'll be able to have your own place."

"I will?" But even as he questioned her, he knew it was true, it was as much his insistence to live as hers. This was something he would have learned to say in the doctor's office; the capacity to say it was within him, the strength with which to utter the words was there. He simply had not been ready to use his own tongue; the bells of echo were beautiful in him as Debby said the words first.

"You can bring Ma some money every week. Naturally we'll all give her enough money. But you don't have to be nailed to the house."

Her voice quieted then. "I'm getting my own place as soon as I have a little money saved. I'll always give Ma enough, I don't have to tell you that. But she doesn't need me in the house. Or you either."

He knew that, too. The knowledge had been inside him for a long time now, and he had been ready to say the words, ready for the truth and ease of the words.

"It's true, Debby. We can be her children even away from the house, can't we? Living our own way. Not having to live their way, that really isn't ours."

The old man's clock struck eleven. The strokes sounded slow, almost friendly.

Debby smiled. "That might be Pa, telling you to go right ahead."

"Yeah." He lit another cigarette, took a deep drag. What if he were to tell Bernie he could call on his uncle for anything he wanted? He might start out by taking him, and Allen too, to a movie. On a Sunday, maybe eat downtown, too.

"You thinking about the kids?" Debby said.

He looked up, sighed. "Yeah. How'd you know that?"

"I don't know," she said. "Except, this is just about the time to be thinking about them."

. . . and in the giving of blood, not only has S been accepted by society, or the world (symbol of authority), but his family has been accepted, too. His sister Deborah, as "different," as "odd," as any one of the family—and therefore, in his mind, the perfect identification for that family—not only was accepted by the Red Cross (in this instance, the world, America at war) but was welcomed, praised, because it was her fourth blood donation.

This is a double acceptance, a double approval. In this offering of blood, S feels strengthened on two counts, one as an accepted member of society, and two as the member of a family accepted by that same society. Not only has he, an individual, offered himself to a major thing and been accepted, but his family has offered itself to America and been encompassed. Jewish blood, in his mind not too long ago a despised thing, has been accepted and now flows in the mixture of American blood. S has proved to himself, in a most obvious way, that he is a member of a group which is of value to the world.

Interesting comparison of values between S and his sister in their reasons for making blood offering. The poetic sister gives as a way of warding off, and fighting, evil: the sins of society against minorities, the evil of society's segregation of Jew, Negro, homosexual. Her blood is offered up against ghettos of any kind, physical and spiritual. When she lies there, in the act of giving, in her heart she hears the cries of subject peoples, tormented peoples.

Basically, S gave his blood for the same reason, to break down the walls of ghetto. With him, however, the reason was not the universal one of Deborah's; with him, it was his individual ghetto, and that of his family. Out of this small reason some day may come the greater issue; his thinking already has stretched to meet the horizons of his sister's. S is a follower of what he admires and respects, and Deborah's strength of belief, her hope for a future for any kind of people, will continue to broaden his own ideals.

And now S has begun to evince his own strength, for which he has fought so hard. When Deborah suggested a social worker for his nephews, his first eager impulse was to welcome the idea. His new strength could not accept this easy solution, however, a solution which could ease his conscience, too. This trained worker knew what to do with "bad" boys, knew how to do it, and S would be in on the workings, perhaps confer, advise, act the man of the family. In his vague way, however, S knew that it would not work. He knew—and will know in more detail and with more actual knowledge as time goes on—that he will have to "do it himself" before it works out for him, as well as for the boys.

S has given his blood. He has made a gesture directly opposite wasteland, a gift of life. He gave as a Jew, and as a patriot, to some degree; but, most important, he gave as Everyman. He wanted to be the anonymous man of America, the man who is the same as the next man, with as much to give and as much to be reckoned with. His acceptance in this role proved of more importance than the Jew and patriot roles, though they stem directly from it. Everyman is alive. He is a member of society, a working part of it; he belongs. Everyman, in other words, is not, and cannot be, a part of wasteland. Everyman is strong enough to say his right name out loud. He has asked his sister to call him Jake. And in the books of society, he has written his name correctly. Nor did society question that name; nor did his sister question his desire to be once more renamed. His new dominance has been accepted.

The giving of this pint of blood is the first small, outward victory in the struggle of S to belong. The other victories, as yet, are within him; recognition of them will come, too.

Inner recognition is there. Within himself he recognized the need to "do it himself," instead of leaving it to a social worker. Within himself, too, he recognized the psychological moment when he could say—in words now, instead of simply desire—that he was strong enough to leave the house. The words are articulate; he knows that "the house" includes mother and family and all the confused ties and bonds he found impossible not only to bear but to identify.

The approval of society, the voice of authority, in accepting a pint of his blood, is the first sign. . . .

Eleven

Jesus, it was so easy! After all his worrying, after all his dopey attempts to sort of rehearse what he was going to say to the kid. Then it turns out to be easy. Not that he said what he had rehearsed; no, it hadn't turned out easy in that way. And the word wasn't really "easy." The word was, well, maybe the word was—natural. Because, as it turned out, Bernie and he just talked, like it was the natural thing for them to do. He felt funny inside, sure, but the talk itself came easy.

He gave Bernie the package in the car, just as they pulled away from the curb in front of the apartment. On the little box-like porch of the apartment, Sarah and Allen and Max sat and stared down after the car. ("For his bithday?" Sarah had said, her eyes bewildered. "You're taking him to a prize fight for a birthday present?" To Allen he had said: "You're going on your birthday, too. Maybe it'll be a baseball game by that time. Or a hockey game. O.K.?" Allen's eyes did not believe one word of it. To Debby, he had said: "Thanks for finding out about their birthdays." To himself, he had said, Jesus, I wish it were over!)

"What's that?" Bernie said. He had a rough, street way of talking, his voice hoarse and deep, and yet Jake could see how the kid was tortured with shyness, how the giggle lapped over the suspicious dark glance, how a brief, sideways look darted up toward him now and again and then was buried in the mannerisms rough as street bricks.

"Birthday present," Jake said, his face hot. "Plus this fight we're going to."

It was just beginning to be dark, and in the car there was a pocket of twilight in which he could see the kid's hands fumbling on the string of the package.

"How'd you know about my birthday?" Bernie demanded. Then the giggle came, one hand slapped the package. "Oh sure, Debby must've told you."

Jake's heart was pounding, but he said very quietly, "Why don't you open it? Sure, Debby told me. Do you like Debby?"

"Sure! She's all right. She never hollers, but oh boy, can she be tough!" Bernie giggled again. "She's like a teacher sometimes. The way she talks. Bet I wouldn't get into so much trouble if she was my teacher in school."

"Bet you wouldn't," Jake said. As he shifted for a traffic light, he said lightly, "What's the matter, don't you open birthday presents?"

The string broke, paper tore, and then Bernie said, "Hot dogs! Hey, how'd you know I like to draw?"

"Debby," Jake said, smiling in the twilight safety of the car.

Then the easy part, or the natural part, that is, began; the hoarse voice next to him going fast and excited about comic strips and freehand drawing. "This a sketchbook?" Bernie asked. "Twelve pencils, boy oh boy! Wait'll I show you this guy I made up for a comic strip, Jack. Bet if I really work on him he'd be worth plenty of dough."

His chest tight, Jake said lightly, "Say Bernie, why don't you call me by my right name? Call me Jake, kid."

"Jake? Everybody calls you Jack, don't they? Except Grandma."

"Oh, Jack's a nickname," Jake said, swinging the wheel. "Might as well call me the right thing, huh?"

"Might as well."

Jake lit a cigarette. As he thrust the lighter back into its dashboard niche, Bernie said, "Boy, this is some car, Jake! This is the kind where you push a button and the top goes down, isn't it? This the car you went to Mexico in?"

"Yeah," Jake said. They were on the main thoroughfare now, with the brightness of street lights and store windows flashing on and off across the boy's face. He had wrapped the notebook and pencil box back into a rough package and slid it between Jake and himself.

After a long silence, Bernie said, "I never saw a real, professional fight before. Who do you think is going to win, the nigger? Or this guy Levine?"

"I don't know," Jake said. He did not know whether to say it now, or later, or not at all. "The papers say Johnson might," he added helplessly.

Driving, he had a flashing picture of Debby's face; her eyes, that sad look that sometimes changed her mouth and eyes so completely. His throat felt dry, but he could not say it.

"Say, Bernie." His voice sounded careless, and this part was easy, very easy, compared to the nigger part. "Doing anything for your skin?"

After a moment, Bernie said, his voice uneasy, "I'm washing with some stuff you call green soap. You think my face looks bad? That big pimple on my nose is a new one, just got it this morning. When I woke up, the Goddam thing was there. You think it's bad, huh?"

And that was easy, real easy. "Green soap's pretty good, sure. You ought to try and not eat too much candy. Or sweet stuff, Bernie."

He put out an easy, a natural, laugh. "Boy, I remember how my face looked when I was as old as you are. A regular holy mess!"

"Yeah?" Bernie cried eagerly. "What did you do? How long did it take to go away? Your face is O.K. now."

"Oh, hell, not long. Maybe two years, all in all. Boy, some days it looked so bad I just didn't want to get in front of a mirror. Honest to God, I was a mess!"

"Yeah," Bernie cried. "It's terrible, all right, isn't it? What do you mean, cut down on candy? Would that do any good? How come? Sometimes I eat a hell of a lot of candy."

And that was easy, too. All the way downtown, Jake talked, his voice casual, his manner hearty and light; and Bernie's hoarse voice chimed in with questions, with agreement or with soft curses of approval.

"Yeah, I read about puberty. Sure, I understand it. This friend of mine, Jerry, got a book. He lets me read it. His face is broken out worse than mine. He's the one who told me about this green soap. Hell, he chases after girls too much, but he's O.K. What do you mean, where'd he get the book? His old man bought it for him. Jerry claims you don't get over it for five years. Boy, that's a hell of a long time! Adolescence? Sure, I saw that word. It's in Jerry's book. Hey, Jake, did you ever use any cream or stuff like that for your face when you had it? Yeah, I get kind of ashamed to let people see me. Sure, I know all boys get it. I know that. All the same, sometimes it's so bad I hate to go to school those days. I used to feel terrible about it, but I guess I don't feel so bad now. Hey, Jake, did you eat any candy at all when you had it?"

It was easy, so easy. And it was wonderful, too. In the jammed Arena, Jake showed his sports desk pass and the usher led them to the first row, and Bernie whispered, "Boy oh boy, we're right on top of them!" And in the kid's eyes, Jake saw how easy it was, how wonderful life could be, how worshipful and wonderful and easy things could be.

Then, not twenty minutes later, in that huge room packed with people and violent with laughter and cries, with hooting calls and stamping feet, quite suddenly it was not easy at all. Suddenly it was a matter of a strange kid studying you with half-closed eyes, something like a brown net over the eyes, and the eyes not steady, darting away from you, the poor crossed eyes shaming themselves by staring at anything but you.

The familiar, smacking thud of gloves against flesh, the intricate, trained steps made by the two men's feet, the rising and falling roar of voices; and then Bernie's excited, tense whisper came to flick at the feeling of ease: "Gee, I hope the Jewish guy beats the nigger! Don't you? Gee, I hope he does!"

Jake's heart sank. Now what? What does a person say to a thing like that? What does an uncle say? In his mind, Debby's eyes flashed, swung like lanterns.

"Don't call him a nigger," he whispered close to Bernie's large, red ear. But he did not know what else to say, and he kept his eyes on the two men, slowly advancing and retreating in the powerful light.

"He's a wonderful boxer," he whispered again. "What's the

difference what color he is? You want a guy to win because he's the best guy, don't you? Not because he's a Jew, don't you? Look at the way Johnson teases him."

No, maybe it wasn't as easy as he had thought. When Bernie's eyes pushed away from the ring, focused on him, with that thin, brown curtain over them. When he saw it was a stranger kid sitting there and looking at him, a kid he had no idea about, or what he was thinking, or if he had even understood one word of the few he had tossed at him.

All he could think of was Debby. She'd say—well, what? Bernie and his little ghetto; that's what she'd say. You give a pint of blood against any kind of segregation, Jake; that's what she'd say. Yes, but what would she do? What do you do to a ghetto when you bump into it?

Johnson won by a knockout. Bernie's dark, rough face turned toward Jake. His eyes were moist and hot-looking. "Boy oh boy," he cried, his voice quavering.

"Come on," Jake said. "Let's scram before the crowd gets going. I'm hungry."

They had ice cream, in the big garish drugstore next to the Arena. "Some fight, huh?" Jake said. "Watch that guy Johnson. Everybody says he might be champ some day."

What do you say to a kid? How do you start smashing up a ghetto? "He's as good as any white boxer I ever saw. And, believe me, I've seen plenty of them."

Bernie's eyes lifted and fell, like little wary animals. It was as if he looked at you until the moment you started to look, until the second you might start to see how his eyes crossed that way, then the look was averted.

"Yeah, he's good, all right," Bernie admitted.

Jake lit a cigarette, watched the boy eat. "Debby and I were talking about that," he said. "About the way some people call them niggers. You know, one of Debby's best friends is a Negro girl. She's a marvelous girl. Smart. Pretty. A lot like Debby."

He flipped cigarette ash into his empty dish. "We think it's pretty dumb to use a word like nigger about people who're just like us. It's like a lot of people call people like Grandma and Grandpa dirty Jews. Exactly the same thing."

The spoon moved steadily up and down. The little, wary eyes rose and scuttled away, rose, fled again.

319

"Think you'll want to see another fight with me?" Jake said then. "Maybe a hockey game? Baseball?"

Bernie's eyes lighted, stayed with Jake's for a moment; the rough, real smile, which came so rarely, appeared. "Boy, would I! Wait'll I tell Jerry about this! Hey, Jake, Jerry says maybe there won't be any baseball pretty soon. On account of the war. You think he's right?"

"Nobody knows. Depends on a lot of things. We'll go if there is any baseball. O.K.?"

"O.K. by me," Bernie said, and pushed his empty dish away. The eyes were steady for a moment, very serious. "You going to be a soldier, Jake?"

Jake stared at him. "Yeah," he finally said, "I think so."

Bernie's eyes stuck to his, a deeply excited look in them. "I'd be a Marine," he said, almost whispering it.

And in the car it was easy again. Maybe that was because of the darkness, because he could not see Bernie's eyes darting away, and back, and away again as he talked.

In the car, after minutes of driving, when the only sound was that of the wrapping paper crackling under Bernie's hands as he kept touching the birthday present, it was easy to say carelessly, "How about some glasses, kid? We could go up to the doctor's and get an examination. A good doctor, a specialist. I could even go with you."

"Nah," Bernie cried very quickly. "I don't want any glasses. What the hell good are glasses?"

That was easy, too. "I was talking to the military editor on the paper," Jake said, shifting at a stop street, then pressing down on the gas pedal again. "You know, the guy who writes all the stuff about the war. He was discussing the exams they put the guys through. They've got some pretty stiff physical qualifications. Know anything about them?"

"Sure, I know. Jerry's brother was drafted. You got to be perfect. Or else they kick you back home. Sure."

"Your eyes, too," Jake said. "The toughest outfit to get into is the Marines. But I guess you know that."

"Sure I know," Bernie said bitterly. "What the hell am I supposed to do? Think I want an operation? Nothing doing!"

Inside, Jake cursed. "Who said anything about an operation?" he asked quickly.

"Aw, Leah did. And my mother. They said you can't fix up your eyes without an operation. Don't worry, I heard them talking!"

"Listen," Jake said earnestly, "I'll make you a bargain, Bernie. We'll go to that eye doctor. Just to see what's wrong. If he says you need an operation, well then, the hell with it—we go home and forget all about your eyes. But if he says all you need is glasses, you get the glasses and I pay for the whole shooting match. But you wear the glasses after you get them! You wear them until your eyes are O.K. What do you say? Is it a bargain?"

"Aw, nuts!"

"You wear glasses for a couple of years, and they fix you up. All the time you're wearing them, they strengthen your eyes. One of these days you can take the glasses off and throw them away. Anybody knows that."

"Aw, he'll cut open my eyes, that's what. I heard Leah tell my mother. They cut your eyes open and tie up the muscles."

"Listen," Jake said very quietly, "I made you a bargain, didn't I? Operation? Nothing doing. Glasses? O.K. Didn't I?"

"Yeah." Bernie's voice had stopped its hoarse raging.

"I'll go with you. You going to do it?"

"Hell," Bernie said, "bet you fifty cents it's an operation."

"O.K., it's a bet. Fifty cents it's only glasses. Shake on it."

They shook hands, Jake guiding the wheel with his left hand. Bernie's hand was hot and hard, barely there before it was withdrawn. Like the way he looks at you, Jake thought.

"Get ready to lose a half a buck," Bernie said.

"Wait and see." Jake turned the car off the main thoroughfare, drove into the short cut leading to the section where they lived. They whizzed through a deeper darkness, the shops and bright lights behind them.

"Any of your friends ever work?" Jake asked after a while.

"Jerry does. He helps out in his old man's store sometimes on Saturdays."

"Does he like it?"

"He has to do it," Bernie said, his voice disgusted. "It's not like you get a job you want. Well, his father pays him, all right. Jerry buys all the comics he wants. He doesn't have to ask his mother for money."

Jake lit a cigarette. "How about if I try and get you a job

working for the *Register*? Saturdays. Maybe after school, too. But that's only if you make pretty good marks and you can spare the time after school. You could help out on the delivery truck, maybe. They've got a lot of boys working in the circulation department."

Bernie's voice sounded stunned. "You kidding, Jake?"

"No, I'm not kidding. Maybe you'd rather have a paper route. That's a good way to get started. I used to sell papers downtown when I was a kid."

"I know! My mother told me. And Grandma told me, too. Gee, Jake, I'd rather be on that truck! That'd be a real job."

It was not too easy to think, at that moment, of how he would go to Jim and say, "This is my nephew, Bernie. Want to put him to work?"

Well, what would Jim and the department see? A big, hulking kid with a pimply face and cross-eyes. Maybe he'd be wearing glasses by then. A kid in sloppy clothes, his neck dirty. So what? Jim wouldn't see the little ghetto Bernie was dragging along at the end of a string. Or hear the way he talked, and, in the echo of his words, the way Sarah and Max talked.

Boys, this is my nephew. How about putting him to work? He's a good kid. The thing is, I want to save him. Yeah, you heard me. From a lot of things. Ghettos. Juvenile delinquency. Wasteland. You can call it anything, boys, but let me tell you, wasteland is the word, all right!

"Hey, Jake! You mean on those big trucks that have steps behind? Where they deliver papers to the stores all over town?"

"Yeah, that's what I mean. Talk it over with your mother tomorrow. And I'll talk to the boss of that department. O.K.?"

Bernie's voice shook. "She won't let me," he said.

Jake smiled in the darkness of the car. "Talk it over anyway. Then, if she doesn't like the idea, maybe Debby will tell her what a good idea it really is. Maybe I will."

"She thinks I'm a baby," Bernie cried. "She always acts like I'm a baby."

"But you aren't," Jake said, with a deep chuckle. "We better prove that to her. O.K., Bernie? Bet she gets the idea after a while."

Bernie started to laugh suddenly. "Bet she hollers at you, Jake!"

"Bet she doesn't."

They laughed most of the rest of the way home, and when they got to the apartment, the windows were lit up, and Bernie took his package and eased out of the car. He looked up at the windows, then looked at Jake. His face seemed solemn and like a small boy's. "If she won't let me, you going to come here and talk to her?"

Jake leaned toward the open door. "You know darn well I will," he said emphatically.

"You going to talk to that guy?" Bernie said, slouching on the curb.

"Yeah. You going to go to the doctor with me?"

"Yeah. When?"

"How about Saturday? Three o'clock?"

"O.K. Guess I'll go up now."

"Good-by, kid. Tell your mother about it now, will you? The whole works, glasses and job, too. What I'll do, I'll call you up tomorrow to see how you made out. O.K.?"

"O.K.," Bernie said, and turned slowly from the car.

Jake drove off with a jerk. Easy? Jesus, how easy, how tough, how he was sweating about the whole evening. . . .

". . . And the hell of it is," Jake continued, rubbing his eyes, "it was only the first little step. I realize that. I realize I'm not going to change that kid overnight."

"But you expect to change him, do you?" the doctor asked.

Jake liked the way he was smiling. He nodded sheepishly. "Yeah, I guess I really expect to change him."

He lit a cigarette. "He paid me off. That fifty-cent bet."

"Is he wearing the glasses?"

"He hates them," Jake said with a wry smile. "They're sissy stuff to him. But I'm hoping he'll wear them. Gosh, you should've seen his face when the doctor said, 'Operation? What kind of operation? Who told you such a stupid thing?' You know he's a good kid, inside."

"Of course he is. By the way, what made you set that doctor's appointment for Saturday, at three o'clock?"

"What?" Jake blinked. As the doctor's smile deepened, he began to smile. "Must be I was missing my Saturday here."

Then, as he put out his cigarette, he scowled. "Say, does

that mean I'm going to depend on you for the rest of my life? Inside of me, I mean? I didn't realize, when I was making the appointment, that I'd grabbed at that particular day and time."

"I wouldn't worry about it," the doctor said. "The rest of your life is a long time, Jake. Don't you think it's rather natural to cling to your physician during the period of convalescence?"

"Convalescence?"

The doctor nodded. "You're well on your way. Aren't you?"

"Yeah, I suppose. I feel pretty good, all right." Jake lit another cigarette, glanced sharply at the doctor.

"What is it?" the gentle voice asked.

"Well. I'd like to ask you something. I've wanted to know about it since—we began." Jake hesitated, then blurted it out. "Why did Debby lie down on the couch when she was here, and I—well, you said for me to sit here during treatments. Would you tell me?"

"Yes, I'll tell you. Certainly you're strong enough to be objective now, to look at it intellectually instead of emotionally. When you first asked me that, at the beginning of your treatments, the answer might have disturbed you."

"It won't now," Jake said, his voice as quiet as the doctor's.

"No, it won't. I wanted your sister to lie down because there was a strong need for her to give herself to something, or to someone. Most of her life, she had made herself overly strong, overly masculine. She had not dared be feminine, or soft in any way; she had not dared give way to anyone or to anything. She was afraid to. Subconsciously, she knew she would break if she did. But while she was here, she had to give up the power of decision over her own actions. She had to give up the conviction of self-confidence before she could achieve real self-confidence. You, on the other hand, had to accept self-confidence in order not to give up. The supine condition was simply a means to an end for Deborah. For you, an erect position was the means to an end."

"I understand now, all right," Jake cried eagerly. "It sure was bothering me, though. I sure wanted to know why. But I knew you'd tell me eventually."

He smiled, his rough, boy's mouth a little shaky. "I've been trying to stand up straight. Like you asked me to. My back doesn't hurt, but it sure is easy to let my shoulders slide right back."

"Yes, it's physical habit by now, Jake. There are some simple, corrective exercises which will help you, now that the source of the stoop is gone. You realize now that the psychological weight you've been carrying all these years has been removed to a great extent. Your realization of what it was you were carrying will help you to stand straight. And your realization, of course, that most of that burden was never yours."

"That feeling of shame, you mean. And the guilty feeling. Yeah, I think so," Jake said slowly. "Corrective exercise, sure. And I hear the army is pretty good at straightening shoulders, too."

The voice was casual, quiet, interested, the way Jake liked it to be. "Have you set a definite date for yourself?"

"I'd like to go down and enlist on my birthday," Jake said shyly. "I'd like to do it that way. I'd like that a lot."

"That's after your Passover holiday, is it?"

Their eyes clicked, and Jake nodded, smiled. "Yeah, just about the same time. I wouldn't leave before the Seder this year. Not on a bet."

"I take it you're attending the Seder this year?"

Jake's smile deepened. "Yeah. I've got only about a week and a half to wait. It's even kind of hard to wait."

He leaned back in the chair, sat there silently for a while, his fingers playing with his pack of cigarettes. When he looked up, to find the doctor's eyes, he said in a half-choked way, "I want you to know I'm not looking for miracles! I mean, I know things won't happen right away, overnight. I know it's going to be a small step at a time for me."

He took a deep breath. "The way I took Bernie to the fights. The business about his glasses. Maybe getting him to trust me a little at a time."

"Yes," the doctor said. "A step at a time."

"But it's so swell to take those steps," Jake cried. "I guess you know! I mean, stuff I couldn't do once. Hell, I didn't even know it was possible to do such things. Let alone have the nerve to do them!"

The office seemed very quiet. Within that stillness, within

the anonymous walls of the room, sitting near the gaze that was so devoid of anything personal, Jake took another deep, satisfying breath.

"I did a couple of other things since the last time I saw you," he said, and his voice was quiet now. "Besides Bernie, I mean. A couple more of those steps. You want to hear about them?"

"Yes, of course."

"Roz and Debby." Jake shook his head. "That wasn't easy. It was easier with Roz, but even that wasn't really easy. I had—a—tough time, Doctor. I started with Roz. . ."

. . . because you knew that the really difficult thing would be to clear up the Debby angle. The Roz thing made you sweat just to think of it, but you knew all the way inside of you, way down and to your feet, practically, that it was the Debby business that would really be tough.

Easy or hard, you do it. You know there are certain things you are going to have to do, sooner or later. The sooner the better, though; you know that, too. No, it isn't that you expect miracles. It isn't that you expect the rest of life is going to be a snap, just because you went to a psychiatrist. But you know that, starting from scratch, it's going to be possible to do things one step at a time now.

No, it isn't that you're going to start all over again. Not miracles; nobody ever starts all over again. But, along with trying to straighten up in the shoulders, you know a few new words and phrases now, and you might as well start right in proving you know them. Strength and weakness; those are two of the words. Adjustment, the psychological moment, knowledge banishes fear; you can really work with phrases like that, especially when you know how they're tied up with you.

Not miracles. You wouldn't call saying the word "sister" to Roz a miracle. Even though last year it would have taken a miracle to make you see a thing like that.

Easy or hard, it's a thing you know you have to do. And it involves your best friends. It has to.

"Come on, we're going out. The drinks are on me. I'm celebrating."

Wally and Kathy look at you. They smile. "Celebrating what?"

You smile back, you wink. "Life. Want to help me celebrate?"

They go with you. They like you. You like them. But you're sweating. No, not miracles. Miracles must be easy compared to the way your heart is ramming your chest.

You're driving. You go, straight as a line, to the Glens. You stroll in, Wally and Kathy behind you. Your eyes are all over the place, but you don't see her right away. Your heart is going like crazy.

Wally says, "Want to sit at the bar? Pretty jammed."

"Nothing doing," you say, and laugh about it, but you want to cry. God knows why. You're not sad, not happy, just excited.

"We can go somewhere else, Jack," Kat says.

"Look," you say, "this is my little party. Wait a minute. Just wait for me here."

You go up to a guy, slip him a buck. "Look, buddy," you say, "we want a table for three. And we want Roz to wait on us."

It's really easy. You feel like you're walking and talking in a dream, but look how easy it is. The guy takes you to a table. You're sitting there, Wally on one side, Kathy on the other. You're laughing.

Then, all of a sudden, she's there.

"What'll it be?" she says.

"Johnny Walker," Kathy says.

"O.K. for me, too," Wally says. "But with water on the side."

Roz is looking at you. Easy? You stand up. She doesn't know anything about miracles either. Her eyes don't even flicker when you stand up.

"Hello, Roz," you say, and you can feel how Wally and Kathy are staring at you, from you to Roz and back again. She's wearing something bright and full of colors. Her hair is up, a red artificial flower in it, so blond, and she's made up to kill. The way a woman really has to make up in a night club, with the kind of dim lights they use in places like that.

"Hello," she says, and her eyes haven't changed a bit. She's waiting for the next step. Maybe she thinks you're drunk.

You walk around the table, and then you're standing next to her. "Roz," you say, and your voice is pretty low but it comes out all right, good and clear, "I want you to meet two of my friends, Wally Lowell and Katherine Adams. They both work on the paper with me."

You look across the table. "Wally, Kat, I want you to meet my sister, Roz Stern."

"How do you do." That's Kathy right away.

And Roz says, "How do you do."

Wally is standing. He makes kind of a bow. "This is a pleasure. Jack's sister. This is really a pleasure."

And it's like Wally really means it. You don't look at Kathy right away. You look at Roz.

What do you see in Roz's eyes? How do you know? She's smiling. She's saying, "Did you ever see a fuller house? It's a wonder you got a table."

But her eyes. Are you imagining? It's like her eyes opened, changed, became—well, somebody you never saw. Or maybe somebody you saw a long time ago. Long, long ago; you've almost forgotten what she looked like then.

"Aren't you drinking, Jack?" she says, and you say, "Oh sure, I'll have some Scotch, any kind. With water, Roz."

"In a minute." She's gone. You walk back to your chair. You sit down. You take out a cigarette, and somebody strikes a match. Your heart—hurts; that's the way it feels.

You bend toward the match. Kathy's holding it. Her eyes are very nice. Soft, with kind of a smile. Very nice.

"She's sweet," Kathy says, blowing out the light.

"Damn good-looking girl," Wally says. He clears his throat.

And then, suddenly, it's not so hard any more. You take a drag on your cigarette. Your voice comes out, and you hear it, and it's the way you wanted it to sound.

"Roz? She's a swell kid. Been supporting herself for years. She's the spunkiest one in the family. Independent as all get out."

Then Wally starts talking about baseball, and spring training, and do you think you're going to enjoy traveling down to the training camp for art? And you say, "How do you know I'm going?"

"I put in a claim, that's how I know," Wally grumbles. "The lousiest photographer on the *Register*, why shouldn't I ask for you?"

And Kathy's laughing at the kid stuff, and then Roz shows up with the drinks. She puts them down, grins at you, says, "Sorry I can't stay. Have fun!" then she's gone again.

Kathy picks up her drink, holds it out. "Here's to it. Whatever we're celebrating."

Wally and you clink with her. You take the first sip.

What are you celebrating? Ten thousand things. But tonight only one. Tonight, drink to your sister Roz, and how you called her sister. Tonight, drink to the look in Roz's eyes, whatever it was. Maybe it was a look of calling you brother. . . .

He planned to take her up on Friday, about two, when they'd all be standing around after the home edition had been put to bed.

He'd asked her to meet him for a late lunch, and when she came into the restaurant she was wearing the green dress, and she looked marvelous. Hatless, her hair fluffed by the wind; she stood near the door for a moment, looking for him, and he could see people starting to stare at her, the short, yellow hair and the strong but shy look of her. He walked quickly toward her and took her arm.

"Hi," she said, and smiled up. "You're right on time, Jake."

He led her to a table, and after a while they ate something or other, and the tough part hadn't even begun for him, just the knowledge of what was coming, the foretaste of what it would be like, walking across that big, clattering room with her.

"What did Sarah say?" he asked. "About moving, I mean."

"Oh, that she didn't know. That she hasn't the money. That she's ashamed of her furniture. That Max hates to move. A hundred different things."

He scowled. "Did you say Bernie ought to have a room? I mean, did she get it at all? How important it might be to him not to have to sleep on that cot in the living room? Allen and he could both use the room, damn it."

"She agreed." Debby finished her coffee, lit a cigarette. "Jake, she means well. You know she does. She's tired, not too well. Why in the devil should we expect her to have any hope for better things? She said, 'Sure, sure, he needs a room. But what can I do about it?'"

"What can she do about it!"

Debby smiled. "Take it easy, Jake. I told her you were so

interested you were going to talk to her. That you had a lot of suggestions."

"What she say?"

"She was flattered." Debby nodded at his look. "That's right. She wanted to know if you really thought they ought to move. I said yes, and what's more, you thought it should be a six-room house. Not a dark apartment."

"What she say to that?"

"She looked sort of helpless. Then she said: 'Maybe I'll talk to Max. But he hates to move!' Then she wanted to know when you were coming up to talk. She wanted to know if maybe you'd talk to Max, too."

"Hell," Jake said, "I'll drop by tonight."

"Good! Here, have a cigarette." She struck a match for him. "It's been nice to eat with you, Jake."

"Where are you going now?" he asked abruptly.

"Back to work. Why?"

His voice stumbled. "I'd like you to come up to the office. I want you to meet some of my friends up there."

Her eyes suddenly seemed to ice over. "What for?"

"Wouldn't you like to?" he said. His voice sounded pleading to him, and he tried to control it. "I—I'd really get a kick out of it, Debby. Wouldn't you like to?"

"No," she said. He noticed then how tight her lips had become. She went on talking slowly. "I'd rather not, Jake. Not today."

"Please come," he said, trying to figure it out.

"What for?" she asked again, her eyes on the ashtray. Her voice sounded dead. "Why should they have a chance to look me over?"

"Debby!" he said. When she looked up, the ice was gone from the blue. She smiled shakily.

"I feel a little timid today," she said. "I get that way once in a while. The idea of walking into that city room, Jake. All of them looking at me. Reporters, editors. Not today, please."

"I want them to meet you." It was painful to talk, but he got the words out. "My sister. I mean, I want them to see you. I want to tell them how you write."

Her smile was deeper now. "That's nice, Jake. That's awfully nice. And sometime we'll do it. Some day I'll want to do it.

I just don't think I can take it today."

"Promise?" he said eagerly. "Promise you'll go up with me some day? Soon?"

"Promise," she said. She lit a cigarette, watched the glowing end for a second.

When she looked up, her eyes seemed tired. "Ask me again soon, Jake," she said very quietly. "That would be a help."

"What's the matter?" he said.

"Nothing too bad. It's just that some days it's still hard for me. Hard to have people stare. To know they're talking about me. Other days it doesn't bother me."

His voice was so low she had to lean forward to hear. "I know the doctor doesn't make a miracle out of it. No hundred-per-cent cure, overnight."

"No. He's the first to tell you that." She pushed her pack of cigarettes toward him. "I'll be all right tomorrow, Jake. Maybe even later today. A person gets tired, a little depressed, then all the old stuff seems to crop up. But it's just for a while."

"I'll know about it when it hits me," he said. "Don't worry about me."

"Oh, that's the wonderful part of it," she told him. Her eyes were eager again. "You know what it is. Really, Jake! It's so wonderful when you know what's happening. It isn't half as hard to take. And it goes quicker, too. When you know. When you can describe it to yourself in words."

He nodded. "Listen," he said, "let's make it sometime next week. I'll ask you then. O.K.? Maybe Wednesday or Thursday. There's a guy I want you to meet. I think I've mentioned him to you. He's retired now. The guy who broke me in, Debby. I'll phone him to come up that day. He drops in all the time anyway, but we won't take a chance on missing him. You'll like him. He'll like you, too. A lot."

He started to tell her about the Old Man, and after a while her eyes looked less tired, and he knew she would go with him some day. He knew, too, that he would remember these minutes for a long, long time; that, when his own time of tiredness came to him, he would take comfort of these minutes. He would remember her unhappiness, but he would remember, too, how she had told him the word—tomorrow.

On some quick tomorrow, she would come with him. He

would have his arm around her, and he would say, "Hey, I want you to meet my kid sister, Deborah."

And if, on that day, she was tired, he would stand next to her and hold her up. Way up. If there were too many eyes on her, he would stand in front of her. But if, on that day, she was the strong Debby instead of the tired one he would stand next to her and get a double kick out of the way everybody would know she was his sister. Everybody would say, "Well, well, kid. Didn't know you had a writer in the family."

On some quick-to-be tomorrow; not a miracle, just another small step to take in the new direction. That was all he wanted. For both of them.

. . . and, whereas S is by no means completely integrated, his realization of his problems and their solution continues to grow. He has achieved a fine maturity, a desire, as well as a need, to make his own decisions.

His behavior toward Bernie, his attempts to break down the barrier of strangeness between his nephew and himself, are evidence of his new strength. He realizes keenly that Bernie is symbolical of family and future. In helping the boy, he not only is attempting to help the family out of wasteland but is making more possible his own tomorrow.

S has begun to think in more universal patterns. The by-play at the fights concerning the Negro, and Bernie's attitude toward this subject, make a good beginning. S has begun to see the larger ghettos of the world in relation to his own.

His desire to recognize his sisters in the eyes of society proves further the extent of his strength. As far as Roz is concerned, this desire is double-edged; he wishes to claim her as sister before his friends, and he wants her to recognize him as brother within herself.

As for Deborah, object of most of his former feelings of guilt and shame, his greatest desire now is to identify her as sister in the eyes of his own world, those people he most respects and admires. Having identified and recognized his sisters within himself, S now has the strength to want society's recognition of them as his sisters.

S stands up well under the shock of recurring manifestations of Deborah's one-time weakness. He accepts this weakness on the part of the strongest person he knows; accepts it and applies it to his own future with no implications of psychosis. It was she who introduced him to the idea and hope of psychiatric treatment; it was she who gave him every evidence of the efficacy of such treatment; and yet, when she shows that symptoms may recur, he is strong enough to accept not only her weakness but the possible recurrences of his own weakness.

S speaks of anticipating the Passover, the Seder ceremony which has been of such importance to him through the years. The ceremony has been put into proper focus. He knows that he may sit down to the Seder table now and find the ritual meaningful and dignified. He need not feel anxiety, or guilt, or shame. He need not search for reasons to sneer and hate. He knows that he does not have to over-compensate now. His family has achieved perspective, as he has himself, and now the holiday may take on its true perspective, too. Both his family and he have the right to be part of this old, meaningful ritual of a people. They have a rightful place within the ranks of such a people. They have the right not only to share in the ritual but to further it.

In recognizing the inadequacy of his father, S has accepted him. In recognizing his mother as weak and diffused, a woman who broke under the rigors of a loveless marriage and the intense economic difficulties of her world, he has accepted her. She, too, has achieved perspective; he may protect her now without feeling bound to her, trapped by her. He may leave the womb without feeling he will destroy her in the leaving.

Meaningless as the Seder ceremony may prove as a symbol of family, S knows now that the ritual and meaning really are contained within himself, and that his self is free. He has a closeness and deep understanding with at least one part of his family, Deborah. The two have joined hands in things, not the least of which is Bernie, symbol of their family's tomorrow.

S has proved to himself and accepted the fact that he needs his sister's hands, her strength and faith in the future. The hands of "family," in other words. He also has proved, however, that he is capable of going ahead even when her hands are taken away.

S will sit quietly with his family at this year's Seder table. Obstacles which have kept him from complete participation have been dissolved. At this year's ceremony, he can recognize without bitterness what is there for him, as well as what can never be there. Recognizing the inadequacies, he knows he need not be hurt by them. . . .

C·H·A·P·T·E·R
Twelve

"Of course," Jake said, "I know I may not go right away. But I definitely wanted to enlist on my birthday."

"As a matter of fact, you may not be called for some time."

"Oh, but that's all right," Jake said eagerly. "It's just that I wanted to make the move on that day. And—and I can keep seeing you until I actually have to go."

The doctor studied him, said quietly after a moment, "How do you feel about being so far away from this room? From your physician?"

Jake stared at him. He had turned rather pale, groped now for a cigarette. "I've been thinking about that," he mumbled. "It's going to be tough. Not even in the same city. I mean, I won't even be able to phone you."

"Do you feel frightened about it?"

Jake shook his head. "No, not exactly. I've been wondering, though. I mean, if I will be all right away from here."

His eyes caught at the impersonal glance. Gradually the color came back into his face, and he nodded.

The doctor struck a match, leaned toward him. Jake put the cigarette between his lips.

"Well, do you think you'll be all right?" the doctor asked, waving out the burning match.

"Yeah," Jake said.

"You know," the doctor said gently, "if you ever get stuck, you can always phone me."

"Yeah. I just hadn't thought of that."

"And there are always letters."

Jake grinned then, dragged deeply at his cigarette. "I'll bet it's natural for a guy to feel this way, too! Timid, as Debby would say. Kind of like a baby learning to walk. Isn't it, Doctor?"

"It's quite natural. You know," the quiet voice went on, "you're walking very well indeed."

"Yeah!" Jake took another drag, scowled thoughtfully.

"Did I tell you," he said shyly, "we've got Bernie signed up with the neighborhood settlement house? He's going to camp this summer."

"Good."

"It wasn't my idea," Jake said quickly. "That friend of Debby's suggested it. That social worker. The nice thing is, the settlement has a drawing class. That's what got Bernie to go. He went once—it's right around the corner from where he lives—and the teacher said he was pretty good. I guess he liked that."

His mouth went crooked as he smiled. "The kid sneaks off his glasses a lot. Sarah told Debby. I suppose that's natural, too. Puts them in the closet and scrams out of the house without them." The smile disappeared. "I'll have to have a couple of serious talks with him. He'd better wear those glasses."

"He's never been to a camp?"

"No," Jake said, his forehead puckered again. "Funny, I'd never of had the idea myself either. I mean, it's funny because when I was a kid I always wanted to go to camp. I wanted it bad. But our family! Sarah's the same. I mean, it never occurs to us to send kids to camp. Maybe Allen can go next year. After Sarah sees it work out for Bernie. Sure, camp, and college the same way." He looked up sharply. "Debby should've gone to college."

"Perhaps your children will go," the gentle voice said.

Jake flushed, reached for the cigarette box. After a moment or two, he said quietly, "You know, Bernie's the kind of kid you have to prove things to. He said to me, 'Camp? Sure, I want to go to camp. Let me know when it's time, Jake!' And he laughed, the kind of laugh that says you don't believe a word of it."

"Most people want to be reassured," the doctor said. "Proof is a very secure thing to have."

"He's going to camp," Jake said, his mouth tight. "Whether I'm here or not. Debby'll take care of that."

"Good. You won't really be gone, will you, with your sister here?"

"That's right." Jake's eyes were very bright. "She knows how I feel. And she feels the way I do. It's like—. Well, it's like leaving a piece of yourself behind when you go."

He stretched back in the chair. It was good to talk today. It had been good from the moment he'd come into the office, a feeling of complete ease and relaxation.

"Bernie's on the waiting list at the *Register*. I explained it to him, how he'll probably get a summer job on the trucks after he gets back from camp. That a lot of kids sign up for jobs like that, and he's got to take his turn. He says he doesn't mind waiting as long as he knows it'll happen." His forehead wrinkled. "Those two kids. Bernie and Allen. They're entirely different. It's kind of nice to watch them, and listen to them talk. One's so damn different from the other. That Allen. Well, do you know the latest about him? He's going to Hebrew school. Somebody in our family going to Hebrew school!"

He put out his cigarette, shaking his head smilingly. "I asked him how come. He said all the kids on the street were going, and he wanted to go, too."

"Did he have trouble persuading his family?"

"Yeah. Bernie laughed at him. Sarah said, 'Hebrew school? What for? You got plenty of homework. Do your homework better.' I went over there one night and talked. The kids were outside. I asked Sarah to let him go. I told her either he'll get tired of it, or he'll like it so much he'll go on with the classes."

He smiled. "A funny thing happened while I was there. Max was sitting near the radio. Most of the time, you know, he never says a word to anybody. Except to squawk at them. Well, all of a sudden, he said, 'Let him take Hebrew. Will it hurt us to let a child be Jewish? I studied Hebrew.' 'In Europe,' Sarah said. 'Who needs Hebrew in America?' 'Listen,' Max said, and he wasn't quarreling or anything, 'if a boy wants to know Hebrew in America, is that a crime? Let him be a Jew here if he wants. Will he hurt anybody if he can write a little Hebrew?'"

Jake grinned at the doctor. "The kid signed up the next day. He still likes it. Debby says he does his homework regularly. Sits in a corner of the kitchen and chants, like a regular little Jew."

"Your father must be pleased," the doctor said.

"The old man?" Jake looked startled. "He is. How'd you know that?"

"Perpetuation of tradition," the doctor said softly. "Continuation of a Jewish family."

"Yeah. I didn't think of that angle. The old man wants the family to go on, too. Sure."

Again he relaxed in the chair. He was silent for a long time then, his eyes dreaming on the wall and window behind the desk.

After a while, the voice caught softly at him. "Did it work out all right, Jake?"

He nodded, his eyes on the doctor's now. "I feel good about it," he said. "Very good. We had the Seder Tuesday night, but I started to feel good about it Monday night."

"You phoned me that evening."

Again Jake nodded. "After I phoned you, Sig came home. It was early, only a little after nine. Debby and I were in the living room, and then Sig came home early, for a change. He went to the bedroom, but in a couple of minutes he came out, walked back into the living room, . . ."

. . . where he sank down at one end of the couch and lit a cigar. Debby smiled at him, went on reading.

Jake was sitting opposite her, in the other deep chair, with a copy of *Time* open on his knees. From the kitchen came odd, whacking noises.

"What's Ma doing?" Sig asked, his head back against the couch.

"Getting chicken ready," Debby said. "Tomorrow's the first Seder, remember?"

"Well, well," Sig said. His head came up, and he removed the cigar from his lips. Smiling, he looked less tired than usual. "Passover, already. Time flies, doesn't it?"

"Going to be here tomorrow night?" Jake said casually, but his heart began to bang as he asked it. Suddenly, for the first time in a long while, he wanted a drink.

"I think I will. I could eat over at Harry's. He's asked me. A month ago; I didn't realize it was so near. He's having a crowd."

"I wish you'd eat here tomorrow," Jake said, his voice harsh with the effort to control it. He felt, rather than saw, Debby's eyes come up from her book. "It might be my last Seder for a long time. It would be nice to—well, to have the whole family together."

"What do you mean?" Sig said, his eyes startled. Again he removed the cigar. "Why, what's happening?"

Jake's mouth felt dry. "I'm going to enlist," he said.

Sig stared at him. "You're not going to wait and be drafted? Maybe they won't take you."

"I want to go," Jake said stiffly. "I want to enlist, myself. Like I said." Groping for a cigarette, his eyes met Debby's. She was smiling.

"On your birthday," she said. "That's tomorrow."

"That's right." He felt uneasy, shy, and lit his cigarette with a crisp motion.

He could not make out Sig's look. Surprise, yes, but there was a lot more to it; oddly enough, his face seemed to have changed. It looked firmer, somewhat as if the flesh had been jolted into sharp lines. He looked younger.

"Say," Sig said rather breathlessly, "that's swell. I think that's swell!" He took out a packet of matches, lit his cigar again. "Army?" he asked, puffing strongly.

"Signal Corps, maybe," Jake said. "I'll have to ask around at recruiting stations. I'd like to go in as a cameraman, naturally."

"Oh, naturally, naturally!" Sig cried. His eyes seemed to have come all alive. "Say, maybe they'll make you an officer. You can't tell."

Jake grinned. "Without a college education? Maybe they'll help me finish high school, huh?"

"I forgot about that," Sig said, looking embarrassed.

"'How many times did I warn you to finish school?'" Jake said lightly, mimicking his brother's tones. "'I warned you. Don't say I didn't warn you.'"

They smiled at one another.

"Hell, don't worry about that," Sig said. "You've got a camera instead of a degree."

"I'm not worried," Jake said. "Not about that, anyway."

"What, are you worried about something?" Sig asked, leaning forward.

Debby laughed. "He thinks maybe Ma will starve to death," she said. "Or be evicted. He thinks he's the only one who can support the family."

"Oh, hell," Sig said. He sounded relieved. "That's a joke, isn't it? Debby and I can support any family. Can't we, Debby?"

"Sure," she said. "Jake, have you got an extra cigarette?"

He lit it for her, and she said, "Roz is going to chip in, too. I've already asked her."

"Say, that's swell." Sig looked at Jake, that oddly youthful expression sharpening his face. "What is this? Are they calling you Jake again?"

Jake reddened, but his voice came out light. "Yeah. All of a sudden I like Jake again. General Jake Brown. How does it sound?"

Sig laughed. "General! Well, you can't ever tell. They say miracles happen every day in America. How does Ma like the idea?"

"I haven't told her yet."

Sig nodded, his eyes serious again. "She'll carry on about it, but she'll get over it. Don't you think so, Debby?"

"I'll take care of Ma," Debby said. "It won't be too bad. After a while, she'll be proud. You wait and see." She grinned at Jake. "I'm going to buy her a blue star flag for the window. And a service pin to wear. That'll help."

Sig stood up, walked over to the mantel and leaned on it, puffing at the cigar. He looked excited, tense. It seemed to Jake, at that moment, that his brother's body had taken on the same sharp, youthful look which had tautened his face.

"I just can't get over it," Sig said. "I think it's wonderful. Wonderful! I never thought you'd do it. Being drafted, that's different. Listen, don't worry about the house. Pa is working these days, too. I'll have a real talk with him, he'll pay some bills, too."

340

"I'm not going to worry," Jake said. "I'll be sending home allotment money, too."

"That's up to you," Sig cried heartily. "You don't have to. On fifty lousy bucks a month."

"But I want to," Jake told him.

"Good, good," Sig said. He began to walk up and down the room, slowly, excitement making his steps heavy. "This war! Hell, this is some war, that's all I can say!" His voice became more intense. "All I can say is, I'm glad you're doing it. You'd be surprised! I feel wonderful about it, just wonderful!"

He was at the mantel again, and he stopped there, looked at Jake, then at Debby, in the same urgent way.

"I feel that way, too," she said gently. "Like he's going to fight for us, too, in a way."

Sig nodded, his eyes eager. "You read about those Nazis in the paper," he said harshly. "What they do to people, not only to Jews. But look what they're doing to the Jews, especially! Everywhere, all over the world!"

He lit his dead cigar, and Jake saw that his hands were shaking. He was born in Europe, he thought with a sudden feeling of pity. Where they're killing Jews by the thousands. A guy must remember where he was born.

"A guy doesn't think he's going to save the world single-handed," Jake said.

"But a lot of guys together," Debby said. "That could be different."

"You read where they burn down a whole ghetto," Sig muttered. "All I know is, I'm glad you're going. And somewhere else they make new ghettos. People have to wear yellow badges."

Jake sat there, remembering when the only ghetto he knew and hated was his own. The walls of thickest stone, the narrow strip of sky a million miles away. When had his own wasteland become part of the world's? When had his individual fight been encompassed by the world's war, and for the same right to walk out of the quicksand of wasteland, to leave the death of waste behind? Yes, for that matter, when had Sig's eyes become so alive?

"There are plenty of ghettos," Debby said. Jake's head came

up. "Anywhere you look you can see them. Maybe it takes a war to wipe them all out."

Sig was nodding.

"I'd like to wipe them out, all right," Jake said. "Any kind. Every single one of them."

In Debby's eyes he saw the words he was not saying: Negro, Jew, your kind of people. In her eyes he saw that she had taken his hand. . . .

Was he imagining the new gaiety, the new laughter? Had he dreamed up the new expressions on faces? Even the old man seemed dignified, the little black prayer cap accentuating his white hair, his trimmed mustache, the gaunt, sharp-boned look of his freshly shaved face. This evening, the old man seemed to resemble many of the peasants in newspaper pictures again, old men of Poland and Czechoslovakia, standing outside their houses in the villages through which the German armies marched. If I saw a picture of him, his face, Jake thought, I'd like him. I'd feel for him. He looks old, as if his back and legs hurt.

Jake had come home first, and in the kitchen his mother was shelling hard-boiled eggs at the sink. In the dusky light of the room, her head came up and her eyes held the familiar peering, half-startled look.

"You're here already?" she said. "Maybe you want to eat supper right away?"

"Heck no," he cried, in the half-Yiddish, half-English mixture; "I'll eat at the Seder."

A moment later, his head popped around the doorway leading to the kitchen. "Ma, is there any hot water? For a shower?"

"The boiler is full," she said. She was putting the fish into a glass dish so that it could cool. "I let it heat all afternoon. You could even take a bath if you want one."

He was out of the shower in five minutes. Grinning at himself, he got into his best suit, the brown tweed one. He spent several minutes matching tie, socks, and handkerchief.

What you would call symbolical bathing and dressing, I suppose, he told the doctor in his mind. He grinned again, but his heart was beating hard with excitement.

He carried his camera and case into the dining room, and as he stood there for a moment, peering at the table through the twilight haze in the room, he breathed deeply of the familiar holiday odors. Then he snapped on the light, and the table seemed to spring up out of darkness.

"Ma. Hey, Ma," he cried, advancing on the table. "Is it O.K. if I pour the wine now?"

He sat the camera on one of the chairs and lifted the wine decanter.

She came padding into the room, and her clean apron shone in the light, and she was carrying the empty fish pot in one hand and a spoon in the other.

"What's the matter?" she said.

"I want to take some pictures," he said, and smiled at her. "How can I take pictures of a Seder table without wine in the glasses?"

"Pictures?" She looked puzzled. "Without people? Why do you want pictures of a table?"

"I'll get the people later." He poured carefully, filling each glass to the brim, and when he came to the extra glass, he chuckled. "I'll take a picture of Elijah, Ma," he said.

She giggled, and went back to the kitchen. As he walked around the table, studying angles, he could hear her occasional quiet giggle between sounds of dishes and pots scraping on the sink. That girlish laughter made him ache a little inside, but it was an ache of fondness, unmixed with loneliness or nostalgia.

He took several shots, quietly happy at the wonderful detail of the plateful of matzoth at the old man's place, the pillow on his chair, the open *Haggadah* at his own place, and the shine and shimmer of the glasses, the rich look of the wine.

JEWISH HOLIDAY, TWENTIETH CENTURY, he thought. Or I could call it, THEY KEEP FAITH IN AMERICA, TOO.

He pulled out a chair, clambered on it, and shot down on a section of table which held the plate of bitter herbs and *charoseth*, the matzoth, and his own place with the *Haggadah* open at the first page.

He was still on the chair when Debby came home. She leaned against the wall and watched him for a moment. After the flash, she said, "That ought to be some one-man show. When you get round to it, Jake."

"Yeah," he said, stepping down. "After the war, maybe. Listen, Debby, I want a couple of pictures with everybody around the table. Before the Seder starts."

"O.K.," she said. "That'll be easy." She grinned at him. "Hey, many happy returns of the day, kiddo!"

"Thanks."

"Jake," she said, her voice very quiet suddenly, "did you do it?"

"Yeah." He smiled soberly. "Signal Corps."

She swallowed, then she said in a low voice, "Best of luck! The very best, Jake!"

After an instant, she turned and walked briskly into the bathroom to wash. "Ma," she called, over the running water, "is everything ready? Did you leave anything for me to do?"

That'll be easy, that'll be easy. Jake walked slowly into the living room with his camera, Debby's words rolling through his mind. He sat on the couch, the camera on the cushion beside him, and lit a cigarette.

Easy to take these pictures he had always been afraid to take. Easy to sit at this table he had been afraid to face all these years. Easy to leave the house and yet to know he need not leave it, to know that it was not dragging at him with chains of mother and iron balls of obligation never faced and never met.

Easy? At what point does a guy start feeling easy about things? Or—as Debby would say it—when does he start to know peace? Cessation of spiritual torment, beginning of self; that's how Debby would say it. This was like dreaming, except that in the dream his heart would not be banging like this, would it? In the dream it wouldn't be so easy to sit here and want to cry, would it?

Sitting there, he remembered some of the words he had read so many times in the *Haggadah*. "Because we were slaves unto Pharaoh in Egypt, and the Eternal, our God, brought us forth thence with a mighty hand and an outstretched arm."

Because we were slaves unto wasteland, he thought.

He was still sitting there, smiling and shaking his head slowly about himself, when Roz and Sig came home. Then the old man came home, and Jake heard him mumble, "Good holiday, good holiday," as he entered the kitchen.

Was he imagining the warm look in Roz's eyes? "Hi there. How are your friends? Miss Adams and Mr. Lowell?"

"Oh, they're swell. They liked you."

"Mr. Lowell comes in a lot," she said. "He always comes over and talks to me now. Course I used to see him around the club a lot, only I never knew him to talk to before you introduced us."

Easy? Jake's face felt hot as he fumbled with the camera. Easy? Now the family was sitting around the table, and the old man had cleared his throat, was turning pages in the big, shabby book. Sig was breaking pieces of matzoth off one broad leaf, and chewing, and Roz was saying, "Take a little sip, Ma. Come on. It won't hurt you." In another minute or two, Ma would giggle, cry softly, "I'm drunk already!"

He took the first shot from the living room, facing the old man at the head of the table, waiting for that moment when the old man's lips had begun to move, and the first whispered, abstract sounds came from him as he thumbed the pages. It was like shooting sounds, as well as faces and gestures.

At the flash, Debby cried gaily in Yiddish, "We're going to be famous. Look how he's making our Seder famous, Pa."

The old man looked up, blinked. "Well, we have to start now," he said hesitantly, but he looked pleased, straightened the book in front of him, pulled the plate containing the bitter herbs closer to the edge of the table.

Jake worked quickly, shooting once from the opposite direction, and once from on top of the chair he yanked into the room from the kitchen. As he worked, he talked smoothly, watching carefully to snatch the moments when the studied, stiff looks on faces disappeared.

"Sig, stop eating for a second, will you? How about putting your hand on the wine bottle? That's right! Pa, why don't we have Sarah's family here next year for the Seder? Allen could ask the questions. That would be a real Seder. With grandchildren."

The old man looked up, his eyes sly. "Why not? At least he could ask the questions in Hebrew!"

"Well, tonight they'll be in English for the last time, huh?" Jake said, grinning, and took the picture. It would be a beaut, the old man's face up that way, and everybody looking directly at him. "Next year in the land of Israel, O.K., Pa?"

The old man smiled. "He has a sense of humor," he said to all of them. "Do you hear how he talks? Like an educated man. Right out of the *Haggadah*."

"You think it's a joke?" Ma said. "Maybe they'll be here next year. Right now Max is making a little Seder in their house. You know why? It's the first time he made a Seder, all the time he's in America. You know what an unbeliever he is. You know why he did it? Just because Allen came home from Hebrew school and asked where is the Seder."

Roz and Sig laughed, and suddenly Jake thought tremblingly, I enlisted today!

"Pa," Sig said, reaching for the matzoth again, "isn't it true a little child shall lead the way?"

The old man nodded, cleared his throat impatiently. "Well, Jake," he said, "enough pictures already?"

And then the Seder had begun, the dream had reverted to long-remembered chant and words so familiar they seemed new in the actual moment of reading them to the refrain of his father's Hebrew.

In the dream, he was sitting opposite Debby's grave eyes and his mother's wrinkled face, to the right of his father, to the left of his brother and sister. In the dream, everything was peaceful, easy; Sig's restless breaking of matzoth, Roz's heavily made-up face, her whispering to Ma, the blueness of Debby's eyes. In the dream, he had never asked them to be any different than they were, and now they were the same but he was different. He was part of the table, belonging in this chair; he was not demanding of his father and brother, not ashamed of his sisters, not guilty before his mother. He was part of the prayer and part of the evening; and soon, at the proper moment, he would take his place in carrying on the service for another year. All over the world, wherever Jews were gathered for this holiday, the youngest son present was ready to speak.

"Blessed art thou, O Eternal, our God, King of the Universe, Creator of the fruit of the vine."

His father's chant began, and Jake read the words in the English column to match the somber sound. Once, when he and Debby had been listening to one of her beloved radio concerts, she had said, "Listen to that cello, will you? It always reminds me of Pa praying on holidays. It's like the voice of a praying Jew, isn't it? Listen to it."

He listened to his father's voice, praying. The wailing, deep tones thrilled him as they rose and waned to a whisper, rose again like walls. Over the walls of sound, his eyes looked into Debby's.

A brief, panicky thought came to him: Will it really do any good? Bernie, will he be all right? Ma, what makes me think her eyes won't follow me? Right into the war, right across the world! Debby, what about the ghetto inside of a guy? How does he know he's wiping that out?

Her eyes were wonderful. He could not keep feeling afraid, looking at her eyes. They were full of different expressions, like the colors of a rainbow but not bright, just soft and changing. Her eyes were a lot like the voice of their father, sad and yet, a second later, hopeful, strong as the walls of sound and yet lamenting what had gone before, grave and devout and yet full of a passionate, searching look.

He wanted to nod to her that he knew, that he remembered how tormented her eyes could be sometimes, but that he remembered how strong they could be, too. He wanted to tell her that he remembered how her voice had sounded when she said the word "tomorrow."

His father's hand fumbled a page, went out to his glass of wine.

Jake followed the words in the column of English. "Blessed art thou, O Eternal, our God, King of the Universe, who has preserved us alive; sustained us, and brought us to enjoy this season."

His father lifted the wineglass. Jake sipped, his eyes on the others as they brought their glasses to their lips.

The quick, pattering prayer said, his father dipped bits of parsley into salt water, passed a piece to each person at the table. Again, one of the fast, muttered prayers came from his lips, and everyone ate, a moment after he had begun to chew the piece he had kept for himself.

It was almost time. Jake watched his father break the middle matzoth and hide away one half. He watched him pick up the dish containing the bone and the egg. As the chant began again, Jake gripped his *Haggadah,* watched his mother fill each wineglass to the brim.

Inside of him, a quiet, tremulous voice said, Oh God—.

Then his father said, "Well, Jake, ask the questions."

He stood up, began reading to them with all his heart: "Wherefore is this night distinguished from all other nights? . . ."

Lightning Source UK Ltd.
Milton Keynes UK
UKHW011920140221
378607UK00014B/589